Praise for a different book

'Not many books make me laugh out loud, but *The Perpetual Astonishment of Jonathon Fairfax* is one of them... A comic gem.'

Francesca Brown, *Stylist*

'It cleverly combines intrigue with comic, astute observation which made me laugh throughout.'

The Bath Novel Award (2014 shortlist)

'You can't help being tickled.'

Alfred Hickling, *The Guardian*

'Shevlin was rightly picked up by the literary agency that represents the likes of David Nicholls. ... the comic hero is caught up in a murder plot that unravels into a political thriller, which is by turns absurd and engaging.'

Ben East, *Metro*

D1310702

About the author

Christopher Shevlin dressed as a cowboy every day until the age of six, making him the most heavily armed child in Doncaster – no small achievement. Other facts about him include these: he distrusts condiments; he dreams in high definition; he briefly worked as a labourer in Tel Aviv, earning the nickname 'astronaut' for his incredible slowness; he has twice performed at the Edinburgh Fringe; he once dug a grave.

His pen is available for hire, along with his writing advice and teaching. He has run a *Guardian* Masterclass, taught bankers to write, invented a giant outdoor board game, ghostwritten articles about diverse and mostly intensely boring subjects, and written a short film script about beer. He also wrote *Writing For Business*, part of Penguin's *Writers' Guides* series.

When life is hard, he has always turned to books for comfort. His favourites include his battered old *Jeeves Omnibus*, Douglas Adams's *Dirk Gently* books, *1066 And All That*, the *Molesworth* books, and *Augustus Carp By Himself*. His ambition is to write books that are even a tenth as comfortingly odd.

His first novel, *The Perpetual Astonishment of Jonathon Fairfax*, was shortlisted for the 2014 Bath Novel Award and became an Amazon UK bestseller.

To find out more about Christopher Shevlin, his books, and the disturbingly assertive squirrels of Helsinki, please visit:

www.christophershevlin.com

Jonathon Fairfax Must Be Destroyed

CHRISTOPHER SHEVLIN

ALBATROSS

Published by Albatross Publishing

ISBN 978-0-9569656-3-9

Version 4c. September 2017.

Christopher Shevlin has asserted his right to be
identified as the author of this book.

www.albatrosspublishing.com

Thank you

I have an unusually huge number of people to thank for this book, which I wrote through a series of mistakes, accidents and disasters rare even for me.

First of all, thanks to Adam Fletcher, Paul Hawkins and Linn Hart, who were there throughout my weird and mistaken stay in a German stroke ward. I owe them a huge amount.

I'm also extremely grateful to my intrepid test-readers: Avery Elizabeth Hurt, Stef Jakobi, Laura Kennedy, Andrew Nelson, John Lenahan, Ben Ross, Emma Rawsthorne, Alice Pott-Negrine and Hilary Jacob.

Then there are the friends who, among much else, let me live in their flats while I wrote some of this book: Adam, Paul and Linn again, Stef Jakobi and Jack Kinsella, Fred Eichelbaum and Sophie Eisentraut, and (almost) Kate McNaughton, Stefan Rother, and Rich Baxter.

I'm also grateful to Scott Pack for editing it, Patrick Knowles for the cover, and my friend, the genius illustrator Edward Ward for coming up with the title and the first sketch of the cover.

Thanks to everyone at the Comedy Cafe Berlin for making me laugh.

Finally, thank you to everyone who got in touch to tell me that they liked my first book, as well as to everyone who gave it nice reviews. That really kept me going.

Thank you all.

Part One

Hey!

Monday

1

Monday, London, the year 2000

Love at first sight is like the London Underground: inconvenient, outmoded, often disappointing – and yet still, somehow, the best option.

Jonathon Fairfax was about to discover this on the Northern line. It was 8.42am, and he was being hurled through a tunnel deep underground.

'Hup. Um, oops,' he said.

He had just discovered that he was standing on someone's toes. When he looked up from the toes to apologise, he instantly fell in love. She seemed to fit perfectly into a gap in him, almost audibly clicking into place.

There was something charmingly ridiculous about her, as though she perhaps did stupid voices when no one was around. She had large green eyes, and the soft curve of her upper lip contained more beauty than anyone else managed to pack into a whole face. Her hair fell to her shoulders in chestnut tresses, as though it belonged to the heroine of an old-fashioned book. It licked down over her red scarf and tickled the lapel of her woollen coat.

Jonathon should have said something, but falling in love at first sight is a distracting experience. It leaves little spare brainpower for conversation, which is in any case strictly forbidden on the Tube.

They stared at each other. The air seemed to have become super-charged, despite the light steam rising from the damp commuters all around them.

And then the train stopped. The doors were opening. The driver was announcing, 'Embankment station, ladies and gents.' The competing announcer on the platform was shouting, 'Please allow all passengers to alight before boarding.' And beneath it all, the recorded announcement was intoning, 'Mind the gap,' in its precise, threatening way.

Their eyes remained locked together, despite the buffeting of the people getting off, despite the icy *excuse me* of the woman who stepped between them, despite the nasty whack on the back of the knees Jonathon received from an unusually sharp-edged suitcase. And then the girl saw the writing on the wall – *Embankment* – and she was leaving, allowing herself to be swept away by the crowd, her eyes on his the whole time.

Two stops later, Jonathon remembered that he too should have changed at Embankment. Now he was going to be late.

Jonathon would have been nowhere near the girl or her toes if it hadn't been for the newspaper article.

That morning, after arriving on the Victoria line, Jonathon had narrowly missed a Tube at Warren Street. This happened every morning. When the next train arrived, he was pushed on and propelled into a seat by the force of all the people behind him desperately trying to get in. This too happened every morning.

Someone beside him was wearing headphones that broadcast the highest register of the percussion part.

Dum-dum smash, a dum-dum smash, a dum-dum smash.

This was also normal.

Usually, Jonathon got out his book at this point and slipped away into another world. But this morning he couldn't help noticing something in a newspaper. It was the name of the company Jonathon worked for, in a story towards the bottom of one of the inside pages.

Farynx's Chief Risk Officer dies in fire.

Jonathon couldn't help reading on over his neighbour's shoulder. After all, the only thing that could make dying in a fire worse would be if your job involved anticipating and preventing accidents. Jonathon expected to die in just such an unfortunate and embarrassing way himself. Or at least, the old Jonathon had expected that. Now, he told himself, he was changing, turning himself into the sort of switched-on go-getter who could understand headlines in the *Financial Times* – including roughly two-thirds of the one on the front page: *Nasdaq breaks 5,000.*

Having finished reading the article, Jonathon was suddenly aware that the man who owned the paper was looking at him with an expression of intense annoyance, as though Jonathon's eyes were casting a shadow over the page.

'Sorry,' said Jonathon, reddening.

The man shook his paper irritably, to emphasise his point, and – after aiming another stinging glare at Jonathon – went back to his reading.

Jonathon looked away: a fatal mistake. There was a middle-aged woman standing in front of him, and he was plunged into the dilemma he usually avoided by reading a book. Should he offer her his seat, and risk making her think she looked elderly or pregnant? Or should he stay where he was, feeling increasingly tense and guilty for not offering her his seat?

He solved the problem by getting up as if he were going to leave at the next stop, so the woman could have his seat without him offering it. But she wasn't fast enough, and the seat was taken immediately by another twenty-something man like Jonathon. He should have offered it after all and risked reading in her eyes, *Oh, am I old now?*

Feeling he needed to put some distance between himself and this small but comprehensive social debacle, Jonathon weaved through the dense crowd to the area near the doors, where he made sure to keep his eyes on nothing in particular. And that was how he came to be treading on the toes he instinctively wanted to spend the rest of his life with.

Jonathon did not know it, but he had just fallen in love at first sight because someone had died 3,515 miles away and 17 hours earlier. It's odd how things work out.

2

Sunday, New Jersey, 3,515 miles away and 17 hours earlier...

Pete Hatcher glanced at his watch: 10.42am. He tucked the mixing bowl under his arm and opened the door to his New Jersey house. Outside, the sky was clear and blue, but obscured by the very big man standing in front of it.

'Hi Pete,' said the man, offering his hand and smiling. He had crow-black hair, a hard, smooth face, and a mouth that curled easily at the edges – like a stone that has learned to smile. Pete always found himself wanting to please him, an impulse that was especially inconvenient that day, given what he had to do.

'Todd! Come on in,' said Pete. 'Barb's out shopping for antiques with her mom, so I'm making buttermilk pancakes. Don't tell her. You want?'

'Sure.'

Pete shook Todd's hand and led the way into a big kitchen at the back of the house. He was nervous, but this had to be done – for everyone's sake. And if you're going to destroy a man, it's best to do it in the kitchen and serve buttermilk pancakes afterwards.

'Nice,' said Todd, looking around.

'Thanks,' said Pete, glad of the chance to distract Todd. 'You like this thing here in the middle? They call it an "island". You can prepare food here, but you can also sit down at this guy, read the papers. Best of both worlds. You want coffee?'

'Thought you'd never ask.' Todd's hard mouth curled into its easy smile.

Pete set his bowl aside and laid a paternal hand on the coffee machine. It looked like someone had adapted it from the front of a fifties Cadillac: it was all gleaming metal, polished lacquer, grilles, pipes and fins.

'We splashed out a little,' said Pete. 'Got ourselves a Flemke 1100. If you've got the beans, it'll do whatever you want.'

'Great. I'll take an espresso.'

Pete set to work grinding beans, flipping levers and tapping pressure gauges. *It'll be easier with a coffee in you*, he told himself.

He served the coffee in the cups with the delicate blue butterflies on them, a gift from his mother-in-law. Then he took a stool at the island, opposite Todd. *Do it*, he told himself. He played with the rollers of a sturdy pasta machine fixed to the edge of the work surface between them. *Do it.*

Pete opened his mouth.

'Hey, nice tie,' said Todd.

It was a new one, a present from Barbara, Pete's wife. But the compliment – the little glow that comes from a fellow human being recognising that your wife has really good taste in ties – would make this all the more difficult.

'Thanks,' said Pete. 'I started going to church again. Just came from there, actually. So I guess you'd say this is my Sunday best.'

'Good for you,' said Todd. He sipped his coffee.

Pete took a deep breath and did it. He got it out. 'I know your uh…
secret, Todd. And I know what you have planned for London.'

This did not have the effect Pete had wanted. He had hoped for
a tearful confession, feared a look of horrified betrayal. But he was
not prepared for the expression of irritation that crossed Todd's face.

'So what do you want?' said Todd.

'What I want is for you to do the right thing, Todd. Go to the board.
Go to Chesborough O'Teece. Say what you've done and make it right.'

Pete knew there would be no way for Todd to make it right, not
something on this scale. But he needed Todd to believe there was.

'Who have you told about this, Pete?'

'No one, Todd. This little chat isn't even in my diary. All anyone
will ever know is that you decided to do the right thing.'

Todd seemed to mull this over. He took another sip of coffee and
then looked Pete in the eye.

'Pete, this is not about doing the right thing,' said Todd. 'It's about
playing like a winner. You think when Bill Gates sold IBM an operating
system *that did not exist* he said to himself, "This is fraud, I should be
ashamed of myself"? No. He just wrote an operating system in *two
weeks*. That's because he's smart. If you're smart, there's a different set
of rules.'

'Todd, there's just one set of ru— Wait a minute, is that why Windows doesn't work?'

'Hey, if a company is smart enough to make money from products
that don't work, I'm buying from them. They *deserve* my custom.'

'What?'

'It's the law of the jungle, Pete. You have to get too big to be eaten.
And you do that any way you can. Seems to me you're the only one
around here who doesn't understand that.'

Pete's head was spinning. He felt like an assassin whose victim
has just looked him in the eye and said irritably, 'Let me explain why
that isn't a gun.'

'Don't try and turn this around, Todd. What you're doing is illegal.
If you won't come clean, I'll tell the board myself. I have a duty to act.'

'That's not how you felt at your last company, Pete. See, I know
a few secrets of yours too: the drugs, the hookers, the collection of
Staffordshire pottery.'

Pete felt his cheeks flush with shame. So Todd knew. He had been
afraid of this. But he would do the right thing even if it cost him his
breakfast island, his house, the remains of his Staffordshire collection.

Everything.

'And I regret that every day,' said Pete, his voice quiet. 'But I am clean now. And if I got this job because someone thought I would keep quiet about something on this scale, well... *someone* made a mistake.'

'You know what, Pete?' said Todd, taking a sip of his coffee and sitting forward. 'I am going to kill you.'

The words hung between them. Pete looked Todd square in the face. He knew what he had to do.

'Then I will kill you too, Todd,' he said. 'Go ahead and tell the board whatever you know about me. But I will tell them what I know about you. And not just the board – the regulators, the press, the whole world if necessary. I am tired of lies and I just want to do what's right. If you make me lose my job, my career even, then so be it. But I will stop you, Todd.'

Todd smiled broadly. 'Pete,' he said, 'you've got me all wrong.' He shook his head, almost laughing.

Relief flooded through Pete's chest. He smiled. 'I can't tell you how much I hoped to hear you say that, Todd.'

'Pete, I don't mean I'm going to *metaphorically* kill you by ruining your career. I mean I'm going to *literally* kill you, right now, in this kitchen.'

Pete's mouth opened and he started to get up, but Todd's hand flashed out, grabbed his tie and yanked his head smartly down onto the counter, stunning him. Todd twisted the long and short ends of the tie together and fed them between the rollers of the pasta machine. He wound the handle so Pete was trapped, his tie knot touching the rollers. While Pete struggled to adapt to this new world in which he couldn't breathe or move, Todd disappeared behind him somewhere.

Just as Pete reached out for the pasta machine's handle, a chopping board hit him in the face. Todd was holding it, wearing oven mitts. Why had he put those on? The board did Pete little damage though: it was the thin neoprene one that folded at the edges so you could funnel vegetables into a pot. He put up his hands to ward off another blow, losing him precious time for freeing his tie. Todd disappeared again, no doubt searching for another weapon. Pete tried frantically to look behind him. He heard the bowl of pancake mix smash on the floor.

'Ah crap,' said Todd. 'I was going to use that to stove your head in.'

Pete grabbed the pasta machine's handle. It wouldn't move. His tie was jammed in the rolling mechanism. *Where have I left the scissors?* he thought. *And will Todd see them?*

Todd was opening drawers and muttering, 'Why is there nothing in this godforsaken kitchen that can kill a man?'

Pete hammered at the handle of the pasta machine, but it just seemed to chew up his tie even more, keeping him trapped. Meanwhile he could hear Todd behind him opening the cupboard beside the extractor hood, pulling out the contents.

'Who has a whole cupboard full of rubber cupcake baking sheets?' shouted Todd. 'Who *needs* that many cupcakes?'

The cupboard door slammed and another one opened. Pete managed to clamber up onto the counter, still secured at the neck. He put his back and legs into the struggle with the pasta machine.

'Plastic colanders!' yelled Todd behind him. 'You have *got* to be kidding me.'

And then, with a loud ripping noise, Pete broke free. He whirled around. All he had to do was hit the yellow panic button on the wall, installed for Barb after the Goldstein kidnapping.

Todd followed the direction of his gaze and spotted the panic button. Pete dived for it, but Todd had a colander in his oven-mitted hand and was there first.

'Uh-uh,' said Todd, as Pete's hand hit the bottom of the colander that now covered the panic button. 'No way.'

Pete grabbed at the colander, trying to wrestle it away from the button. But Todd held it fast with one padded hand, the other scrabbling on the counter just behind him.

Pete felt something clamp on his windpipe, cutting off the air. He looked down: his salad tongs made of dark-finished walnut wood, a present from his sister Mary. He grabbed at the gloved hand holding the tongs. Todd pushed him away from the panic button, dropping the colander and searching for a new weapon with his free hand.

Behind Todd, right next to the stove, was a vertical drawer containing a wide selection of Japanese molybdenum steel kitchen knives. If Todd found them, Pete was finished. But if Pete could somehow get to them first…

Todd stretched out his hand, feeling around behind him. He grabbed Pete's Stir-o-Matic, a present from his brother Paul, and hit him with it until the mercifully feeble wooden paddles broke off. Todd threw it aside in disgust and grabbed behind him for another weapon. Pete tried to pull away, but Todd was too strong, forcing Pete to his knees.

Todd said through gritted teeth, 'I am gonna find something lethal in this kitchen, Pete, if it's the last thing I do.'

After that, Pete was hit in quick succession with a bookstand in the shape of the word 'Cook', a packet of resealable freezer bags, a nest of measuring cups, a small scale shaped like a seashell, a packet of fresh oregano, a lunch box, an innovative vegetable scrubber, some kitchen roll, an empty ice tray, a side plate, two spoons and a jar opener. All the while, Pete clawed at the horribly robust salad tongs, trying desperately to rise.

Then Todd brandished a thick wooden spaghetti spoon.

'I guess this means golf is off this Saturday, Pete,' he said.

And with that, he laboriously beat Pete to death and set his house on fire.

3

Returning to Monday morning in London...

By the time Jonathon arrived at work, everything had changed. That moment when he had looked into the girl's eyes and known beyond doubt that he and she were destined to spend eternity together – that hadn't happened. Or, if it had (which it hadn't), it had been just one of those mad half-thoughts that pass through your brain all the time – like wondering whether your life is really a film, or thinking you'd look good in a hat.

Despite the fact that the moment indisputably hadn't happened, Jonathon felt a deep, gnawing guilt about it. The fact was that he already had a girlfriend, a soulmate. Her name was Emma and she worked in human resources. He was in love with her. She had a light tan, abdominal muscles and the sort of face they put on magazine covers. She was definitely not the sort of woman he had ever expected to end up living with. They were happy. Life was perfect. He had a girlfriend, a flat with oak-effect floors, and a sensible job in a big company. He was definitely happy.

He rushed into the revolving doors and did his customary involuntary hoedown as the sensor brought the doors to a halt, forcing him to do a half-step back before moving forward again into the vast lobby. The floor stretched away in all directions, the ceiling soared high above, and light poured in through the windows, illuminating the huge Farynx logo on the wall.

The clock above the long granite reef of the reception counter said 8.49. He had one minute to reach his desk. He hurried over to the metal security barriers.

'Pass please, sir,' said the short security guard in his Yorkshire accent, glaring at Jonathon. The guard was remarkably intimidating. In fact, per foot of height, he was probably the most intimidating person in the Western world.

As Jonathon fumbled for his pass, he almost dropped the yellow free-ads paper, *Loot*, he had picked up on the Tube. The girl had let it slip from her charmingly ridiculous fingers, but that wasn't why he had picked it up. He just needed a copy of *Loot*.

'Um, I've been here a few months,' he said, searching his pockets. 'My name's Jonathon Fairfax.'

'It's not my job to remember your name,' said the security guard.

But by now Jonathon had found his pass. The security guard examined it minutely, as though he suspected Jonathon might have counterfeited it in order to gain access to the building and covertly perform administrative tasks. Finally, he grunted and opened the security barrier.

By the time Jonathon got out of the lift on the fourth floor, it was 8.53. He was meant to arrive ten minutes early for his nine o'clock start. Livia didn't like it if he was late for being early.

The lift doors opened and Jonathon rushed to the reception booth opposite. It was crewed by two female temps of his own age who dealt with so many people that they often turned their personalities off as a power-saving measure.

'Good morning. How can I help you?' said Nicci, as though she had never seen him before.

'Hello. I'd like to book a desk, please.'

'No worries.' She typed something on a computer. 'Number 412. Have a great day.'

He thanked her and hurried off, muttering '412, 412' under his breath. The reception booth and the lifts were moored in the middle of the floor. Clustered around them were the coffee area and a huddle of meeting rooms, break-out zones and private offices. And on both sides of this central area, stretching out to the toilets and staircases at either end of the floor, were the wide-open expanses of deskland.

Jonathon struck out north, found desk 412 and staked his claim, laying out his things before going and retrieving his company laptop from its security drawer. Only then did he risk sneaking a glance at Livia's office in the corner of the room, between the printing station and the knowledge-management area. It looked empty, so he decided to get a coffee while his computer booted itself up and went through its impenetrable on-screen mutterings about caches and integrity checks.

The floor's coffee area was a vision of a clean and successful future – the future he was sure he must want. Though small, it was expertly lit, with carefully chosen colours and lots of light wood and brushed steel. Along one wall was a counter with three neat, squat coffee machines. In the handful of other places Jonathon had worked, there had always been huge, old-fashioned vending machines that would charge you fifty pence for something that reminded you of coffee. Here, the coffee was free and made from pleasingly futuristic rectangular foil pouches, of which there were seven different varieties. Jonathon, feeling like a connoisseur, selected an Ethiopian and clicked it into place. The machine took just long enough, and made just the right sounds, to give him the impression it was brewing his coffee rather than simply squirting hot water through some foil.

As he waited, he glanced at the copies of the *Financial Times* and *Business Week* that were strewn neatly on the little table. He frowned slightly, as though he fully understood what *NASDAQ breaks 5,000* meant. Then he frowned again, because his brain had decided to show him a picture of the girl from the Tube that morning.

He sat down at desk 412, took a sip of his Ethiopian, entered the password written on a Post-it note stuck to his screen, and flinched. Victoria was staring at him from above the partition that separated his desk from the one in front.

'You were *late*,' she said theatrically. 'Livia won't like that.'

Victoria said everything theatrically, as though it were a joke. She jokingly pretended that there was a fierce rivalry between them, and she was so persistent in this joke that it had become indistinguishable from a genuine fierce rivalry.

'Hello Victoria,' he said. 'How are you?'

She looked at him mock-suspiciously and disappeared behind the partition. A minute later she appeared at his elbow, making him flinch again.

'*Before you got in,*' she said, mock-pointedly, 'I took a call from Darblat Altonero. He wants you to call him back. Here's his extension.'

She handed him a Post-it note with a number and name on it.

Farynx was packed full of members of the international executive class, and Jonathon could not get used to these people's shiny, untroubled perfection or the silliness of their names.

Jonathon had grown up in various places in England where everyone had names like Ian Smith or Sarah Brown. At most of his schools even his own name had been considered suspiciously exotic. That was why he still couldn't quite accept that someone could blithely sail through life calling himself Darblat Altonero. At any school Jonathon had attended, a Darblat Altonero would have been ritually strangled on his first day. But here there were quantities of people with even sillier names, loudly and unselfconsciously proclaiming them on phones and in corridors all over the building.

'Oh and Dawn from Eager Beavers wants to talk to you about last week's timesheet,' said Victoria as she left.

Jonathon winced and flushed, feeling like someone in a period drama who is revealed at dinner to be the son of a tradesman. Now all the members of the international executive class around him would know he was a temp.

They continued to stare into their laptop screens or speak into their phones, their shirts crisp and their hair perfectly combed. Many of them had those mysterious, unplaceable accents people acquire at international school. It was the accent of Business English, which had its own vocabulary that Jonathon was only just beginning to decipher. He was acutely conscious of only being able to speak Normal English.

Jonathon dialled the extension Victoria had given him.

'Hello Darblat. It's Jonathon Fairfax from MBA recruiting. You asked me to call you?'

'Jonathon. I need to interface with you with regard to the current interview process conducting at Kellogg School of Management. Going forward, our alumni capability should be leveraged.'

'Um,' said Jonathon.

Over the next ten minutes, Jonathon slowly worked out that Darblat just wanted him to look something up on the database that occupied most of Jonathon's time at Farynx. It seemed strange to Jonathon that they were still putting so much effort into interviewing people. After all, the American manager who had taken over Farynx's consulting division had introduced a 'headcount freeze', which meant that it was almost impossible for them to actually offer anyone a job.

Jonathon had finished the call and was finding the information for Darblat when a shadow fell across his desk. He looked up and there was Livia, with anger in her eyes and a fur coat on her shoulders.

'Good *afternoon*,' she said, as though she somehow knew he had been four minutes late. 'So good of you to join us.'

'Oh, hello Livia,' he said, sitting up straight in his chair and trying to look efficient.

'Question,' she said – this was her favourite way to begin a question – 'have you made the database changes I requested?'

'Er, not yet. I've…'

'Please attend to it as a matter of urgency. You'll have to do better than this if you want to be a permanent person.'

Livia spoke a mixed Business-Posh dialect, which meant Jonathon was never exactly sure how English she was. She said 'prep' instead of 'homework', but she also called her female friends 'girlfriends'. She was deeply confusing.

Jonathon found most people deeply confusing. But there was something about Livia that seemed to stop his mind functioning at all. Her birthday, three weeks ago, had been his worst moment. The twenty-sixth of February was now engraved on his mind.

It had been ten in the morning, and about a dozen people, including Livia's bosses, Sarah Melchior and Adrian Salazar, stood in her small office. Victoria jabbed Jonathon in the ribs, and he held out a parcel containing a livid floral scarf.

'How thoughtful,' said Livia.

'Happy Christmas!' said Jonathon.

It took him a second to hear what he had said. And then everyone laughed at him, some shaking their heads at what an idiot he was.

'*Not* the sharpest axe in the tool shed,' said Adrian Salazar, and everyone laughed again.

Jonathon, his face bright red, said, 'I'll just go to the, um…'

He turned around, walked into the doorframe, and then went and hid in the knowledge-management area, where no one ever went. It was a small room, full of brochures with titles like *Solutionising the FMCG Space* and *Total Resource Utilisation Process*. There he had stood until his face returned to its normal colour.

And now his face was bright red again, and Livia was standing over him.

'You'll have to do better than this if you want to be a permanent person,' she repeated. 'You don't want to end up in the Data Services Department, do you?'

And with that terrible threat, she was gone.

4

On the other side of the Atlantic, Lance Ferman was facing no terrible threats, except perhaps the creasing of his jacket. Everything had been going his way for a very long time now.

In fact, Lance had won a whole series of genetic lotteries and had been living on the proceeds all his life. He had won a pair of cheekbones set at exactly the right angle, hair that fell across his brow just so, a masculine jaw, and a pair of eyes that seemed to have something going on behind them even when he was thinking about socks. And all that was just on his face.

He carried the face around on a tall, slim body on which clothes hung perfectly. He was charming and nonchalant, always looked healthy no matter what he ate or how late he stayed out, and women everywhere found him irresistible.

In combination, these attributes were as unlikely as a child wandering into a casino with a penny, betting at random, and emerging an hour later a billionaire. But whereas in England people resented that kind of good fortune, in America – where Lance was now living – everyone wanted to get as close as possible, hoping some of it would rub off on them. Lance liked living in America.

Lance particularly liked living in New York. He walked along the chunky, sun-dappled pavement, making for the subway. His apartment was in Chelsea, in a red-brick building with tall, dark windows, delicate lintels and rugged green fire steps bolted to the front. Like all bohemian places since people had discovered money in the early eighties, it was now a) not bohemian and b) breathtakingly expensive. But it suited his self-image. He was, after all, a TV presenter with a background in private investigation.

He made for the subway, past the liquor stores, past the salons and the delis, the gyms and galleries, and as he walked the buildings pumped themselves up from the old five-storeys near his apartment to grander and marginally less old ten-storeys a couple of blocks away. At Sixth Avenue, he looked south and could see skyscrapers – as exciting in their way as the first glimpse of the sea on childhood holidays.

Lance was looking forward to cancelling the plane he'd booked for the next day and telling his brother – a doctor marrying a human-rights lawyer – that he wouldn't be able to make his wedding in England.

'Sorry,' he would say, 'but my MTV series has finally got the green light – I'm going to be busier than the pope at a small-white-hat-wearing contest.'

After a year in development hell, his series was finally going to happen, as it had in Britain five years before, but on a larger scale. Everything here was on a larger scale. To an Englishman, everything in America – cars, chairs, people, toilets – seemed to have been made one-and-a-half-times life-size.

Lance took another look at the skyscrapers and then turned in the opposite direction, walking a couple of blocks north to take the F train at 23rd Street. All around him, the people looked as though they'd been cast as themselves in a film and were determined to dress and act the part. They were all the central character in a movie about someone fighting for their dreams, with a little luck, a lot of heart, and no doubt a series of astute bribes.

Lance descended into the subway, which was just as big and solid as everything above ground, packing in just as much metal and concrete. He went down to the big empty platforms, the huge carriages, the hard plastic seats. There was a thrill of danger on the subway and it made people carry themselves a certain way: chins out, alert even as they slouched.

At 2nd Avenue, Lance poured out of the station with the others – cocky, chin up. He felt so capable here, like he could punch a man out cold or drink an elegant new kind of martini, without really caring which.

Lance walked the couple of blocks to Katz's, with its old-fashioned neon signs and its big windows.

'Meeting Sol Spender. He here yet?' he said to the man who met everyone as they came in. After a journey on the subway Lance always sounded a little more New York. He had better rein that in: being British was supposed to be part of his charm.

'Right in the corner.'

Lance made his way over, threading between the giant meaty diners wielding their giant meaty sandwiches.

Sol Spender pulled his attention away from a TV set opposite his seat as Lance approached. He was a heavy man, with a powerful face and slicked-back white hair. He wore glasses, a brightly checked jacket and a yellow shirt.

'Lance. You're right on time,' he said, checking his watch. 'I had a good feeling about you, kid.'

'Mr Spender. Good to see you, sir.' Lance had picked up the American habit of calling older men 'sir'.

'Sit down. What'll you have?'

'Pastrami on rye?'

'Two pastrami on rye,' said Spender to the waiter. 'And get us a couple coffees, will you?'

Lance sat down.

'Lance, I'm just going to lay it right out there. You're fired.'

'Fired?'

Spender sighed and picked up the menu again. 'Why does everyone say that when I fire them? What am I gonna say, "No"?'

'Sorry. I didn't mean to put the question mark on the end. What I mean is, why?'

Spender looked up from the menu. 'That's better. You know, I like you, kid.'

'And you're firing me. What do you do to people you don't like?'

'I fire them too. But I don't bring them to Katz's to do it. I get C to call them.'

'I'm honoured. But why?'

'I don't know. You got chutzpah. And nice hair. You can go a long way with nice hair. I like to look at it while I eat. Reminds me what my bathroom mirror used to show me in the mornings.'

'I meant why are you firing me?'

'Listen. This project's been in development for a year now. If *MTV Undercover* was ever going to get made in the United States, it would have happened by now.'

'But you're the executive. You could just green-light it.'

'Weren't you listening? I said it's done.'

'But why? That's the thing I'm trying to find out.'

'This spy stuff is old. I mean, hello, the Cold War is *over*. People aren't interested any more. That's the kind of thing people like now,' he said, waving at a TV on the opposite wall, 'something with a bit of excitement.'

Lance turned in his chair to see. There was a news report showing aerial footage of a small burning mansion in New Jersey.

'You mean the local news? That's what people like?'

'Don't get fresh, it doesn't suit you. I mean house fires, human drama, rich people suffering. Wait a minute.' He pulled a phone out of his pocket and pressed a button. 'Hey, C. Make a note: I want a show that combines urban music, human drama, bad things happening to rich, cute people. You know, like a mansion lights on fire, that sort of thing.'

He put the phone back in his pocket and returned to his menu.

Lance said, 'But the Cold War ended more than ten years ago. It was just as over twelve months ago when you brought me over here to develop this project. I cancelled my contract with MTV Europe to come here. And the show was a hit in Britain, where the Cold War is equally over.'

Spender shrugged.

Lance continued, 'It's mostly about me in a trench coat introducing songs that are tenuously linked to secret activities. I mean, house fires can also involve secrets. We can put them in the show.'

'Listen,' said Spender, leaning back to accommodate the giant pastrami on rye that was set down before him, 'I never told you this before, but I had a bad feeling about this show from the start.'

'So why did you bring me over here?'

'It was a good format.'

'But you've just spent twelve months making me change the format. It *was* good: I play some songs about spying, I spy on bands, I interview some semi-shady characters. I do most of it in a moodily lit alleyway in a studio. It worked. Why change it?'

'Weren't you listening? There's nothing to change. It's been cancelled.'

'By you.'

'Who else is gonna cancel the goddamn thing? Now eat your sandwich.'

'Had you even decided to fire me and cancel the show before you saw that news report? Is this just a whim?'

'It's not a whim. It's a gut decision.'

'Would you consider me for another show?'

'Jesus, no. You're too strongly associated with *MTV Undercover*.'

'But no one in the US has seen me on TV, how can I be too strongly associated with anything? What's the problem?'

Spender leaned forward, his voice a whisper. '*Your show got cancelled*. Besides,' he said, picking up his sandwich, 'people are looking for a little more emotional depth than you provide.'

5

'What have you *done*, Jonathon?' said Victoria in mock-horror.

Jonathon flinched. He hadn't realised that Victoria was standing behind him. And his nerves were already somewhat strained by Livia's casual threat to send him to the Data Services Department, which would be disastrous for his chances of becoming a permanent person.

'I'm just making the database changes that Livia asked for,' he said.

'But you've *ruined* Michael Bartagharsley – all the information about him is *gone*.'

'It's all right,' he said. 'This is my test version. It hasn't changed anything about Michael Bartagharsley in the real version that you use.'

Michael Bartagharsley was one of Farynx's many job candidates from international business schools. Jonathon was in charge of the database that kept track of them. When Jonathon was working out how to make the changes Livia asked for, he always used Bartagharsley as his guinea pig. Over the months, Jonathon felt he had come to know the man better than any of the people who sat in the chairs around him. Bartagharsley attended Wharton School of Management, he held Italian, Bulgarian and British passports, he had represented at least one of these countries in synchronised skating, and he played the bassoon.

'But under "Business School" it just says "green",' said Victoria. 'Michael Bartagharsley goes to Wharton.'

'Yes, but it's only the test version. It hasn't changed in the real version. Livia wanted the screen's border to go green for candidates who have passed the first round of interviews.'

'But he passed and the border *hasn't* gone green.'

'No, I know. I'm still trying to work out how to do it.'

Jonathon was having a bad morning. Sometimes he could coax the database into doing what he wanted. Other times it would crash at the tiniest provocation and refuse to understand the little programs he wrote for it. Today it was behaving like a malignant genie, exploiting any tiny ambiguity in his phrasing to fuck him in the most egregious way possible. Instead of turning Michael Bartagharsley's border green it had replaced nearly every piece of information about him with the word 'green' – or, in some places, its hexadecimal equivalent.

Part of the problem was that Jonathon's brain was still insisting on flashing up pictures of the girl from the Tube every few seconds.

He didn't know why it would do this, as he definitely hadn't fallen in love at first sight.

'But if you don't know how to do it,' said Victoria, 'why did you promise Livia you *would* do it?'

'Because I know it's possible. I just haven't figured out how yet.'

Victoria stood beside him and looked down at him with mock-serious, accusing eyes.

'Michael Bartagharsley's starting in two weeks' time,' she said. 'You'd better have his information fixed by then.'

'His information hasn't changed. This is just my te— Wait a minute, what about the headcount freeze? How come he's got a job?'

'Someone obviously wanted him enough to find a way. *He's* an expert on the Japanese automotive industry, you know.'

Jonathon was suddenly overcome with an intense desire to be an expert on the Japanese automotive industry too, so that he could be a permanent person with a proper job.

Victoria shook her head in mock-sadness and walked away. Jonathon sighed. He could never work out whether she really couldn't understand what he was saying, or if it was just a ploy to unsettle him.

A picture of the girl from the Tube flashed up in front of his eyes.

He needed a break.

There was nothing for it; he would have to go to the toilet. When you're locked in a vicious mock-rivalry with someone who seems to observe your every move, and everyone around you works constantly, going to the toilet becomes the only legitimate way of having a break.

He walked to the end of the floor and pushed through the fire doors, into the carpeted area beyond. Opposite the toilet doors hung a piece of corporate art. Jonathon stopped and looked at it. That was how desperate he was for distraction from Victoria, the programming genie, and the face of the girl on the Tube with whom he had definitely not fallen in love at first sight.

It was difficult to tell what the painting was. The thing seemed to have been done at some speed, and not necessarily by a painter. To Jonathon it looked like an old man in a waterproof coat yelling at the sea, but it could equally have been a banana left in the rain or an unusually elongated fried egg. As he looked at it, feeling angry that someone had been paid for it, he realised that he had not thought of that beautiful upper lip for several seconds.

After a bit, Jonathon started to worry that Victoria would see him there, so he decided to climb the stairs and see the corporate art on the next floor. He pushed through the double doors and into the stairwell, which almost no one used. The windowless walls were whitewashed, and his footsteps rang out as he climbed the concrete stairs. This was a building that expected you to use the lifts, unless there was a fire.

On the next floor up, the picture was a nude who seemed to be made from a kind of chunky phlegm, lying on a couch in a room missing at least one of its dimensions. This made Jonathon angry enough to forget the girl from the Tube for a whole minute. He felt that if he could make it to two minutes without thinking of her, it might break her hold on his brain, allowing him to successfully turn Michael Bartagharsley's border green and take one step closer to becoming a permanent person. He decided to go up to the next floor.

On the sixth floor the picture was a giant but watery oil painting of a woman in a suit floating midway between what was probably a cradle and what was almost certainly a briefcase. It looked like more time and care had been spent in hanging it on the wall than in painting it.

This annoyed Jonathon even more than the last two. He had done a degree in illustration and had got a first. He accepted that this had been a foolish thing to do, and that he needed a proper, sensible job. But he couldn't help feeling that there was something unjust about the fact that he was programming databases and taking recreational toilet breaks while someone who very clearly had no ability to depict things was selling pictures.

In fact, Jonathon was so annoyed by this painting that it took him within a whisker of forgetting the girl. There was only one more floor above him. Perhaps the painting there would be so bad that it would drive the girl from his mind altogether, allowing him to get on with his life. He climbed the stairs.

On the seventh floor there was no picture.

There was nothing else there either. Through the glass of the fire doors, Jonathon could see that the floor was completely empty. This was odd, because Jonathon had talked to Lynton Chinafat there about a month earlier. Then it had been crammed with desks, chairs, combined photocopier-printers and people talking loudly about shareholder value. Now there was nothing. Jonathon pushed open the fire door and stepped in.

The layout was identical to the fourth floor, where Jonathon worked. And yet, empty, it felt both far larger and much smaller. The blue carpet tiles seemed tattier. The wooden walkway that ran the length of the floor seemed forlorn, leading only to more emptiness. Things that psychologically loomed large on the fourth floor – like Livia's office – were revealed to be tiny. He felt cheated, as though they had been deceiving him all this time. Farynx was just a big space with some things in it.

It would look bad if someone found him here. How would he explain what he was doing? He looked at his watch. Twelve minutes had passed. He had better get back to work before Victoria noticed and told Livia.

Back on the staircase, he hesitated. There was the sound of footsteps, climbing up the stairs with measured tread. He thought of hiding – in a corner of the empty floor, or in its toilet. But if he were caught it would be far more difficult to explain hiding than to explain just walking down some stairs. He continued downwards.

He reached the landing where the stairs turned. Then he was halfway down the second flight, nearly at the sixth floor. By now the footsteps were louder. He could see someone mounting the last few steps of the staircase up from the floor below. It was the short, intimidating guard from that morning. Jonathon tried to walk as though everything was normal. It was, of course, because he hadn't done anything wrong. He had just taken a walk to clear his head. So why did he feel so guilty? It was the same when he saw policemen. He always had to walk past them pretending to be innocent, and it's hard to pretend to be what you really are.

Jonathon did the same now with the tiny, intimidating security guard, neither looking at him nor ostentatiously not looking at him. But the guard was very definitely looking at Jonathon.

''Scuse me, sir,' said the guard.

'Ah, yen? I mean, yes?' said Jonathon.

'Pass, please.'

'Oh yes. Here it is. I'm Jonathon Fairfax,' Jonathon explained. 'We met this morning.'

'It's not my job to remember your name,' said the guard, scrutinising the pass. Then, looking up, he said, 'What were you doing on seventh floor?'

The guard had one of those Yorkshire accents that make it impossible to say 'the'. Instead, he left a tiny gap, as though he expected Jonathon to add his own 'the' if he felt one was needed.

'Just, um, taking a break. I wanted to clear my head and see what the picture was.' It sounded such a pathetically unlikely excuse.

'What picture?'

'The corporate art. There's a picture on every floor. I just thought

I'd see what it was.'

'I see,' said the guard, suspiciously. His name tag said he was Carl Barker.

'How come the floor's empty?' asked Jonathon. It was what he would have asked if he were innocent, just a legitimate employee taking a break he was entitled to, looking at the pictures that had been put there for people to look at. And he was. They had. All of that was true.

6

'I killed a guy,' said Todd. He was sitting on the edge of his sofa, clutching his phone tight in his hand.

The person on the other end of the line turned off a TV set. 'What?'

'I said I killed a guy,' repeated Todd.

'What, *again*?'

'What do you mean *again*?'

'I mean you killed a guy *before*, Dad. Remember?'

'That was *two years ago*,' said Todd.

'That's right. Maybe that's why I said you killed a guy before. What the fuck, Dad?'

'Listen, Duke, could you be a little more supportive?'

'Oh, supportive. Right. Like you are?'

Todd got up from the sofa and walked over to the window of his apartment.

'Is this about how I was when you came out? Listen, Duke, I'm sorry. I'm sorry about how I acted. As a matter of fact, I'm ashamed of it. Okay? But I've done a lot of work on myself since then. You know, I can even admit that I have some of those same feelings myself. I think Patrick Swayze, for example, is a very attractive man.'

'Dad, you do *not* have the hots for Patrick Swayze.'

'I do. A little. Hey, I'm not claiming to be a full-blown gay.'

'*A full-blown gay*? What is that? Who says that?'

'You know what? I'm sorry I called.'

'Me too.'

'Fine.' Todd looked at the cell phone in his hand, sighed, pressed the red button, and threw the thing at his sofa. It bounced off, scratching his polished parquet floor.

'Fuck,' he muttered under his breath.

He turned back to the window. East 72nd Street. Just a little too far from Central Park. *That park's a hell of a walk from your apartment*, some billionaire had said to him at a party. The sky was dark already but the street was lit up gold by the cars, the street lights, the windows of other apartments. Not long now and he would have a penthouse overlooking the park.

He retrieved the phone from the floor, punched a couple of buttons on it, and flopped back into his black leather sofa.

'Yeah, hi. It's me again. Listen, Duke, can we start over?'

There was a pause. 'Okay.'

'So, sorry. It's just that I'm a little down right now. Like I said, I killed a guy. When it's happening, I feel like I'm invincible, like I'm this god. And then afterwards I just feel… kind of empty, I guess.'

'You know, Dad, I hate to say what's obvious here, but you've really got to stop killing people.'

'I know, I know. But what can I do? My therapist says I have a strong need to kill. I mean, we all have it to some degree, but I… it just gets too much for me. And I try to put it into perspective. I mean, hundreds of years ago my drive to kill, my killer instinct, wouldn't have been a problem. The opposite, in fact – it would have made me a valued member of the community. I'd have killed the guy from the other tribe who was stealing our horses, or whatever. It's really just an accident of history that it's seen as a problem now, as something to be ashamed of. It's like, years ago being gay was a crime. That was something you had to keep secret, to lie about.'

'Okay. That is the most ridiculous and offensive thing I have ever heard, right there.'

'Come on. This is a tough time for me. I'm just trying to get a little perspective on this…'

'Uh, yeah. By saying being gay is morally equivalent to murdering people.'

'That is not what I said. I'm sorry. You know that's not what I meant. Just, you know, I killed a guy – and that doesn't automatically mean I'm a bad person. That's all I'm saying.'

'Dad, it's *murder*. It kind of does automatically make you a bad person.'

'Yeah, well, so does smoking pot and dropping out of college. Know anyone who fits *that* description?'

'Are you crazy? Those things don't *hurt* anyone.'

'Don't hurt anyone? You're telling me *Mexican drug gangs* don't hurt anyone? Give me a break. And dropping out of college hurts my bank book. Performance Art MAs don't come free, not even at Kent State. That was meant to be an investment.'

'Yeah, well, maybe if you were a little less critical I'd have the self-esteem and confidence to stick to a college course. And maybe I wouldn't need to self-medicate if you and Mom had stayed together. You ever think about that? Perhaps I just needed better role models.'

'Hey. I am a good role model! Don't I make a good living? Don't I provide? Don't I achieve what I set out to achieve? I am head of the fastest-growing divisions of Farynx. I am going to remake business as we know it...'

'Yeah, Dad, you're a great role model – *apart from all the killings!*'

'*All* the killings. There's been like *two* killings in my life.'

'OH WELL THAT'S FINE THEN!' shouted Duke.

Todd writhed in his seat, his lips drawn back, angry words ready, his face flushed and sweating, the veins standing out on his neck. And then suddenly, he was aware of all those things. He saw himself in his mind's eye. *Is this the kind of father I want to be?*

He let out a long breath, wiped his forehead with the back of his hand.

'I'm sorry, Duke,' he said. 'We're fighting again. Why do we always get like this?'

'I don't know, Dad. I don't know.'

'It's me. It's me. I'm just too aggressive.'

'But that's your strength, Dad. That's how you've got where you are.'

'Yeah, with an ex-wife and a son who hates me.'

'Dad, I love you. It's just, *what the fuck?* I mean, *what the actual fuck?* You killed a guy. Wait. I hadn't even thought of this. Are you going to jail? Are they going to execute you?'

'What? No. Of course not. I'm good. I just... I have this *instinct* for it. I erased the security tape of my car arriving at the gates – guy had his password stuck to the monitor. Then he had this ridiculous coffee machine—'

'What kind?'

'What does it matter?'

'Just curious.'

'It was a Flemke.'

'My God, he had a Flemke? *I* would kill for one of those.'

'I'll tell you something, it made the best coffee I have ever tasted.

I'm missing it already. I think maybe that's what pushed me over the edge. You know how a really good coffee makes you feel like you can do anything?'

'Dad, you were telling me about why you're not going to jail.'

'Oh yeah. So, I laid the coffee machine's power cable over this thing he had, this raclette grill—'

'For the cheese?'

'Yeah, you put the Swiss cheese on and then you scrape it off when it melts. It's good. I mean, it's not *great*, but it's fun for a change if you're at a dinner party.'

'Man, when I get invited to a party it's just a bunch of guys smoking weed and watching *Ren and Stimpy*. I only see dinner parties like that on TV.'

'Well you should visit more.'

'You're always too busy.'

'Well if you would arrange things in advance a little instead of just calling up and saying like, "Can I turn up tomorrow?"'

'When I arrange stuff you just cancel at the last minute.'

'When? When have I ever cancelled you at the last minute?'

'Like *all the time!*'

'Jesus! I… Wait a minute. This is happening again. We have got to get ourselves out of this cycle. Okay. I will not cancel you last minute again. I mean, I don't specifically remember a time I have done that. But if you're telling me that, I take it on board. I hear it.'

'And that's all I ask.'

'Right. Right. Anyhow, I put some dish towels next to the raclette grill, and I wait a couple minutes – and his wife could be back any second…'

'Oh fuck. He had a wife?'

'Sure.'

'And you don't think that makes it worse?'

'Listen, this is not something I'm proud of. But this is a part of me. And I'm trying to share with you here, Duke. Are you going to help me?'

'Okay. I'm listening.'

'So, pretty soon we've got ourselves an electrical fire…'

'No sprinkler system?'

'I shut it off. He has the same system as your uncle.'

'Dan?'

'No, Ruben – your mother's side. But it makes me think that

someone – some power – wanted me to kill him. Because he also just happens to have a security system I know how to operate. So those are the two big hurdles that are going to get me caught, right there – security system, sprinkler – and both of them are neutralised. I know it sounds crazy, but maybe *fate*—'

'It sounds crazy.'

'Maybe. Anyhow, we've got some dish towels and we've got some cognac leading the fire down onto the floor, and then we have wooden units and a wooden floor, and that kitchen goes up like a Christmas tree. No one's going to be able to tell he was beaten to death with a spaghetti spoon now—'

'With a spaghetti spoon?'

'Don't ask. Anyhow, there's no evidence I've been there, no DNA evidence of him on me, because of the oven mitts.'

'The oven mitts?'

'Sure. I put on some oven mitts before I killed him, so I wouldn't get his DNA on me. I didn't want to get pulled over on the way back, get a swab taken under my fingernails and spend the rest of my life in jail – over *this* guy…'

'That's forward thinking, I guess.'

'Right. Like I said, I have a gift for this stuff. So, no one sees me drive out of there. An hour later I'm back in my apartment. Two hours later the clothes I wore are burned down to nothing and in a public trash can on the other side of town. And twelve hours later I'm hearing on the news about a death in a house fire and some fire department captain's saying it's early days but they believe it was caused by a coffee machine. Now I hear his wife is looking to start a class-action suit against Flemke.'

'So that's it?'

'The cops are not treating it as a murder. Looks like I'm in the clear.'

'But you're through with the killings now, right?'

'Yes, I'm through with the killings. I'm all business now. Heading off to London tomorrow…'

7

Jonathon clicked the key in the lock and eased open the front door of the new flat he shared with Emma. He knew she must be at home because the radio was singing quietly to itself about what a girl wants.

'Hello?' he called.

The door slammed behind him, making him flinch. The flat was fitted with self-closing safety doors. They made it marginally less likely that he would die in a fire, but much more likely that he would die of hypertension brought on by constant flinching.

He hung up his coat and put his briefcase in the bedroom, then stuck his head around the doorway into the kitchen and living area. Emma, chopping carrots, paused and looked up at him. He was always somehow surprised to see her. There was something unfamiliar about her, as though they were still essentially strangers even after living together for four months.

'How was work?' he asked. He was tired and would have liked a beer.

They kissed, each mistaking the position of the other's head, so that he got her nose and she got his chin.

'Fine,' she said. 'We started the payroll systems upgrade pilot today.'

'Oh,' he said. 'Was it… um?' He could not for the life of him think of a response. 'Will it… upgrade the payroll systems?'

Emma, mercifully, seemed not to hear this as she bent to take a large and noisy casserole dish from the cupboard.

'How about yours?' she asked.

'I found an empty floor,' he said.

Emma nodded absently, as though this was something that happened regularly, like a fire drill. She poured some chopped tomatoes into the casserole dish.

'It wasn't empty a month ago, and now it is. It's strange. Farynx is doing well. They say it was the world's sixth-best-performing company last quarter. But they've emptied a floor.'

'What?'

'They've emptied a floor.'

'Oh.'

Jonathon peeled a sweet potato.

'Emma,' he said, 'when you worked for Farynx, did you understand what it does?'

'Of course,' she said, laughing at the idea of anyone not understanding. 'It delivers solutions strategically.'

'But what does that mean?'

'What do you mean?'

'What?'

'What?'

'I mean, I know it has different divisions doing different things, and that the division I work for does consulting. But when I try to work out what consulting involves, I can't understand. I tried reading the brochures but they all have titles like *Automotive Solutions, Evolved*, so they only really mean anything if you already know what Farynx does.'

'Read their website.'

'It just says what the brochures say.'

'Well, you know that your division does management consulting in Europe.'

'Yes, but as far as I can work out, that means that the people paid to manage other companies pay my company to tell them what to do.'

'Well, you could put it like that.'

'But… the people who manage those companies are paid a lot of money to manage them. But then instead of doing their jobs, they pay my company even more money to do their jobs for them. Why don't the companies just recruit someone from Farynx to manage them? That would be cheaper.'

'That's not how it works.'

'But that's it – I don't understand how it works, or why.'

'Don't be silly,' she said, laughing nervously. 'I don't know what's got into you tonight. I hope you don't talk like this at work: you'll never become a permanent person.'

They went for a run, ate their healthy casserole, prepared their things for the morning and went to bed. He rolled over and brushed her perfectly brushed hair away from her face. It immediately fell neatly back into place. He tried again.

'Ah, er, sorry,' he said. 'I've got my watch strap caught in your hair.'

'Ow,' she said, laying aside the copy of *Healthy Woman* she had been reading.

'It's all right, I've got it now. There. Sorry.' He took off his watch and put it on the bedside table, next to the alarm clock that Emma walked around the bed to turn off every morning.

'Sorry,' she said.

'Do you, er…?' he began.

'What? You mean… er?' she said, lying back in a way that could equally mean 'come and get me' or 'now for some refreshing sleep'.

'What?' he asked, confused.

'Yes?' she said. But why did it sound like a question?

'Oh, er, I mean, you have to be up in the morning. Sorry.' He let his hand drop.

'Sorry. No, it's fine.'

'Oh, right. Thanks.' Was that what he should say? What would Casanova have said?

'I mean, um, good,' he added.

She turned the light off. He moved his hand to caress her ear, kissed her. And then the embarrassed fumbling began. They sounded like a pair of very polite fat people trying to get into the same small lift, and the words of their formal intimacy could be set down in any order.

'Sorry.'

'What?'

'Is that…?'

'There?'

'Right.'

'Sorry.'

'What?'

'Thanks.'

'Oh.'

'Good.'

'What?'

And afterwards panting slightly and holding her, and trying not to think about this stranger in his arms, or the girl on the Tube.

Tuesday

8

The fourth time the buzzer rang, the woman in Lance's bed punched him in the head.

'Mffgh?' he said.

'There's someone at the door,' she said.

'Oh, right.' He mulled it over. This seemed reasonable. And then the buzzer sounded, lending the idea even more credence. 'Weird. I got it confused with someone punching me in the head.'

He rolled over and pushed his face into the pillow.

'Hey!' she said. 'Aren't you going to see who it is?'

This had not occurred to him. Apart from the obvious problem of requiring him to get out of bed, it seemed a sound plan. He threw off the covers and lurched elegantly to the intercom by the door. A fuzzy black-and-white picture of a man in a hat and a moustache appeared.

'Good morning, sir,' said a voice from the speaker. 'We're here to collect your Flemke 1100.'

'What do you mean?'

'Ah, I don't know any other way to say it. We're here to collect your coffee machine?'

'Does that mean I won't have it any more?'

'Yes, sir. I'm afraid it does.'

'You'd better not then.'

'Ah, is this Lance Ferman?'

'No, *this* is. *I'm* Lance Ferman.'

'Sir, a representative called you yesterday and made this appointment with you.'

'Oh, he must have made it with drunk me. I got fired yesterday. You're talking to hung-over me.'

'Sir, we have a lot of collections to make today. Could you please just let us up?'

Lance pushed the 'disconnect' button. Then, to even things out, he pushed the 'open door' button.

He went into the kitchen and put some coffee on. That was when he saw the clock. Twelve minutes to nine.

His flight.

His plane to England was going to take off in an hour and twenty-seven minutes.

After his meeting with Sol Spender, he had immediately gone to a bar and begun to methodically make himself drunk by consuming booze. This was no simple thing for a man of Lance's genetic blessings; it required time and commitment.

The afternoon and evening began to reassemble themselves in his head. There had been a wonderful period of several hours when he had so many new best friends he had not cared about being fired. And then at a certain point, he had met the love of his life. Now the friends were gone and he was dreading what the woman might have turned into.

There was a knock at the door. He opened it a few inches. There were two men outside, both wearing moustaches, green baseball caps and uniforms with 'Flemke' written above the pocket.

'Yes?' he said, unnecessarily. He wanted to buy a bit more time to think.

'Sir, we've come to pick up your coffee machine,' said the wider of the two men. He had the sort of determined polite reasonableness you can only acquire by constantly dealing with people who are allowed to be rude and unreasonable to you.

'But why?' said Lance.

'Well, sir, following an accident, we believe your machine could, ah, burn your apartment down.'

'Oh.' Lance considered for a moment. He had obviously considered this same question yesterday and decided that, almost unbelievably good though the coffees were, they were not quite as nice as not being burned to death.

A voice behind him said, 'Quit being a jerk, would you? Let these guys do their job.'

He turned around and saw a slight woman with black hair hanging in fronds over her round blue eyes. She had art-deco cheekbones, fair skin and the kind of legs that do more than just keep a torso from hitting the ground. Looks-wise, he had certainly not disgraced himself: she was gorgeous. But he didn't like the way she talked. And he suddenly remembered that she had punched him in the head.

However, when a gorgeous woman wearing one of your shirts tells you you're being a jerk, and two polite men with moustaches are telling you with their eyes that you're being a jerk, then, he reasoned, you're probably being a jerk.

'Come on in,' he said. 'Take it. I'm going to stop being a jerk. And also put some clothes on.' He was, after all, completely naked.

He grabbed both coffees from the machine and made for the shower. But the woman with art-deco cheekbones stopped him and took one on the way.

After drinking a coffee, taking a shower and dressing himself in some of his most airline-upgradeable clothes, Lance was beginning to feel like himself again. He walked out of the bedroom to find the two moustachioed men leaving, carrying his beautiful coffee machine in a plastic crate.

'Between you and me, sir,' said the one who did the talking, 'there is no way there's anything wrong with this machine. But Mr Flemke's a good guy. He says if there's even the smallest chance this machine caused that fire out in New Jersey, that's too much for him.'

'Oh. Can I have it back then?'

'Sorry. We're just following orders.'

And with that, they were gone.

In the kitchen, Art Deco sat on a stool at the breakfast bar, making her coffee last. She looked up, taking him in.

'Well,' she said, 'I guess I didn't disgrace myself last night. Looks-wise, I mean. Don't like the way you talk though. And I get the impression there's not much going on behind those big blue eyes of yours.'

Lance considered his next remark carefully, but ended up settling for, 'What?'

She laughed. 'Your face. You look like Jonathon Fairfax.'

'What?' he said again. It wasn't his finest repartee, but he had severely depleted the world's alcohol reserves last night, and this woman kept saying things that struck him as being very surprising.

'You know, Mr Astonishment.'

'How do you know Jonathon Fairfax?' he asked.

'He's my husband.'

Lance gave her a hard look, signifying that he knew this was impossible.

'You seriously don't remember?' she asked.

He narrowed his eyes to suggest that he might remember, but that she should go on anyway.

'You were telling me about him last night. Said he was your best friend. I mean, you said everyone was your best friend, so… But you tried calling him.'

'Did I?'

'Why would I lie?'

'Listen,' he said, looking at his watch, 'I've got to go. But I'll call you.' He switched his eyes and voice into sincere mode, as he always did at this point. And, as ever, he neglected to mention that he might not use a phone when he called, so there was a good chance she wouldn't hear.

'You think I want you to call me?' she said, puzzled.

He was equally puzzled. 'Do you think you don't want me to call you?'

'I know it. I don't do second dates.'

'You mean you only do one-night stands?'

'I prefer the term "microrelationship". But sure. That's the fun bit. Why carry on chewing the gum after it's lost its flavour?'

'That's what I think,' said Lance. 'I just pretend not to.'

'Why?'

'I find lying is convenient.'

'Weird. I just say what I think.'

'Me too.'

She looked pleased for a second, then confused.

'Convenient lie,' he explained. 'See how much easier it makes things?'

'Not really.'

'Never mind. The important thing is that we both agree on our preference for microrelationships. And that means I can be up-front in asking you to please get out of my shirt and my apartment so I can get my plane.'

'Screw you. I'm taking a shower.'

'Then you leave me no option.'

'What are you going to do about it?'

'I'm going to leave you in my apartment and hope that what you lack in personality you make up for in not stealing my things or setting them on fire.'

'Well, I guess you're just going to have to find that out, aren't you?'

9

Jonathon found himself lying in a large white box full of noise. There was a glowing square at one end of the box. Something was covering him. There was a body lying next to him. It was all awful.

It was, however, not quite as bad as where he had just come from: taking the wrong path through the woods, pursued by a shadowy figure with a scythe.

'Could you turn the alarm off please?' said the body. It was a woman.

'What?' he squawked, panic-stricken.

Another consignment of consciousness arrived. His memories started to plug themselves in. The white box was his bedroom. The glowing square was the window. The thing covering him was a cover. The woman was Emma, his girlfriend.

He was Jonathon Fairfax. This was his flat. Its laminated floors were his laminated floors. Its chrome-effect mixer taps were his chrome-effect mixer taps. And the shadowy figure in the woods had been a dream. *But what could it possibly mean?*

'The alarm's still going off,' said Emma.

'Yes,' he agreed. 'I'll turn off on it.' *How do you speak again?*

There it was beside him: a small, terribly angry box. It was making a horrible noise.

Emma sprang up, opened the curtains, walked around the bed and pressed a button on the angry box. The noise stopped. She walked back around the bed and out through the door, which closed itself behind her with a bang, making him flinch.

The problem was that he required such a long boot-up process in the morning. Emma seemed to open her eyes and be instantly functioning, starting immediately on the to-do list of getting out of bed, switching off the alarm and having a shower. He needed a couple of minutes just to remember that time and matter existed, and then reason his way from those basic principles to the existence of noise, mornings, jobs, alarm clocks, and the necessity of turning them off and getting dressed. He could change though, he knew it. He could become the sort of switched-on achiever that he needed to be.

The door opened and Emma was back in the room, dry and immaculate, wrapped in a neat white towel.

'Aren't you up yet?' she asked. The door slammed itself shut. He flinched.

'No,' he admitted, and went off for his shower.

The flat's shower was, by some way, the most stress-free place in Jonathon's life – easily better than Farynx's toilet cubicle. In this watery Eden he found himself singing 'Perfect Day' by Lou Reed. He had liked it as a child, when he had heard it on the kitchen radio. Back then, he had assumed it was mainly about a man having a really nice day. Now, of course, he knew it was really about how heroin can bring you a brief moment of peace, the perfection of which is already tainted by the knowledge that it's an illusion that will undermine your health and eventually kill you.

The water began to cool and Jonathon realised that once again he'd spent too long in this anti-worry chamber. He towelled himself down and rushed out of the bathroom. Emma was standing by the front door, looking at her watch.

'I'm going to have to go,' she said, giving him a tight little smile. 'The payroll systems upgrade pilot…'

'Ah, oh. Sorry. Yes,' he said.

He should have been ready to take the Tube in with her, break-fasted and with some delicious healthy sandwiches neatly packed in Tupperware. Instead he had spent too long booting himself up and singing in the shower. He felt embarrassed. He would change though. He just needed to become one of those efficient, easy-waking, short-showering, in-the-real-world-living, switched-on achievers.

Should he kiss her goodbye? Did she want him to? Was she annoyed with him? He found her difficult to read. Just as he decided that he would kiss her, he looked up and saw her elbow disappearing. And then the door banged behind her, making him flinch. She was gone.

It was 8.09. If he didn't hurry he would be late for being early for work again. And he ran the risk of being on the same train as the girl he had seen yesterday. He hurriedly dressed and packed. He wasted a small amount of time being distracted by some new coasters Emma had bought, and a larger amount of time being surprised by his phone showing a missed call from America. Then he fell over the ironing board, absent-mindedly packed the coasters and was gone, flinching as the door slammed behind him.

He set off at a run, briefcase in hand. He ran down Brownswood Road, right onto Blackstock Road and kept running, past its many rotisserie chicken shops, all hard at work cooking their breakfast chickens, past its equal number of estate agents, past the one nice cafe, past the small groups of Turkish men who strode up and down the road all day shaking hands with one another. The Turkish men stopped and openly laughed at the foolish sweating man with the sticking-up hair who chose to fill his days with suited running instead of pursuing a simple manly life of handshakes and rotisserie chicken.

He ran past the phone box that was exclusively used for buying and taking drugs, past the pub that people with teeth never went in, past the Happening Biegel Bakery, past Ken's Plucky Fried Chicken, the area's second most upmarket chicken shop, and past the Arsenal Shop. He ran across Seven Sisters Road, glancing up at the sign on the rusting railway bridge where, beneath a yellowing sky and amid bluey-green clouds or trees, faded letters spelled out the words, 'Welcome to Finsbury Park.'

He ran into the mouth of the station, down the stairs of its gullet, and after being thoroughly metabolised by the Tube, London's large intestine, he was flushed out the other end into Temple station. Despite changing correctly at Embankment, he had not seen the girl, and was deeply relieved. Now he could get on with forgetting all about her and becoming a permanent person.

In the early afternoon, a shadow fell across Jonathon's desk. He whirled around and there, standing over him in a houndstooth suit, was Livia, her eyes flashing.

'Question: have you still not made the changes I requested? Yes or no?'

'Um,' he said, trying to work out the logic of the possible answers.

'It's a perfectly simple question. Yes or no?'

'Ah, no, I haven't not made… I mean, um. Yes? I've made the changes.'

'Then why are the borders not turning green?'

'They are on mine.' He found the database entry for Michael Bartagharsley, who had passed the first interview. The border, to Jonathon's relief, was green.

'Go to Chad T Shook,' she said sternly.

Jonathon did. The border of the screen was not green, but standard grey.

'But that's because we haven't finished entering the results of the Wharton interviews yet. Look, if I tell the database that he passed…' Jonathon chose 'Passed' from a drop-down menu.

The border turned green.

'Oh,' said Livia, turning on a sixpence from rage to girlish delight. 'That's wonderful. Aren't you a clever little chipmunk?'

He was not sure how to answer this, so hedged his bets with a quiet, 'Possibly.'

'Oh, that's marvellous. Victoria! Have you seen this?'

Victoria's face rose above the partition and gave Livia an ingratiating smile.

'Yes?' said Victoria.

'Isn't it wonderful? The computer can sense who's passed the first interview, and it turns the border green, so you can see at a glance.'

'Is it *that* helpful? I mean, we still have to tell the computer the information. It doesn't really "sense" it. And how long did it take him?'

'You know,' said Livia, 'you should be more supportive of your colleagues. You'll never become a permanent person with an attitude like that. That's more a Data Services Department attitude.'

Victoria blanched.

Livia continued, 'If you had a good mental attitude, you would have taught yourself to program like Jonathon here. Jonathon, I'm very pleased with you.'

She smiled graciously at Jonathon, then turned and gave Victoria a hard stare that lasted long enough to bring her to the verge of tears. Then she turned smartly and strode back to her office, closing the door behind her.

Victoria gave Jonathon a look of hatred from narrowed eyes.

'You're only her favourite because you're a man, you know,' she said.

'But she usually hates me!' said Jonathon. 'Did you not hear her on Friday screaming at me for being useless?'

'Well you *are* useless. And if you were a woman she'd take you into her office and talk quietly to you until you cried. I'm going to get a coffee.'

And with that, Victoria marched off.

Jonathon sat down. He had always assumed that his maleness made Livia treat him worse. And when Livia took the female temps into her office, he had thought she was carefully mentoring them and giving them advice that would help them become permanent people. But perhaps he had it wrong. Perhaps he *was* benefitting from thousands of years of horrific and systematic male oppression of women, and yet was still only a temp who operated a database. Worse yet, he was feeling sorry for himself instead of doing anything to end the injustice.

The image of the girl from the Tube floated up in front of his eyes.

It made him feel even more guilty. He was supposed to be in love with Emma, but was being mentally unfaithful with a stranger. And his thinking about her was almost certainly a form of oppression. He had appropriated her image into his mind's eye without her permission, and he was using it to grossly disrespect his girlfriend. Of course, he was also doing it without his own permission: he didn't *want* to think about her. He was trying hard to avoid it. Everything was great. Emma was great. His flat was great. His job was going well. And hadn't his knowledge of Microsoft Word's 'Compare Documents' feature enabled him to score a record-breaking 97 in Eager Beavers' Software Proficiency Test? He was bound to become a permanent person.

He needed to clear the unwanted thoughts out of his head so he could get back to entering the results of the Wharton interviews in the database. Now was a good time for a walk, with Victoria still getting coffee and Livia in her office talking loudly on the phone.

Through the first set of fire doors. His eyes glided over the picture of the old man or banana, and he was walking up to the fifth floor, and then on, barely glancing at the phlegm nude. He wanted the emptiness of the seventh floor.

But when he got there he found it was not empty.

The floor was fully equipped and redecorated. There was even corporate art. It was abstract: a green triangle standing unhappily on a purple square.

He walked to the inner fire doors and looked through the safety glass. There were still no people. But the floor had now been fitted out in a way that made it much better equipped than his own. There were huge flat-screen displays mounted on the walls as well as on the desks, which were gracefully curved and arranged in clusters, rather than rows. The computers on them were gleaming black, instead of beige. Not one had a scrawled password stuck to it. And the walls were now painted a very dark blue, giving the place an air of importance and dynamism.

How had it been so thoroughly transformed between one afternoon and the next? And why? Jonathon felt that if he could understand just this one floor, he would understand Farynx. If he could understand Farynx, he would understand the economy. And perhaps if he could understand the economy, he would understand life.

He gingerly pushed open the door, half expecting to hear an alarm go off. There was silence.

He took the most tentative of tentative steps into the floor area.

Nothing happened.

He took another extremely tentative step in. Nothing continued to happen.

He looked around. There was no sign that anyone had been there. It seemed like someone had just conjured it all up with the wave of a magic wand.

Jonathon briefly wondered whether he was on one of those TV programmes where they lure you into a ridiculous situation and then show millions of people how badly you deal with it. But who would want to watch a man walk into a suddenly redecorated office floor? That wasn't ridiculous, just boring and slightly weird. Nonetheless, he looked around for cameras. He even bent down to see if there were any hiding under the desks.

There weren't, of course. But there was something slightly shiny just beside the nearest cluster. He walked cautiously over to examine it, still not entirely sure that a TV presenter wasn't going to leap out from the military-grade photocopier in the corner.

The shiny thing was a laminated pass. The name on it was Alistair Fordham, presumably one of the people responsible for this rapid transformation. It was a special pass, valid for three days, ending tomorrow. Had they expected it to take longer?

Jonathon, suddenly sure he was being watched, whirled around.

DADDLE-A-DADDLE-A-DADDLE-A-DOO. DABBLE-DABBLE DAA-DAA, DABBLE-DABBLE DAA-DAA. DADDLE...

There was no causal connection between his whirling around and his phone going off, but his heart was thudding violently against his ribs. He fumbled with his phone and pressed the button to reject the call.

There was no one behind him. Carl Barker was not standing there looking sternly through the glass of the fire door. All the same, Jonathon felt he should leave this place. He should not be here.

'Hello,' said a tiny, tinny voice.

He whirled around again. There was still no one there.

'Hello!' said the voice again.

It was his phone. He must have pressed the 'answer' button by mistake. He raised it to his ear.

'Hello?' he whispered.

10

Lance was standing in a queue at John F Kennedy airport saying 'hello' into his phone.

'Jonathon?' he said. A man in front of him turned. Lance waved him away.

There was a faint crackle on the other end of the line.

'Hello?' Lance said again. The woman who worked on the gate turned. Lance pointed at his phone and smiled charmingly.

Then there it was on the other end of the line, a faint whisper: '*Hello?*'

'Is that Jonathon?' said Lance.

'Um,' said the whisper. It was definitely Jonathon. 'Yes.'

'Why are you whispering?'

'I'm at work.'

'Where do you work?' whispered Lance – very few people can resist matching a whisper. 'A library?'

'No, it's a company called Farynx. Is that Lance?'

'Yesamundo. How's it going, hotdog?'

'I'm, um, embroiled in a mystery. And don't call me hotdog.'

'What kind of mystery, big guy?'

'It's the top floor of the building I work in. It was a normal floor a month ago, then yesterday it was completely empty, and today it's been fitted out like some kind of futuristic command centre.'

'Oh,' whispered Lance. It was a surprisingly tricky thing to whisper.

'Yes,' whispered Jonathon.

'I've got great news for you, Jonathon,' whispered Lance. 'I think I've solved the mystery.'

'Have you?'

'Yes. Your company has quickly turned its top floor into a futuristic command centre.'

'Um. Right. Well, when you put it like that…'

'It means we can stop whispering.'

'It's just that there's no one here.'

'Which means there's no need to whisper.'

'But I'm not really meant to be here.'

'So go where you're meant to be and I'll call you back.'

'I'm not allowed to take personal calls in the place where I'm meant to be.'

'What would happen?'

'My boss would probably scream at me. Which would cause problems with Victoria.'

'Victoria doesn't like it when you get screamed at?'

'No, she thinks it shows favouritism towards me.'

'Where did you say you work again?'

'Farynx.'

'Well, it certainly sounds like Farynx is a great company!' whispered Lance, sarcastically.

'Can I call you back later?'

'I'm just about to get on a plane. That's why I wanted to talk to you. I'm coming back to London for a few days. Want to meet up for a beer?'

'What? Oh. Yes. Definitely,' said Jonathon.

'Great. Where do you live now?'

Lance looked up from his phone just as the woman at the gate finished a whispered phone call of her own. It ended with her saying, 'Dead? That's horrible.'

Their eyes met and Lance gave her a smile of phone-whispering solidarity.

The woman smiled back, composed herself, and said to him, 'Sir, we are delighted to be able to offer you a complimentary upgrade on your flight today.'

'Whoa,' said Lance. 'Really? That's great.'

He hoped he sounded convincing. Actually he almost always got upgraded because of the several genetic lotteries he had won, and because he was always nice to the gate attendants when he arrived. Also, he just looked too well dressed to be in standard class – the attendants probably worried that people would start to feel bad about themselves if they saw Lance among them. And today he had made the upgrade slightly more likely by clipping his MTV badge carelessly onto his jacket, as though he had forgotten to take it off. This was overkill though. If his jacket had turned up at the airport on its own it would probably have got an upgrade.

Lance did prefer business class, of course, with its large seats that meant you hardly ever had to sit with part of someone else's body jammed into you. And there was enough legroom to accommodate Lance's legs.

The one drawback of business class was that he sometimes ended up sitting next to someone who wanted to talk about business for the whole flight. Some executives felt that the flight was a chance to kick back and relax by telling a stranger about their new inventory-management system. And these tended to be men who had got to the top by persistence and determination, men who would not let Lance's lack of interest or even consciousness deter them.

That was why Lance casually asked, 'Who will I be sitting next to?'

'I can't give out names I'm afraid, sir.'

'No problem,' said Lance. 'It's just some people's companies are so… boring.'

She giggled. 'I could tell you the company names. We now have two openings – one next to a gentleman from Heidelberg Cement, and the other beside a gentleman from Farynx. A colleague was supposed to be travelling with him, but we've just heard that he's…' She mouthed the word 'deceased', which Lance was quite proud of himself for recognising.

That was handy. Perhaps he could solve Jonathon's mystery even more completely than he already had. It might make him feel like a private detective again.

'I'll go with Farynx – if there's a choice,' he said.

'Sure thing. I hold Farynx stock – it's a strong buy. Cement's a little Old Economy for my tastes.'

'Thanks very much.'

'Thank you, sir. I hope you have a great flight.'

Lance stretched out in his huge business-class seat, put his book aside and took a sip of champagne.

'Gimme yours any day,' said the man in the next seat, gesturing to Lance's book and then holding up his own reading material – Farynx's annual report. 'There's mistakes all over this thing. I need to get someone to check it before we send it out.'

Lance gave a sympathetic grimace. 'Yes,' he said. 'I'm hoping to make it to book number two today.'

'You finished a book already, before you even got on the plane?'

'I mean in my life.'

Lance smiled and patted the book – The Firm by John Grisham – then took a swig of champagne and settled into ignoring the safety announcements.

Within the last twenty-four hours Lance had lost his dream of having his own TV show in America and left an aggressive stranger alone in his expensive apartment. A person with functioning emotions would feel, well, something. But Lance was wrapped in the nonchalant hug of a hangover, which he was warming with free champagne. Lance always drank champagne when he flew.

'I lack emotional depth,' Lance continued, 'and I hear that reading's an easy way to get it.'

The man chuckled and raised his whisky glass.

'You Brits with your – what do you call it? – *self-deprecation*. I never know where I am with that.'

'Yes, we really should stop doing it. Silly habit.'

'Todd, by the way. Todd Stuckers.'

'Lance. Lance Ferman.'

They shook hands. Todd's was big: it seemed more like a fist that could be temporarily unclenched than a traditional hand. It was tanned and backed with a sleek coat of black hair. His head was a slight remodelling of the same idea: solid and smooth, with a long knuckle of nose and a big meaty thumb of jaw. And yet he had a mouth that curled into an easy smile and there was a twinkle in his eye.

Todd loosened his tie, took off his cashmere jacket, probably Milanese, and slipped off his John Lobb shoes. When he moved, his muscles seemed to be having a competition to see which of them could stick out furthest from his body. Even in a business-class seat, his triceps were just a whisker away from violating Lance's airspace. Lance didn't mind though. Not today.

'You Brits,' said Todd. 'You make out everything's going down the pan the whole time. But look at you. You got a beautiful jacket, nice hair, you're sipping champagne, sitting in business class…'

'Thanks very much.'

'I mean, your ticket cost more than some people make in a month, but give you half a chance and I bet you'll make out you're on skid row. Me, I'm a simple guy from a simple country: we make out everything's going great even if we live in a hole and some guy pours shit in it every day at five.'

'Inconvenient.'

'Exactly. That's not me, by the way – the hole. I've got a giant condo right by Central Park, a summerhouse in East Hampton. I pull down money like you would not believe, I'm president of four divisions and I'm going to be CEO within six months, tops. I'm doing great.'

'What's the company?' asked Lance, already knowing the answer.

The stewardess indicated where the emergency exits were.

'Just a little thing called Farynx,' said Todd. 'Heard of it?'

'Of course,' said Lance, as though he had known of the company for longer than forty-seven minutes.

'What did you hear?'

'That it's a great company,' said Lance, failing to mention that he had heard this from himself in his phone call with Jonathon, and that he had said it sarcastically. 'Mysterious and futuristic,' he added, on a sudden inspiration.

'You know, that might just be the most astute summing-up of Farynx I have ever heard.'

Lance waved this aside. 'I don't know anything, really,' he said.

'I am on to you,' said Todd, wagging his finger in Lance's face.

What, already? thought Lance.

'With this self-deprecation,' continued Todd. 'I am on to you with that.'

'Busted,' said Lance, smiling modestly.

A voice told them to buckle their seatbelts and prepare for take-off. The plane trundled forward.

'So, greatness, mystery, the future,' said Todd. 'What most people don't realise is that those three things go together. The way my divisions make money – that's a secret. That's like our secret sauce. You get other companies giving their secret sauce away, saying exactly what they do to make every million dollars. That's dumb. With us, we're smart, so we'll tell you *what* money we're making, but we're not going to tell you *how*. You like the way we perform? Okay, then you got to trust us. That is the way of the future, and that's what makes us great.'

'Because you don't get great by giving away your secret sauce.'

'Exactly – you really get this. You know, sometimes people come to me and they say, "Farynx is a black box – I can't look inside and see how it works." And I say, "Yeah. It is. That's our strength. We're a big black box that prints money. You want some of it? Buy our stock."'

'Why do people have such a problem with black boxes?' said Lance, as though this were a source of constant frustration for him. He wondered dimly what Todd meant.

'Right!' said Todd. 'But in all fairness, it feels like the market accepts that about us now. You beat the analysts' profit targets every quarter, that speaks for itself.'

'People don't care what colour your box is then,' said Lance, knowledgeably.

'You got that right,' said Todd, and clinked glasses again. 'So, what line of work are you in? Investment banking?'

The plane began to make the concentrated whooshing sound that signalled it was trying its hardest to haul them up into the air.

'You could say that,' said Lance, leaving out the crucial detail that anyone who did say that would be wrong. 'Actually, I do a few things. For instance, I have this investigative solutions consultancy in London – we tracked down the prime minister when he was kidnapped five years ago...'

Lance flipped out a card from his wallet. He didn't 'have' the company in the sense of owning even a tiny part of it, only in the sense of having worked there a few years ago and still carrying around the cards because Bob Plover gave him a cut of any business he introduced. Lance wasn't lying, just using words differently than other people.

'... and I do some TV work on the side,' he said, flipping out another card. 'I have a show in development at MTV.'

Twenty-four hours earlier this had been true, so he wasn't lying, there was just a delay in his honesty.

'Wow,' said Todd. 'TV. My son, Marmaduke, is looking to get into TV work. He's an actor – studied at Kent State.'

'Marmaduke, good name for an actor.'

'It's kind of a family name. Anyway, if you could...'

'Absolutely, yes. Put him in touch. Maybe I can...' Lance left the sentence hanging, since there was nothing he could possibly do for any actor. He wasn't sure if there was anything anyone could do for any actor.

'Anyway,' said Todd, 'seems like you have a lot going on.'

'I have a few connections,' said Lance.

Todd put his hands to either side of his mouth and said, 'Self-deprecation alert!'

By this time, Lance felt ready to begin a bit of digging – or possibly fishing. Something rural anyway. He wanted to prove to Jonathon that there was no mystery on the seventh floor.

'So,' he said, 'I hear big things are going on for Farynx in London – you know, *upstairs*.'

Todd looked at him, eyes narrowing, though he maintained his smile.

'What did you hear, specifically?'

There was a rattle and thump as the plane shook itself free of the ground, pushing them back in their seats as it rushed for the sky.

11

After Lance had sat in the sky for seven hours – drinking champagne, exchanging business cards and being offered jobs by Todd – the plane rushed back down to earth with a bump. Lance promised Todd he would call him, adding his usual silent caveat. Then he took a cab to Finsbury Park, pausing only to drop off his luggage in an Islington hotel.

Getting out of his cab, Lance absent-mindedly shook hands with a group of Turkish men and inhaled the fumes of a rotisserie chicken shop – the skewered carcasses in the window mechanically rotating like the men in their groups.

Here it was: London, with its black cabs, its red phone boxes, its karaoke pubs full of shouting alcoholics, just as he'd left it a year ago. And yet, after New York, it seemed different. Its buildings were puny. Its streets lurched in all directions, as though they had been planned on a small pub table during an epic lock-in. Even the pavements seemed fragile – a patchwork of slabs, tarmac and bricks, lacking the stout metal kerbs of American cities. Almost nothing in London was made of metal. It was all brick, and it looked like one hard shove could push it over. In fact, Blackstock Road looked like it was already mid-shove. Lance wondered whether Jonathon would have changed as much.

He arrived at Jonathon's building, Coleridge Court, and pressed the buzzer.

There was a crackle, a clatter and then a fuzzy voice said, 'Um. Ah. Are you there?'

'Hey,' said Lance. 'Any Jonathons at home?'

'Oh, Lance. Yes. One or two. One actually. Come in.'

There was a click and a buzz and Lance pulled open the front door. He took the lift up to the fourth floor and knocked at Flat 23. From inside there came the sound of someone saying, 'I'll get it' and falling over. Then came a second voice saying, 'What?' and then the first voice saying, 'What?' again.

But by then the door had opened and Lance was looking at someone who could never in a million years be Jonathon's girlfriend.

It wasn't just that she was too attractive for Jonathon, though she was. It was more the air of quiet, brisk certainty that she had, of things boxed and neatly stored in her mind. There was a no-nonsense look about her, where Jonathon had always appeared fundamentally pro-nonsense.

She was wearing blue running shorts, a pink vest and a pair of white sports socks. Her legs were long and lightly tanned. Her straight, glossy hair hovered just above her shoulders in a tidy bob, held back by a yellow hairband, and her face was neat and symmetrical: it would not have looked at all out of place on the cover of a sensible magazine.

'Hi, I'm Lance.'

'Hello. I'm Emma. Come in.'

'And you live here with…' Lance stopped to push the disbelief out of his voice.

'Jonathon,' she finished.

At that moment Jonathon appeared from a room around the corner. At first the man who stepped into the hall didn't look anything like Jonathon. He was slightly taller and a bit more three-dimensional in a way that Lance could not quite fathom. His hair lay down neatly on his head, and he wore a long-sleeved polo shirt. He also wore the newest pair of jeans Lance had ever seen – somehow darker and less creased even than the ones in the shops. He looked very, very tired, but also haltingly pleased to see Lance.

'Sorry,' said Jonathon. 'I fell over the ironing board.'

And as Jonathon said this, he seemed to flicker and dissolve and he was instantly the Jonathon who Lance had met five years earlier.

They had become friends by accident, after sitting too close to each other in a cafe. There had been an instant, if slightly unlikely, bond between them, and then they had almost immediately been drawn into that odd business with the stolen documents. It had ended with Lance being in the news, leading to his job offer from MTV. Then Jonathon had gone to university, Lance had got serious about his TV career and gone to America, and now it was somehow five years later.

Lance hugged him, and Jonathon hugged back, like someone who had read about it in a book, but never actually tried it before.

'Absence makes the heart grow fonder,' said Emma.

'Um, what?' asked Jonathon, amiably.

'What?' said Emma.

There was a silence.

'Well,' said Lance, 'here we all are in the hallway.'

'Sorry,' said Emma. 'Come through.'

She gestured towards the kitchen.

'Yes, come through,' said Jonathon. 'Mind you don't fall over the

48

ironing board.'

The kitchen was really a small alcove at the end of the living room, which contained a circular dining table, a green sofa, a TV, a bookshelf and a vase of flowers. Beyond, through the floor-to-ceiling windows that occupied a corner of the room, lay Blackstock Road's chicken shops and Turkish camaraderie.

'I brought you some wine,' said Lance, putting a bottle wrapped in tissue paper on the table.

'Lovely,' said Emma, putting it on the side. 'The old vino.'

'Sorry,' said Jonathon to Lance, 'I thought you were coming tomorrow.'

'We've already eaten,' said Emma.

'Good,' said Lance pleasantly, eyeing the remains of something viciously healthy in a casserole dish that would no doubt soon be put in Tupperware, labelled and possibly colour-coded.

'Will you come to the pub with me and Jonathon?' Lance asked Emma.

'I was just about to go for a run,' she said.

'Or we could stay here,' said Jonathon loyally. He turned to Lance. 'Have you eaten? We've still got some…' He gestured at the casserole dish.

Lance gave him a smile that plainly said, *Do you think I'm fucking insane?*

Jonathon laughed.

'What?' said Emma.

'What?' said Jonathon.

'What were you laughing at?' said Emma, with a little baffled smile.

'Um. Lance's face, I suppose,' said Jonathon.

'Oh.' She looked confused. 'Well, laughter is the best medicine.'

They all smiled at each other.

'Well, I'll have that run,' said Emma. 'You boys have fun.'

'Hey,' said Lance, 'enjoy your run.'

Jonathon was too preoccupied by his coat, which had got caught in the ironing board, to say anything.

Out on the street, Lance said, 'Well look at you, J-Dog, you old stud.'

'Don't call me J-Dog,' said Jonathon, settling back into their old routine, 'or an old stud.'

'No problemo, F-bomb. So, how did you and Emma meet?'

What Lance really wanted to ask was, 'Have you two ever met before?' He had never in his life encountered a couple who, despite the evident polite goodwill on both sides, communicated less well with each other.

'It's a bit complicated,' said Jonathon. 'I'll tell you in the pub.'

The Faltering Fullback was a homely place, full of panelling and painted wood, with a very old framed rugby shirt hanging on one wall. It was not one of those pubs where everyone turns and falls silent as strangers enter. In fact, as Lance and Jonathon entered, the dense throng of people set their backs a little more squarely to the door and bellowed all the louder.

Lance reached his hand out in front of him at about head height and took advantage of Londoners' unconscious desire to avoid strangers touching their ears. By this means he melted a narrow path through the crowd. When they reached the bar, he turned to Jonathon.

'So, what do you want?' asked Lance.

'Nothing – I've got the flat, the job, Emma. It's great,' said Jonathon tiredly.

'I meant in a glass, not in life.'

'Oh. Oh yes, we're in a pub. Let me get these. It's my um…' Jonathon did a complicated mime, the gist of which was that because the pub was near his house, he had to buy the first round.

'Well, I won't punch you in the face over it,' said Lance. 'Thanks.' He knew better than to get into a politeness competition with another English person.

With drinks in hand, Lance and Jonathon made their way into a cosy but crowded room furnished like an old study, with bookshelves, globes, stuffed animals and mismatched chairs and tables. Like magic, an old couple rose to leave as they entered, so Lance and Jonathon were able to get a table immediately. This made them part of the landed element in the pub – a little less than half its population – and so able to look pityingly at the mere standers.

Lance turned to Jonathon. 'Sorry, by the way, for not keeping in touch.'

'No no, it was my fault,' said Jonathon, flushing with embarrassment.

'Then I accept your apology,' said Lance, to avoid an English apology stand-off. After spending a year in America, there were now even more bits of English culture that he found himself refusing to get involved in.

There was a moment's silence while they both took the ceremonial first sip of beer. Then Lance said, 'So, now you can tell me how you and Emma got together.'

Jonathon took a deep breath, a gulp of beer and another deep breath.

'Okay, well, it was like this…' Jonathon began, but stopped when Lance started wiggling his fingers about in front of his face. 'Why are you doing that?'

'That's the screen going wavy. This is where the flashback would be if this was a film.'

'Oh. Is it?'

'Yes. If you live in New York it's pretty much mandatory to take screenwriting classes. It's like LA. Everyone's got a script. But it means you start looking at life like it was a film.'

'Maybe it is. Maybe we're in a film right now.'

'We definitely aren't,' said Lance.

'Hm. How do you know?'

'Because no screenwriter would write this line bacon.'

'Because you said "bacon" at the end for no reason?'

'No, that's fine. No one cares about small stuff like that. But the line doesn't advance the story, so it would get cut. That's the problem with real life: the story's all over the place. And so you have to sit through people actually telling you stuff – and, I suspect, saying "um" a lot – instead of getting everything in neat, efficient flashbacks. Anyway, go on. Tell me the story.'

'Um, well, it was like this…'

Lance wiggled his fingers again.

12

Six months earlier…

'Where's bloody Emma gone now?'

Suzanne was Hansen Underhead's secretary, and arranged the monthly team-building drinks for the temp and secretary castes. This was the first time Jonathon had been invited.

'Honestly,' said Suzanne, 'it's like herding cats, this is. She was with us a couple of streets ago.'

'Um. I think she's fallen behind,' said Jonathon.

Suzanne smiled at him. 'No shit, Sherlock,' she said.

Jonathon heard this so often that he sometimes felt it would be easiest if everyone just wore a 'No shit, Sherlock' badge and tapped it whenever he spoke.

'Why don't you go back,' said Suzanne, 'see where she's got to, and then meet us in the Progress Bar?'

He agreed and hurried off.

'You know where it is, don't you?' she called after him.

He gave her a thumbs up.

'Good lad. See you there.' She turned to the others. 'Tim! Wrong way! I said wrong way – the Progress is over here.' She walked on, shaking her head, 'Herding cats…'

Jonathon went back the way they'd come, muffled against the autumn cold in his new thick black coat. He walked away from the neon speckle of bars just off the Strand, leaving the light and people behind, back through the narrow streets.

And there was Emma ahead, in the middle of the thin, dim street, talking to two male friends. He waited, but they didn't notice him. They were too wrapped up in their conversation. One of them affectionately rested a hand on Emma's bag.

Jonathon felt he should make his presence known. If they turned and saw him now, they might think he was the kind of weirdo who silently watches other people's conversations from a distance, not daring to join in. They might, in other words, draw the right conclusion about him. So he called over to them, a friendly, casual 'hey'.

This was his first 'hey'. He had just noticed people in American sitcoms saying it, and it had instantly made 'hi' sound foolish and old-fashioned. But as soon as his 'hey' left his lips, Jonathon realised he had got it badly wrong in every possible way: volume, tone and intonation. His was not the kind of 'hey' that fits easily in the sentence, 'Hey Chandler, let's go grab a coffee.' It was more the sort of 'hey' that Ian Paisley might have shouted if he'd noticed the pope hanging around at the bottom of his garden.

In fact, Jonathon got his 'hey' so wrong that it made Emma's friends run away at top speed. She dropped her bag and looked around with a horrified expression.

Jonathon thought about running away himself, but that would have put his behaviour completely beyond the pale. So he walked over to Emma, who was looking at the ground. He picked up her bag and handed it to her, as though this could make up for frightening her friends away. She took it, then looked up, met his eyes, and simultaneously burst into tears and threw her arms around him.

'Um,' he said, 'sorry. I…' But how could he explain what he had done?

'Thank you,' she said. And then she unhugged him and took her bag. 'I was rushing to catch everyone up but those two men stopped me to ask directions and it was really weird because they kept changing their minds about where they wanted to go and then I realised they were just keeping me talking to get me on my own and then one of them put his hand on my bag and I said 'no' and he reached into his inside pocket and I think he had a knife and then suddenly you were there and saw what was going on and – and you just stopped them. Thank you,' she finished. She had been speaking very quickly.

He was about to explain, but the words dried in his mouth. How could he tell her that he was so awkward that he was able to entirely mess up the intonation of a newly imported friendly greeting?

She looked around. 'We should get out of here,' she said.

'The others are in the Progress Bar,' he said. 'Shall I carry your bag?'

He carried her bag and she held on to his arm. Soon Jonathon realised he had been entirely mistaken in telling Suzanne he knew where the Progress Bar was. He and Emma went to a nearer bar and Jonathon called the police from their payphone. He didn't have a mobile phone at the time: it seemed self-important to imagine that people would want to talk to you even when you weren't at home.

While he and Emma waited for the police, he tried to be reassuring, but couldn't think of anything to say. 'My casual salutations make grown men flee' was too grandiloquent. Whereas 'getting mugged is horrible' sounded ridiculously self-evident. It was nonetheless what he found himself saying. He half expected her to tap her 'No shit, Sherlock' badge, but instead she grabbed his arm again.

Then the police arrived – two short, muscular, fattish men, bulging out of stab-proof vests. They took Emma's statement with the air of people getting through a pointless formality, and then said, 'So you haven't lost nothing, madam? You haven't actually been… *mugged*?' Emma started crying and the police went back to their car.

Jonathon had no idea how to deal with the situation.

'Shall I walk you home?' he said.

'Yes please.'

After a silent Tube ride and a ten-minute walk, they reached the door of the house where she lived.

Jonathon was wondering what to say. Emma kissed him and pulled him inside, closing the door behind them.

13

Lance wiggled his fingers again.

'So we got together,' concluded Jonathon, 'and then we moved in together about four months ago.'

Lance raised an eyebrow and Jonathon felt suddenly defensive.

'Emma says we're a bit behind the relationship timetable, so we need to catch up,' he explained. 'And we were both living in horrible, expensive places – though obviously hers was clean and had flowers in it. So we borrowed some money for the deposit and letting fees. We're hoping to buy a place next year. Banks are desperate for everyone to borrow their money at the moment, for some reason. I've probably been pre-approved for two major loans and six exclusive new credit cards just while we've been sitting here.'

'Epic,' said Lance, smiling but shaking his head. He picked up his glass and waved it. 'Hey – it's your round,' he said.

'Oh, right,' said Jonathon automatically, getting up. 'Same again?'

'The prosecution rests,' said Lance. 'We have no further questions at this time.'

'What are you talking about?'

'You know you bought the last round,' said Lance, somehow contriving to shift in his chair as though he were turning to face a jury. Jonathon laughed at Lance's dextrous sitting technique.

'And yet,' continued Lance, 'when I ask you to get another round, you do so without question. Ladies and gentlemen of the jury, why is this?'

Lance looked around at the other drinkers packed into the pub's cosy library-effect room. They continued mostly to eat crisps and talk about football, but Lance behaved as though he held them in rapt attention.

'One word,' said Lance. 'Politeness.'

'Oh, well that's all right then,' said Jonathon.

'What I'm saying,' said Lance, suddenly ceasing to be a hotshot New York lawyer, 'is that you're a polite person and so's she. You're going out with each other out of politeness. Just like you were going to buy the round out of politeness.'

Of course, Jonathon had known that he had bought the last round. Like every English person, there was a region of his brain devoted exclusively to remembering how many beers he owed everyone. So why hadn't he said anything?

'That's not true,' said Jonathon. But he could hear the uncertainty in his voice.

'Or is it, Mr Fairfax?' said Lance, echoing Jonathon's confusion, and with eyebrows raised for the benefit of the jury. 'Okay, I'll stop doing the lawyer thing now. But are you and Emma always like that with each other, the way you were tonight?'

'No. No, no. A bit. Yes. Sort of.'

'When was the last time you laughed together?' asked Lance. He held up a warning finger and added, 'At the same thing, I mean.'

'Um, it was…' Jonathon couldn't think. They had laughed at the same time, but Lance's stipulation that it be at the same thing, rather than just a coincidence, made the task more difficult. Two Saturdays ago, Emma had laughed at Jonathon for leaving the salad in the fridge at lunchtime, and he had joined in. Did that count? He suddenly felt annoyed at Lance for calling one of the fundamentals of his life into question.

'That's not the point,' he said. 'Our relationship isn't like that. You can have a bond with someone without going around laughing all the time. And anyway, she says I'm…' He paused, suddenly unwilling to finish the sentence.

'What?' asked Lance.

'Well… she says. Um…'

'Come on.'

'I'm, er, the strong, silent type,' said Jonathon, blushing.

At this, Lance laughed so loudly and so helplessly that he got the attention of all the people who had ignored him when they had been his jury. It was a full-body laugh which lasted a good minute and left him stretched out on his chair, wiping his eyes.

Jonathon stood up. 'I will go and get those drinks now,' he said, wanting to leave the embarrassment behind.

'I'll have whatever he's having,' said a woman at the next table.

When Jonathon returned, Lance still seemed to be experiencing little laughter echoes, making him smile and shake slightly every few seconds.

'I'm stronger than I used to be,' said Jonathon as he sat down. 'I go to the gym all the time now.'

'Maybe I went a bit overboard there,' said Lance, wiping his eyes again. 'But still – no matter how much you go to the gym and how little you speak – you'll never be the strong, silent type.'

Jonathon scowled, which made Lance laugh again.

'I mean that in a good way,' said Lance. 'I'm the same. Brooding silence can be cool, but it's also pretty much the same as just having no conversation.'

Jonathon, as if to make a point, took a sip of beer and said nothing. The beermat fell off the bottom, making him jump and spill some. Lance looked at him with sympathy.

'I didn't mean to oversimplify it. It sounds like she's running her life to a timetable and has decided to simplify things by pretending you're a completely different man than you are. And you're flattered and grateful that a woman who looks like she could be on the cover of a sensible magazine has accidentally chosen you. So you're politely pretending to be in love with her.'

Jonathon stared at him, horrified that Lance should have recognised the situation so perfectly wrongly.

Lance added, 'I'm a detective, don't forget.'

'You're a TV presenter.'

'Well TV presenters are also unusually perceptive.'

Jonathon stared into his beer. This was going horribly.

'Anyway,' said Lance, 'didn't you used to have a different girlfriend? One you got on with? The one with the really brown hair?'

Jonathon forgot to take the rest of the sip he was in the middle of. He froze, the glass lodged in his mouth. Lance reached out and gently guided Jonathon's glass back to its beermat.

'Rachel?' said Jonathon. 'Oh God. I... well, we had a bit of a thing...'

'A thing?'

'A... relationship. I think. I mean, we definitely did. We saw each other all the time and, you know, and then.'

'And then?'

'And then she went to visit her dad in France. He's a plumber,' said Jonathon, as though that helped to explain why he lived in France. 'She was meant to be gone for a month, but then about three months later I got a friendly letter from her. It was exactly the kind of letter you'd send to a platonic friend who isn't completely in love with you. It said she'd just got engaged to a French farmer. She even invited me to the wedding.'

'Wow. You made her go farmer.'

Jonathon gave him a stricken look.

'Sorry,' said Lance. 'I'm sorry. That sounds... well, would "shitty" cover it?'

'It might.'

56

'That's not cool. She was obviously insane. Or maybe she just got a bit freaked out and ran away.'

'I was completely in love with her.' Jonathon stopped and looked at the moon. But it was impossible because they were in a pub. He flashed Lance an embarrassed glance.

'Well, there's your mistake,' said Lance. 'This is why I prefer to have stable, committed and fulfilling microrelationships. I mean, why buy a big bag of frozen peas when you can get fresh ones from the market whenever you want?'

'Because some of the fresh ones have little grubs in them?' suggested Jonathon, glad of a distraction from the huge towel of doubt that threatened to absorb him.

'What?'

'Maybe I'm thinking too literally. Are we talking about you… having sex with peas?'

'Strictly figuratively, yes.'

'Well then, the only possible reason for buying them would be because you and the frozen peas are in love with each other.'

Jonathon lapsed again into worry about what was happening between him and Emma. Perhaps she had grabbed what looked like a packet of frozen peas and then, finding when she got home that they were actually sprouts, decided nevertheless to press ahead with her pea soup recipe. And perhaps he was afraid that if he had something in common with a packet of frozen peas, it would leave him in a horribly painful way. *This frozen pea metaphor isn't helping*, he thought.

'So,' said Lance with the tone that is universally used to shift the conversation to an easier subject, 'guess who I sat next to on the plane today?'

'Mike Tyson?'

'What? No. Why would that be the first person you'd guess?'

'I don't know. Gloria Estefan? Gore Vidal? A man with no arms?'

'No. What's going on in your head? No. Weirder. After you told me you work for Farynx, I managed to get myself upgraded to a seat next to Todd Stuckers.'

'Oh,' said Jonathon.

'You've never heard of him?' said Lance.

'No. What does he do?'

'He controls about a third of your company – and rising. He's head of Farynx's gas division, their energy trading bit and the management consultancy.'

'Oh, that's the bit I work for,' said Jonathon.

'And yet you've never heard of him.'

'Maybe I have. All the names blur into one after a bit.'

'Anyway, I've solved the Mystery of the Suddenly Redecorated Floor.'

'You didn't tell him I'd been up there, did you?'

'Relax. I just mentioned I'd heard there was something big going on. He told me there's an analysts' event tomorrow and they're unveiling some kind of new trading floor in their main London office.'

'What's an analysts' event?'

'You know, an event,' said Lance vaguely. 'For analysts. I don't know. A normal business thing. Something to do with the share price.'

'This is a thing I've never understood,' said Jonathon, wanting to move the conversation decisively away from the big personal subject that he didn't understand to a smaller impersonal subject that confused him in a more manageable way.

'What?'

'Why companies care about the price of their shares.'

'Why wouldn't they?'

'Maybe I've got it all wrong. But when a company floats onto the stock market, it stops owning itself and instead lets anyone who buys a share own a bit of it.'

'Right.'

'I understand why they want the price of each share to be as big as possible then,' said Jonathon, 'because they get that money. That's how much they're paid for giving up owning their company. And they can spend it on… new trading floors or something.'

'New trading floors,' said Lance, as though it were a toast.

'But once they've sold the shares, why does the company care about the price after that? Then it's just shareholders selling their shares to other people. The company doesn't get any money for that.'

'No, obviously,' said Lance, steepling his fingers like a financial expert.

'So why do they care?'

'*Do* they care?' said Lance, raising his eyebrows like a financial expert.

'Yes. Farynx has a display in the lobby showing its share price. And I can't go to the toilet without hearing people talk about shareholder value.'

Lance shrugged. 'It's a mystery,' he said. 'Unlike the seventh floor.'

Wednesday

14

He was in a white box, with a loud, insistent noise in his ears. He looked around in panic.

'Could you turn off the alarm, please?'

'What?'

And then, again, his life slotted itself back into his brain.

He was in bed. He was Jonathon Fairfax. This was his flat, complete with integrated utility closet, recessed lights and Juliet balcony.

Their morning routine unfolded exactly as usual. His recurring dream had been of driving a car in the wrong direction, constantly taking the wrong turn. *But what could that possibly mean?*

In the shower's damp paradise, he found himself singing 'Norwegian Wood' by the Beatles. It had been one of his favourites as a child, when his dad had played it in the car. Back then, he had assumed it was mainly about how good forests are in Norway. Now, of course, he knew it was about how John Lennon could get so annoyed with a woman pretentiously showing off about her pine furniture and not sleeping with him that, when he woke up alone in her bath the next morning, he would get revenge by burning her flat down.

As Jonathon was about to leave, he spotted an ominous note from Emma, reminding him that she had the day off on Friday and that her dad was visiting. He seemed to avoid coming at weekends, when Jonathon might be around. This threw Jonathon into a troubled contemplation of the new coasters, and an agonised replay of his conversation with Lance the night before. Luckily, his phone rang, saving him from being late. It was Lance, asking if he fancied lunch.

And after that came his usual run down Brownswood Road and up Blackstock Road, past the toothless pub, under the rusting cloudy bridge and into the Tube.

The crowd pulled Jonathon up the steps from Temple station, towards Arundel Street and Farynx's offices. *Do-se-do*, through the revolving door, across the stone ocean to be met at the great metal barrier reef by Carl Barker, the security guard. The clock above reception said 8.47.

'Pass please. Sir,' the guard said.

Jonathon put his hand in his pocket and his fingers closed around a felt-backed coaster. *Shit*.

'Hello,' said Jonathon. 'We talked yesterday.'

There was a flicker in the guard's eyes. 'Pass,' he said.

A wave of relief swept over Jonathon. The guard had remembered him – and why not? After all, they'd spoken yesterday, as well as having seen each other most days for several months now. *Carl Barker*, he would definitely remember his name.

'Thank you very much, er...' Although Jonathon had read Carl's name, he was suddenly unsure whether it was all right to use it. *Best not*, he thought. He stepped up to the turnstile and pushed at the bar. It didn't move.

'Sir,' said Carl. 'You need to show me your pass.'

'Oh, sorry,' said Jonathon. 'I thought you were saying "pass".'

Carl looked Jonathon up and down. Despite the guard's small stature, his immaculate military bearing suggested that he had been seconded from an elite regiment to protect Farynx's lifts.

'I was. Sir,' said Carl.

'I mean, I thought you meant it as a verb.' Did he mean verb? Or was it one of those other things?

Though Carl stood only a whisker over five feet tall, he nonetheless contrived to look down his nose at Jonathon. This trick suddenly gave Jonathon the feeling that the laws of perspective had been badly damaged, as the small man towered under him, leaving him reeling in a high, queasy pit of inverted vertigo.

'Sir. If you do not produce your pass, you will be required to vacate the premises.'

'Right. Sorry.' Jonathon couldn't help noticing the way Carl was keeping the word 'sir' cordoned off from the rest of his sentences, as though to indicate that it was discipline, rather than respect, that compelled him to use it.

Jonathon checked his pockets again. There was still only a coaster there. He felt dizzy. Somewhere far below him the ceiling soared.

He was going to have to go home and get his pass. And that meant he was going to be world-endingly late. Victoria had the day off, but even without her, Livia would be sure to notice him being an hour and a half late.

He moved back, out into the stony deeps, and opened his briefcase, rooting through database printouts that he should have thrown away, the charmingly ridiculous girl's *Loot* that he should never have picked up, the box where he should have kept the sandwiches he should have made, and the lost pass that he should have handed in yesterday.

He pulled out the lost pass. It was even more temporary than Jonathon's: a piece of paper in a plastic envelope with a fabric band. The photo printed on it was too low definition to make out – it looked like a thumb with a face sketched on it.

It was now 8.48. If he used this pass, he could get to his desk on time. In four minutes' time he could be sipping an Ethiopian and getting on with entering the final batch of Wharton interviews. He could have a normal day.

After what Lance had said last night, a normal day was exactly what Jonathon needed, especially if he was going to see Lance at lunchtime. And he needed to believe he could become a permanent person, despite the headcount freeze which plainly made it almost impossible.

He suddenly felt angry. Why was ordinary life so *difficult*? Evolution had equipped him to roam the forests and plains as a hunter-gatherer (or, more realistically, just a gatherer). So why did he instead have to spend his life worrying about the numbers on clocks, packing himself into underground trains, remembering passes, and cajoling computers into turning borders green in certain tightly defined circumstances?

It would all have been easier to deal with if he hadn't been to university. At least school had the honesty to prepare him for a life of boredom, futility and relentless low-grade bullying. But then university had come along – with its late nights, freedom and loose moral code – and prepared him instead for the life of a minor beat poet. Now it was taking all his effort to forget that and accommodate himself to reality.

Jonathon closed his briefcase and stood up. The pass was clasped in his hand. He advanced towards Carl, holding it before him. *It's not my job to remember your name*, Carl had said. Well, he would find out whether that was true.

At the barrier, Carl took the pass and inspected it, seemingly micron by micron, then raised his walkie-talkie to his mouth.

'C5381 to Control. Give me a ten-eight on this pass number.' He read out the number.

After a long wait there came a burst of static that must have contained some words because Carl said, 'You can now enter building. Sir.'

Carl pressed a button on the turnstile, and Jonathon was in. He had done it, and ahead of him were the lifts that would take him to his desk and his normal day.

'You need Lift Four,' said Carl. 'Wait with others till it's available. And you need to wear your pass at all times.'

Jonathon hung the pass around his neck, like an albatross. He wondered why Carl wanted him to use a particular lift. Glancing back, he saw Carl still watching him, so he continued to walk towards the people standing around Lift Four. There were twenty or thirty of them. *Who were they?* As he drew closer, Jonathon saw that their jaws had the kind of definition you only get by having no surplus body fat, their necks were toned, and their faces were much more facey than you might expect, as though they had been assembled in a panic from a bucket of strong features.

Jonathon planned to stay close to the group and then, when he was sure Carl had stopped watching, jump into Lift Three. That was his favourite lift anyway: there was a slight delay between some of the words in its automatic announcements, which gave it an appealing air of vulnerability, as though it had dreamed of being more than a lift but had found the strength to live with its limitations.

Lift Four went *bung!* and opened its doors. A man beside it ushered people in. He was tough-looking, with a lined face, a grey buzz cut and a slight paunch hanging over the waistband of his pinstriped trousers.

'Okay folks, in you go, one at a time,' he said in an American accent, clicking a little metal device to count each one as they went past. 'Right to the back, right to the back. Someone press the button. Floor seven.'

They were going to the seventh floor.

The American leaned into the lift, checking how much space was left. He hadn't seen Jonathon, and Carl had stopped watching him. This was the perfect moment to subtly alter his course and make for Lift Three.

But he did not. He carried on walking towards the group.

And then he was part of the group, and the American had seen him. The moment was past. Jonathon could no longer leave.

15

'Henry!' said Todd, clasping Henry's hand, pulling him in and slapping him on the back in one giant, fluid move.

'Hey Todd,' said Henry, returning the slap on the back. 'I hope this conference room is satisfactory as a temporary office. The fourth floor has incredibly low meeting-room utilisation rates.'

'It's okay. We both know I'll be somewhere way better before too long.'

'And how did the flight perform? Positive experience?'

Henry leaned against the table. He was Todd's right-hand man, and looked a little bit like Todd might if you turned down all his attributes by around ten per cent. He was tall and broad, but in a Clark Kent way, with neat dark hair, square glasses and a sober blue suit. He spoke Business natively, which complemented Todd's from-the-gut style. Together, they were an ideal team for world domination: Todd supplying the charisma and Henry reassuring middle management.

'Not bad,' said Todd, clicking one of the foil coffee pouches into place and pressing the button. 'Not so productive – but I got talking to a guy who might be useful to us, so...'

'Great,' said Henry, who hated anyone else getting close to Todd. 'Identity?'

'Another time,' said Todd. 'I know you've got to be up there in like *minus* ten minutes, so I'll make this quick. I wanted to say this last night, but I had a ton of work to catch up on.'

'*Minus* ten minutes: that's great humour, Todd.' Henry laughed a little too hard, as he did when he was nervous.

'So, number one: I know you are going to go up there and kill them. I *know* you're going to do that. I don't even have one doubt about it in my mind. You are Henry Rearden and you are a fucking killer.'

'Ah, thanks, Todd.'

'Number two: tell them I would be there myself, but I have to be in a board meeting. You'll handle it better than me anyway. You have a way with words that these people really appreciate. I'm more your crowd-pleaser for tonight's event.'

'Way with words: check.'

'Number three: what we are doing is real, and I trust you absolutely. Okay?'

'Thanks, Todd. The trust is bi-directional here.'

'Great. Now I'm going to prove my trust by telling you that Pete Hatcher's death was not an accident. I murdered him.'

'What?'

'Yes.'

Henry said nothing, just stared at Todd.

'You need a coffee? You need to sit down?' asked Todd.

'No. I'm fine. I'm… I'm pumped. It's just, my expectations were not fully calibrated for that information. I heard it was a fire.'

'I set the fire. The Fire Investigation Unit's still investigating but they say there's not much to go on. So, looks like it worked. I wanted to get rid of the evidence that I'd beaten him to death.'

'That is a strong move, Todd.'

'Well, you know, we talked about this. We said, if it becomes necessary, we're ready to go all the way. Survival of the fittest. *The Selfish Gene*…'

'Absolutely, Todd. And *Atlas Shrugged* really speaks to this point…'

'Sure,' said Todd, glancing at his watch.

'I mean,' said Henry, 'I want to process this at a higher level of detail, but I guess we can do that later, right?'

'Right,' said Todd. 'For now, just know that we are overcoming all of the challenges. Thanks, by the way, for swinging into action on the fit-out of the seventh floor once Hatcher was out of the picture.'

'No issue, Todd.'

'After the board meeting today, I predict we will be significantly closer to achieving our plan. The Chief Risk Officer is the one person – apart from Chesborough – who can poke his nose into my business. If I'm CRO our lives will get a lot easier. But only if you go upstairs right now and you do what you were born to do. Can you do that?'

'Yes! I will deliver, Todd. I will execute on that.'

Todd stood and clapped his hands on Henry's shoulders.

'I know you will, Henry. I know you will.'

Henry opened the door and was about to leave when Todd called him back.

'One more thing. Number four: take off your tie, Henry. We've gone internet.'

16

'Good morning. How may I help you?' said the woman on reception, turning on a mid-level smile.

'Okay, so this is the thing: I haven't got my pass. I have looked *everywhere*' – Alistair Fordham half-sang the word – 'and I just cannot find it – bags, pockets, washing machine, you name it. *Aaarrgghh!*' He did a little mock-frustrated scream and laughed.

'What's your name, sir?'

'Alistair Fordham.'

'And how are you spelling that?'

He spelled it, and she said, 'And who are you here to see?'

'This is the thing: I don't know the name. It's for the corporate. There's an Andy, Andy someone? And another one who looks a bit like Clark Kent...'

'I'm sorry, sir, but I *will* be needing a name.'

'It's just – aaaarrrgghh!' Alistair did the little laugh-scream again. 'I'm meant to be with the people over there by the lifts. They're going up right now.'

'Well, we do advise to keep all passes with you at all times, sir.'

And then his phone went off. Alistair looked at the screen and his heart leapt in horror. It was his agent.

17

Bung!

'*Seventh floor*,' said the lift.

There was a long moment, as though the lift aimed to build suspense before revealing what was going on beyond its doors. Jonathon had recently seen *Saving Private Ryan*, so he could say with certainty that this moment was absolutely not like waiting for the doors of a landing craft to open on D-Day, showing the hell of sand, water and bullets beyond. It would have been absurd and offensive to suggest that.

Nevertheless, young men exchanged uncertain glances. By the door, the tough-looking American with the grey buzz cut checked his watch. And Jonathon gulped nervously and tried to steady himself by staring at an incredibly toned neck in front of him.

And then the long moment ended. The doors opened, revealing the previous liftloads of personnel standing in the disembarkation area in front of the empty reception booth. Jonathon filed out of the lift with the others. Over to his left were the fire doors through which he had entered the day before. Now a camera crew was setting up its equipment there. The huge flat-screen displays he had seen yesterday were now switched on, flashing up numbers and graphs, or showing financial news.

The American with the grey buzz cut went and stood in the entrance to the reception booth, on a step, silencing the crowd with his eyes. He did not speak. They all stood mute for two minutes, then three. And then the lift behind them went *bung!*

They all turned.

'*Seventh floor,*' muttered the lift as it opened its doors.

A tall man in a blue suit stood there for a second, then strode out, parting them like the Red Sea. The American with the grey buzz cut relinquished his spot on the reception booth's step, and the man in the blue suit took his place, turned and held up his right hand, as though calling for silence. No one had spoken.

'Okay. Listen up, guys,' said the man in the blue suit, revealing himself also to be an American. His glasses made him look a bit like Clark Kent. 'First off, I want to recognise and celebrate the success of the rehearsal you guys executed yesterday morning. You guys have some *seriously* high levels of acting talent.'

Actors! That explained why they were all so toned and facey. Jonathon shrank away from them. Like most people, he was afraid of actors, worried that if he got too close to them he might find himself emotionally blackmailed into sitting through an experimental mime piece based on *Macbeth*.

'Today,' continued the man in the blue suit, 'your performance will be filmed. So I need you all to do exactly what you did yesterday – and ten per cent more. Admins, I need you to walk super-fast and look super-efficient – but you've always got time for a smile. Managers, I need you to be super-decisive, thoughtful or morale-building, depending on the type you have been allocated. Senior traders, you have a super-important role here today. I need you to be aggressive, aggressive, aggressive. You are not talking on the phone, you are killing super-tigers. What are you doing?'

About a third of the group – tall men with glossy hair – shouted, 'Killing super-tigers!' as though they were in the marines.

'And finally,' continued the American, 'junior traders, I need you to be super-keen, so you are drinking in the experience you are getting on this trading floor and you are learning to be hunters. What are you doing?'

A smaller group looked at each other and shouted a mixture of things, among which 'drinking experience' predominated.

'You are learning to be hunters. Let me hear you again! What are you doing?'

This time the smaller group – thinner and less tall, with shorter hair – shouted, 'Learning to be hunters!'

'Okay, now everyone: are we going to smash this?'

'Yes!' they all shouted.

'What are we going to do?' shouted the American.

'Smash this!'

'What are we going to smash?'

'This!'

'Okay, now get to your start positions.'

There had been a number of points at which Jonathon could have admitted the truth. The first, and most decisive, had been at the security barrier. The second had been when he had joined the group by the lift. Then there had been a debatable third when they had emerged from the lift and stood in silence. But if he spoke up now, he would have to explain not just about the pass, but about why he hadn't said anything before.

How had he come to be in this position? He had let his natural human curiosity get in the way of his professional need to be on time. The decision had been made mostly by his legs, which had carried him closer to the group by Lift Four almost in defiance of the rest of him.

And how could he possibly salvage the situation? Even if he somehow managed to slip away he would still be horribly late. And now he had to work out how to smash this, drink experience and learn to be a hunter, as well as get downstairs in – he checked his watch – minus ten minutes. It was a predicament for which none of his previous experience had prepared him. He decided that, since making a bold move had got him into this mess, he should default to his standard operating procedure when dealing with the obstinately difficult real world, and just shut up and try not to upset anyone.

Everyone around Jonathon was going over to the workstations

and chairs and forming small clusters. He walked slowly and spotted a group that did not seem to have a thin, short-haired man of around his age.

One of the big, glossy-haired men in the group turned to him. He had a face like an elegant boxer's – perfect, you might think, for playing an emotionally complex villain or flawed hero.

'You look a bit different today, Alistair Fordham,' he said, looking at the pass hanging around Jonathon's neck.

Jonathon felt as though someone had quickly and efficiently cut his stomach out. He stood and goggled.

'Ill, is he?' asked the elegant boxer.

Jonathon had never felt so grateful to any human being in his life as he did for this casual offer of a lifeline. He nodded, then recovered his voice.

'He, er, I'm, they, I… I'm standing in for him,' he managed.

'Well, it's a corporate,' said the actor. 'Piece of piss. They're making a video about trading, but they don't want to disturb the real traders. Between you and I' – the actor raised a theatrical hand to cover his mouth – 'I think they're just not good enough performers.'

'Ah, and what do I have to do?' asked Jonathon.

'You just sit down, typing – they said to use a well-known phrase, so it looks like real typing. It won't appear on screen. We'll be shouting into telephones or arguing over the charts. If we look like we're running out of steam, you just say, "San Fran to LA is breaking out," and we'll do our nuts about it. Oh, and one strict rule: don't break character till the whole shoot's over.'

'Okay everyone,' called the man in the blue suit, from the centre of the open-plan area. 'This starts in three minutes. Once again, if you break character, I will break you – and you will not be paid. But I know you're going to deliver a great job. You are all great actors. And you're going to give one hundred and ten per cent to your portrayal of highly successful businesspeople on the world's most advanced trading floor.'

As the applause for this threatening pep-talk rang out, the man with the blue suit walked into the lift and disappeared. When the doors had closed, the American with the grey buzz cut took his place in the open-plan area.

'You heard the man,' he said. 'Any questions?'

'Can I go to the toilet?' someone asked.

'No,' said the man. 'Anything else?'

There was silence.

'Cameras?'

A man with a hat and a beard gave a thumbs up.

'Action!'

On his word, the floor sprang to life. Over a hundred people set to their pretence with a will. The admins fetched coffee and rushed about with printouts, the senior traders shouted into their phones, the managers pointed to things on charts, and the junior traders looked keen and typed frantically on their keyboards. Jonathon typed over and over, *Oh God, I have made a huge mistake.*

At the very edge of Jonathon's hearing – which had been tuned by months of listening out for Livia's approach – the *bung!* of the lift sounded again.

Through the maelstrom of drama came the blue-suited American, leading a gang of perhaps two dozen suited men and women, and addressing them in a loud and confident voice.

'… our bandwidth-trading platform can support over one million trades per minute, ladies and gentlemen.'

The group stopped right next to Jonathon's team. He glanced up and the elegant boxer met Jonathon's eyes, just for a split second, and raised his eyebrows. The signal.

'San Fran to LA is breaking out!' said Jonathon, his voice hoarse and high, louder than he had meant it to be.

It was, it seemed, the signal for everyone to step up their performances to a state of almost hallucinatory intensity. If the performances had been big before, they must now be visible from the moon. Not even the subtlest and most nuanced of them was giving anything less than a hundred and thirty per cent.

'I need to cover my position,' someone yelled.

'Buy as much San Fran to LA as you can, goddamn it,' shouted another into his phoney phone.

'We need to make this deal happen right this second!' shrieked the elegant boxer.

The man in the blue suit was saying to the group, '… for example, enterprises are undergoing high levels of expenditure for internet bandwidth capacity that is severely underutilised outside of office hours. We decided to create a platform that would allow businesses to sell their excess capacity, enabling bandwidth-intensive services such as online video. Imagine renting a movie without going to the video store…'

There was much sage nodding from the group as they observed

the pandemonium all around them. The man in the blue suit began to move on, saying, 'Now I have a great PowerPoint presentation that I just can't wait to share with you folks.'

The group filed back into the lift, the doors closed behind them, and the grey-haired American shouted, 'Cut!'

18

'Why do you wear a tie?' Piper asked her dad suddenly, turning around in her swivel chair and setting her slightly extravagant eyebrows to 'question' mode.

They were sitting together in his office, the sudden March sunlight pouring in through the skylight above their heads and running like white paint down the edges of the highly polished old furniture. That morning she had moved from her seat in reception to his office, so she could explain the accounts to him. But, as ever, he had been distracted by something else, and was now staring intently into one of the monitors that clustered anachronistically on his beautiful old leather-topped desk.

'What?' said Gus, still typing. And then the part of his brain that wasn't involved in the typing seemed to kick in and he followed up with, 'Hm, why do I wear a tie? Well...' *clickety-clack-clack* '... why don't you wear a tie?'

'Because it's not 1926 and I'm a girl and I work in my dad's office-stroke-house most of the time – I don't need to. It would be weird.'

'Well then.'

'But most of that's the same for you too. I mean, you're not a girl...'

'And nor will I ever be.'

'Obvs. So, why the tie, Dad?' She said it with a sing-song emphasis, like it was the name of a game show.

Clack, clack. Clack. Gus stopped typing, peered at his screen for a moment and then turned towards her in his old and preternaturally adjustable chair.

'What's that?' said Gus again. His blue eyes looked at her from within the thick black frames of his glasses.

Piper sighed, 'Never mind,' and turned back to her desk.

'Why do I wear a tie?'

'Now you've got it.' She instantly swung back around on her chair, her chin cupped in both hands, head tipped to one side, eyebrows again inquisitive.

Gus put his hand to the small knot of his knitted, rust-coloured tie, nestled between the collars of his blue shirt and partly covered by a grey waistcoat that faded into the warmer grey of his tweed jacket and the brown of his corduroy trousers. It was an outfit that could have been worn without comment in any of the three most recent centuries.

'I just do, I suppose,' he said.

'Oooh,' Piper said mournfully. 'Nope. That's not an answer.'

'It's what a chap does.'

'But other chaps don't – other people's dads. And you're only fifty-seven…'

'Fifty-eight, aren't I?'

'Oh. When did that happen?'

'My last birthday, I suppose.'

'What did I get you?'

'Something lovely. Absolutely lovely. Beyond description.'

'You don't remember,' she accused.

'Neither do you.'

'That's not the point.'

'It just makes me feel comfortable, that's all. A slight comforting warmth about the neck. You should try one.'

'Maybe when I'm dead,' she said brightly.

'Suit yourself.'

She turned back to the spreadsheet on her screen, with its rows of numbers, its fiercely embedded calculations. It was a shame she was so good at accounts, when she had so little interest in them.

Gus, typing again, asked distractedly, 'What's the minimum amount of its shares a company has to offer when it floats on the stock exchange?'

'Twenty-five per cent on the London Stock Exchange,' she said, then, 'Sorry, I don't know why I know that.'

He grunted something that might have been thanks.

'What I really mean is,' she said, 'why are you… like you are?'

'What do you mean?'

'You were an orphan from Hungary. You could have decided to be anyone, and yet you decided to be, well…' She made an opening gesture with her hands, as though welcoming him to a small invisible stage.

'Well,' he said. 'Let me answer that thusly.'

'No,' she said, in a horrified whisper. 'Not a poem.'

'*How happy is he born and taught, That serveth not another's will; Whose armour is his honest thought*— By the way, did you pick up a copy of *Loot*? Was our advert in it?'

Piper blushed and looked away. 'I picked one up on Monday but I, er... left it on the train. The advert was in it though.' And then, as though it made things better, she added, 'I circled it.'

'Any more replies yet? Two people isn't nearly enough.'

'Not yet.'

'Oh well. There'll be plenty of chances to get the advert right once we've floated the company on the stock market. It's only a week on Monday now.'

19

'Okay,' said the American with the grey buzz cut, clapping his hands. 'That's it. We've decided to cut filming short...'

People exchanged surprised looks. 'That's *it*?' said one of them. Jonathon looked at his watch: it was only 9.25. With Victoria being off, there was a chance – just a chance – that he could make it to his desk without Livia noticing. He felt a soaring sensation in his chest, a sudden giddy lightness.

'... so make your way over to the lifts.'

The soaring sensation crashed. The giddy lightness turned to sickening dark. Of course. They were going to be shepherded into the lifts and out of the building. He would be in exactly the same position as he'd been in earlier, except that it would be later. He would still have to go home and get his pass.

He trudged over with the rest of them.

'Nice delivery on that "San Fran to LA" line,' said the man with the elegant boxer's face. 'Interesting choice to put so much *fear* in it. But kudos to you: it *worked*.'

'Oh, ah. Thank you,' said Jonathon. They were all pooled together now by the lifts, congratulating each other while the American with the grey buzz cut did a headcount. Jonathon found himself standing at the entrance to the reception booth, where the man in the blue suit had stood to give his threatening pep talk.

'Your line about making the deal happen was good too,' said Jonathon. *Good* sounded a bit feeble, so he added, 'It worked.' He had never used the phrase before, but he was suddenly grateful for its air of meaning something while not needing to specify exactly what.

'Pshah!' said the elegant boxer, glowing slightly. 'Where did you train?'

Shit. 'Oh, the usual place.' What places were there? He needed a diversion.

Luckily, someone clapped the elegant boxer on the shoulder at that moment and told him he'd been marvellous, so Jonathon was able to sink out of the conversation, muttering something about tying his shoelace.

There was a restful and secluded feel at kneeling level, away from all the congratulations, looking out at a forest of shins. Perhaps it would be even more restful and secluded if he crept into the reception booth and hid under the counter. He could wait till everyone had gone and then creep down the stairs to his own floor. In ten minutes – if Livia hadn't noticed his absence – he could be sitting at his desk sipping an Ethiopian.

The idea was stupid, he had to admit. But then everything he had done that morning had been stupid, starting with putting a drinks mat in his pocket and progressing to committing fraud and acting the part of an actor.

He shuffled along in his kneeling position, withdrew into the booth and then gently toppled onto his back. But before he could roll under the bottom shelf of the counter, a face appeared: the elegant boxer again, craning his neck around the entrance to the booth.

Jonathon gave an apologetic look and raised a shushing finger. The actor pulled a face that seemed to say, *I respect your process*, and disappeared. Jonathon completed his roll and lay there under the bottom shelf, thinking how difficult it would be to explain his actions if the actor's expression had actually meant, *I'll summon help*.

Shortly afterwards, he heard a *bung!* And then the hubbub began to drop as the actors were shipped out, evacuated from their beachhead. And all the while, Jonathon lay in a state of petrified tension in case he was discovered.

When the last *bung!* had knelled, Jonathon lay there a little longer, listening intently, sending tendrils of attention snaking out through his ears and into that great space beyond the reception booth. Nothing.

He tentatively rolled out. He had never thought a roll could be tentative, but now he found it was possible. Then he pulled himself up into a kneeling position and stuck his head around the entrance to the booth. Left, then right. No one.

He grabbed his briefcase and left the booth, crouching as though he expected to be set upon by one of the tigers the man in the blue suit had mentioned. The open-plan area was deserted, and he moved through it quickly, walking with light steps so as not to make a noise.

He reached the door, softly opened it and stepped into the carpeted airlock beyond. Past the painting of the unhappy triangle, through the next door, into the stairwell. Just three floors to descend. But there was the sound of footsteps on the stairs – heavy steps climbing upwards, towards him. He looked down the gap in the middle of the staircase and saw, three flights below, a muscular hand on the bannister, a sleeve of Farynx blue. Security. Jonathon did not want to be caught coming down the stairs from this empty floor, especially when he didn't have his real pass with him.

Jonathon eased back through the door and into the toilet. He went into one of the cubicles, bolted it, put the toilet seat down and crouched on top of it so that no one would see his feet beneath the door.

Two minutes later, the toilet door crashed open and a voice called, 'Anyone in here?'

A Yorkshire accent. Carl Barker.

20

Lousy museum piece, thought Todd. He hated this long, narrow boardroom, with its huge oak table and ebony chairs. The tiles on the floor each bore a crown and the letters *RABWARGC*: the Royal Anglo-Belgian West Africa Rubber and Gas Company – Farynx's distant ancestor. This cramped building on Piccadilly was somehow still the headquarters of the multinational corporation it had become.

When Todd became CEO, his first act would be to sell this draughty piece of period real-estate. History was a bunch of shit. Just a lot of people who dressed weird, had poor technology and couldn't even come up with a catchy acronym. What could you learn from them, apart from how to build cold and depressing boardrooms?

No, Farynx's boardroom should be at the top of the tallest building in London – all glass, metal, rare wood and polished stone. He, Todd Stuckers, would be there at the head of the largest boardroom table ever devised. And at his side would be someone like the blonde executive he had chatted to that morning.

'So, gentlemen – and lady – we come to the first item on the agenda,' said Chesborough O'Teece, looking around at the board members and glancing at Todd. Farynx's Chairman and Chief Executive Officer was a chubby American from the Mid-West, of middle height, with pink skin and flyaway sandy-grey hair. With his flabby cheeks, broad nose, little eyes and jowly neck he looked a little like a large, shell-less turtle.

'Now, I am sure you have all heard of the death of our very respected colleague, Peter Hatcher, our Chief Risk Officer. But it falls to me to inform you officially, at this board meeting, that he is in the arms of the Lord.'

Chesborough addressed them a little like they were a prayer meeting. This annoyed Todd, but he had years of experience pretending it didn't. And today it was particularly important that none of his annoyance leaked out. Todd put his hands up to cover his mouth and nose, and closed his eyes for a second, as though a new wave of grief had hit him.

Chesborough continued, 'Boy am I glad that all of you non-executive members of the board could make it today. Thank you. It was, ah, convenient that we had a board meeting scheduled for today. So in that respect, Pete's death was well-timed.'

He began a smile and a chuckle, purely out of habit, but then – catching sight of the faces around the table – back-pedalled on both of these enterprises before they had really got going. He looked again at his piece of paper.

'But, of course, death always comes before time – the Reaper is seldom welcome when he – or she,' he added, glancing at their new, female member of the board, 'knocks at the door. And at what door could that Reaper be less welcome than Pete Hatcher's? We knew him as a friend, a valued colleague and an exemplary Chief Risk Officer, cut down by fire at the young age of just forty-seven.' He rocked back on his heels and frowned at his paper.

'So, let us observe a one-minute's silence, while we think of what our colleague meant to us, and I read out some of the highlights of his two years here at Farynx.'

'Hear, hear,' said Patrick Swire, the longest-serving member of the board, and a reliable sycophant.

They closed their eyes and bowed their heads.

'The roll-out of RMC-certified risk workshops,' said Chesborough, soft and sonorous. 'The Navajo risk-management system,' he added, and then, after a longer pause, 'Goldwater risk-assessment templates, reports and bi-annual updates.'

Finally, Chesborough said, 'Thank you for that minute of sweet silence. I know Pete would have appreciated that. Any questions?'

'This fire – was anyone else killed?' asked the female member of the board, Dame Margery Kempe. She was a white-haired woman, polished and venerable like a Queen Anne sideboard. She looked severely at Chesborough over her little glasses.

'No, ma'am, praise be. His wife and mother-in-law were out shopping for antiques.'

'And do we know the reason?'

Chesborough blinked and then gave his preacher's smile. 'I guess a combination of investment potential and genuine appreciation.'

'I mean, do we know the reason for the fire? What caused it?'

'Ah, the police and fire department are still investigating, but it seems the probable cause was a coffee machine. It's now being withdrawn from the market, and our lawyers are looking into the potential for a class-action suit.'

Todd successfully stifled a smile that wanted to break out on his face, and also refrained from shouting, 'I fooled you all! I'm a genius!'

Chesborough looked around the room, and then continued, 'Well, if there are no further questions, let me just say that Pete would be delighted that this news has not materially impacted Farynx's share price. Nor have we allowed this bad news to disrupt our UK analysts' event, which concludes today. It is my sure and certain hope that the analysts will raise their target price for Farynx stock.'

'Amen to that,' said Todd, to murmurs of approval, particularly from Patrick Swire.

'So, I propose that we move directly on to the first item for discussion: choosing a new Chief Risk Officer. Now – as you'll have guessed from the fact that he's sitting here – my pick would be Todd. As you know, I like to move folks up from the inside, instead of bringing in strangers—'

'Surely we should look at candidates from inside and out,' said Dame Margery, 'following established best practice.'

Todd tensed. He looked around the table at the thirteen non-executive directors. Only five of them – older men with somewhat flushed cheeks – had been there before Todd had orchestrated Chesborough's stunning coup d'état three years before. And yet two of these were nodding their agreement with Dame Margery.

'Well, we can talk about best practice,' said Chesborough. 'When I was a kid – around about a hundred years ago now' – he looked around with a puckered smile and Todd led the room in a loyal laugh – 'they told us to eat up all of our fat, said it was good for us. Now of course we know different...'

The other seven men had sharper suits, deeper tans and a certain eagerness about the eyes. They were smiling, nodding along with Chesborough, no doubt keen to keep their fees for being on the board.

'The latest studies actually show that it depends on the type of fat...' put in Dame Margery, but Chesborough talked over her.

'So it seems to me,' he said, 'that best practice can change.'

Around the table the loyalists were nodding again.

'But one thing that's never changed is common sense. When you find a good man, a man you can trust, well, you stick with him. And it seems to me that Todd Stuckers is one of the best.'

There was a round of applause. The old hands looked at Dame Margery. She was here for her first meeting. Her predecessor had retired, and Chesborough had wanted to look modern and appoint a woman. He had apparently – as with Pete Hatcher – chosen badly. Chesborough was losing his touch.

Todd wished he had supervised the selection process, but he had been too busy. Taking over the world is extremely time-consuming, and there are all sorts of apparently insignificant details that can trip you up. Still, he was close. And after this meeting – despite Dame Margery's opposition – he would be one giant step closer.

'His divisions are our best performers by a country mile,' continued Chesborough. 'They already have the most advanced risk-management systems. And this is not the time for us to have an empty saddle right at the head of the posse. If we're going to complete our takeover of United Biscuits, we need to keep up our stock price. And one thing the stock markets we're listed on have in common? They love Todd and the way everything he touches turns to gold.'

Another round of applause broke out. But again, the inconvenient thirteenth man, the woman, spoke up and ruined the moment.

'Among Mr Stuckers' *growing number* of divisions is our energy trading operation,' she said, 'which is inherently by far the most risky part of Farynx's business. Putting him in charge of the company's risk management would be like appointing a poacher as gamekeeper. Would that not be a clear conflict of interest – an egregious risk in the very part of the company meant to manage risk?'

At this there were some muted murmurs of approval.

'I take your point about the poacher and the gamekeeper, truly I do,' said Chesborough. 'But who knows the birds better? Who knows the woods and paths better?'

Dame Margery looked at him again over the tops of her glasses.

'That is not an argument,' she said. 'When you appointed me, you assured me that you valued my business experience, that you weren't just looking for a token woman. But I now see that a token was exactly what you were looking for. A board of directors is supposed to make sure the CEO and senior executives are acting in the company's best interests. But you seem to have packed this one full of the worst kind of noodles and yes-men.'

She glanced around the table and added, 'I'm sorry.' But it was clear she regretted what they were, rather than what she had said.

'Well now,' said Chesborough, 'let's you and me have a talk after our business here is concluded. But for now, let's go for a vote. All those in favour of appointing Todd here our new Chief Risk Officer?'

21

Lance, having arranged to meet Jonathon for lunch at one o'clock, was surprised to find himself arriving at the sandwich place exactly on time. It was a new chain called 'Sup, and Lance was sure it hadn't existed when he'd left London a year ago. Now there seemed to be branches on every street in the centre of town.

Inside it was all brushed steel and light wood, with signs printed in white capital letters on a cardboard-brown background. Lance was amused to see that all the staff wore long white coats and tall chef's hats. He selected a sandwich and took it to the counter, where he found he was standing behind Jonathon.

''Sup,' a man dressed as a chef said to Jonathon. 'What can I get you?'

'Um, I'd like this, please,' said Jonathon, holding up a sandwich, 'and a small cup of coffee to drink here.'

The man behind the counter gave a slight frown of annoyance. 'Tall brew, eat in,' he corrected. 'And with the sandwich that'll be £4.65.'

As the man shouted the order to someone behind him, Jonathon fumbled with his wallet, upset some plastic forks and retired, wounded, to wait for his coffee.

Lance handed over a sandwich and some money, pointed at the coffee he wanted, stepped around Jonathon, bagged them a table nearby that a couple of elderly priests had been making a beeline for, and reached out for his coffee. Jonathon sat down beside him, wrestling with a plastic lid.

'Tough world,' said Lance, glancing at the disappointed priests.

'Sorry,' said Jonathon. 'I can never order right here. I get distracted by chef's hats. I don't understand how the puffy bit on top helps.'

'It's a problem,' said Lance.

'Come to think of it, I get distracted by all hats,' continued Jonathon, discarding the lid. 'They're really odd. I mean, why is it that the three groups who have adopted the beret are intellectuals, onion sellers and soldiers? What's going on?'

'No one knows.'

'And then something strange is happening with language. Why do I have to eat a tall brew in? And now we're all switching to "hey" instead of "hi" – but how come no one mentions it?'

'These are big issues.'

'Sorry. I've been trying not to obsess over how weird everything is. I'd made myself believe it was all normal. But then this week…'

'The mystery of the seventh floor had to show up, on this of all weeks.'

'Well, you were right about the mystery. There isn't one. I went up there this morning and saw what's going on with my own eyes. I accidentally became an actor in a corporate video, and those analysts you were talking about were in it.'

'I hate to say this, but what are you talking about?'

Jonathon explained what had happened that morning: using the found pass, being unable to resist getting in the lift, the actors, the filming, and the sneaking off and hiding in the toilet.

'Wow,' said Lance. 'Busy morning. And good for you, by the way. Lying, cheating, using someone else's pass, all just to find out about an empty floor. You've taken your first step into a bigger world.'

'I hope not,' said Jonathon.

'So what happened after the guard shouted, "Anyone in there?"'

'I thought someone must have tipped him off. I was going to say something, but I couldn't. And then I heard him open the door to the other cubicle.'

'And?'

'And then he said, "Chuffing hell," in his Yorkshire accent. And there was a kind of clicking sound, and then cigarette smoke. I've never been so relieved to smell cigarettes. And then after a couple of minutes he sprayed air freshener and left.'

'What did you do?'

'I waited another five minutes and then sneaked down the stairs and got myself a desk. I thought Livia, my boss, would be bound to see me, but she must have been in a meeting or something. I kept waiting to hear her footsteps behind me and for the shouting to begin. But when she eventually appeared she just asked me something about the Wharton interviews and called me a chipmunk.'

'Is that good?'

'I think so. She even went off humming.'

'Maybe she's in love,' said Lance.

'So anyway, the mystery is now solved.'

Lance looked at Jonathon, frowning. Jonathon looked back, not frowning.

Lance said, 'I hate to say "What are you talking about?" again, but what are you talking about? Now, for the first time, there is a legitimate mystery. None of this empty floor nonsense.'

'Oh. Now there's a mystery?' Jonathon looked at the ceiling. 'How does everyone else know what's a mystery and what's just the world being normal? How do you distinguish between tall brews, which everyone seems fine with, and... whatever this seventh-floor thing is?'

Lance looked at Jonathon more closely. Sometimes he suspected his friend of being an elaborate practical joke. 'How can you not see the difference between using words to make people feel like they're getting a bigger coffee, and hiring actors to fool investment analysts about what your company can do? One's marketing and the other's fraud.'

'Oh. Doesn't anyone else have difficulty telling the difference between them?'

'No. Apart from your company's management.'

'But is it definitely fraud? I mean, maybe they have got a floor full of bandwidth traders somewhere but they don't want to disturb them.'

'I've met traders in New York. They aren't shy, sensitive types. They spend all day drunk and coked up, shouting into phones and pulling their pants down whenever they make another million bucks. They don't get disturbed if you lead a few analysts past them.'

'Oh.'

'And I bet they'd be a lot more convincing playing themselves than if you got a load of people who'd rather pretend to be a Scottish king or something.'

'Well, when you put it like that…'

'I do. You know, I've still got Todd Stuckers' card. He mentioned something about a job on the plane, though he was quite drunk by then. Still, I could give him a call, maybe see if I can find out about this.'

Lance had been back less than twenty-four hours, but already he could feel boredom's hand on his shoulder. Besides, he actually didn't have a job. Not that he wanted to think about that.

'Anyway,' he concluded, 'it'll be fun, like being a private detective again.'

'But why would he tell you anything about it?'

'We have a bond. Hey, he confided that his son's called Marmaduke.'

'He might not know anything about this anyway.'

'True. But he might. Are you sure they said "bandwidth trading"?'

'Yes. I wouldn't make something like that up. I don't even know what it is.'

'Neither do I, but it sounds exciting. This is the internet age, Jonathon. If you put all the internet's data on floppy disks, the pile would be high enough to reach the moon, or something.'

'Oh, but everything reaches the moon if you pile it up.'

'True. Maybe it's not that. Maybe it's Mars. Or maybe it's if you use Zip disks.'

'What are Zip disks?'

'They're like normal disks, but cool. They look better. And each one holds the equivalent of a hundred floppy disks. Or possibly a thousand. Or ten. Anyway, a lot.'

'I feel like we're all in over our heads with this internet stuff.'

'Hey, maybe you are. But you've just admitted you're in over your head with the concept of hats. I'm fine with the internet.'

Just then someone laid a hand dramatically on Jonathon's shoulder, causing him to flinch and spill a small amount of coffee.

'Hello *Alistair Fordham*,' said a man with glossy hair and a mauled but sensitive face.

'Oh, hello,' said Jonathon. 'Thanks for not saying anything back there.'

'Not a problem,' said the man. 'I respect your process.' And then to Lance he said, 'This is a *great* actor. You should have seen his performance this morning. So powerful. So authentic.'

'You don't have to tell me,' said Lance, to stop the man telling him. Lance was suspicious of actors: he didn't like competition in his specialist areas of looking good and lying.

'Sebastian Brett, by the way,' said the actor.

They introduced themselves, Jonathon admitting his real name.

'So you were at the filming this morning?' Lance asked.

Sebastian gave a slight bow.

'Did you notice anything weird about it?' asked Lance.

'It was a *corporate*,' said the actor, with infinite disdain, as though it were beneath his dignity to bestow any attention on it. 'They're always weird.'

They chatted a bit more, then Sebastian gave Jonathon and Lance his card and said he must dash. Shortly afterwards, Jonathon looked at his watch. 'Shit. I'd better get back.'

Lance was visiting his parents the next day, but he and Jonathon arranged to meet again on Friday, after Jonathon finished work and before he went home to Emma. Perhaps by then Jonathon would have found out more about the fake trading, and Lance would have met Todd and prised the truth from him.

22

At eight o'clock that evening, as Jonathon packed his briefcase, he glanced at Livia's office and saw that she was also packing up. He had stayed late to make up for the work he had missed that morning, and also to repay the karmic debt of having got away with it. There was no way of telling whether that was how karma wanted to be repaid, but it was all he had.

Jonathon sat down and slowed the pace of his packing, so as not to leave at the same time as Livia. At last, he saw Livia leave. He gave it two minutes, then made his way over to the lifts. But no sooner had he pressed the button than Livia appeared from the coffee area, throwing a paper cup into the bin behind her.

'You're leaving late, chipmunk,' she said. 'Beavering away at your database, eh?'

'Oh, ah. Er, yes.'

'Watch out. All work and no play makes Jack a dull boy.'

Livia's slightly mysterious business-poshness made it all the more difficult to respond properly. 'Yes, he is a bit,' said Jonathon.

The lift arrived and Jonathon had no alternative but to follow Livia inside. He prayed that while they were in the metal box together she would not ask him what time he had started work. He was no good at lying, except when it came to well-drilled subjects such as football.

'I'm meeting a few of my girlfriends tonight for a glass or two of wine,' said Livia, laughing.

Jonathon never knew how to deal with people who laugh at their own uncontroversial statements. And he had never got used to people using 'girlfriends' to mean 'friends who are women', rather than female lovers. His mind was now inescapably full of Livia indulging in a large, laughing, lesbian orgy, and this made it difficult for him to think of any way of replying.

'I'm having a girlfriend tonight,' was the formula his brain pushed out of his mouth.

Livia looked at him and then laughed. Jonathon reddened.

'I mean,' he explained, 'I'm meeting my girlfriend tonight.'

'Oh, where is that?'

'Um, in, er, in our flat.'

Livia frowned slightly and then hoiked her smile back up and said, 'We're going to Brown's Hotel.'

'Yes,' agreed Jonathon. *Surely this lift ride must be over by now?* Were there awkwardness sensors linked to the lift's brakes, slowing it down in case the social tension snapped its cables?

Finally, 'G' scrolled onto the display and the lift said, 'Ground' – vulnerable pause – 'floor'. *Bung!*

And then they were out, saying, 'Thanks, bye,' to Carl as he glanced over their passes, walking through the metal turnstiles.

Livia turned to him.

'Question,' she said, 'why are you using a pass with the name Alistair Fordham on it?'

Thursday

23

That night Jonathon's dream abandoned symbolism.

His dead grandpa came and sat beside him, on the bank of a river where they had once eaten some jam sandwiches. He put a hand on Jonathon's shoulder and said, 'All this corporate stuff's wrong for you, you know. Follow your heart. Stick with the music.'

'Um. The music?'

'Yes. Isn't it music that you do? Or is that your cousin?'

'David plays the guitar, but…'

'Oh, right. What is it you do?'

'I do some drawing. I used to, I mean.'

'That's it,' said his grandpa, adjusting his trousers to stop them bagging at the knees. 'That's the thing that makes you human. Do that.'

'What about money?'

But the dream had ended. There was a loud noise and Jonathon was in a white box. Soon after, he remembered it was his bedroom, in his flat with its heated towel rails and soft-close drawers. Emma turned the alarm off, and a few flinches later Jonathon was in the shower.

He found himself singing 'Every Day' by Buddy Holly. His dad had played it on a caravan holiday in France. Back then, Jonathon had assumed it was mainly about how fast and fun roller-coasters are. Now, of course, he knew it was about how quickly the time goes while you're procrastinating over asking out the girl you love, so that you still haven't done it when you eventually die in a plane crash at the age of twenty-two.

After his shower, he failed once more to kiss Emma before she left. He dressed, flinched, packed his briefcase and fell over the ironing board. Then he set off for work, running down the road, through the Turkish laughter and under the bridge with its yellowing clouds.

Would Livia tell someone he had used the wrong pass?

24

'Come in!' Todd called, putting the spoon aside and making sure he held his coffee so that his bicep was fully flexed.

The door swung open and there she stood, popping out of a blue striped shirt, her hair gleaming like cast bronze. She wore a tight, grey skirt and red shoes with heels high and sharp enough to punch a hole in a man's heart. Under her arm was a plastic folder.

'Good morning, Mr Stuckers,' she said, looking into his eyes and batting her lashes.

'Todd. Call me Todd. Great to see you again, Livia. Glad I bumped into you yesterday. Coffee?'

'Brazilian. Tan. Thanks.'

'Brazilian. So you like the strong stuff?' He clicked the pouch into place.

'I like everything strong.'

'Then we should get along just fine,' he said, picking up a fresh coffee cup like he was doing a rep with it at the gym.

'I brought what you asked to see,' she said, lightly caressing the plastic folder. 'What's your interest?'

'I'm interested in people,' he said levelly, looking her up and down. 'People are fascinating.'

He handed over the coffee in its immaculate white cup. She took it and sipped, watching him, then slowly spread out the pages from her plastic folder on the large table.

'If you need to see more,' she said, 'just say the word.'

Their eyes met.

'Maybe you can take me through what you've got,' he said, sitting down and running his hand over the figures and graphs.

'I have a system that produces a comprehensive suite of reports in a timely manner, showing the state of play live, vis-a-vis the recruitment of MBAs against our projected needs,' she breathed huskily.

Todd was nonplussed by the lack of erotic subtext in her answer. He quickly ran through it again. Nothing.

She seemed to spot her mistake, adding, 'And our needs are… huge.'

'Impressive,' he said, a little gruffly.

'You can see we are maintaining extensive contact with over six hundred candidates who are projected to graduate from tier-one business schools this year. We already have a shortlist of a hundred, fully interviewed and fitting our criteria.'

Has she missed it again? he wondered, just as she added, 'They're hot prospects.'

'Hot prospects,' he repeated, meeting her eye. 'You know what? What you have brought me is stunning. I can't recall seeing anything like it before. Do any other parts of our recruitment process have something similar?'

'No, just my part,' she whispered.

'I see. Well, maybe we could expand your part, spread it over other areas of recruitment.'

She gasped. 'For the whole of consulting?'

'Maybe beyond that. Sky's the limit. Did you hear I've just been made Chief Risk Officer, as well as running four divisions?'

'Congratulations. I can see your role is growing.'

'Thanks. It didn't just land in my lap though. I had to fight hard for it. But I'm used to getting what I want.'

'And how did you fight to be Chief Risk Officer?'

'I made my case to the board, overcame certain… objections. Some dame says my divisions are the most risky in Farynx. Says it's a "clear conflict of interest" having me run the fastest-growing division in Farynx *and* look after its risk.'

'How did you deal with her?'

'Don't worry. I was gentle. I said, "You know what a business is? It's a way of getting paid for taking a risk. Business *is* risk. The art is handling it. And that is my speciality."'

'So, for you, handling risk is an art form, is it?'

'What's with the "is it"?' said Todd.

'I'm sorry?' said Livia.

'That "is it" sounds sceptical. You sceptical about something I said?'

'I'm sorry, I didn't mean…'

'What didn't you mean?'

He had tensed up, moved into attack mode. *Calm*, he told himself. His therapist had told him he had a preference for the attack – something else that would have been a strength for his ancestors but which now sometimes unfairly made it harder for him to sleep with women.

'I didn't mean to sound sceptical,' she said. 'I'm full of admiration for your approach to risk.'

'Right. Maybe I've been drinking a little too much coffee lately. But, you know, getting back to what we were talking about, risk is actually a good thing. Without risk, there's no business. And if you're smart you can hive off the bad risk and leave yourself with guaranteed rewards.'

'And how big are these rewards?' asked Livia, standing up and moving around the table. She had her coffee cup in her hand, as though she meant to refill it. But she put it down beside the machine and turned to him, looking down, her body side-on.

'Unbelievably massive. If you know how much risk to take on.'

'And how much risk do you take on?' she asked, stroking the coffee machine.

He stood. 'As much as possible,' he said, 'and no more.'

He put a hand to the back of her neck and drew her to him. She put a hand on his shoulder.

Their lips met. She moved her other hand to the top of his thigh. He stirred.

And then the door opened and in walked a thin young man with large, startled eyes. He looked from Todd to Livia, back to Todd, down to Livia's hand. His face turned a shade of deep red.

Then he fixed his eyes on Todd's laptop and, as though addressing it rather than either of them, said, 'Oh, sorry, it um… Victoria said to… You, um, said I should… ah. I'll, um, I'll comen't barg lighter.'

He turned and walked into the doorframe, apologised to it, tripped over the bin, said something that sounded like 'yeg', and was gone.

'Get rid of him,' said Todd to Livia.

25

'Question,' Livia's arms were folded, her face a bright sharp axe. 'What is wrong with you?'

This was a question that Jonathon had asked himself many times in his life. The answer was, of course, that he was himself: Jonathon Fairfax. And he seemed unable to make any kind of permanent dent in that awful fact, no matter how hard he tried to be someone else.

He could feel his face reddening. His heart pumped a wholly unnecessary amount of blood around his system, as well as what felt like some small and very cold razor blades.

She had appeared behind him at his desk in the open-plan area. Jonathon could feel everyone looking at him: the temps, the secretaries and the members of the international business elite who could work fourteen hours and then play Olympic-standard hockey and give a Chopin recital.

'Well?' asked Livia, her voice ringing out, her hands on her hips, her eyes spewing flames of hot anger.

Jonathon could still think of no easy summary of what was wrong with him. Someone had once told him he was autistic, but he had looked it up and found that – unlike most psychological conditions – he didn't really have the symptoms. He could read facial expressions and usually knew what people were feeling, it was just that he had no idea what to do about it. No one else seemed to have much idea either; they just didn't mind upsetting people as much as he did.

'I…' he began, but he had nothing to follow it up with.

What could he say that wouldn't just upset her more? After all, the real problem was that he had seen her with her hand on the front of a man's trousers.

He had tried hard *not* to see it. He had averted his eyes, stared at the table, at the laptop and the printouts. Now, every detail of that was etched into his brain. The crescent of lipstick on the rim of the coffee cup, the grain of the table's light wood, the pixels of the Windows 95 screensaver, the screen-edge Post-it note on which was written 'todd_stuckers' and 'Marmaduke021380'. And immediately after that he had walked into the doorframe. The world was a complex series of traps.

'I'm sorry, I didn't quite catch that,' said Livia, still vibrating with anger. 'I'm still waiting to hear what sort of disorder makes a person think it's completely fine to just *waltz* into someone's private office without knocking.'

'But when I used to knock you told me not to. I didn't mean to…'

Alarm appeared in Livia's eyes. She glanced around to see who was in earshot, causing Victoria to duck back below the partition between the desks. Livia's face went pink.

'Oh, er, don't worry,' Jonathon stammered. 'I'm not going to, um…' But how could he tell her that he wasn't going to mention the trousers without mentioning the trousers?

'But that is not what I… wanted to discuss with you,' said Livia in a quieter voice, her face still glowing. 'The real issue is your use of a discarded pass in place of your own.'

Oh. Yes. That was why he had gone to her office.

'I only, um…' he began.

She cut him off, speaking quickly. 'Do you have your pass with you today?'

He showed her the pass.

'Good. In future if you forget your pass, will you use one that you found on the floor?'

'No.'

'Well then, let's leave the matter there,' she said briskly, glancing at the people around them. 'There was an email asking for volunteers to check figures in a report. You have volunteered. It will mean going down to the basement for a while. Down to the Data Services Department.'

Victoria, still hidden by the partition, revealed her presence with an audible intake of breath. Jonathon felt the colour leave his face.

'Did you say the Data Services Department?' he asked.

The lift deposited him in the basement. With its whitewashed walls and concrete floors, it was clearly a place where no one of any importance was expected to set foot.

Jonathon followed the signs to the DSD, past the toilets, as the lighting grew dimmer and yellower. From somewhere, perhaps in the printing department, Cockney voices could be heard, shouting to each other in their angry, cheerful way – a reminder that he was not among the international business elite anymore. There was no light wood here, no brushed steel.

He halted before the scuffed black door, then knocked. It opened slowly. In the doorway, looking Jonathon up and down, stood a tall, plump man with rosy cheeks, big fluffy greying hair and one shoulder higher than the other.

'Yes. What can we do you for?' asked the man in a serious, suspicious tone.

Beyond the man, Jonathon could see the room: the strip lights, the desks lining the two longer walls, the small table with a kettle and a plastic bucket on it.

Around half the room's chairs were occupied. Nearest the door was a very tall man crouched over like a wounded spider. Beside him was a man with curly hair that rose up like smoke towards the ceiling. And beside him sat a man with surely the thickest glasses that could be supported by a human nose. There were three more with their backs to him, men warped and misshapen by the unbearably dull things they had to do. There were no women.

'Come on, come on,' said the fluffy-haired man. 'We can't stand around all day waiting. What can we do you for?'

'I, er… Livia Cavendish sent me. I'm Jonathon Fairfax. I'm meant to be working here today – checking some figures in a report? I'm a temp.'

'Oh. Well. Sit down, sit down. Good to have another pair of hands for the annual report. We're stacked! Absolutely stacked.'

The poor, scattered gulag creatures looked at him with goggle eyes; one or two waved limbs in greeting.

'Where should I sit?'

'Anywhere. Not by the kettle. Here, use this one – she's not such a bad piece of kit.'

The fluffy-haired man wobbled along the desks and patted one of the beige monitors with alarming force.

Jonathon sat down.

'Oh, *briefcase!*' said the fluffy-haired man, pointing at Jonathon's case. 'Thought you said you were a temp.'

Jonathon looked for signs the man was teasing him, but found none.

'Um, I am,' said Jonathon. 'I just, er…' He tried to think of a different way of finishing the sentence, but failed. '… have a briefcase.'

'Not to worry.'

'What's your name?'

'Alan. Alan Handler. With an H. And you are?'

'Jonathon Fairfax.'

'Right. Well, no point introducing everyone. You'll only forget. Going clockwise we have Roger, Blount, Keith, Brian, Layton and another Blount.'

One or two of them turned at their names and nodded. Jonathon nodded back and tried not to say, 'Two *Blounts!*'

As with the briefcase, he entirely failed.

'Two *Blounts!*' he said.

'Yes, unusual. Now, you know how to log on? Good…'

With that, Alan Handler began a long and involved account of how Jonathon should check the figures in his section of the annual report and mark it on the Design Department's copy. He had to begin by working out where to find the original figures in the shared drive where Farynx's accounts were kept.

'There are two folders,' Alan explained, '"External" and "Internal". We always use the External one.'

'But we're internal, aren't we?' said Jonathon.

'Of course we are, with our briefcase and fancy tie.' Alan gave Jonathon's BHS tie a completely earnest sidelong glance. 'But down here we use the External folder.'

'So who's internal?'

Alan looked at him sharply and adjusted his glasses. 'That would be for the top brass: Chesborough O'Teece, Todd Stuckers and the like. No, if there's something that we in the poor bloody infantry need, it usually makes its way into the External folder.'

Alan wobbled over to his desk, picked up a battered pink Post-it note and handed it to Jonathon. 'Here's the username and password for the External folder.'

Scribbled on it in biro was *Guest* and *Pass123*.

After a few minutes it became clear to Jonathon that everything in the External folder had been exported in an odd format from a central accounting database in the Internal folder.

'It would be much quicker if we could just look at the database in the Internal folder,' said Jonathon.

'And it would be much quicker to get from A to B if we were Class A4 locomotives like the 1938 *Mallard*,' said Alan, who had a Post-it note saying *pw:Mallard1938* stuck to his monitor. 'But we aren't.'

'No, but if someone with access to that database just exported everything in the same order as the figures in the annual report, then the job would hardly take any time.'

Alan was humming softly to himself and peering at his screen.

'If we did that,' said Jonathon, faltering as he realised no one was listening, 'we could move the numbers into Microsoft Word and check them using the "Compare Documents" feature.'

He looked around at the creatures hunched over their computers. 'It would only take a few minutes,' he added, quietly.

Jonathon sighed and set to work. After a few minutes, he felt as though he had been labouring in the Data Services Department for years. He saw why even the bravest temps shuddered at the mention of its name. They were condemned to sit in this windowless room with its buzzing strip lights, in back-breaking swivel chairs, staring at tiny numbers on punitively small, old and flickery monitors, using the world's most heartbreakingly slow computers. Even the pointer on the screen could not quite keep pace with the speed at which a human hand moved the mouse.

Already, Jonathon's back ached, with deep knots of pain at its base and between his shoulders. His eyes felt as though they were about to drop shrivelled from his face, and a headache pounded redly in the very centre of his skull.

'John!' a voice behind him called.

Jonathon flinched and wrenched around in his seat, badly hurting his already painful back and neck. A couple of desks away, a man with a very tall head was craning around his neighbour to make eye contact. It was the wounded spider.

'Hello?' Jonathon said.

'Hi, I'm Blount – well, one of the Blounts…'

The man with gigantic glasses said, 'Blount Two.'

Blount laughed. 'Oy, no. You are,' he said to the other Blount, and then to Jonathon, 'Do you like football, John?'

Jonathon instantly relaxed. It was a football conversation. Though he didn't really like football, he did know the answer to this question.

'Yes, I do,' he said.

'So who do you support?'

'Plymouth Argyle.'

'Oh, right,' said Blount, instantly losing interest. Jonathon had chosen his team expressly to get this reaction, since it freed him from having to know anything at all about them.

Blount said, 'I'm an Arsenal man myself. See the Arsenal–Man U match on Saturday?'

'I missed it.'

'We won, one–nil. Gooners!'

'That was always going to happen,' said Jonathon, deftly deploying his football-conversation skills.

'Totally agree. Of eighty-seven matches between Arsenal and Man U since 1958, we've won thirty-three, including one FA cup, and drawn twenty-four. Just thirty losses.'

'Wow. Um, did you know that in 1878, Charles Wollaston became the first player to win five FA cups?' It was a clumsy return, Jonathon would be the first to admit, but it seemed it had been allowed.

'Talking of cups,' said Blount, 'anyone fancy a tea? My round. John?'

At that moment, Jonathon realised that he had never before been offered a cup of anything at Farynx. There was something so simple, touching and everyday about it that he felt as though someone had very gently inflated a balloon inside his heart. He could have cried, except that it would have undone the good work he had done in the football conversation.

The tea, in its cracked mug, tasted on the one hand much worse than an Ethiopian in a fancy paper cup, but on the other hand almost infinitely better and more satisfying.

92

They all sat and drank their tea together, occasionally bringing up a fact about football or – in Alan Handler's case – trains.

'What gets me,' said Alan, 'is that no one ever remembers the *Bittern*, one of thirty-four sister locomotives to the more famous *Mallard*.'

'In thirty-eight league games last season, Seaman conceded just seventeen goals,' put in Blount.

Perhaps it was a more statistics-dominated conversation than Jonathon would have chosen, and certainly it was happening underground and away from any people with normal-shaped heads, but it was a conversation nonetheless.

It occurred to Jonathon that, on their own and in any other department, none of these men would seem remarkable. It was only because they were concentrated together and stuffed into this room in the basement that they seemed strange. And he was one of them, with his thinness, his slight resemblance to the Cat in the Hat, the way the hair at the back of his head liked to stick up sometimes.

Two hours later, this feeling of belonging had faded. He was close to collapse from the backbreaking chair. His headache pulsed from the strobing screen. He could feel himself slumping forward, his face greying over, his eyelid starting to twitch. He stretched his aching back, rubbed his ruined eyes. Of the several pages of small-type figures he was supposed to check, he had done almost none. What made it worse was knowing that it was unnecessary to do it in this slow and painful way.

If only he had knocked. He shuddered, thinking again of Livia's hand on Todd's trousers. The crescent of lipstick, the Windows 95 logo, the Post-it note on the screen's edge.

Ah.

Was it possible that the Post-it contained Todd's username and password for the shared drive? Did Jonathon dare to find out? His heart said he didn't, and the idea made him feel sick. But his brain couldn't bear the alternative.

Jonathon glanced over at Alan Handler, who was scratching the back of his neck with a toothbrush as he rhythmically clicked his mouse, eyes staring blindly into his screen.

There was no harm in trying, surely? Jonathon clicked on the Internal folder. A grey box appeared, asking for a username and password. First, Jonathon tried the guest password he'd been given for the External folder.

'*Access denied. Error 4302. Check your password and try again.*

Attempt(s) remaining: 2.'

Right. Well, he hadn't expected the guest password to work. Was he really going to try Todd's? He looked around again. Everyone continued to hunch and stare and click. His heart was beating hard in his chest. It was partly fear that someone's eyes would flick over to his monitor just as he typed Todd's username, and partly excitement at the amount of hunched, straining boredom he could avoid.

With shaking hands, he typed 'todd_stuckers' in the 'username' box. And for 'password' he typed 'Marmaduke021380.'

He glanced around again. *Hunch, stare, click.*

He pressed 'enter'.

The computer, with agonising slowness, drew itself a new screen.

He was in. He couldn't quite believe it.

The mouse trembled in his hand. He found the database in the Internal folder, exported the figures he needed in the right order, and copied them into Microsoft Word. *Glance: hunch, stare, click.* Then he copied the figures from the report into a separate document. Finally, he chose "Compare Documents" from Word's menu. He felt like one of the cleverest men alive, but of course all he was doing was using a standard feature of the world's most widely used piece of software. After a long wait, the computer highlighted the numbers that were different. Jonathon carefully marked all the mistakes on the draft annual report.

Jonathon didn't immediately tell Alan he had finished – that would have aroused suspicion. But with his job done, he was able to waste much of the afternoon surreptitiously looking at files in the Internal accounts folder and trying to work out what Farynx actually did. This hurt his head almost as much as checking the numbers, because it seemed that Farynx made most of its income from selling its own buildings. He must be reading it wrong. At four o'clock he told Alan that he had finished.

When Alan had checked Jonathon's work, he said, 'That should have been two days' work, but you've done it in less than one.' He shook his head in wonderment. 'All the mistakes you've found check out. I suppose Livia will be wanting you back, so go and report to her.'

Jonathon got up, briefcase in hand.

Alan put out a hand. 'Just so you know,' he continued, 'I've asked if she'll lend you to us for a few days longer – at least till we've finished this Annual Report. We're absolutely stacked.'

And then, flushing slightly and looking at the floor, Alan added, 'And we'd be glad to have you back. Your face fits.'

26

'… so if we do that, my divisions' earnings hit our targets for the quarter. So what's the annual figure?' asked Todd.

Henry adjusted figures in a spreadsheet and clicked his mouse. 'That would produce a figure of twenty-eight point seven per cent.'

'And that gets dragged down by the divisions I don't control. So what's the overall number for Farynx?'

'Fourteen point seven-nine-four. That is it.'

'No, Henry, that is not it. Farynx needs to grow by fifteen per cent per annum. Not "almost fifteen per cent". Fifteen per cent. That's what we did the last two years. Is there something scheduled to sell next quarter that we can bring into this one?'

'Well, there's the premises where we're currently located.'

'Too much,' said Todd. 'And we'll never have the other floors cleared in time.'

'I'll conduct another pass through the database. Trust me, something *will* be identified.'

'That's what I employ you for. That and your silver tongue. It'll get easier again once this big takeover's out of the way in two weeks' time. With United Biscuits under our belt we'll be unstoppable. And everything will get a heck of a lot easier once I step into Chesborough's shoes.'

'The probability of that was significantly uprated at the event last night. The analysts there experienced a paradigm shift, Todd. They loved your presentation.'

'I think your little walk-through put them in the mood. Didn't I say you would kill them?'

Henry grinned, modestly waving Todd's compliment away.

'I'm serious,' said Todd. 'I talked to every one of those guys, and they all said how impressed they were with our new bandwidth-trading operation. HBCI has already sent out a memo saying that we should now be considered an internet stock. No wonder the stock price is up to forty-two dollars eighty-six today in New York and thirty-two pounds in London.'

'We should celebrate,' said Henry.

'Damn right we should celebrate – after you find a way to hit fifteen per cent. Do that for me today, and we'll go celebrate tomorrow night.'

'Okay, Todd. That is a one hundred per cent commitment from me.'

'Great. Now, if you'll excuse me, I need to go check on my date for our celebration tomorrow night.'

Todd looked through the window in the door. She sat at her desk, straight-backed, bronze-haired, magnificent. It was a small office, and windowless, but he would change all that for her.

He knocked. She looked up, recognised him, flushed. She rose from the desk, smoothing her skirt, and opened the door.

'Mr Stuckers,' she said, formally.

'Todd, please,' he said, careful to keep his tone just the way it would be with anyone else. 'Livia, I uh took a closer look at these reports, and there's one or two details I'd like to run over with you.'

'Of course, please come in.'

He stepped inside and she closed the door behind him. She turned to him as he put his hand on her rear, and whispered, 'Not here, someone will see us.'

'They shouldn't be looking,' he whispered back, trying to kiss her.

She moved her face away, looking at the window in the door, but smiling, still flushed.

'We're interviewing twelve per cent more candidates this year,' she said loudly, indicating with her eyes a spot where it would be impossible for anyone to see them – against the wall beside the door.

'I'm sensing a lot of growth,' he said.

'But there's one figure in these briefs that you should double-check,' she said.

She stood with her back against the wall, raising one leg, so that her skirt began to ride up. He came over to her and put his hand against the wall so his bicep bulged. She undid the top button of her blouse. He undid the next button. She reached out her hand and touched the front of his trousers.

The door opened and a thin young man with large startled eyes walked in, turned, saw them, jumped back two inches, said something that sounded like 'yark ardslargh' and coloured bright red.

'I thought I told you to get rid of this guy!' said Todd.

27

At shortly after six thirty, Jonathon opened the door of the flat and stepped inside. He had spent the whole of the Tube ride home trying to work out how to tell Emma that he didn't have a job any more, but had got no further than the line, 'I haven't got a job any more, Emma.' He felt something more was required, but had no idea what.

Closing the door gently behind him, he stretched out an exploratory ear. The radio was on, howling quietly to itself about what it would do for love. He braced himself and walked into the living room. Emma was there, sitting at the small circular table that had come with the flat.

'I've made you a cup of tea,' she said, indicating the mug opposite her.

'Oh. Thank you,' he said. How long had she been sitting there? He felt she wanted him to sit down opposite her, behind the cup of tea from which no steam rose. He sat.

'I think it's best,' she said, and took a deep breath.

'What?' he asked. 'What's best?'

'I hadn't finished.'

'Oh. Sorry.'

'I think it's best,' she said again, and this time left such a long pause that Jonathon was sure she must have finished.

'What?' he asked again, helpfully.

'If we split up.'

'If we split up what?'

'What?'

'Split up what?'

'What?'

'What do you think we should split up?'

'I think it's best.'

Jonathon had by now penetrated to the very essence of the thing.

'Oh. You think it's best if *we* split up,' he said.

'Yes,' she said.

What Jonathon's mind had grasped several seconds before now reached his body. He felt as though he'd been kicked in the stomach with both feet. Both his own feet. Breaking his legs in the process.

'What?' he said again, weakly.

'You're not the person I thought you were.'

The living room seemed to take off and swirl around his head.

'Um, I'm trying really hard to become that person though,' he said. And then he remembered Lance's full-body laugh at the idea of Jonathon being the strong, silent type.

It was true. Lance had been right. And that was why he was sleeping so badly.

Jonathon was never going to become the person Emma thought he was. And he didn't even want to be that person. He didn't like organised, go-getting, strong, silent executives. He was surrounded by them every day and he had never even made it to the second sentence of a conversation with any of them. He very definitely didn't want to be one.

You could have told me sooner, he rebuked himself.

'I realised it when your friend came over,' she said. 'He talked such *nonsense*, but you understood him. And it made me think. And actually, you were only ever really *yourself* that day you made those muggers run away. I keep looking for that man, and he isn't there. Just this other one who sings in the shower and draws rabbits in waistcoats.'

'I said "hey" wrong...' Jonathon began to explain. But his voice once again demonstrated its autonomy by delivering the words in a broken falsetto, followed by a small coughing fit.

Emma gave him a look, as though to say this was exactly the sort of thing she was talking about.

'I want you to move out. I've made a list of all your things and where they are, to facilitate the process. My dad will pay your part of the rent, until...' She stopped. *Until I find a real organised, go-getting, strong, silent executive man* was probably the phrase that fit best, thought Jonathon.

'Right. I'll go tonight.'

'Don't be silly. It's late. I've got the day off tomorrow and Dad's coming, so we can—'

'I'll definitely go tonight.'

When talking about Emma's dad, people always said, 'He doesn't suffer fools gladly.' As a result, he tended to frown a lot when Jonathon was around. He was a no-nonsense paper executive – practical, organised, go-getting, strong and, now Jonathon came to think of it, largely silent. Ah.

'I'll definitely go tonight,' he repeated.

'Take a sandwich,' she said.

'What?'

'A sandwich,' she repeated, ever-practical.

28

Todd held up a hand to Henry to stop him speaking, and turned his attention back to the phone. It was six thirty, and he was catching up with his calls – business and personal.

'I can't wait till tomorrow. Come for a drink tonight. We could grab some dinner,' he said.

'When?' asked Livia, on the other end of the line.

'Eight thirty. There'll be a car waiting outside the office.'

'Where are we going?'

'Probably somewhere impossible to get into.' Todd put the phone down.

Henry, who had shrunk back towards the doorway, advanced again. The two lines on his forehead, just above the bridge of his glasses, were particularly prominent.

'So, what's the bad news?' asked Todd.

'Who says it's bad news?'

'Your face is shouting it all over town. Spill.'

'I… okay. I'm just going to lay it right out there. I interfaced with a security guy here, a Carl Barker. He advised me that one of the actors didn't leave the building on Wednesday till eight.'

'When did the others leave?'

'Nine thirty AM.'

Todd, who had been leaning back and twirling a pen between his fingers, now sat forward, his shoulders flexed.

'You fucking what? One of your actors stayed here for over *ten hours*?'

'Uh, that would be affirmative.'

'I thought I told you to take a headcount in and out.'

'We did—'

Todd stood up. 'So you miscounted? Or you just did it out of academic interest, published the results in the *New American Journal of Being Fucking Useless*?'

'I was with the analysts. Andy Kassowitz conducted the headcount. You know how robust and process-driven he is.'

'Kassowitz is *your* guy. If he messed up, it's on you. So what's his story?'

'I'm not currently able to advise on that. He has a client engagement in Geneva.'

'Bullshit. I want him to call this phone,' Todd pointed at the phone on his desk, 'in the next three minutes or he's fired.'

'Okay, it's just' – Henry laughed as he did sometimes when he was nervous, which always infuriated Todd – 'he's at a client dinner with Bruckhausen and Rorschach. You really want me to pull him out of that?'

Todd didn't answer. He just stared hard at Henry until he got the message. Henry disappeared from the room, and three minutes later Todd's phone rang.

He picked it up. 'This fucking better be Andy Kassowitz.'

'Uh, good evening, Mr Stuckers. Andy Kassowitz speaking.'

'What the fuck is this I hear about one of your actors staying in the building for ten goddamn hours?'

'I… I don't know where that story comes from, Mr Stuckers. We did a headcount at the beginning and the end of the process. The numbers matched. Is security sure of its facts? I mean, those guys aren't the brightest…'

'Shut up. You do not get to pass the blame off onto someone else. Tell me exactly how you did these headcounts.'

'Uh, the first was carried out as they entered the elevator from the lobby—'

'Let me stop you there. You had a hundred actors waiting in the lobby?'

'Yes.'

'Why not just put up a massive billboard saying, "Something weird's going on, folks"?'

'What else could we have done?'

'Stagger their arrival times. Take them up as they arrive.'

'Sorry, Mr Stuckers. I received no instructions—'

'Let me ask you a question. Why do I pay you?'

'Uh, well I'm Associate Vice-President of Six Sigma Project Execution—'

'Shut up. I pay you to solve problems before they happen. That's your instructions. So now tell me how you fucked up the headcount on the way out.'

'Well, to avoid the problem you just alluded to, the headcount was conducted as they entered the area in front of the elevators on the seventh floor.'

'What?'

'The headcount was conducted—'

'In a half-assed way that means you can't guarantee all of them left the seventh floor. And don't insult my intelligence by saying it was to avoid the problem I just told you about.'

'But Mr Stuckers, with all respect, they're actors. All of them had been on the acting agencies' books for over a year, they all signed non-disclosure agreements, we have all their names and addresses. Even if one of them stayed in the building – which, you know, has not been absolutely proved, I mean he probably just sat in the canteen, learned his lines, talked to his agent, whatever these actors do…'

'For ten hours?'

'As I understand, these are time-rich individuals.'

'You know what? I should fire you right now. I should make you a fucking time-rich individual – and a very, very cash-poor one. I'm going to consider your future very carefully, Andy, and keep a very close eye on you. Now get off my phone line. You're embarrassing it.'

With that, Todd ended the call.

Henry, who had evidently been waiting just outside the door, now entered the room again. The two lines were even more deeply etched into his forehead. His face was ash grey.

'Todd, I tracked down the head of security for this building.'

'Tracked him down?'

'He had already departed for home.'

'He's head of security and he goes home before six thirty?'

Henry nodded.

'Unbelievable. And?' Todd got up and clicked another pouch into the coffee machine.

'There are security cameras in all the communal areas – lobby, corridors, stairs, elevators. I've tasked security with processing the footage for Wednesday, so if this individual was snooping around, we should get a visual image of him.'

'Right. And what about the other areas?'

'Ah, there is specific legislation in place that prevents us from record-ing the working areas.'

'You fucking what? You're telling me the places where we've got stuff we want to keep secret, they're the places where we cannot record?'

'That, uh, would be affirmative.'

'Unbelievable. This fucking country. Henry, I want you to take responsibility for security. Do not drop the ball again or I will take the ball away from you. And why didn't your security guy stop this actor who's trying to get out *ten hours* after the others?'

'As I understand it, their primary focus is on preventing unauthorised ingress. And this individual possessed a valid pass. What you're talking about would be an arrest, and they can only perform those if an actual crime has been committed.'

'What about trespass, isn't that a crime?'

'In the UK that is not a criminal offence. We could sue him, but he could not be arrested for it or sent to jail.'

Todd ripped the mouse from his laptop and hurled it at the wall, where it embedded itself. He stared at it fiercely, then threw himself down in his chair.

'Government,' he said, 'has one job: to secure property rights, so that people like me can create wealth. Seems like that's just about the only goddamn thing it doesn't do.'

Henry said, 'You know, that is exactly what Ayn Rand says in—'

Todd held up a warning hand and Henry stopped.

Just then, the phone on Todd's desk rang. He picked it up.

'Mr Stuckers,' said his PA, Janet, 'you have a three-minute scheduled call with a Lance Ferman of LPA. You met him on the flight over. He's on the line now.'

Todd sighed.

'Do you want to go ahead or should I cancel?'

'I'll take it.'

Clack.

'Hey, Todd?'

'Lance. I hope you're calling about a job because right now I feel like I'm surrounded by idiots.' Todd said this for Henry's benefit, looking him full in the face.

'I'm calling about a job,' said Lance. 'Can we speak some time? Buy you a coffee?'

'Buy me a drink. Come here tomorrow at six.'

29

Jonathon took his battered *A to Z* map and the copy of *Loot* that he'd been carrying around since Monday and went to a pub a few streets away: *The Bank of Friendship*.

It had a darts area, a huge old TV burbling about some football, and lots of worn and dirty purple benches clustered around the sides. The orangey-grey carpet was either patterned or just intricately dirty, and the ceiling was a mottled, nicotine yellow-brown. In the centre of the room was a wooden Victorian bar, scuffed, scarred and missing bits of its ornate carving. It was, in short, exactly the most comforting sort of pub to visit if you have that day lost your job, your girlfriend and your home.

One of the most comforting things about it was the lack of choice. There was no food, apart from KP dry-roasted peanuts and salt-and-vinegar Golden Wonder crisps. There was only one kind of wine, and anyone who drank it went back to beer afterwards. Of its four beers, people only ever drank two. And then there was cola, lemonade, gin and Bells whisky.

Ministering to this tiny range was a couple in late middle age, as plump and lumpy and full of ash as their purple benches. The man wore a brown-and-orange striped shirt, half open, and the woman wore a sleeveless velour top in off-pink. They had matching glasses.

'What can I get you, squire?' asked the man in a cracked and gentle voice.

'Um, I'll have a Carling please.'

'Barrel's just gone, boss.'

'A Fosters then, please.'

The man nodded at him as at someone who has wisely chosen the only available option.

'That'll be £2.70, chief.'

Jonathon handed over the money and took a seat in one corner, near some comforting old men. If it was humanly possible, he would move out that night. The alternative was the sofa and Emma's dad the next day. An event like this break-up would make Emma and her dad even more briskly effective than usual. By nine thirty they would have accomplished their standard father-daughter trip to Waitrose and would probably be repainting the flat and giving him disapproving looks.

He flicked through *Loot*, unable even in this urgent situation to entirely skip the irrelevant sections, as though something in him had always yearned to know how cheaply he could pick up a used drill nearby. It took him five minutes to arrive at 'Accommodation', by which time he felt a bit calmer. He was now absorbed deeply enough into the ash and beer of the bench, gentled by the clinks and murmurs of the old men two tables away, and soothed by a third of a pint of Fosters. He circled the five cheapest adverts, and then began phoning them.

When he got to the fifth number, someone actually answered the phone.

'Aye, what do you want?' said a Scottish voice.

'Um, somewhere to live?' said Jonathon.

'Is *that* a fact?' said the voice.

'Yes it is,' said Jonathon.

'Better come round then, loon. Have a look at the place. We'll decide if you're a numpty.'

Even at eight o'clock in the evening, Whitechapel was worrying.

Jonathon had only been walking for two or three minutes before an ill-looking woman said, 'You want business, love?'

'I'm um… I've already got some, thank you,' he said.

He wasn't entirely sure what she meant, but he guessed she wasn't a backstreet management consultant. Nonetheless, out of habit, he glanced suspiciously into the small car park behind her to see if there was a flip chart with the words 'shareholder value' written on it. She told him to have a nice night and he walked on, past a couple of chicken shops that seemed somehow brighter and louder than the ones around Finsbury Park. There were no Turkish men but some pretty big gangs of kids instead.

Following his *A to Z*, he turned left, down Greatorex Street, which was smaller and darker. He remembered that this area was where Jack the Ripper had enjoyed his most creative period, and shivered.

Kingward House was a brown and looming six-storey building, a layer cake of concrete and bricks that had spread itself over a wide area. At the main entrance there was a panel full of buzzers for the flats, but the door hung open. The concrete staircase had the smell of urine that is traditional to them, reminding him of his schools. So, this was the only cheap room left in *Loot* after four days. There was no way it could be so horrible that he would turn it down in favour of the head-collapsing awkwardness of staying with Emma and meeting her dad the next day.

There he was: Number 42. Jonathon pressed the bell on the chipped and faded turquoise door. It was silent, so he knocked loudly. The third time he knocked he heard someone shout, 'Darren! *Darren!* Go and get the fucking door, will you?'

A few seconds later the door swung open and Jonathon was facing a thin man with a pair of glasses and a smile.

'Hulloo,' said the man.

'You must be Darren,' said Jonathon.

'Aye – come on in.'

Jonathon stepped into the hallway, kicking down the edge of the carpet that curled up to trip him, dodging around the two bikes propped against the wall.

'This is the hall, like,' said Darren.

'Nice,' said Jonathon, taking in the bikes, curling carpets, the pile of coats, the knotted bin bag, the magazines and the dead pot plant.

'You think this is nice, you should see the kitchen,' said Darren.

The kitchen had an ancient white cooker that had gone brown, and some brown cupboards that had gone black. Then Craig appeared, wild-haired but also smiling, and they showed him the empty room upstairs. It was small and forlorn, with a sloping ceiling and a microscopically thin blue carpet that shrank from the walls.

'Nice,' said Jonathon again. 'Can I take it?'

'What do you reckon?' Darren said to Craig.

'He's a numpty, like, no mistake. But he's all right.'

'Aye. Never seen that before.'

This seemed a fair assessment to Jonathon. They shook hands and he said he would be back in an hour with his stuff, and the deposit.

'Is there anything else I should know?' he asked.

'Bog's a bit slow to drain, like,' said Darren.

Part Two

This Fairfax Guy

Friday

30

'Good morning, Miss Cavendish,' said Todd, cuddling the phone into his shoulder muscles. 'Great brain-storming session last night. Very stimulating.'

'Why yes,' said Livia, on the other end of the line, giggling. 'I think we tossed some good ideas around.'

'Are you—' There was a knock at the door. He looked up irritably. The Trafalgar Room's blinds were open, and he could see Henry waiting outside.

'Yeah. What is it?' he said loudly. Then more softly to Livia, 'Sorry, I got to go. Maybe we can uh… resume proceedings later on.'

He put the phone down and sat back in his chair as Henry came in. Once again, the worry lines were deeply etched into Henry's forehead, just above the bridge of his glasses.

'Shoot,' said Todd.

'Okay, now this may be nothing, but you tasked me with keeping you updated on security, so—'

'Would you just get to the point?'

'I talked with our network security guy. He said there was an unsuccessful attempt to access the Internal folder of the Accounts drive.'

'And let me guess, this happened Wednesday, when our actor friend was visiting.'

'Actually it happened yesterday. So it may be nothing – just someone clicking the wrong directory by mistake. But I just wanted you to know that when you say, "I am concerned about security," I make it a personal priority to oversee that whole area and keep you updated.'

'Okay, I get it. You want to make up for your mistake with the actors – make me forget that Andy Kassowitz is a useless piece of shit. Appreciated. Do we need to worry about this attempt? Where did it come from? Is this hackers?'

'Our network security guy believes it came from inside the company – a guest account on a computer somewhere in the basement.'

'He can't be more precise than that?'

'He's working on it. I'll get back to you when we know more.'

31

Jonathon woke from a dreamless sleep and found himself looking into a pair of dark, blank eyes.

The mouse, sitting just beside his pillow, broke eye contact first. It shivered, twitched its nose, wrung its pale pink hands, and then turned and scampered back through an invisible hole in the skirting board.

Jonathon looked around the room. His bed was a mattress lying on an ancient blue carpet so thin that it could almost have been electroplated onto the floorboards. The walls were green and the curtains were a rival green. A rickety canvas wardrobe stood in the middle of one wall, near where the mouse had disappeared. There was a chest of drawers beside the window, and next to them his belongings: two suitcases, a rucksack, three cardboard boxes, a carrier-bag, his briefcase and an uneaten sandwich.

It was, looked at objectively, horrible.

On the other hand, he felt a curious sense of peace. He hadn't been woken by an alarm clock. There were no slamming doors. He hadn't flinched once. He didn't have to go into Farynx.

He felt a sudden sensation of weightlessness. It was as though, after many months, a very fat man had just apologised and got off Jonathon's chest. He could breathe freely at last.

Maybe this was just what he needed. He could redo his CV and get another temping job today, an easy one, and start drawing again in the evenings and at weekends. He decided to begin his job hunt immediately by calling Eager Beavers. He needed the money: after paying the deposit and rent on this place he had only fifty-three pounds before he hit his overdraft limit.

He found his phone and dialled the number.

'Hello,' he said, 'can I speak to Dawn?'

There was a pause and a series of clicks.

'Hello Eager Beavers Dawn speaking how can I help you?' said

Dawn, just letting the words pile on top of each other with no punctuation.

'Hello Dawn. It's Jonathon Fairfax here.'

'Right,' said Dawn.

'The, um, job at Farynx... came to an end yesterday,' he said, and cursed himself for saying it in such a mealy-mouthed way.

'Yes, Livia Cavendish said she'd had to let you go. She explained the circumstances fully. I won't lie, I'm a bit disappointed in you.'

What could he say? When Livia had sacked him, she had said it was because he was always late and had used someone else's pass. She had dwelt at some length on what a serious moral and personal failing this was. And Jonathon had to agree that, seen from a certain perspective, using a pass he had found on the floor was really quite a worryingly dishonest thing to do.

But he had only done it to avoid being late. And ultimately, his lateness (for being early) was a consequence of having become obsessed with the mystery of Farynx and its seventh floor. And that had only been his way of avoiding thinking about the possibility that he had fallen in love at first sight with a girl on the Northern line. And he had been trying to avoid thinking about her so that he wouldn't have to admit to himself that he was living the wrong life. And because of all that, he had seen Livia and the American boss in a compromising position, for which he had been sacked.

It was a tale as old as time, but how could he translate it into something that Dawn would understand? After all, switched-on go-getters neither become fascinated by empty floors nor walk in on people when they're touching the front of other people's trousers.

'I'm still here,' said Dawn.

'I left my pass in a pile of coasters and had to use one I found on the floor,' Jonathon heard himself say.

'Well that sounds *perfectly reasonable*,' said Dawn, with the startlingly blatant sarcasm that, he now remembered, was her defining characteristic.

'Do you, er, have any more work?' he asked.

'There's nothing for you *just at the moment*. We'll let you know as soon as something does come in,' said Dawn.

Jonathon thanked her very much and they said they would talk soon. It had, as he feared, been a disaster. Still, at least he was English, and therefore knew it had been a disaster. If he had been from one of those countries where people expect everyone to say what they mean, he might have thought the problem had been neatly resolved and expected a call from her within hours.

His phone's battery was almost dead. It was him in telephone form, requiring colossal amounts of energy to do almost nothing. And he had accidentally left his charger in what was now Emma's flat. Well, perhaps it would be better to go and visit the other agencies in person anyway.

At the first agency, Angelic Assistance, he met a woman exactly like Dawn in every way, but with black hair. It was as though the world could not be bothered to make up a whole new woman from scratch. She was even called Dawn.

'Temp or perm?' asked Dawn, filling in a form.

'Oh, er, both,' said Jonathon.

'What shall I put?' asked Dawn, looking at him with the expression of an undertaker who has just asked 'burial or cremation?' and been given the jovial reply 'oh both'.

'Temp,' he said.

'Experience?' said Dawn.

'I've just been, um, programming a recruitment system in Microsoft Access.'

'Okay, you can operate Access.'

'Er, not just operate it. I can do all the reporting and programming in Visual Basic.'

Dawn gave him the undertaker look again, turned to his CV and said, 'You've got no programming qualifications.'

'No.'

'Okay. You can operate Access. Any other packages?'

'Word, Excel, PowerPoint.'

'The usual.' She made a faint mark on the form. 'Any other skills?'

'I'm a trained illustrator. I've got a degree in it, a first.'

'*Lovely*,' said Dawn. 'I meant *useful* skills, obviously.'

Jonathon said nothing. He had felt when he arrived that there wasn't much to him, but now it seemed he barely existed.

'And your specialist sector is HR slash recruitment.'

Is it? thought Jonathon. *Oh God.* 'Erm, I suppose…'

'And when did your last position end?'

'Yesterday.'

'A Thursday. Right. Was the assignment terminated?'

'I suppose so.'

'You *suppose* so. And who terminated it? You or the client?'

'Ah, the client.'

'*I see*. Reason?'

'Um, there was an empty floor.'

'*Right.*'

'And I left my pass in a pile of coasters.'

It was hopeless. He felt as though everything that made him human
– all he had ever managed to achieve, all he could do – was an obscure
type of gas which recruitment agencies lacked the technology to detect.

'*I see,*' said Dawn. 'Well, there's nothing for you *just at the moment.*
We'll let you know if anything comes in.'

Jonathon then had almost exactly the same conversation in another
six recruitment agencies. He was, without question, fucked.

32

Todd looked at his watch: two minutes to six. He put aside the report
in his hand, leaned back in his chair and addressed the conference
call phone.

'So, I want you to push back *strongly* on the idea that we do some
of this deal in cash, right? This is an *all-share* deal. And if that means
you have to give a little ground over their valuation of the Jammy
Dodgers component…'

There was a soft knock on the door. It eased open and Livia poured
herself into the room. Todd gestured with his eyes at the conference
phone and Livia put a finger to her lips, advancing slowly on him.

'Todd,' said a voice on the phone, 'we have a couple of doubts here
as to the validity of certain claims about their jam-research capability. Should we—'

Livia had her hand on his thigh.

'Uh, listen, Myron? Something big just came up. I think we're pretty
much done here. All. Share. Deal. Okay?'

Todd put the phone down. His desk phone rang immediately. He
picked it up reflexively. 'Yeah?'

'Good evening, Mr Stuckers,' said his PA. 'There's a Lance Ferman
here for your six o'clock.'

The guy from the plane. Should he cancel? Todd had a lot to do.

But then he thought again of how annoyed he was with Henry for the mistake with the actors. Besides, jealousy is a good motivator. It couldn't hurt to make Henry think he had a rival.

'Send him up,' he said, and hung up.

He stood, put a hand to the nape of Livia's neck, tipped up her face and kissed her. A molten feeling surged up in him.

'We can't fool around like this in the office,' he said. 'I have a position to maintain.'

'I know,' she said. 'I can feel it against my stomach.'

There was a knock. Todd sat down and picked up a piece of paper, which he frowned at fiercely. Livia picked up a folder.

'Come in!' called Todd.

Henry stepped into the room.

'It's okay,' said Todd, feeling a mixture of relief and annoyance, 'it's only Henry. What is it?'

Henry cleared his throat. 'I've liaised again with our network security specialist. He reports that the access attempt originates from a network node traced to the Data Services Department in this building. And…'

'And?'

'Our network security guy also confirmed that, subsequent to the unsuccessful attempt to gain access utilising a guest account, there was a successful attempt.'

'What did you say?' said Todd, very quietly.

'Uh, there was a successful attempt. It utilised your account and password, and it too appears to have originated from that same computer in DSD.'

Todd picked up his desk phone and pressed a button. 'Janet. Put the head of DSD on the line.'

'Right away,' said his PA. The line clicked twice and then a ringtone sounded. Thirty seconds of tense waiting, then it was answered.

'Alan Handler, Data Services Department. What can I do you for?'

'This is Todd Stuckers.'

There was a surprised cough, then, 'Oh. Mr Stuckers. Good evening.'

'Listen, someone in your department tried to get access to the Internal folder of the Accounts drive yesterday. Who was it?'

'Er, none of us. I mean, we are absolutely stacked, so—'

'Shut up. Who was it?'

'Well, there was a temp here yesterday – John Something. Livia Cavendish sent him down to double-check your department's figures for the annual report. Very fast he was too—'

'You get up here right now. Fourth floor. Trafalgar Room. You're not here in two minutes, you're fired.'

Todd put the phone down and turned to Livia.

'So. He says our spy is the guy you sent down to DSD yesterday – the guy I told you to fire.'

'Jonathon Fairfax? There's absolutely no way he's a spy. And you just said, "Get rid of him." I didn't think you meant permanently.'

'Okay, let's not go over all that again.'

'But that's why I sent him to the DSD. That's what we do with temps who need a bit of… straightening out.'

'Let me ask you a question. Did you ever threaten this Fairfax guy with that in the past?'

'Yes…'

'So he knew if he did something wrong – like walking in on… an important meeting – you'd send him there?'

'Yes, I suppose so. But I was going to punish him that morning anyway. That was why he was coming to see me.'

'Oh yeah. What for?'

'He used someone else's pass.'

Todd and Henry looked at each other.

'You fucking what?' said Todd, very, very quietly.

Livia looked at him appealingly, but he didn't move a muscle. He just stared hard at her.

'I left a bit early on Wednesday, at eight,' she said. 'He was leaving at the same time. At the security barrier, I saw the pass he was using. It was a special pass, and it said someone else's name.'

'And you didn't report this to security?'

'They checked the pass on the way out.'

'But they didn't know it wasn't his pass.'

'But he worked here, so I thought there was no point saying anything to security. He said he had found the pass – someone had lost it. And he was going to hand it in that morning, but then he found he had forgotten his own pass, and he didn't want to be late, so he used the pass he had found.'

'And you believed him? You believed this bullshit!' Todd hit the table hard with his fist, making everything on it skip nervously.

'Of course I did,' said Livia defiantly. 'He definitely isn't a spy. He's too awkward. And he trips over bins all the time.'

Todd turned to Henry. 'Get his HR file.'

Henry ran from the room, pushing past a plump man with a hunched shoulder and fluffy, greyish hair.

Todd stood up, put on his jacket and picked up his phone. He could feel his breath hard in his nostrils, the pricking of sweat on his forehead and the back of his neck.

'Hello, Mr Stuckers,' said the plump, fluffy hunchback. 'Handler, Alan Handler. With an H. From DSD.'

'Handler with an H, if you say one more word or move a fucking muscle, I am going to kill you and then I'm going to fire you,' said Todd. 'Is that clear?'

Handler blinked his comprehension and stood rooted to the spot.

'What do you want his HR file for?' Livia asked.

Todd gave her a look and said sarcastically, 'I want his address so I can add him to my Christmas card list. What do you fucking think? I'm going right now to talk to this Jonathon Fairfax – *obviously* fake name, by the way. I'm going to find out why he's doing what he's doing. And I am going to square him. If he knows anything, it is *not* going to come out.'

'Shouldn't we use lawyers?'

'Yeah, tomorrow. What are they going to do right now?'

Henry ran back in, shoving aside Handler, who was blocking the doorway.

'Here's the address,' he said.

'I want a car right now,' shouted Todd, grabbing the piece of paper out of Henry's hand, pushing past Handler and running from the room, along the corridor, past a thin girl he recognised from the reception booth, and Lance Ferman.

'Lance, I'll call you,' he said in passing.

He could hear Henry chasing after him, saying into his phone, 'A car is required, in a timely goddamn manner!'

33

Lance stepped smoothly from Farynx's revolving door and out onto the street. He had got into a lift seconds after Todd, and had followed him out through the lobby. Todd was climbing into the back of a Mercedes, and Henry was saying something to the driver. Todd slammed the door and the car pulled off, leaving Henry in the street, hurriedly pretending that he hadn't been about to climb in too.

Lance looked around. A man in a grey suit had just flagged down a black cab.

'Look!' called Lance, walking over and pointing into the sky behind the man's head. As the man turned around to see what Lance was pointing at, Lance glided into the cab and slammed the door behind him.

'Thanks, Graham,' he said, so the driver would think the man was an assistant who had hailed the taxi for Lance.

Then Lance said the words that guaranteed the driver would not wait to check what had happened, the words that every taxi driver longs to hear.

'Follow that car.'

'Blue Merc?'

'Yes, mate. There's an extra twenty in it if you don't lose him.'

The taxi pulled off at speed even while Lance was talking. Within four seconds it had caught up with Todd's car, which had reached the end of Arundel Street and begun the long process of waiting to turn into the Strand.

In the forty-three-minute journey that followed, there was never any point at which the front bumper of Lance's taxi was more than six feet from the rear bumper of Todd's Mercedes. It was by a long way the least exciting car chase Lance had ever been involved in. Todd's driver took no evasive action at all. After all, it's normal in London for a black cab to be driving so aggressively close that it appears to be trying to park on your back seat. And the car's speed rarely exceeded eight miles an hour. Lance began to regret offering a reward.

Lance had heard Todd say Jonathon's name in an angry voice, mention lawyers and imply that Jonathon knew something inconvenient. All this was further evidence that something odd and mysterious was going on at Farynx. Had Jonathon somehow discovered what that was? Lance had found, during that odd business five years ago, that Jonathon possessed an unexpected knack for almost solving mysteries.

But Lance severely doubted Jonathon's knack for self-preservation, and that was why he was going to follow Todd and see what he was up to. He was supposed to be meeting Jonathon in the pub that evening anyway – at six thirty, which now seemed a bit optimistic.

Lance called Jonathon.

'*The* number *you have called is*… UNOBTAINABLE… *Please leave a* message… *after the tone.*'

MEEEP.

He sent a text instead: 'tod stbkers mn way 2 yr flat i;m boming'.

Bloody phone. He wished his American one worked in England.

Every ten minutes he tried again to call Jonathon, but each time the phone went straight through to voicemail. Had something happened to Jonathon already?

When the Mercedes pulled up outside Jonathon's building, Todd got out and strode quickly towards the door. Lance was delayed by his initial unwillingness to believe he could possibly owe the driver fifty-four pounds. By the time Lance got out of the taxi, Todd was already upstairs.

Lance couldn't remember Jonathon's flat number, so he just pressed the buttons by the door at random until someone buzzed him in. Then, not wanting to arrive out of breath, he called the lift.

Bing! Here he was: the fourth floor. Lance stopped admiring himself in the lift's mirror and turned. He could hear Todd's voice from around the corner even before the doors had opened.

'So, let me get this straight: your boyfriend—'

'Ex-boyfriend,' said Emma's voice, but it was steamrollered flat by Todd's. Lance stepped out of the lift to hear better, but kept one hand on the doors to prevent them closing.

'—packed and moved out last night, right after you broke up with him, and you don't know his new address.'

There was no sound from Emma, but she must have nodded, because Todd continued.

'Well that's pretty convenient, wouldn't you say?'

Lance couldn't catch what Emma said.

'Okay. Fine. That's the way you want to play it. You *will* regret it. Just give me his number and I'll deal directly with him. And I mean his real number – not the one that goes straight to voicemail.'

'I haven't got any other number,' said Emma. 'And if I had, I wouldn't give it to you. I don't even know who you are.'

'Bravo,' said Todd, beginning a slow, sarcastic hand clap that Lance winced at, having seen it deployed by the villain in so many films. 'Great performance...'

Lance put his head around the corner, looking at Emma, a hushing finger to his lips.

'Hey!' he said as Todd turned to follow the direction of Emma's gaze.

'Lance?' said Todd. 'You followed me here?'

'Sure. It seemed like no one else was giving you back-up.' Then to Emma he said, as though meeting her for the first time, 'Hi, I'm Lance Ferman. Here's my card.'

After all, if someone's under suspicion, admitting you know them will just make you look suspicious. And then you can't help them. Or nose gratuitously about in the mystery they seem to have stumbled upon.

Emma said nothing, just glanced at the card Lance had pressed into her hand.

'I'll say it again,' said Todd. 'You *followed* me here? Who *does* that?'

'A private investigator turned TV star who's now looking to move into the corporate world. And I can't resist an opportunity to say, "Follow that cab."'

Todd considered this for a second, eyes narrowed and lip curled, as though someone were holding a jar of gherkins under his nose.

'Pretty snappy answer,' he said.

'Pretty snappy guy,' said Lance snappily, not even allowing a millisecond of silence between Todd's line and his.

Todd glanced at Emma, who'd had all expression wiped from her face by the confusing turn of events.

'Hi,' Lance said to her again. 'If you're wondering where you know me from, it's probably *MTV Undercover*.'

'We don't have satellite,' said Emma.

'Let's not get distracted here,' said Todd. 'I have come here perfectly legitimately, because some guy committing corporate espionage had this address on his personnel file.'

Todd looked at them both, then addressed Emma.

'Now I don't care what you say about this *convenient* break-up and moving out, you need to tell him to get in touch with me so we can… resolve this situation. I assure you it's in his own best interest to do that – and yours. You have my card.'

'I can't—' began Emma.

'We are *done*,' said Todd. 'Now close the door. I want a private conversation with this man.'

Lance gave her a sympathetic glance as she closed the door with a bang.

'Too much, following you here?' asked Lance.

'A *little*,' said Todd, with heavy understatement.

'Okay, I understand.' Lance turned towards the stairs. 'If you're interested in working together, give me a call. If not, no problem. I'll leave you alone.'

And after that, they walked down the stairs together in silence, something that only a man of Lance's supreme non-awkwardness could have pulled off.

34

Jonathon had been in the Faltering Fullback for an hour and a half. Lance was thirty minutes late. That was fine though, since Jonathon had Nicholas Emir Brunsengett's new book with him, *White Swans: The Power of the Expected*. The pub was not, now, near to where either Jonathon or Lance was staying, but Jonathon had not been able to face telling him what had happened. It would come up in conversation. Besides, there was something comforting about being in a familiar place. It was busy, but not so inhumanly crowded as it often was. Sometimes it felt like everyone was packed in so tightly as to be in imminent danger of collapsing into a single super-dense person.

Jonathon had got there early enough to reserve a whole table in the nice part of the pub. But as the place filled up, the idea of one person holding sway over a whole table came to seem laughably unrealistic. Jonathon re-enacted in miniature the history of the Native Americans, losing his territory bit by bit: first the far end of the table, then the middle, and finally the stool he was saving for Lance. The man who took it swore he would give it up as soon as Lance appeared, but President Jackson probably said a similar thing to the Cherokees.

Jonathon tried to concentrate on his book. The current chapter was making its point in the form of a story about a 1970s baseball team. Somehow, by expecting the expected they had turned around a losing streak and fulfilled the hopes of their coach, who was dying of cancer. Jonathon was struggling to work out how the story related to the book's theme. But he was sure that when he did work it out, he would be able to use it to turn around his own situation, whereby a nagging curiosity about an empty floor had rapidly spiralled into the loss of his girlfriend, job and home.

He was distracted partly by the sense that his presence at the table had become an aboriginal inconvenience to the men who had colonised it. But he was also wondering what had happened to Lance.

Jonathon's phone had finally given out, so he could not text Lance to find out where he was. His charger was still in the flat, Emma's flat, plugged in next to the bed.

'Um,' he began, tapping the man next to him on the arm, 'have you got a phone charger?'

'What's that, mate?' asked the man, looking sidelong at him.

'Have you got a phone charger?' asked Jonathon again. It was a long shot.

'What's he want?' asked the man in Lance's seat on the other side of the table, shouting above the music and the voices.

'Wants a phone charger,' said the first man.

'Who brings a phone charger to a pub?' said the man in Lance's seat.

'Who brings a book to a pub?' said the first man. The second man laughed, and the first man added, 'Nah, you're all right, mate. It's good to read.'

'I'm waiting for a friend,' said Jonathon. 'But my battery's gone, so I can't see if he's sent me a text message.'

'Course you are,' said the man in Lance's seat.

The first man turned to another at the end of the table. 'Oy Col, you got a charger with you?'

'Yes, mate,' said the man at the end of the table.

'What phone you got?' asked the first man. 'Nokia, yeah?'

'No, it's a Sagem 815.'

'A what?'

Jonathon took his dead phone from his pocket and showed it to the man, who instantly did a full-body laugh, just like Lance had the last time he had been in this pub.

'What's that, Dan?'

Dan took Jonathon's phone and passed it to the rest of the group, who also burst out laughing.

'Is that even a phone?' one of them asked.

'I bought it by accident,' said Jonathon.

'How do you buy a phone by accident?' Dan asked.

There was no way Jonathon could explain that he had mis-pointed in the shop and then been too embarrassed to correct the mistake because he felt sorry for the shop assistant. It could never have happened to any of the men at the table.

Col, still wiping tears of laughter from his eyes, did try to plug the cable into Jonathon's phone, but the charger was too sleek and well designed.

'You sure it takes electricity?' he said.

'I'd better go and see where he is,' muttered Jonathon, taking his phone back. He fled from the pub, the laughter chasing him out.

He was clearly not going to be able to live without his phone charger. And he was almost sure now that Lance was not going to come to the pub. He felt in his pocket for his key to the flat, which he'd forgotten to give back, and decided that if Emma was out he would sneak in and pick up the charger now.

35

After Todd had been whisked away in his Mercedes, Lance doubled back to Jonathon's flat and knocked on the door. It opened a crack and Emma looked out suspiciously.

'Hey,' said Lance. 'Are you okay?'

She opened the door and burst into tears. 'Thank you,' she said. 'That was horrible. What's going *on*?'

Lance put a hand on her shoulder. 'It's okay,' he said. 'Come on, sit down.'

He took her into the living room and sat her down at the table.

'You need tea,' he began. Then he noticed the bottle of wine he had brought on Tuesday, sitting on the side, still in its tissue-paper wrapping. 'Or wine. Tea *and* wine, that's what you need.'

He went into the kitchen area and put the kettle on, then rummaged through the drawers for a corkscrew.

'You probably need biscuits too,' he called. He had noticed that people tend to feel better when they have biscuits.

'We don't have any!' said Emma. 'I mean, I don't have any.'

Lance looked around at the Waitrose bags that Emma must have been in the middle of unpacking.

'Really?' asked Lance.

'They aren't good for you.'

Lance thought for a second. 'How about dips?'

'Oh, we've got those,' said Emma, brightening.

Lance set the tea and wine in front of her, then went to the fridge to get the dips. He glanced over at Emma, who put the tea to her lips, pulled the universal 'too hot' face, and then set it down and immediately took a drink of the wine.

'I don't really drink,' she said.

'That's all right,' said Lance.

He put the dips on the table, sat down beside her and poured himself some wine. Emma dipped a carrot stick in some slightly exotic hummus and ate it, then took another sip of wine.

'Sorry,' said Emma. 'Crying like that. It's not what I'm like at all. Who was that? Why was he like that?'

'That was Todd Stuckers. He's one of the bosses at Farynx. Did he say why he was looking for Jonathon?'

'No. He just said—'

But she did not get any further because, without either of them noticeably initiating it, she and Lance were kissing.

36

Jonathon walked down Stroud Green Road, past its smart new bars, old wig shops, sudden estate agents, unidentifiable vegetable sellers, upmarket bath boutiques and illicit snooker clubs.

For the moment, the bars seemed to have gained the upper hand in their struggle against the wigs. But their victory was thrown into doubt at the end of the road, near the station, by Rowan's Tenpin Bowling. It was a long, smudged building nestling under a gigantic faded poster of a very young woman in red hot pants. She lounged uncomfortably across a bowling lane, above the traffic, smiling through her pain.

He crossed the Seven Sisters Road, hurrying past the terrifying corner pub in which he glimpsed drunk people performing unspeakable acts of violence and karaoke. It was a relief to reach the chicken shops beyond it, with their Turkish men shaking hands and smiling at each other. And beyond them, around the corner, was the flat that had been his flat.

He looked up from the cold street. The lights were off. Emma must be out. He realised he had been holding his breath slightly.

He touched his fob to the sensor by the door, pulled it open and started to climb the stairs. The door buzzed again. There were footsteps in the hallway. *Emma's?* He stopped, listening. The footsteps passed the stairs and headed for one of the ground-floor flats, reserved for people who didn't mind passers-by seeing them watch TV in their underwear. Jonathon, finding he had pressed himself to the wall, prised himself away from it and continued upstairs.

Here he was, outside Flat 23, familiar but already not home. Should he knock to check Emma wasn't in? It seemed strange to knock on the door of his own flat, even though it was no longer his. He put his ear to the door. There was no sound.

His key turned quietly in the lock, and he pushed open the door. Inside, he stretched out his metaphorical ear again. Nothing, just the faint sound of the neighbours having sex. He closed the door softly behind him. There was no need to do it softly because there was no one in. But he shouldn't be here, and so he closed the door softly and he tiptoed soundlessly along the hallway. He opened the bedroom door and inaudibly switched on the light.

Lance and Emma, both almost (but not quite) naked, turned and stared at him. Jonathon stared at them, one hand on the light switch, the other on the door handle, one leg still raised in the action of stepping.

The moment stretched out. Galaxies were born and died. All the days of men's lives blew away like chaff.

And then he turned and ran. The bedroom door closed behind him. *Bang. Flinch.* He fought his way through the front door and out. *Bang. Flinch.* Down the stairs and into the street. *Flinch. Flinch.*

Saturday

37

The next morning, Lance woke with a guilty start. He didn't really do guilt, so at first he thought it was indigestion. But then he saw Emma lying next to him and he remembered Jonathon last night, framed by the doorway and looking like the model for Munch's much more disturbing follow-up to *The Scream*.

But why should he feel guilty? Jonathon and Emma had split up, and Jonathon was not supposed to live there any more. It obviously could not be guilt. More likely it was just a vague apprehension that Emma would want to talk about what had happened. That would make his least favourite part of one-night stands – the bit in the morning – even worse. There was no one he enjoyed talking to in the morning.

If Lance brought women back to his own flat, he could sometimes just pretend to be asleep until they left. But that tactic worked best with polite early risers, who were not the demographic best represented in the sorts of bars he went to.

Luckily, his non-guilty start had not woken Emma, who lay neatly on her back, her breathing perfectly regular, as though she were plugged into a recharging unit. He believed he had the skill and experience to get up, get dressed and leave without waking her. That was the gallant thing to do.

Lance moved his right leg closer to the edge of the bed. A lot depended on the mattress, but the aim was to move his weight sideways without pressing down. The right-leg move went without mishap. Next he floated his right arm to the edge of the bed. Then he moved his left arm and leg closer to his torso. Emma slept on. Now came the dangerous part: a gradual slight tensing of the left and then the right limbs so as to transfer his torso to the right-hand edge of the bed.

Softly, softly. This was an art form like t'ai chi, depending on power, grace and control. He was a waterlily, his weight perfectly evenly distributed as he floated gently to the edge of the mattress, ready to slide to the floor. Just a couple more inches...

Emma sprang out of bed, opened the curtains and froze. Lance could feel her eyes on him. *Damn*. Well, if he was going to do a plausible waking up, he had better do it now.

'Mwag, huh,' he said.

'What?' said Emma.

'Nothing,' said Lance. 'Just waking-up noises.'

'Oh, I woke you up. I'm sorry.'

'Hey. It's fine,' said Lance, yawning and stretching.

He sat up and pulled on his trousers, which were beside the bed, then looked around for his shirt. Emma had already put on a tasteful grey hoodie and leggings, and looked fresh and groomed.

'Do you want a coffee?' she asked.

'Does the pope shit in the woods?' said Lance, spotting his shirt.

'What?' said Emma, smiling in polite confusion.

'Er. What?' said Lance, trying to do his grin that made everything all right and feeling that the grin must be losing its power. He grabbed the shirt and pulled it on.

They gave each other the kind of tight little smile – Lance had once heard someone call it a *yink* – that is exchanged by work colleagues as one leaves a toilet cubicle that the other is entering: a situation where goodwill clearly needs to be maintained, but all the immediately obvious topics of conversation are off-limits.

'Well, rise and shine,' said Emma, after a little too much time had passed.

They both laughed politely.

'I'll rise, you shine,' said Lance, doing his grin. He didn't mean even the remotest thing by it. It was just some words.

'Er, what?' said Emma, jacking her smile up a couple of notches to compensate for her confusion.

'Let's get that coffee,' said Lance, buttoning up his shirt and making for the bedroom door, which he held for her and gave an instinctive nudge of his foot as he left, so that it wouldn't slam.

'Do you want some muesli?' asked Emma, again with a little laugh.

'I'd like to not have some,' said Lance, as though modifying her suggestion only very slightly.

'Oh. What? Is that a yes?'

'No, thanks,' said Lance.

A few minutes later, they sat at the table, taking rapid little sips of

126

their scalding-hot coffees.

'So,' said Emma, 'I really have to…'

'Listen,' said Lance at exactly the same time, 'I've got to…'

'What?' said Emma.

'What?' said Lance simultaneously.

They exchanged a yink.

'You go first,' said Lance.

'I was just saying I really have to go for a run and then get to IKEA.'

'And I have to change my clothes and then drive to Sussex or possibly Hampshire for my brother's wedding. He's marrying his own fiancée.'

'No rest for the wicked,' said Emma. 'Not that you're wicked. I mean…'

Lance got up, did his grin which usually produced such great results but which now seemed to be broken, and swallowed the last of his coffee, only magma-hot by now.

'I'll call you,' he said, adding his usual silent disclaimer.

38

Todd sat on a bench in Hyde Park, sipping a coffee and distractedly throwing bread at the ducks. The sun flashed silver off the water and lit up the tips of the oars waved about by the tourists in rowing boats.

Sensing movement behind him, he whirled around, a piece of bread screwed up in his fist.

'Oh,' said Livia. 'I was trying to sneak up on you.'

'Can't be done,' he said, relaxing and throwing the crushed bread at a swan's head.

He handed her the extra coffee that sat beside him on the bench.

'Got you a coffee,' he said. 'Tall skinny caramel latte, right?'

'Perfect,' she said, sitting down beside him.

'And a donut: Krispy Kreme.'

'I can't,' said Livia. 'My figure…'

'Right,' said Todd. 'Me either. I gave mine to the ducks.'

'Is that why there are so many ducks?'

'No, that's because of the bread. Actually, who am I kidding? I ate the donut.' He took hers from the tray and stuffed it into his mouth too. 'Just means I got to lift a little extra in the gym.'

'Forget it,' she said. 'You look good big.'

'Big?' he said. 'Do you mean fat?'

She pulled back a little but held his gaze.

He almost said something angry, but held it in. The anger faded.

'About last night,' he said. 'I guess I just wasn't in the mood for celebrating.'

'No problem.'

'I was starting to think you wouldn't show today.'

'Tiggy was being impossible this morning, and the childminder was late.'

'You should bring her. I love kids.'

'Do you even love them when they have a tantrum because you won't let them wear a hat in the bath?'

'Sure. I mean, they're frustrating, don't get me wrong. But they're a blessing.'

'Do you have children?' Livia asked.

'Yeah, one. My boy, Duke – Marmaduke.'

'Marmaduke?'

'My grandfather's name. My middle name. It's sort of a family tradition. Why, you think it's funny?'

'Oh no!' she said. 'It's a wonderful name.'

They caught each other's eye, she smiled, and then Todd laughed softly.

'I guess it is kind of a funny name,' he said. 'Still, what are you going to do?'

'How old is he?'

He hesitated. 'Twenty. Makes me feel ancient.'

'I've always preferred older men,' said Livia. 'They're more responsible.'

'What are you?' he said. 'Twenty-nine?'

'I wish. I'm thirty-six.'

'And Tiggy?'

'She's two. What does Marmaduke do?'

'He's a student – Kent State, performing arts major. It's a good programme. Actually, who am I trying to kid? It's a shitty programme, and he's dropped out. He's a pot-head, got no job, just lives on the allowance I give him. But you know, I've really been working on my relationship with him the last couple years. We're close. He'll turn around.'

'I'm sure he will.'

'Yeah, he's a good kid.'

There was a silence. Todd dug out some more bread.

'This Fairfax guy,' he said finally, 'or whatever his real name is, he's shut down his fake identity and disappeared.'

'I really don't think he's a spy,' said Livia.

'Okay, well, I go over to his address last night. There's a woman there says they broke up the night before and he left that same night.'

'Do you believe her?'

'I believe her. I mean, maybe she's just a great actress, but I believe her – for now. She was scared of me, and confused, and she got a little angry in that British way you guys have where it still kind of sounds like you're apologising. I don't know, it just had the ring of truth to it. Like I said, I think this guy shut down his fake identity and disappeared. I think he used her for a few months and now he doesn't need her any more.'

'But why do you think he's a spy?'

'Because if I didn't think he was a spy and he was one, then – bang! – Farynx is gone, my career's gone, it's all gone. I mean, what he might know is so dangerous that I just can't take that chance.'

'But what could he know that would be so dangerous?'

'You know what? Let's not go into it. In business, you're strong if people *think* you're strong. It's all about market sentiment, perception. Anyone smart does what they can to influence that. And I am very smart. But, I'm not going to lie, this is a tricky moment – in my career and in the development of Farynx and my divisions. If this all pans out the way it's supposed to, then in a month's time I will be *bulletproof*. But right now, we got a big acquisition coming up and I am still… consolidating my power base within Farynx.'

'Okay, I understand that you have to take this seriously, this idea that he's a spy. But honestly, he isn't.'

'So tell me about him.'

Livia nodded thoughtfully. 'I'd say he has some skills in data entry, checking, filing, general admin and basic programming, but poor time-keeping, and he really does trip over the bin every single day.'

'Listen to yourself: every single day? Doesn't that sound like he's trying to make you underestimate him?'

'But he also—'

'Wait, did you say computer programming?'

'Yes, he made the system that creates those reports I showed you. Of course, I told him exactly what I want. And when I—'

'If he can program computers, why is he a temp doing an admin job? This is the internet age. Those guys can pull down serious money.'

'Well, he couldn't when he arrived. He read the manual, picked it up.'

'He learned programming just from reading a manual?'

'Yes. That's what the manual's for, isn't it?'

'You know, the more I hear about this, the less reassured I feel. He does not sound like a temp.'

'Victoria's an award-winning playwright. She had a seven-minute piece performed at—'

'I mean, we know that our management accounts were accessed using my password from a computer in the DSD. If he's a hacker, that explains how he got my password. And we don't know what else he might have done, sitting in the office for months, connected to our network, all our systems...'

'But it took him two days just to make the border go green when someone got through the first interview.'

'Yeah, well maybe he wasn't putting all of his time into making the border go green.'

'I would have noticed. I keep very close tabs on my temps, you know. A tight rein. Besides, spying's illegal, isn't it? You just need to set the lawyers on him.'

'But all the lawyers can do is send letters to that tiny apartment I went to last night. I mean, maybe it's worth doing that. But basically, I'm just sitting here waiting for him to get in touch, tell me what he's got and how much he wants for it. I don't know who he is, where he is or who he's working for.'

'Why don't you get someone to find him? The police—'

'I am *not* getting the police involved. Period.'

They were silent for a while. A couple of ducks lifted themselves out of the water and began to strut about.

'There *is* this guy who's been sniffing about for a job. You know, he actually followed me when I got mad and went after Fairfax last night.'

'He *followed* you?'

'That should have been Henry, right? He saw how mad I was. I mean, not that I did anything I regret. I know more about this whole spy thing now...'

'I really don't—'

He cut her off. 'Sure, it creeped the hell out of me at the time. But I guess he's just trying to show he's keen. I mean, everyone wants to work at Farynx, so... But this guy, I met him on the plane and, you know, there was this kind of a *bond* between us. He owns this investigative agency – they found that prime minister who got kidnapped a few years ago.'

'It *sounds* ideal. But why would he be looking for a job if he has this agency?'

'Well, I guess he's looking senior level, you know, not like…' He stopped, to avoid saying 'not like your job'. 'Keep the other stuff going on the side. Basically, break into the seriously big bucks.'

'I still think you should at least talk to the police—'

'Yeah, I could give him a shot, I guess. I mean, at least I know what his agenda is, and that he can do this kind of work. Otherwise, where do you start, looking for someone you can trust with this kind of thing? You know, it's been really helpful talking this through with you. I appreciate that.'

Todd pulled out his wallet, sorted through a small pile of business cards and dialled Lance's number.

'*You* have *reached the* VOICEMAIL *for…* Lance Ferman… *Please leave a message after the—*'

'Okay, he gave me another card. I'll try that. I am going to find this Fairfax guy. And when I do…'

Monday

39

'Come in,' called a voice from the room. A nervous temp pushed open the door and ushered Bob Plover inside.

Stepping in, he was brought to a halt by the hard stare of a tanned man of prodigious muscular size. The man had a sleek head like a polished stone and the kind of startlingly white American teeth that Plover could never get used to.

'Todd Stuckers,' said the man, taking Plover's hand and squeezing it to a fine pulp.

'Bob Plover,' he replied, trying to recover from the devastating handshake and do the tiredly cheerful smile that was usually so effective at establishing rapport.

It seemed to bounce straight off the huge American. This irked Plover a bit, both because his company, LPA, desperately needed to get this job, and because he prided himself on his rumpled charm and ability to gently set people at ease.

Plover's charm, when it worked, had a lot to do with his rumpled appearance. Someone had once told him that he looked like Jeff Goldblum in *The Fly* – if, at the crucial moment, it had not only been a fly that blundered into the experimental teleportation device but also Columbo, Les Dawson, Tony Hancock and a dozen Walter Matthaus.

'Take a seat,' said Todd, sitting down. 'So Lance couldn't make it, huh?'

'I'm afraid his schedule made it impossible,' said Plover, forgetting to mention that Lance's not knowing about the meeting had also been a factor. 'But he says that anything you would tell him, you can tell me.'

Plover held out his card, with the title Managing Partner carefully picked out in silver.

Todd put a card of his own on the desk, face up, as though they were hands of poker and Plover had just made an unwise call.

'Lance tells me your company found the prime minister five years ago, when he went missing.'

'Yes, that's true. I managed to track him down to a cellar in a small Welsh town called Llandudno. He was unharmed but had gone completely mad. Been kept in a rolled-up carpet for God knows how long.'

'He ever recover?'

'He hasn't said a single word since.'

'And how did you find him?'

The truth was that Plover had found him by the simple expedient of having kidnapped him in the first place. It had been during that difficult time five years ago when he had been blackmailed into supporting a massive government conspiracy, got tangentially involved in a murder and ended up serving time in prison.

'Well if I told people that, I wouldn't have a business, would I?' said Plover, in his most reasonable tone.

'Don't want to give away the secret sauce, huh? I get that,' said Todd. 'I get that. I need you to find someone.' He pushed a manila file across the desk.

Plover opened it. Inside, there was an overexposed identity photo, a two-page curriculum vitae, and a five-page printout from a personnel file, which on closer examination turned out to contain only an address.

'So,' said Plover, looking up, 'you want us to find this, er, Jonathon Fairfax based on just this photo, a CV and an old address.'

Had he heard that name before? No, he didn't think so.

'If you don't want the job I'll give it to someone who does.'

Plover definitely wanted this job. Getting into blue-chip corporate counter-espionage was exactly what LPA needed to finally become a big success. These gigantic corporations must be stuffed full of industrial espionage. Or, better still, easily encouraged paranoia about industrial espionage.

'I'm not going to lie to you,' said Plover. 'It's going to be tough with so little to go on. I mean, all I can tell from this photo is that Fairfax has a head, at least one eye, and maybe part of a mouth. If it wasn't for the body underneath and a kind of hair-shaped shadow on top, I'd say this was a picture of the moon.'

'Well that's all we've got. If I could hand this guy to you on a plate, I'd find him myself.'

'Any security-camera pictures?'

'We've asked for them. You'll get them when we do.'

'We haven't discussed the fee.'

'Shoot.'

'Twenty grand up-front and another twenty when we find him. Plus expenses.'

'Whatever,' said Todd, shrugging. 'But Lance will be working on this, right?'

'Absolutely,' said Plover. 'Absolutely.'

40

By Monday, after his brother's wedding in either Sussex or Hampshire, Lance had a) started smoking again and b) realised he was going to have to find Jonathon and apologise to him for sleeping with his recent ex-girlfriend.

He didn't feel guilty. Why should he? Jonathon and Emma had split up. And things like that aren't under anyone's control; they just happen. Besides, who could have predicted that Jonathon would appear there in the doorway, looking like a horrified seahorse? No one. That was why Lance didn't feel guilty. Anyway, he was too nonchalant for guilt.

But there's nothing like your brother's wedding to a human-rights lawyer for kicking a chunk out of your nonchalance. Over the course of the weekend, dozens of Lance's extended family had asked him when he was going to get married. Lance had explained to them about fulfilling microrelationships, but they seemed to regard this as shallow and adolescent. He knew this because several of them, including his dad, had said, 'That's a bit shallow and adolescent, isn't it?'

There was also the fact that Jonathon had just lost his job, home and girlfriend, and so might be particularly sensitive to a friend betraying him. Not that Lance had betrayed him. But it had become clear that a man of Lance's depth and maturity would find Jonathon, apologise – however unnecessary that might be – and make sure he was all right.

Lance began by calling Todd. He had promised not to, but he only had two possible leads – Emma and Todd – and it seemed best to start with the one he hadn't slept with. Besides, surely the best way to find someone is to ask another person who is also trying to find him.

There was no answer, so Lance left a message. At eleven o'clock he got a call from Todd's PA.

'Mr Ferman, you wished to arrange a meeting with Todd Stuckers for today. Am I correct?'

'Yes, that's right,' said Lance.

'I'm a little confused. We already had you booked in to see Todd at nine, in your capacity as owner of LPA. I spoke yesterday with your colleague Robert Plover to arrange it.'

'Ah, of course,' said Lance, smoothly papering over his great surprise at this news. 'Yes, I'm sorry. There was a' – what was the phrase that made it all right? – 'scheduling conflict.' Yes, that was it.

'I see.'

'Could I get ten minutes with Todd later today?' asked Lance. 'He'll know what it's about.' Lance didn't himself know what it was about, but he hoped Todd would.

'I will check that for you,' said Todd's PA, sounding dubious, 'but, you understand, he's a very busy man.'

Five minutes later she called back, sounding surprised. 'Mr Stuckers will see you at two.'

Perhaps top business executives aren't as busy as they try to make out. Or perhaps Todd thought this was really important. Whatever this was.

41

'Henry, this is important.'

Todd clacked a foil coffee pouch into place. He turned in his chair and looked hard at Henry, standing on the other side of the table.

'Comprehended, Todd.'

Todd took the coffee and blew on it, then flicked his eyes back to Henry.

'Just, if I seem to be riding you a little hard at the moment, that is why. You know I've been a little disappointed in your performance around this whole spy thing.'

'Todd, total focus is being invested here to deliver proof that your confidence in me is merited.'

'Yeah, I can see that. Appreciated. Just… you know that this is make-or-break time for our whole plan, right? For the whole idea of Conceptual Business.'

'There is one hundred per cent clarity from my side, Todd.'

'Because if we do this right, then we are going to be the richest, most powerful men, ever. *Ever*. I mean, forget all the kings and all the emperors. Forget them. In a couple years, I could just like, one afternoon, buy every Picasso – everything he ever did – and light it on fire in Times Square, just because I felt like it.'

'Full buy-in from me, Todd.'

'Because I have been working on this a long time, Henry.'

'Ah, there has never been total visibility on my side, Todd, vis-a-vis the genesis of Conceptual Business. Could you fill me in? I mean, I know the three pillars…'

'You want coffee? Venezuelan, right?'

'Sure.'

Todd clacked another foil sachet into the machine and leaned forward.

'We're talking ten years ago – I was still with Norma – at some bullshit conceptual art exhibit. It got me thinking, art is whatever the art guys say it is. They say a chair next to a fucking *photo of a chair* is art, then it's art. Same for business. Profit's what the auditor says it is. Shares are worth what the analysts say. Etcetera. And we know these guys – geniuses they are not.'

'No intersection on that Venn diagram, Todd.'

'Exactly. So, if you can be a great artist without paint, you can be a great business without products, customers and staff. You want to be a great business, cut out all that stuff and just put all your effort into *looking* like a great business.'

'*Total success equals total commitment to sustaining the illusion of success*, to quote a certain someone.'

'Right. And that's why we have the three pillars of Conceptual Business. Pillar One: de-meat. Cut people, sell assets. Make that look like phenomenal profits using financial engineering. That's why I switched us to mark-to-market accounting, by the way – if your assets are complicated cross-holdings in companies you set up, you can say they're worth whatever you want. Pillar Two: spend like crazy on auditors, analysts, ratings agencies and so on. You want it so that if a junior auditor thinks they see a problem in your accounts at nine o'clock, their firm fires them at one minute after nine. And Pillar Three: when your share price goes up – as it will if you have phenomenal profits and everyone constantly says how great you are – you use those shares to buy another company. No cash, all-share deal.'

'And *repeat*, right? It is genius, Todd. Once you're CEO and we've got United Biscuits, the plan will just run itself.'

'Till we own everything,' said Todd, passing Henry a coffee.

'Although…' said Henry, hesitantly.

'What?'

'Nothing. Just, in a sense, not *totally* optimal, employment-wise – I mean, for the broader economy.'

Todd gave Henry a long stare.

'Just in a sense, short-term,' said Henry.

'Henry, this is *exactly* how the economy is meant to work. This is a competition here. You look after yourself. Those people who get fired? They should have invented Conceptual Business and taken away *my* job. You've got to follow your dreams. Make yourself immortal. You think Pharaoh thought, "Oh, what about the people? Maybe they want some houses instead of dying to build me a fucking huge pyramid?" No. He built the pyramid. That's why we remember him.'

'Which pharaoh?'

'What? *Pharaoh*. You know, the guy with the gold fucking head.'

42

Plover pushed open the door to LPA's meeting room. Twelve people were jammed into it, some on chairs, some perching on tables, all with paper cups of coffee. They had the air of American TV cops in the morning briefing scene.

Barry Lenin, Plover's business partner, glanced up from his agenda. He was as thin as a rail that worried too much, and had an immaculate coiled quiff balanced on his tall, thin head.

'G-good-good morning, Robert. Status rep-port?'

Plover looked disappointedly at the floor. 'I'm afraid,' he said, and then raised his head and smiled, 'we got the job.'

There was a cheer. Sally, who co-ordinated their work for Possum's Holidays, clapped her hands. 'Well done, Bob – I knew you'd get it!'

Plover held up his hands. 'Let's not get ahead of ourselves – whatever that means. It's just one job, and there's approximately fuck all to go on. But the person he wants us to track down is a corporate spy. And we can invoice twenty grand now with another twenty if we can find out who he's working for.'

'B-bravo, Robert. This could be v-very signific-cant for us. I have always said that the fu-fu-fu-fuckit-future of LPA lies in blue-chip c-corporate work.'

Barry had not always said this. He had, it was true, always said that the work they actually did – mostly investigating insurance claims – was not what they should be doing. But roughly every six months he changed his mind about what it was that would rescue them from insurance work and halt their decline.

They had been forced from their old offices in Soho Square when the rent had rampaged out of control. They had lost their reception desk, their security guard, their talking lift. And in their new quarters, they shared a floor with a modestly successful firm of chartered surveyors. Its expansion was helping to keep their rent down, but pushing them into an ever-smaller space. Now only Plover had an office of his own.

They were in a drab post-war building in Baker Street, above a shop that sold expensive bacon sandwiches to tourists who had come to be confused and disappointed by the lack of a real Number 221b. At first they had been excited about finding this place, just a few doors down from where Sherlock Holmes had never worked in his non-existent address. They thought it would impress potential clients and bring in more work. But it had turned out that their clients made their buying decisions on the basis of price, quality and need, rather than the literary connotations of the address, and so business had continued its steady downward drift.

Not long before, the big hope for saving the company had been changing its name from Lenin and Plover Associates to LPA. It was more professional, less specific, and it removed the unsavoury tang of communist revolutionaries and obscure birds that went with their actual names. But it hadn't worked.

Now, however, they had a new client, a new line of business. Though Plover had told everyone not to get ahead of themselves, he was already imagining taking over the top floor of one of those glass and steel buildings in the City. He pictured a corner office for himself with a view of St Paul's and a big desk made of some really rare kind of wood.

All he had to do was find this Jonathon Fairfax.

43

Jonathon stared into the Whitechapel toilet that had become a metaphor for his life. Never entirely satisfactory, it had just about functioned until Friday night, when something unutterably terrible had happened to it, filling it up with an overwhelming pungent darkness.

'I don't know if I can deal with this shit,' he said to the toilet/life.

On Friday night he had stumbled numbly back. Darren and Craig were in, having spent the evening eating chilli, smoking weed and passing some truly outrageous matter from their bowels. It half-filled the toilet, lying there as though all the world's evil had been somehow expressed by two Scottish men's bottoms.

In fact, opening the bathroom door had been nearly as disturbing as opening the door to Emma's bedroom. Again, he stared in horror and then fled, this time taking his toothbrush to the late-opening Sainsbury's down the road.

In Sainsbury's toilet he stood dazed, endlessly cleaning his teeth and replaying the scene in his mind: the door opening, the light flicking on, Lance and Emma turning and freezing. In that instant of recognition, he had felt as though a precisely aimed cue ball had cannoned across a pool table and neatly knocked his heart out of his chest and down a hole.

What hurt was not the break-up with Emma – that was quite a relief because it meant he could stop pretending to be happy. What hurt was that Emma would immediately sleep with a man who slept with everyone. It showed how empty it had all been, how poorly he had pretended to be the man she mistook him for.

He wasn't even cut out for friendship. Lance preferred yet another one-night stand to being friends with him. Well, now the friendship was over. He would have deleted Lance's number from his phone, if his phone had possessed the capacity to store it in the first place. And, of course, if he had been able to turn his phone on.

After Sainsbury's, he trudged back and lay on the mattress in his little room, the stink curling under the door like an octopus's tendrils reaching in to wrap themselves around his dreams.

When Jonathon had risen from his bed on Saturday afternoon, he found that the darkness now lurked a mere inch below the rim. Again, he was forced out along Whitechapel High Street to Sainsbury's.

After relieving himself and brushing his teeth, he returned to his room. It was horrible but, unlike Whitechapel, it didn't ask him for seventy pence, try to tell him about the healing power of Jesus, or yell 'pound a pound of bananas' in his face.

Sunday was the same as Saturday, except that Craig and Darren somehow filled up that final inch.

Now it was Monday. The situation was desperate, but perhaps it was no longer physically possible for it to get worse. That was the closest he could get to hope. If the toilet had not overflowed, it must – however slowly – be draining.

Jonathon sprang slowly into action. He took the Lake District tea towel his dad had inexplicably given him instead of a Christmas present, tied it around his mouth and nose, and went to look at the problem.

He opened the window. It didn't do much for the smell, but at least it distracted him with the sound of the alcoholics and truanting kids quarrelling with each other in the ragged car park below.

Jonathon studied the problem as long as his smell receptors would allow. Then he took off his tea towel, went to Whitechapel High Street and spent three pounds fifty on a mop, some heavy-duty plastic bags, a bucket and a ladle.

When he returned, he realised he had forgotten to buy anything to cover the floor with. Luckily, a large proportion of his possessions were newspapers he had forgotten to throw away. He laid them on the floor and got to work, making several trips downstairs to the gutter with the bucket. Once the bowl was empty, he tied a plastic bag over the mop, turning it into a giant plunger. He pumped vigorously, forcing air down the pipe.

After three bouts of pumping, he tried the flush.

The water rushed in, hesitated for the merest moment, and then hared off around the U-bend, leaving only the small, placid pond that should always have been there. It was perhaps the proudest moment of Jonathon's life.

Was it possible, he wondered, that he was not altogether useless? A teacher had once told him that he hid his light beneath a bushel. Maybe it was true. Perhaps he was not, as he tended to assume, a human bushel occasionally confusing others by squatting over a light. Perhaps he was the light, and it was time to get this bloody bushel off his head.

As he was clearing the newspapers away, Jonathon came upon a job advert with a ring drawn around it. It was in the copy of *Loot* that the girl on the Tube had dropped. He did not remember circling anything in the job section.

Do you evoke pity in strangers? asked the advert.

Jonathon stood and looked into the cracked and flaking mirror on the wall. Staring back at him was a thin man with wild hair, wearing a Lake District tea towel.

Holding his own gaze, he said in a determined tone, 'Yes, I evoke pity in strangers.'

As soon as he had finished clearing away, he called the number on the advert.

'Good morning, Albatross. Piper speaking. Can I help you?'

'Sorry,' said Jonathon, 'I thought you said, "Piper speaking."'

'I did. It's my name, I'm afraid. What can I do? My mum chose it because she's American, and my dad failed to stop her because he has some kind of undiagnosed personality disorder. Is that what you were calling about?'

'No, sorry. I was calling about the job.'

44

'Todd – good to see you,' said Lance, walking into the conference room Todd was using as an office. He remembered that Todd was the hand-crushing type, and so opted to surprise him with a slap on the shoulder followed by a brief clasp.

'You too. This is Henry.'

Lance shook Henry's hand more formally, calculating that he could survive it.

'Henry, could you give us a minute?' said Todd.

'Sure,' said Henry, smiling as though this dismissal had no effect on his status, but unable to resist giving Lance a sharp look as he left the room.

'Take a seat, Lance. Nicci, have you asked Lance if he wants anything – coffee, water?'

The nervous temp smiled apologetically, looking a little unsettled by her proximity to both this big American boss and, Lance was pretty sure, the most handsome and languid man she would ever lay eyes on – i.e. him.

'A coffee would be great,' said Lance. 'Just black.'

'Of course,' said the temp. 'Milk? Sugar?'

'Yes please,' said Lance. This was a private rule of his, always saying yes to the offer of milk in his black coffee. He liked to watch the reactions chase each other across people's faces: first simple acceptance, then confusion, and finally a sort of stymied dumbness that came with the realisation that, since they had offered to put the milk in the black coffee, they could say nothing about it. Lance felt it helped, in a small way, to chip a few more flakes off the veneer of rationality that the world tried to wear.

Nicci did a particularly fine example of the expression, with the first phase lasting a good two seconds before the second two smashed into it.

Once she had closed the door, Todd turned to Lance and said, 'Any news?'

'This is more a courtesy visit,' said Lance. 'I'm sorry I couldn't make it this morning: scheduling conflict. I just wanted to check that you're happy we've got the full brief.'

'Right. Well, there's not much of a brief. Basically, a guy who went by the name of Jonathon Fairfax worked here as a temp. I discovered that he saw something he shouldn't have seen. And then he got access to confidential accounting information for my divisions.'

'Is that a problem?'

'Only four people get to see that information. So, yeah, it would be serious if it got out. Remember we talked on the plane about black boxes? I don't want people to know how my divisions make their money. If they copy it, there goes my competitive advantage.'

'Absolutely,' said Lance. 'Do you mind if I ask what this Fairfax saw? Something to do with the recent analysts' event, maybe?'

Todd grew very still and looked at Lance for a long moment, like a cat that's suddenly unsure whether it's playing or hunting.

'What makes you say that?' asked Todd.

'It's just the most recent event I know of,' shrugged Lance.

'For the moment, you don't need to know what he saw.'

Lance was a tiny bit disappointed that Todd didn't trust him with insider information. He could not deny that, as well as wanting to find Jonathon, he was getting more and more curious about what was going on in Farynx. How could he get Todd to let him in on the secret?

'By the way,' said Lance, 'what fee did Bob quote you? I just want to make sure he factored in the discount.'

'Twenty up-front, twenty when you tell me who he's working for – or what's going on with him. Plus expenses.'

'Great,' said Lance, wondering how much Plover would tell him it was, and whether he would ever get the introduction fee. 'That does include the twenty per cent Friendship Discount.'

'Flattered,' said Todd.

'And do you have any leads?' Lance asked.

'We got his résumé and a not-great ID photo.'

'Do you think the CV's genuine?' he asked. He had just thought of how he could use it to find Jonathon.

'I don't know. I'm paying you to tell me.'

'I'll tell you,' said Lance.

'So, how much time are you going to put into this case, person-ally?' asked Todd.

'I've cleared out my schedule,' said Lance. This was a double lie, because he didn't have a schedule and because he was hoping to find Jonathon that very afternoon, apologise to him, report to Todd that he wasn't a spy after all, and then carry on with his holiday. The job would be over so quickly that there wouldn't even be any point in charging for it. Apart from his finder's fee, obviously.

'Good,' said Todd. He pulled out a card. 'The second you find something, give me a call. Here's my UK cell number.'

Lance could feel that Todd was much warier of him than he had been on the plane. The idea of a spy in his organisation had obviously shaken him, as had Lance's following him on Friday. Plus, people are just generally less relaxed once they're no longer sitting in the sky, reclining in one of the world's most exactingly designed comfy chairs and being served free alcohol by attractive women. If Todd was going to be suspicious, Lance wanted it to be for the wrong reason. He needed Todd to think he was desperate for a real job at Farynx.

'I've thought a lot about what you said on the plane, about a job,' he said.

'Oh yeah?' said Todd.

'Yes. I'm not going to be young forever,' said Lance, though he privately thought he would be young forever. 'I can't be an MTV presenter all my life.' He absolutely could. 'And LPA is a nice source of income.' That he didn't have. 'But I have bigger ambitions. I'd like to be a part of what you're doing here at Farynx.'

'Which is what, exactly?' asked Todd, giving nothing away.

'Reimagining business,' hazarded Lance in a tone of absolute conviction.

Todd was silent for a few seconds.

'You…' Todd shook his head, then broke into a big smile. 'You have hit the nail right on the head there. That is exactly what we are doing. That is what *I* am doing. So, okay. Bring me your résumé.'

'I don't have one,' said Lance. 'I've never needed it.'

'Cute. Get one. Now, I am *stacked*. I have a meeting in like' – he glanced at his watch – '*minus* ten minutes.'

45

After the high of winning the business, after all the optimism and congratulations, Plover had retired to his office and realised that he was actually going to have to do some work on this new case.

He had looked at the photograph of the moon perched on a collar and tie. He had looked at the CV and the almost blank personnel file. And, four and a half hours later, Plover had drawn a blank every bit as complete as the one that stared out from Jonathon Fairfax's identity card.

Plover was throwing balls of crumpled-up paper into the bin when he heard a combined high-pitched shriek from the desks outside his office. His first thought was that someone had just brought in a baby, because something had simultaneously hit the entire female population of the office. But that couldn't be it: no one was saying *aah* or *shush*.

His professional pride insisted that he work out what was on the other side of the door without looking. Tom Jones? No, there were male voices adding their deeper undertone to what had begun as a shriek but was now indisputably an excited hubbub. What could have equally affected the male and female populations of the office? Free cake? An incredibly fun website? A kitten with a gun? And then suddenly he had it.

Bob opened the door and said, 'All right, Lance mate.'

Lance looked up, smiled and waved. He was being hugged by Hedda, who had always seemed very wary of him when he had actually worked there. Lance broke off from his explanation of how nice Ethan Hawke was in real life and said, 'Hey Bob.'

Bob was a bit annoyed that Lance had picked up the American habits of saying 'hey' and having a tan, but hid his irritation beneath the front of tired and rumpled good humour that gave him such an easy rapport with everyone. Lance came over and they did a male hug, slapping each other on the back.

'So,' said Bob, 'what brings you back here?'

'Well, a couple of things. I'm in London for a bit, so I wanted to see everyone. And I've just been to see Todd Stuckers. He really wants me to work on this Fairfax case with you.'

'Really?' said Plover, managing a grin.

'Don't worry,' said Lance, 'I'm not going to ask for any money, apart from the finder's fee, obviously. But Todd was very insistent – you know how excited these Americans get – and I thought: why not? It'll keep me in practice.'

The office had fallen silent. Everyone stood behind Lance, expectant expressions on their faces, as though this were the pivotal scene in a musical and Plover only had to say 'yes' for them to burst into a gigantic song-and-dance number about a) old friends, b) the joy of saying yes, or c) staying in practice.

Where was Barry? He was the one who said no and took unpopular decisions. Bob's role was to look on with an expression of crumpled ruefulness.

Bob gave a big, creased grin that made everyone cheer and then he said, 'Wait here, I'll just check the details with Mr Stuckers.'

It was a way of buying himself time, so he could emerge again in a few minutes with a disappointed look on his face and tell everyone that unfortunately Lance would not be working with them after all.

46

'Great idea,' said Lance. 'I'll come with you.'

He walked into the office ahead of Plover. There was no way Lance was going to allow Plover to call Todd alone.

Plover followed, sat down and dialled.

'Good afternoon, Bob Plover here from LPA. Could I speak to Mr

Stuckers, please?'

Lance could hear the faint electrical chirping of a voice on the other end of the line.

'If you could ask him to call me at his earliest convenience. Thanks.' Bob gave her the number, put down the phone and sighed. 'Sorry, Lance mate. I need to get this cleared with the client. It's a legal thing.'

'No problem,' said Lance. He pulled out his mobile phone and pressed a couple of buttons.

'Hi Todd,' he said.

'Hey Lance.'

Plover beckoned to Lance for the phone. Lance responded by putting it on speaker.

'I'm with Bob Plover at LPA. He just wanted to check we have your approval for me to work on this case – it's a paperwork thing.'

'What? You're calling me for this? Of course. Just so we're clear, you also have my approval to breathe and drink coffee. Now stop wasting my time.'

'Thanks, Todd. Great talking to you.'

'Yes, thanks very much, Mr Stuckers,' put in Plover.

'Whatever,' said Todd, and the line went dead.

Lance smiled at Plover, as though he would be pleased at this.

'By the way,' said Lance, 'how much are you charging for this job?'

Plover squidged his face about a bit, as though trying to remember. In fact, he was probably buying time to speed-read Lance's body language, so he could gauge whether Lance already knew the answer to his question.

'Twenty grand,' said Plover, with a little smile. 'With another twenty if we find out who he works for. Finder's fee's still seven per cent.'

Lance nodded. 'Not bad,' he said.

He had almost forgotten this about Plover – how exhausting it was to be with him even when he was being pleasant and honest, because you constantly had to try to work out why he was being pleasant and honest, and when it was going to stop.

'Well, this is what we've got to work with,' said Plover, indicating, with an untidy sweep of his arm, the material from the manila file, laid out on his desk. 'What do you reckon we should do next?'

Lance stood beside Plover's chair and looked down at the motley collection. He picked up Jonathon's ID photo.

'I know,' said Plover.

Lance put it down again and picked up the one thing that might help him: Jonathon's CV.

'Where have you got so far?' asked Lance, looking through the CV.

'Called the number for his previous address, which he left four months ago,' said Plover. 'Bloke answered it saying he didn't know any of the "old-timers" who'd been there before him. I asked if there was any post for this Fairfax and he said they just threw all the post away. Kids, eh?'

'*Cuh*,' said Lance.

'By the way,' said Plover, 'does his name sound familiar to you? *Jonathon Fairfax*?'

Lance pretended to consider it and then said, 'No, don't think so.'

Though this lie was eminently convenient, it was slightly risky. Plover had met Jonathon once, in rather odd circumstances, and he might have come across his name at the same time. Lance was almost certain though, from their talks when he had visited Plover during his fairly brief stay in prison, that Plover would not connect the name with the face. Lance looked up at Plover to see whether he suspected the lie, but Plover was lost in contemplation of the lunar ID photo.

'Anything else?' asked Lance.

'I called the most recent address, the one he shared with the ex-girlfriend, but there was no reply – as you'd expect on a Monday lunchtime. And I called the temp agency he worked for – Eager Beavers – and said I was interested in booking him.'

'What did they say?'

'They said of course I could book him, that they would just give him a call. And then they rang back twenty minutes later to say Nigel Someone was free. I said I wanted to book Jonathon Fairfax. They said of course I could book him, they'd just give him a call. I haven't heard back. I can't work out whether he knows I'm onto him and has given them instructions to be obstructive, or if they're just a bunch of idiots who never really listen to anything anyone tells them.'

'Hm,' said Lance. He briefly considered telling Plover the truth. But that would mean confessing to having slept with a friend's girlfriend, and then having lied to Todd about knowing Jonathon. Plover would then spot that he could avoid having to work with Lance or pay him his cut of the fee if he threatened to reveal those secrets to Todd.

Of course, if Plover actually did reveal those secrets to Todd, Todd might decide that Jonathon was not a spy and so halt the search for him. Or Todd might decide that Lance was part of the spying conspiracy too, and set other spies or – worse – lawyers on him. When Lance tried to think any further about it, his head started to hurt and asked him not to do any more thinking. All in all, it was safest to stick with two tried-and-tested rules of thumb: a) don't trust Plover and b) lie conveniently at all times.

'Anyway, what are your thoughts, Lance mate?' asked Plover.

'Well, we're after a "proactive team player", said Lance, looking at the CV. 'There can't be many of them in London.'

'I've got to tell you, I'm not sure we're going to find this Fairfax. He's a mystery. When Todd first gave me the brief, I thought it sounded like a misunderstanding with a temp. But there's just so much that's suspicious about him: the photo, his movements, the timing of his disappearance. And then there's the CV: it just doesn't ring true.'

'What do you mean?'

'I mean, who does English and illustration? It's exactly the sort of thing I'd choose if I had to make up a false identity – just obscure enough to sound convincing. But who would actually do that degree? No one. And then there's the personal statement at the end: "I have always admired the work of the great Victorian illustrators such as John Tenniel and Edward Linley Sambourne, whose drawings are like poetry." Again, it's what you would make up for someone who's done a degree in English and illustration. But who would actually put that on a CV they're using to get temping work? And spelling *Jonathon* with an *o* at the end, instead of an *a*? Yet again, just obscure enough. It's like the CV's been designed to give credibility to this persona they've made up, instead of to get someone a job. The more you read it, the less sense it makes. And then there's something about the mixture of typefaces that's just not… right.'

Lance read the CV again and had to admit that there was something not quite right about it. And, now he came to think about it, he thought it would explain an awful lot about Jonathon if he were a spy, and everything about him were just an elaborate cover. Was it really plausible that he would get into a relationship with a woman with whom he had absolutely nothing at all in common, then move in with her, all within a month or so? Why would he prepare for one career and then immediately settle for life as a temp? Could he really have learned to program but not thought of getting a well paid job doing it? And then there was his neat hair and polo shirt: it was like he was trying to be someone else.

'There's a way we can work out whether the CV's real,' said Lance. 'Have you got the internet on that?' Lance pointed to the computer on Plover's desk. It looked like a piece of the future had been cut into an interesting shape and polished to a high sheen.

'No,' said Plover. 'That one doesn't work. Never has. I can't even find the "on" button. It just looks really good. The one under there does though.'

Plover pointed at a big plastic rectangle, coloured two shades of beige, that squatted under his desk like a troll under a bridge. He pulled a keyboard tray out from under the desk and scrubbed at his AOL mouse mat until the screen of the little monitor on his desk lit up. Then, being fifteen years older than Lance, he glanced at a manual and spent such a long time hunting around the screen for the right icon to click that Lance had to grab the mouse and do it himself.

'B-DONG... ck-ck-ck-crrrr... B-DONG B-DONG... screeeee... chick-chick tuck screeeeee,' sang the computer, showing the AOL logo and happily scrolling messages about all the connections it was making.

'I would have done that,' said Plover. 'I was just finding the right little picture.'

'Please let me work this computer or I will have to destroy the world in my rage and frustration,' said Lance levelly, pointing the mouse at Plover.

'All right, mate, go for your life,' said Plover, raising his hands as though afraid Lance might right-click and close him down through a context-sensitive menu.

They sat in silent, companionable distrust as the computer finished its song. Lance went to Alta Vista and typed the name of Jonathon's university, his course and his year of graduation. On the third page of results he found what he was looking for.

'I hoped so,' he said. 'Someone who did Jonathon's course has set up a website.'

He clicked the link.

'Benjamin Fox' appeared at the top of the page, and beneath it, 'Web design, graphic design, illustration'. Beneath that was a low-resolution cartoon of a man with wild hair and three pairs of arms, drawing something and operating two computers.

Lance picked up the phone and dialled the number on Ben's 'contact us' page.

'Hi, this is Ben,' said a voice.

'Hey Ben,' said Lance. 'Long time no see. It's Michael.'

'Oh... cool, hi Michael!' said the voice at the other end of the line, trying to make up in enthusiasm what it lacked in memory.

'Listen, I was talking to Blarnky' – this fake name only worked on the phone, where people could hear it as more or less anything – 'the other night, and he said he needs to get in touch with Jonathon Fairfax. I said I'd ask you for his number.'

'Er, cool, wait, let me… I've got all those in er…' There was a sound of piles of paper being moved around and a little rash of swearing. 'Cool. Did you say it was Mark who asked for it?'

'Yes, that's right.'

'Cool, cool. Mark the Beard or Mark the Hat?'

'Beard. Met up with him in Enfield.' This was one of Lance's favourite lie places, because everyone has heard of it but relatively few know exactly where it is.

'Oh, cool,' said Ben.

'You got that address?'

'Yes, cool. It's his dad's: 12 Pilbright Gardens, Crewe CW9 4AX, and the phone number's 01270 935286. Dad's name's Peter.'

'Hello?' said Lance.

'Hi, er, cool?'

'Oh, sorry. The line went a bit strange there. So listen, how's—' said Lance, clicking the button to end the call.

He turned to Plover. 'Old trick. Make it look like you got cut off, so you can end the conversation when it gets boring but still call back if you need to. And now we know his CV's at least partly real, and we've got an address and phone number for his dad.'

'Maybe,' said Plover. 'But how do you know that's his dad's real address and phone number?'

'You think this guy did a degree and gave friends a fake parent's address at the end of it just to throw us off the scent?'

Plover pulled a face to indicate that he would not rule anything out. 'Probably not,' he conceded, 'but maybe the spy's using a real person's identity. We'd need photos to check.'

They called Jonathon's dad. Lance realised that he had already known who he was: the author of airport novels set in airports. These had enjoyed a brief vogue during the irony-filled mid-nineties but had now been comprehensively forgotten. Lance said he was calling from the police's missing persons unit. Jonathon's dad said that he was sure it was all a misunderstanding and that Jonathon would turn up soon. He also said he had no photos of Jonathon after the age of nine or so.

'Why not?' asked Lance.

'I already know what he looks like,' said Peter Fairfax. 'What do I

150

need a photo for?'

After work, Lance and Plover went for a beer together. Lance wanted to keep an eye on Plover, as well as to catch up. He thought Plover probably had the same mixture of motives.

And after that, Lance sloped off to see Emma, who wasn't in. He slipped a note under her door. Would she read it? And, if she did, would she play along?

Tuesday

47

Jonathon arrived for his interview at shortly before half past five. It was a red-brick building in Clerkenwell, built at that time when the Victorians abandoned any semblance of sanity in their architecture and turned even the meanest building into a sprawling collection of turrets, rotundas, steeples, ledges, porticos, stairs, cherubs and chimneys.

Jonathon eventually found the green door to Number 7 hiding at the top of a small decorative flight of stairs, beneath some carved cherubs. There was a sign beside it and two buzzers, one marked 'Do not press' and the other 'Albatross / Palgrave'. Jonathon pressed the second and waited.

'Hello, Albatross,' said a jaunty female voice, thinned and tinselled by its journey to the speaker.

'Um. Hello. It's… I'm Jonathon Fairfax.'

'Come on up, Jonathon Fairfax.'

Tzzz.

The latch vibrated and yielded to Jonathon's push. Inside was a small black-and-white tiled entrance hall, papered in light-blue stencilled flowers and lit by a large, glowing dish hanging from the centre of the elaborate ceiling. Opposite him was a staircase leading upwards.

At the top of the stairs, set in a white-painted frame, was a door of old, golden wood. He knocked gently and stepped through.

Beyond was a large room with a double-height ceiling and floorboards that shone in the golden dusky light that tumbled in through a large curved window. Between him and the window was an oak reception desk. To his right was a waiting area with a small kitchen beside it. To his left was the main working area, sprinkled with old wooden desks and diverse people, including a man in a boiler suit tuning a lute, and a woman dressed as a cowgirl. Beside him was a narrow spiral staircase in cast iron, leading upwards.

Jonathon approached the reception desk, intending to say, 'Hello, I'm Jonathon Fairfax. I'm here for my interview.'

He did not say it, for three reasons.

The first was that the girl at the reception desk was the girl from the Tube.

The second was that she smiled.

And the third, caused by the first and second, was that in his mind a montage had broken out, heavily based on the sort of TV advert that, despite your mockery, awakens a wild and uncontrollable yearning.

Jonathon and the girl were cycling across a rustic bridge at sunset, tripping through soft lapping waves, riding a carousel, with a wistful guitar starting up and a heartworn voice joining in, dancing a Samba, kicking up autumn leaves, laughing at a blob of ice cream on her nose, kissing in a field, holding hands on a sofa beside a crackling fire, the image fading and the guitar quietening as the singer softly whispered the refrain, and where you would expect the final, warm-toned voiceover, there was nothing, because it wasn't an advert but a trick of his mind, and the girl was smiling but with perhaps a slight look of concern in her eyes, no doubt prompted by the fact that he was still standing in front of her desk and hadn't yet said anything.

'Um, hello, I'm Jonathon Fairfax,' he said. 'I'm here for my interview.'

'Ah, hi. Hello Jonathon,' she said in a voice that played each syllable on a small piano inside her. Her large, expressive eyes reminded him of the ones John Tenniel had drawn for Alice in *Through the Looking Glass*.

She paused and smiled again, perhaps disconcerted by the way he was looking at her. He shifted his gaze to the desk, but his eyes immediately snapped back on to her.

She said, 'Gus needs five more minutes to do whatever it is he does in his office. You could wait on the sofa, perchance, if you'd like?'

She sketched a picture of the sofa in the air with an unconscious wave of her hand, and pointed behind him. It was an old-fashioned green velvet sofa, with two very clearly defined bottom shapes no doubt worn into it over many decades. He sat down. Its high, straight sides gave him nowhere to rest his arms, compelling him to pile up his hands in an awkward heap on his lap. A little too far in front of him was a coffee table piled with magazines, newspapers and books.

'Perhaps you'd like something to drink?' she asked. 'Not coffee.'

She seemed to decide against explaining why he couldn't have coffee. Perhaps he just looked too tense already, with his pile of hands in his lap, and his unsuccessful attempt to lean casually back against a support that he now found was further away than he had hoped. Had she seen the montage happening in his eyes? He reddened. A new one threatened to break out, and suppressing it absorbed the brain power he would otherwise have used to answer her question.

'Er,' he said.

'A cup of tea then,' she said, nodding in agreement with her own decision, and disappeared into the kitchen, stumbling a little on the stairs.

She clearly didn't remember him. And she never would, because he was the sort of man who can't even answer a question about what drink he wants. But it didn't matter anyway: he wasn't cut out for romance. At some point he would fully accept this, and then there would be no more montages or uncontrollable yearning.

To distract himself, Jonathon picked up an old book of poems lying on the coffee table – *Palgrave's Golden Treasury* – and leafed through it, picking up an indistinct impression of nature, noble suffering, childhood diseases and the power of fate.

The girl shimmered clumsily down the stairs from the kitchen. She was no longer wearing her glasses, perhaps so nothing would interfere with the look of boundless pity she bestowed on him as she handed him his tea in a Willow Pattern cup and saucer. He was definitely not cut out for romance.

She sat down at the oak desk, pulled out what looked like a fabric tambourine, tested the tension of its surface, and then set to work with a needle. By this time, Jonathon had realised that the girl's presence here was not, as a voice in his mind had timidly suggested, because of the power of fate. She was here because he had picked up her copy of *Loot* and called a job advert that she had drawn a ring around.

Jonathon tried to read a poem about a curfew that was tolling the knell of parting day, but his head was swimming. Minutes passed. And then from above came the sound of a door opening.

'Ah, Jonathon?' said the girl, playing the middle register of her inner piano. 'You could go up now, if you'd like.' Her hand traced the spiral of the staircase.

Jonathon stood, picked up his briefcase and negotiated the staircase, concentrating hard on keeping the tea in its cup. At the top was a walkway running the whole width of the double-height room, with iron railings and a wooden handrail. On the walkway, in front of a door, stood a tall man with a slight paunch. His grey hair had gone out like a tide, exposing a great foreshore of pink scalp. In the middle of his face was a large, beaked nose, architecturally necessary to support a huge pair of square, black-framed glasses. They looked like two huge 1960s televisions, each broadcasting a large blue eye.

'Jonathon,' he said. 'Come on in.'

Jonathon followed the man into his office. The warm lighting chimed off the rich, pea-green walls. The furniture was beautiful and old, polished to a high sheen, and ruined by the assorted computer equipment that dotted every surface – sharing the space with knick-knacks and tottering piles of books and paper.

Jonathon put down his briefcase, turned, tripped over it, and caught his tea cup only by a miracle. The man seemed to regard all this as just the usual preamble to sitting down.

He held out his hand and said, 'Augustus Palgrave. Call me Gus.'

'Jonathon,' said Jonathon, and shook Gus's hand.

'Good to see you have tea in a proper cup and saucer. The mark of a gentleman,' said Gus, as though Jonathon had brought them with him from home.

Gus sat down on a chair that seemed capable of both swivelling and reclining, though it seemed to date from a time when chairs generally did neither of those things. He indicated that Jonathon should take the seat in front of the desk.

'Now, let's have a quick look at your CV...'

Gus picked up the CV and trailed off, his eyes blinking slowly in their deep black frames.

'Oh dear,' he said. '"Proactive team player"? No, I'm terribly sorry to have wasted your time.'

48

Chesborough O'Teece lowered his copy of the *The Economist* and gazed into the fireplace, the apartment's main showpiece. It was, strictly speaking, a lack of fireplace: the fire floated a foot above the silk Isfahan rug that covered the floor. The blaze seemed to spring out of nothing, its little licking tongues of flame miraculously leaving the fabulously expensive carpet untouched.

The flames actually sat on a horizontal sheet of glass through which ran invisible gas conduits. Chesborough clicked his remote control and the flames danced a little higher. Over by the far wall, a large glass-valve hi-fi system was softly, but with immense detail, playing Meatloaf's *Bat Out of Hell II: Back into Hell.*

Chesborough patted his comfortable paunch, took a sip of Japanese whisky and stretched his legs out a little more comfortably along the Mies van der Rohe sofa. He looked out of the penthouse's window, over the city. Beside him, illuminated, was the dome of the big white church everyone made such a fuss about, and beyond it the wheel the British had mysteriously put up to mark the recent millennium.

There was a knock at the door. Chesborough's heart sank. No visits were scheduled for this evening – there should have been nothing to interrupt his reading. And why was it a knock and not a buzz on the intercom?

He put his glass on the coffee table and went to the door, still holding *The Economist.* Looking through the spy hole, he saw no one – just the empty corridor and the lift.

He unbolted the security lock and opened the door.

'Hi Chesborough,' said Todd, who was standing next to the door with his back to the wall.

'Todd! Why, I… I wasn't expecting you.'

'I can see. Is that why you're holding that *Economist* like you're gonna beat me to death with it?' Todd laughed easily. 'Because I warn you, it'd take a *Forbes* to knock me out.'

Chesborough looked down at his hand and saw that he had rolled his *Economist* up and was holding it like a cosh. He pretended to hit Todd with it and Todd obligingly pretended to reel from the blow.

'Ow,' he said.

'Don't complain,' said Chesborough, 'I'm beating you with your own success.'

Chesborough unrolled the magazine and found the article, with its small picture of Todd punching the air at the analysts' conference.

Mr Stuckers has triggered a surge in the share price with his launch of its bandwidth-trading platform, convincing investors that this otherwise unwieldy trading, energy and consultancy conglomerate is really a buzzy dotcom.

That 'unwieldy' had made Chesborough frown until he had read:

Ultimately, that may reflect CEO Chesborough O'Teece's ability to pick managers who excite shareholders – above all, his long-term protégé, Todd Stuckers.

They had nailed it. Chesborough had always said his genius was knowing who to trust and giving them the freedom to do great things.

'Someone look familiar?' asked Chesborough.

'Sure,' said Todd, pointing at his picture. 'This handsome fella right here. Wonder why he's not on the cover.'

'Hey, they haven't put *me* on the cover yet. Come on in,' said Chesborough, showing Todd into the living space and closing the door behind him.

Todd looked around and asked, 'Did you have this flying fire last time I was here?'

'The weather was probably just a little warm for it,' said Chesborough. 'It retracts into the wall. Now, what'll you have? I'm drinking a little of this Yamazaki – it's a Japanese whisky.'

'Sure, I'll take a Yamazaki. I'm dry as a *Harvard Business Review* here.'

Chesborough poured Todd a drink and brought it to him by the fire.

'I got a little something for you,' said Todd. 'Close your eyes.'

Chesborough put the drink down on the coffee table and closed his eyes. He heard the click of Todd's briefcase opening.

'Can I open my eyes yet?'

'Sure.'

Chesborough opened his eyes and saw before him a head: specifically, the head of Marvin Lee Aday, better known as Meatloaf. Todd flipped the album over to show him the front cover. It was the original *Bat Out of Hell*.

'First ever demo pressing,' said Todd. 'This is one of only twelve now in existence.'

'My goodness,' said Chesborough. 'Where did you get this?'

'Oh, a little place in Camden I happen to know.'

Chesborough took the LP and removed it reverently from its clear plastic bag.

'I've been looking for this for the longest time,' he said. 'Imagine what Meat'll say when he sees this baby.'

'Well aren't you going to put it on?'

'I'm not sure…'

'Come on. You got like the best record player in the world. It's not going to scratch it.'

'I guess.' Chesborough drew the record out of its sleeve and crossed to the turntable while Todd took a seat on the sofa.

'Is that St Paul's?' asked Todd, looking out of the window.

'The church? Ah, yes. Sure. I guess.'

Todd looked up at something on the ceiling, but when Chesborough followed his glance, all he could see was the recessed head of the apartment's sprinkler system. The music started up, and Meat began to sing urgently about some fires that were howling way down in a valley.

'You mind if we go out on the terrace and take a look from there?' asked Todd.

'Sure.'

Chesborough went to the entrance area and pulled on a coat. Then he pressed a button on his remote control and the door to the terrace opened.

They walked over the oak decking of the terrace, beneath the stand of beech trees, past the rose garden and over to the rail that stopped you falling sixty-four storeys to the street below.

They stood there, side by side, leaning on the rail and sipping their drinks.

'To Conceptual Business,' said Chesborough, holding up his glass.

Todd clinked the rim of his crystal glass against Chesborough's.

'Conceptual Business, and the United Biscuits takeover,' said Todd.

A silence fell. They stood, staring out at the big white church. Then Chesborough felt Todd's hand between his shoulder blades.

'Chesborough,' said Todd, 'I think you should step aside.'

49

'But every job advert says you need to be a proactive team player,' said Jonathon.

'So?' said Gus.

'Well, I've had jobs. So I must be one.'

'A neat piece of inductive reasoning. And yet the question remains, what does the phrase mean?'

'Um, that I can work as part of a team.'

'Oh, so you're a worker, rather than a player?'

'Yes. I think the playing thing is a football metaphor.'

'And what about the "proactive" part?'

'Well, it just means I do things without having to be told.'

'Ah, so you're a person who can work alongside other people without having to be constantly supervised?'

'Yes.'

'Hmm. That does seem, as you say, to describe the basic qualities required for doing any job whatsoever. You do not attack your co-workers or lapse into passivity when your boss isn't present.'

'No. Hardly at all.'

'Perhaps there is more merit in it than I first assumed. Very well, I shall read the rest of the CV. There is, after all, something in the juxtaposition of fonts that bespeaks a mind at work.'

And so Jonathon sat uncomfortably, sipping his tea, in this grand, eccentric old-fashioned room crammed with new technology. He still had no idea what the company did, but he desperately wanted to work there.

'Oh, good lord,' said Gus. 'You like Tenniel and Sambourne?'

Was it the last straw? First the proactive team player thing and now this? Well, Jonathon could not bear to deny it. The bit about these two illustrators was virtually the only part of his CV that felt like it had anything at all to do with him.

'Yes,' he said stoutly. 'They're my favourites.'

'Then all is forgiven. I have a small album of Tenniel illustrations which I shall show you at some juncture. But if you're a qualified illustrator, why have you been' – Gus peered at the screen – 'programming databases in Microsoft Access?'

'Because I like drawing, but I don't know how to get anyone to pay me to do it. And then… well, it seems so niche and embarrassing, putting lots of time and effort into drawing pictures of rabbits in waistcoats when everyone else is being proactive team players and internet billionaires. And after university I didn't have any money or anywhere to live. I suddenly realised what the real world is like, so I gave up my dreams and started temping. I decided to be sensible and rational, like everyone was telling me to, and get a proper job, a flat, a pension.'

'I see. Unfortunately this means putting your faith in corporations, banks and, via pension-fund managers, the stock market – some of the most profoundly irrational institutions ever to exist.'

Jonathon thought unhappily of the headcount freezes, empty floors, fake trading and flip charts saying 'shareholder value'. There was really nothing he could say to this.

'But let us get back to the issue at hand,' said Gus. 'I have a job to give someone; you are looking for a job. It may not be quite what you're looking for, but I feel it's more likely to interest you if I explain what it is.'

Jonathon did not stop Gus to explain that he had no alternatives and was prepared to do absolutely anything.

'Of course,' Gus continued, 'there would be a probation period to see if you are quite right for it. But on with the explanation.'

He stopped, looked at Jonathon, and Jonathon nodded.

'I am completely unable to draw,' said Gus. 'But the "niche and embarrassing" thing that I like doing is thinking. I have ideas. People pay me – us, Albatross – to have ideas for them. For example, what do you know about whale song?'

'Um, it's what whales sing?' hazarded Jonathon.

'Exactly so. It has two particularly interesting properties. The songs can travel almost two thousand miles through the sea and, while they gradually change, old ones never recur. Thus, if an old one did recur, we would know that it was not started by a whale. So, we're working with an aircraft company on a device that broadcasts old whale songs if the plane crashes at sea, so that rescuers can find it.'

'That's amazing.'

'Of course, a lot of our work is less interesting. It was our idea to add wheels to suitcases, for example, and signs of wear to new jeans. We also design placebos, an enterprise which led us into the communion-wafer business. And there are hundreds of other things, large and small, that we do – I shan't interest you with them now. But I am growing older, and would like to contribute something more to the world. I want Albatross to come up with ideas for solving social problems, then test them, and either put them into practice or hand them over to other organisations.'

'Won't that be expensive?'

'Phenomenally so. I hope that the enterprise will ultimately pay for itself. But getting it going will require a lot of capital, which I'm work-ing on acquiring – we're about to float Albatross on the stock market. I have the prospectus we wrote for potential investors somewhere...'

Gus briefly hunted about through some piles of paper.

'Meanwhile,' he continued, abandoning the search, 'I can't wait to start, even if only in a small way. That's why we placed our somewhat cryptic advertisement, and that's why we invited you for this interview, which I must thank you for attending.'

'Um, you're welcome. Thank you.'

'But what, you may be asking, does all this have to do with you?' said Gus.

'Um, what does all this have to do with me?' asked Jonathon obligingly.

Gus nodded his head in acknowledgement of this small service.

'Well,' he said, 'have you noticed how many homeless people there are begging in London?'

'Um, yes,' said Jonathon, omitting to mention that he feared he might soon join them.

'Well, the homeless people need money. And people such as ourselves' – he generously included Jonathon in this – 'like to give money. But unfortunately our sympathy is most easily roused by presentable, polite people sitting in convenient places. We don't go into backstreets and find the dirtiest, angriest and sickest people. And we give most on sunny days, when we're feeling good, and least when it's cold and rainy. In other words, when people most need our help, we're least likely to give it to them.'

'But how could you change all that?' asked Jonathon.

'I don't know,' admitted Gus with a smile. 'But I'd like to find out. We could try to change the habits of the people who give money. But people are always in a rush, and it makes them feel good to give to nice people. So, I suspect it makes most sense to concentrate on the people with the greatest incentive to change.'

'You mean the homeless people?'

'Probably. I suspect that if we trained people to beg more effectively they would earn more. The refreshing thing about poor people is that their problems actually can be solved by having more money. For the rest of us, that's just an illusion – albeit one it's almost impossible to dispel,' he said, looking sadly around his ornate room full of toys.

Jonathon said, 'Couldn't you, er, just…'

Gus raised his eyebrows, encouraging Jonathon to continue.

'… give them some money?'

'Oh,' said Gus, surprised. He blinked and the televisions on his face briefly ceased broadcasting. 'But you know the saying, "Give a man a fish and he'll eat for a day. Teach him to fish and he'll eat for a lifetime."'

Jonathon had always doubted this wisdom. He couldn't imagine giving a man a fish and getting any response other than baffled hostility. 'Why have you just given me this fish?' the man would ask angrily. And teaching a man to fish seemed even less likely. 'I'm busy,' the man would say. 'Can't you just go fishing by yourself?'

'In any case,' Gus continued, 'I believe the first step is research, and this is what I would like you to help with. I have already assembled

161

most of the essentials of a begging laboratory: a small collection of dogs, various blankets, clothes of different sorts. I have two operatives who began last week. You would be our third. Initially, the work would largely consist of… well, sitting on various streets. But you could help us to design the next stage of the experiment, which should begin soon after we float on the stock exchange, on Monday. And it is not remotely out of the question that you might join the company in a more permanent – and indoor – capacity. So, are you interested?'

50

'I'll take over as CEO,' said Todd. 'You be Chairman.'

'Well, ah, yes,' said Chesborough in confusion. 'That's what will happen. I've already made it clear to the board that you're my chosen successor – that you share my vision for Farynx.'

'That's bullshit,' said Todd, matter-of-factly.

'What? I've said to them on numerous—'

'No, I mean the part about sharing your vision. It's not *your* vision. It's *my* vision. It's always been my vision. And I'm the one making it happen. You don't even understand what Conceptual Business is – you think it's just a neat phrase.'

'What is this, Todd? Of course I understand what Conceptual Business is – I invented it.'

'You invented it? Okay, so how come it's only my divisions putting it into practice? How come I'm the one making our share price go through the roof? How come I'm the one who identified United Biscuits as our next target?'

'Todd, no one's saying you aren't doing a lot. You're the best I've got. But there are lots of reasons for our success—'

'Yes, and every one of them is me: Todd Stuckers. So step aside, old man.'

Chesborough's jaw dropped open. The greater part of his mind was taken up with trying to believe what he was hearing.

'I, ah…' He struggled for words. 'Have I nurtured a viper in my ah…' He stopped, suddenly feeling that 'bosom' would be an embarrassing word to say in this situation.

'You haven't nurtured me,' said Todd. 'I nurtured myself. You're nothing in all this. You just like jetting around and sounding like Obi-Wan fucking Kenobi at conferences and symposiums.'

'Todd, I have driven this company with my bare hands. I am at the coalface twenty-four seven and—'

'You know what? I won't even take it away from you. You can keep it. Keep the jet, keep the apartments, keep the salary. I'll make sure you get a big leaving bonus as CEO.'

'But why now? Wouldn't it be wiser to wait until after we've taken over United Biscuits? Leave it a year, let the markets adjust to Farynx being an internet and biscuits company.'

'That just shows that you don't know what you're doing. You don't know what's going on here. If I become CEO now our share price is going to go so far through the roof it'll bust out of the atmosphere. That would give us a window of great opportunity, but it won't last forever – unless we do everything right. We'll need to buy the right companies, lightning fast, in all-stock deals – no cash. I can do that. Farynx can eat the world.'

'But Todd, buying companies, eating the world – this has always been our plan. Why are you trying to kick me out?'

'Maybe that's always been *my* plan.'

Todd was standing very close to Chesborough now. The hand that had started off on his shoulder in an I'm-going-to-give-you-a-few-home-truths sort of way was now gripping his shirt in what was alarmingly close to an I'm-going-to-kill-you sort of way. Chesborough was suddenly aware of how large and muscular Todd was, and how short and tubby he himself was. He looked at the Yamazaki in his hand, at the city spread out below him, at his rooftop garden and the welcoming golden glow of the hovering flames in the penthouse.

Very, very faintly, he could hear Meatloaf roaring about his heart breaking out of his body and flying away.

He could keep all this, without a fight. Or he could take Todd on just for the sake of those three little letters: CEO.

'Okay,' he said. 'You win. I'll step down. You can be CEO.'

Todd looked in his eyes for a second or so, as though trying to decide whether Chesborough meant it. At length he released Chesborough's shirt, and smoothed it down at the shoulder.

'Right,' said Todd. 'Good call.'

A silence fell between them. The sounds all around amplified to underscore it – the sirens, Meatloaf, the roar of the cars as they accelerated between traffic lights, the hoarse cries of the bankers in their wine bars.

'My goodness,' said Chesborough, shivering, 'it's turned a little chilly out here. Let's go back indoors.'

'Sure,' said Todd. He shook himself out, like a football player after a game.

Chesborough strode ahead, Todd moving more slowly behind him. He badly wanted Todd to go, so he could have some more of the whisky and phone his wife. But he was afraid Todd would sit down, that this horribly uncomfortable conversation would continue.

How could he make him go? 'Well, goodbye Todd' would sound too abrupt – and Chesborough was afraid now, really afraid of what Todd might do if he got angry.

Chesborough had an idea. As they stepped into the apartment, he said, 'Ah, how about a tour of the place, Todd, before you go?'

That made it sound like Todd had been on his way out and Chesborough was asking him to stay a little longer.

'Sure,' said Todd. 'Why not?'

Chesborough had hoped Todd would turn down the invitation. Still, just a few minutes now and he would be free.

'So, you've seen the living space,' said Chesborough, moving through to the point where the open-plan space became a kitchen, marked by a breakfast bar of polished obsidian. 'And maybe you're right,' he burbled, 'maybe I'm not close enough to the business any more. I should put some time into getting acquainted with it, visiting your divisions, seeing how this machine works.'

'Great,' said Todd.

Chesborough was still reeling from the suddenness of what had happened. Nothing seemed quite real, and the main features of the penthouse, as he came to explain them, added to that unreality.

He showed Todd the study. 'Ah, the desk and chair are attached to invisible cables,' he said, 'so once you've got seated, you can just float that whole thing to wherever you want it – answer your emails suspended in mid-air looking right down on that big white church.'

'Neat,' said Todd.

Chesborough hurried on, accelerating through the master bedroom with its pink ivory bed, then the guest rooms, the mezzanine wine cellar, the pool, and finally the main bathroom.

It lit up as he walked in. It was a huge expanse of marble with a round stone bath, comfortably lined in silica, with in-bath lights and a fountain feature that he really didn't feel like demonstrating.

Todd whistled. 'Wow. Beyond neat.'

'Ah, thanks,' said Chesborough.

And then he was shoved from behind with an incredible force that sent his head barrelling into the edge of his luxurious stone bath. All was black.

It was black for a very long time, a time of nothing at all. And the next time it wasn't black, he was nosing aside fragments of shell, struggling with raw flippers over sand, and then flopping into a cool pool of water with the other new terrapins.

51

Emma was sitting on the sofa reading an article in *Personnel Today* about Human Resources' twelve competencies. She found her attention wandering, her eyes still mechanically reading the words while her mind replayed Friday night and thought about the note Lance had left yesterday while she was at her evening class.

How could she have been so wrong about Jonathon? She thought of what her dad had said in Waitrose: 'Warned you – whimsical chap, that.' Still, she hoped Jonathon was all right.

She set her magazine aside, deciding she had read enough to tick it off her to-do list. She should really be doing the ironing anyway, before going for a run. The devil finds work for idle hands.

She got up from the sofa and took the iron out of its cupboard. As she was unwrapping its cord, she thought she heard a knock at the door. She turned the radio down, so the words disappeared mid-line.

'... 'cause we were *umble-mumble-dee-mumble-mumble-dess.*'

Knock, knock, knock.

She suddenly wished she were wearing more than her running kit. She looked through the spy hole, but then remembered it had been fitted backwards, so you could only use it to look in. She opened the door.

'Hey.'

He seemed to occupy the whole of the doorway. His hands were in his pockets and he wore a calm smile on his stony face.

'Oh, hello,' she said, and moved her mouth muscles upwards at the edges.

165

'Todd Stuckers,' he said, putting his hand out. She shook it, but only as much as was necessary.

'Listen,' he said, 'I'm sorry about Friday: I was angry, I was out of line. I shouldn't have yelled at you like that.'

She suddenly realised that she should be angry with him, since he had badly upset her on Friday. But then immediately after that she had slept with Lance, which was really not like her at all – totally uncharacteristic, in fact. Well, to err is human. And then there was Jonathon walking in on them, which she should also be angry about but instead felt guilty for. Between them, those two things had put Todd completely out of her head, which made it the more startling to see him on her doorstep.

He shifted his weight, and she instinctively took a step backwards. He responded as though this had been an invitation to come in.

'Sure, thanks,' he said, and stepped across the threshold. She found herself mechanically stepping out of his way, holding the door open so it didn't get caught on his muscles. He walked ahead of her into the living room.

Seeing that she was unavoidably committed to talking to him, she called, 'One second,' and slipped into the bedroom, closing the door softly behind her. She quickly changed into a hoodie and leggings.

When she came out he was sitting on the sofa, leafing through her HR magazine. She sat down on the chair beside the door.

'So listen,' he said, his eyes taking in her changed clothes. 'Like I said, I'm sorry. I just got a little carried away on Friday. I thought your boyfriend was involved in corporate espionage and it rattled me.'

'Well you thought wrong. And he isn't my boyfriend.'

'Right. What makes you so sure he isn't a spy though?'

'He just isn't. He falls over the ironing board.'

'Okay, okay. You must have heard he quit his job…'

'He said he was fired.'

'Right, well. That was a mistake on our part. I would love to take him on again, because he is a great… employee. You know how I could get in touch with him to talk about that? Phone number? Address?'

'You've already asked me this. And I told you I don't know.'

'Right. So you're not in touch with him at all? You guys have no contact now?'

'I don't feel it's appropriate to discuss that with you,' she said, but blushed.

'Right,' he said. 'You know, I didn't mean to press. I came here just

166

to apologise, explain and get out of your hair.' He looked at his watch. 'It's six forty-five already. I have used up way too much of your time. Already six forty-five. Again, I apologise.'

'Oh no, not at all,' she said reflexively, looking up at the clock and feeling relieved that it was still early. And then, because she was polite and he was, after all, a senior executive, she could not help adding, 'Would you like a cup of tea?'

52

Plover enjoyed pretending to be irritated with Lance, and he was good at it. He made his performance convincing by tapping into the sense of genuine irritation he always felt whenever Lance was around. It did get a bit tiring after a while, especially when they were together all day. But if they had been apart it would have been harder to work out what the fuck Lance was playing at. All that business five years ago had taught Plover the vital importance of knowing this. Of course, Lance wasn't responsible for the fact that Plover had spent seven months in prison for assault. Then again, he wasn't not responsible for it either.

However, now was no time to be thinking about all that. They were walking up the stairs to Emma Hughes' flat, to talk to her about this Fairfax case. The building was so new that its fresh white walls had, so far as he had seen, only a single penis drawn on them.

He knocked on the door.

'What if she's out?' Lance said.

'She won't be.'

'How do you know?'

'I thought you'd been in this game long enough to know that at half past seven on a Tuesday night absolutely everyone in England is at home. You can talk to anyone you want.'

He knocked again.

'What about you?' said Lance. 'You aren't in.'

'Why would I want to speak to myself?'

This time Lance knocked. They waited.

'She's not in,' said Lance again, like a man who didn't want someone to be in. He had very clearly slept with her.

'She's in,' said Plover. 'If she's not answering the door it can only

167

be because she's wearing headphones or she's been murdered. We'd be quite justified in calling the police: they know about Tuesdays too.'

'What? You can't call the police just because someone isn't in on a Tuesday. It's not the same thing as murder.'

But on the word 'murder' the door opened, and there stood Emma in a hoodie and leggings, with a large pair of headphones around her neck.

'Oh, hello,' she said. She seemed surprised to see them both, but not quite as surprised as she should be.

'Hi,' said Lance.

Plover noticed that Emma gave Lance a quick look – more suppressed worry than post-coital anger.

'Evening,' said Plover, with his most tiredly rumpled smile, unable to avoid glancing at the headphones and looking triumphantly at Lance.

'My radio's just broken,' said Emma, catching the look.

'Can we have a few quick words about Jonathon Fairfax?' asked Plover.

'Great minds think alike. Come in. I'm late for my run though. I don't know what's happened to my sense of time this evening.'

Plover let Lance go in first, and then followed, walking with heavy steps down the narrow corridor, glancing through the bathroom door on the way.

In the kitchen part of the living space, Emma looked regretfully at an expensive-looking digital radio with a dead display. She put the kettle on.

'Would you like tea?' she asked.

'What did you mean, "Great minds think alike"?' Plover asked.

'Oh, just that there was someone here not long before you. He was asking about Jonathon too.'

'What was his name?'

Plover noticed Emma's quick glance at Lance, and tiredly rubbed his eye so that Lance could give her an almost imperceptible nod.

'Todd Stuckers.'

'Oh. Our client,' said Plover, massaging the folds of skin around his temples but nonetheless noticing the surprised glance Emma shot Lance, and his furtive reassuring smile.

When the teas were poured, they took them into the living area, where Lance and Plover sat on the sofa, facing Emma on the armchair. Plover leaned back, as though tiredly stretching his neck muscles, but actually doing a quick survey of the room. Nothing unusual, apart from a slight mark on the wall by the clock.

'So, Emma,' said Plover, 'do you have any idea where Jonathon's living now?'

'No. I was just saying to Mr Stuckers that he left on Thursday night.'

'And were you expecting him to leave?'

'Not that night. I'd just broken up with him, and he said he'd try to move out that same night. I didn't think he would manage it but… "There is nothing impossible to him who will try."'

'So in one evening he found a new place to live and moved all his stuff out?'

'Yes. He didn't have much – it was only a few boxes.'

'Did he leave anything behind?'

'Only his phone charger.'

Lance blinked slightly longer than usual.

'And have you seen him since?'

She hesitated, and then said, 'No.'

'Are you sure?'

'Yes. Sure as eggs.'

'What?'

'What?'

Plover decided to leave her cryptic eggs remark for the moment. She seemed to be trying to distract him. She also seemed to be lying to him, though he wasn't sure what she was lying about.

'He didn't come back then – for the phone charger?' asked Plover.

She blushed and said, 'No.'

'Thanks for helping us, by the way. Farynx thinks he's a corporate spy…'

'He isn't.'

'Exactly. So the sooner we find him, the sooner we can do our jobs and show Farynx they're wrong. If we find Jonathon it'll be the best thing for him.'

'Well, "Seek and ye shall find."'

'Er, yes. So, you will tell me, won't you, if you see or hear from him again?'

'If I do, I'll ask him whether he wants me to tell you,' she said, looking down at the slightly too orange laminate floor, and then suddenly looking Plover in the eye.

'And do you have any photos of him?' asked Plover.

'No.'

He looked at her in surprised confusion – always the best trick

169

when someone tells you a particularly implausible lie.

'I'm no good with cameras,' she said. 'I've got no eye and two left hands.'

Plover smiled and nodded, as though he shared Emma's weird defects and had never taken a single photograph of his wife Debbie. At some point in a conversation like this, you had to stop pushing to get to the truth and just watch how the lies come out. He moved the conversation on to how delicious his cup of tea was, though it actually tasted like the water a real cup of tea had been washed in.

Once he saw she had relaxed, he stood up and said, 'Excuse me, I need to go to the little boys' room.'

'What?' said Emma.

'The toilet.'

'Oh. Right. Yes, the bathroom's just down the hall on the right. Mind the door – it slams.'

Bob stood and walked with a finely calibrated heaviness to his step, out of the living area, closing the door softly behind him, and down the hallway. He turned on the bathroom light and noisily opened the door and then let it bang closed.

'Sorry!' he called.

Then he moved noiselessly to the bedroom, eased open the door, took a small torch out of his pocket, and began to look around.

He searched the chest of drawers, finding that two were empty and the other two neatly filled. He searched the bottom of the wardrobe, one side of which was empty, the other full of tidily paired summer shoes.

He searched the pockets of the pair of jeans folded on the clothes chair, but found only a tissue and a to-do list. He searched the bin, but found only more tissues and a nicely executed doodle of a rabbit wearing a waistcoat. And he searched the drawer under the bed, where, beneath a stack of back issues of *Personnel Today*, he found a note from Lance.

He put the note in his pocket, crept out of the bedroom and listened for a couple of seconds at the living room door.

'What?' Lance was saying.

'What?' Emma was saying.

Plover then completed the charade in reverse, spiriting himself into the bathroom, flushing the toilet, washing his hands, stumping back down the corridor, and reappearing in the living room.

53

The glass partition between Todd and the driver slid smoothly up, sealing him in silence amid a giant expanse of leather and carpet. Outside the window, the lights of London eased past. He adjusted his grip on his phone.

'It just feels so right, Duke,' he said, 'like I have this sixth sense for it. So, okay, no judgements: I did it again today – last time, I promise.'

There was a silence, then, 'Go on.'

'Okay, so the guy shows me the bathroom…'

'He what?'

'He shows me the bathroom.'

'Who *does* that?'

'He offered me a tour of the apartment. You know, there's no way I could plan for him to do that. It's just… he offered. It's like there's some… I don't know… some spirit, some force helping me.'

'Helping you *randomly kill people*?'

'I mean, I nearly couldn't stop myself from throwing him off of the roof. If I'd done that I'd be in jail right now. But I calm down, and he says, "Let's go inside," and then he gives me this tour – I have to admit he has some pretty neat stuff in there, like this floating fire that—'

'Dad, you're getting sidetracked.'

'Okay, so we step into the bathroom, and I just know what to do. I can see it all play out in my mind. And it works, it just works. You know the deadliest room in the house?'

'Let me guess: the bathroom?'

'Right. I don't remember the exact statistics, but more or less half of all accidental deaths happen in the home, and more or less half of *those* happen in the bathroom. Kitchen is a close second, by the way. And how do people die in the bathroom? They slip. You know, you're more likely to die of a bathroom slip than an automobile accident.'

'Where do you get these statistics?'

'I don't remember. *New York Times*? I'm interested in stuff like that. So I just give him a shove, flat of my hand in the middle of his shoulder blades, so no marks – and he ploughs his head into the edge of the bathtub. He's gone just like that… You hear that, by the way? I just snapped my fingers.'

'What? People don't just fall over for no reason, Dad. The police—'

'Way ahead of you. I put on rubber gloves and I dropped a towel in the doorway. I was thinking, *Sponge*? *Soap*? But soap, I've got to put some on his shoe, so… I kept it simple.'

'But you must have left DNA somewhere in the apartment, Dad. They're going to catch you.'

'Sure, there'll be my DNA somewhere in the apartment. I've been there before. And why wouldn't I? I know the guy—'

'You *know* the guy?'

'What, you thought I was killing *strangers*?' Todd was horrified.

'Yes. How can you kill people you know?'

'You think it's *worse* that I know these guys?'

'These guys you're *murdering*? Yes, I think it's worse. Jesus, Dad.'

'So now you're shaming me?'

'No, I'm just—'

'Let me tell you, what I'm doing is a hell of a lot healthier than killing randoms off the streets. You know, in tribal culture, you kill people from neighbouring tribes. You know their faces. That's what we are evolved to do. It's this modern, anonymous killing that—'

'I can't believe I'm hearing this, Dad. I mean… How well did you know him? What was he? Rival, co-worker, what?'

'It was Chesborough.'

'Chesborough O'Teece?'

'Sure.'

'Dad, you were at his *wedding*. He gave you like a hundred promotions. He was your *friend*.'

'Hey, this is an important part of who I am. And I am trying to get through this. Are you there for me or not?'

There was silence. Todd was tense, sitting forward in his seat, the phone held so tightly to his ear that he could feel the sweat on it.

The car had stopped in traffic on a bridge with a castle at each end – exactly the sort of bullshit that annoyed Todd about Britain. But he could feel that he was close to water. It calmed him somehow.

Finally, Duke said, 'I'm there for you. But Dad… *Stop. Doing. This*. You're going to get caught.'

'No way. In the news report here, the cop said they had "no reason to believe the incident was suspicious". People are talking about this "curse of Farynx" because of Pete and now Chesborough, but the stock price is up. There's going to be an inquest. But even if the cops suspect it's a murder, which they won't, how are they going to convince a jury? And where's the proof I did it? There's no weapon. There's no evidence

I was there at the time of death.'

'What, there's no cameras?'

'Sure, they got cameras in the lobby downstairs. But you know what? Cameras are never any use to the cops. They've sure as hell been zero use in getting a decent picture of this spy—'

'The corporate espionage thing?'

'Right. Okay, so if we find the spy, *that* will be my last murder. Anyway, the size of that hotel lobby, all the cameras can tell is that *someone's* walking through. It's a big guy in a suit, like me, but guess what? He has a hat and a limp – again, instinct. So there's another couple of reasonable doubts for a jury. Plus I have a great alibi.'

'You have an alibi?'

'Yeah. I had this idea afterwards – and I'll say it again, none of this is planned – I went to see someone. She doesn't like me, but I just know she would never lie to the cops. So I go there by Tube, fastest way, still wearing the hat. She's out of the room, so I turn her clock back fifteen minutes and break her radio, because it also showed the time. And then I get her to look at the clock. So now she's gonna say I was with her at six forty-five – and there's no way I could get from the *scene* to her apartment in twenty minutes. But afterwards, when we've drunk some tea and we've talked a little more, I set it back to the right time. She'll never know.'

'But how do they know what time *he* died?'

'His watch stopped. With that kind of sudden-impact accident they mostly do. I mentioned that.'

'You didn't.'

'I'm pretty sure I mentioned it. Is this... Are you trying to undermine me? Because I feel undermined.'

'Dad, I'm not undermining you. You just didn't mention it. Okay?'

'Okay? No, not okay, as a matter of fact. You know, I am under a lot of pressure here – this takeover, Chesborough, the spy, Henry's not reliable, and... You know what? I just... I don't need this. So goodnight, Duke.'

Todd clicked the button on his phone and pushed his head back against the cushioned seat, breathing hard, his forehead and collar damp with sweat. *Every time!* How did Duke manage to get under his skin like that? *You try to open up to someone...*

Wednesday

54

'Is there a dress code?' Jonathon had asked.

'Oh no, just wear whatever makes you feel comfortable,' Gus had said airily.

Jonathon suspected that was beyond the power of mere clothes. But if he had ever felt comfortable it was probably at university. So he set aside his neat, Emma-era clothes, dug out his old green jumper, a T-shirt and some jeans, and set off for his first day at his new job.

On the bus, he felt a curious sense of calm. There was something simple and honest about accepting how bad everything was. He was not cut out for romance or friendship, and would always be alone – the girl from the Tube's look of pity the day before was a reminder of that. And he would never have one of those shiny, corporate jobs he had thought he wanted. Maybe he would never even have another indoor job.

But that was a relief. He could start drawing again, just for the fun of it. And he was now forever free of Farynx, Livia, Todd Stuckers, fake trading floors, shared drives, passwords, corporate art and mysteries. Failure was a huge, huge relief.

When he arrived at Albatross's office, the reception desk was empty. Off to the left, people in every possible type of clothing were staring pensively at their screens or having intelligent-looking chats in soft voices.

And then the girl from the Tube, with her beautifully drawn eyes, appeared from the kitchen.

'Oh, hello,' she said, stumbling gracefully down the stairs. She righted herself, and treated him again to a look of boundless pity.

Her hair was loose, and she was wearing a white blouse and jeans. Instantly, the heartworn voice and the guitar started up, and Jonathon was pushing her on a swing, weaving flowers into her hair, putting his coat around her as they watched fireworks, pulling into a rainswept bay in a slightly battered iconic car with her at his side… He stopped the montage. It was foolish. He had said only about twelve words to her in his life, at least half of them 'um'. And if he somehow managed to say more, she would only find out what kind of person he was.

Gus walked past carrying a teapot.

'Morning, Jonathon,' he said, 'and welcome. I'm glad to see Piper's kitted you out already.'

'Um,' said Jonathon.

The girl from the Tube – Piper – gave Gus a look.

'Ah,' said Gus. 'It appears I have made a faux pas of horrifying proportions. I was… But no, my ingenuity is not great enough to extricate me from the situation. May I then accompany you, and hope that the grave offence I have given can somehow be washed off with sustained pleasantness?'

Piper looked at Jonathon and rolled her eyes to the ceiling, which – with its being such a high ceiling and hers being such large eyes – took a surprising amount of time.

'Try to ignore him,' she said to Jonathon, waving a hand at Gus as though to cover him with an invisibility field. She apologised to Gus for this, then said to both of them, 'Well then, let's all go and get Jonathon ready. You can explain everything to him, Dad, if you'd like.'

They reached a basement room with old stone tiles on the floor. A pair of tiny rectangular windows near the ceiling let in an undercoat of light, washed over by a single bare bulb. This illuminated a large washing machine, an ancient tumble dryer and several sets of rusty shelves bearing neat piles of old clothes.

'As I mentioned,' said Gus, 'this is a scientific endeavour, so we're controlling all variables: what you wear, where you sit, and so forth. You're our third operative, so you'll be following exactly the same itinerary as our other two. This way we can establish the base level of money-giving. Now, Piper, what will Jonathon be wearing?'

Piper consulted a clipboard, then picked up a small pile of clothes from the shelves.

'This is your outfit,' she said. She held up a pair of grubby white trainers, some worn jeans, and a blue jumper with a ribbed neck and a small hole near the shoulder. All three of them regarded the ensemble solemnly.

'It's very like the outfit he has on,' said Gus, 'except not quite so… well, *perfect*. But I suppose we must stick to our methodology.'

175

'Yes, Dad,' said Piper, looking apologetically at Jonathon. 'And you know how long it took to find three almost identical sets of clothes.'

'I have an approximate inkling,' said Gus.

Piper consulted her clipboard and said, 'You'll also need a… *green* blanket, medium-dirty.'

She found this on another shelf and handed it to him. After that, he was issued a grey woolly hat, some tattered fingerless gloves and a badly beaten, bright-blue nylon sports bag. Then there was a crumpled paper coffee cup for donations, which had to be emptied into a locked security box every twenty minutes. The box automatically recorded times and amounts.

Gus said, 'We also keep a record of the day of the week, what the weather was like, and even if there were any particularly big world events or football matches, so we can look for correlations.'

'And that's how we're going to solve the problem of homelessness,' said Piper, her musical tone occupying an unusual middle ground between sarcasm and hope.

They gave Jonathon a box to put his clothes and shoes into, and left him to change. When he emerged, they looked at him slightly ruefully, and Piper handed him a thick, battered paperback.

'We have certain working assumptions,' said Gus. 'One of them is that books help. Again, I'm afraid everyone has to read the same thing.'

Jonathon looked at the book: *The Idiot* by Dostoevsky.

'Thanks,' he said.

And then Gus looked at them both excitedly and clapped his hands. 'And now off to the dog pool.'

'The dog pool?' asked Jonathon.

'What got me started on this whole endeavour,' said Gus, 'was the observation that I was more likely to give money to someone with a dog than to someone without – irrational though that is. That's another of our working assumptions. So, you'll begin every day by checking a dog out of the dog pool.'

'Also known as our kitchen,' said Piper.

'Yes, I may not have told you that, as well as being Albatross's offices, this is our house. This basement connects the two.'

He led them through two dingy, grey-painted passageways and up some stairs. As Gus's foot touched the bottom-most stair, a dog behind the door at the top began to bark.

'Don't worry, Alice!' called Piper. 'It's only us, not the murderers.' And then, turning to Jonathon, she said, 'She worries.'

The dog, its face visible in silhouette through the translucent glass in the door at the top of the stairs, muted its barking in favour of heavy breathing and jiggling the door handle.

Gus turned to Jonathon and said, 'We're still getting used to the peculiar ways in which dogs go about their business: barking, howling, sloshing water about on the floor, depositing hairs.' Gus opened the door and a small white West Highland terrier leapt energetically at Jonathon's crotch. 'And then there's the overt interest in one's private parts. Get off him, Potato.'

The kitchen was large and full of light, with patterned tiles on the floor. Outside the window were some small trees and bushes – a narrow garden before the brick wall that separated them from the quiet street beyond. In the middle of the room stood a huge table that looked like it had been made a couple of hundred years ago by slicing up the thickest tree available and hammering the bits together. All around were kitchen units: newer, but made in approximately the same way.

'I'm afraid we've lost the key to the back door,' said Gus, 'though we do have a key for this door,' he patted a huge old-fashioned key hanging next to the door with translucent panes, 'which we never lock.'

The terrier had turned its interest to Gus's shoes, which had been worn, polished and resoled so often as to be more like foot-gloves, clearly showing the contours of every toe. The large Doberman that had been visible through the glass leapt up and placed its front paws on Jonathon's chest, snuffling urgently at his face.

'Alice!' said Piper. 'For shame, you barely know him. Sorry, Jonathon.' Alice got down and instead walked around Piper as many times as possible.

A third dog, who looked like a soft-eyed white wolf, with tall ears and a serious expression, sat neatly beside a towering hi-tech fridge, beating its tail on the mat. It looked at Jonathon and let out a sort of quiet rumbling groan.

'This one's called Cess – for short.'

'For short?' asked Jonathon.

'Her full name's Sir Cecil Chubb,' said Gus, 'after the Victorian gentleman who gave the nation Stonehenge. Her owner's an expert on the subject. A fine man: his only real shortcomings lie in naming puppies and determining their gender. Isn't that right, Cess? See how seriously she listens.'

Sir Cecil Chubb regarded Gus soberly as he continued, 'Our canine colleagues are, as you might gather, an oddly assorted bunch for the moment. We are dog-sitting Cess for two weeks while her owner's away, and I have prevailed upon friends to loan me the other two during working hours. I think I would be right in describing all of them as friendly, open characters, keenly interested in events around them, particularly if they involve bottoms. If this venture goes well, we shall look into acquiring our own modest fleet of dogs.'

Piper turned to Jonathon, consulted her clipboard and said, 'You'll be with Cess, for the moment.'

'Is she growling?' he asked.

'Oh, don't worry about that,' said Piper brightly. 'It just means she... likes you.'

Jonathon had been given a lead for Sir Cecil Chubb, and was very glad to find that the dog trotted along at his side, only very occasionally glancing up at him and doing her ambiguous deep groan.

Piper too was walking beside him. She would accompany him for his first day. This fact was making walking and breathing somewhat difficult, since he constantly had to stay on his guard to prevent further montages breaking out.

What was it about her that had such a huge effect on him? There was something in the way she spoke, the timbre of her voice and the expression of her eyes that just seemed exactly *right*. It was just a fact, and there was nothing he could do about it.

This was not helping him to make conversation, however. And Piper seemed suddenly sad and withdrawn, no doubt deflated by the prospect of spending all day with a phoney homeless person who could barely speak.

But as they got closer to Farringdon Tube, she said, 'I was thinking we could start somewhere quiet this morning.'

He nodded dumbly.

'It's your first day,' she continued, 'so we can do whatever's most comfy for you. Not that sitting on the street's comfy, obvs, but you know what I mean. And all you need to do is sit down, read your book and keep an eye on your collecting cup. I'll show you where to go and give you feedback on your sitting technique.'

'My sitting technique?'

'Yes. It turns out that sitting's really tricky. Some people sit really aggressively. And others sit so subtly that people keep falling over them. But you'll be splendid – if that's a word you're allowed to use when you're twenty-four. Just sit like yourself.' And again she gave him the look of infinite pity.

'Sit like myself. Right,' said Jonathon. 'But what if people talk to me? What if they ask me how long I've been living on the streets? Or what I feed my dog? Or where I sleep?'

'Oh, no one will talk to you. This is London. But it's best to move if anyone asks you to, try not to sit in people's way, and just ignore anyone who… you know, says anything bad to you. Anyway, we're all allowed to sit on the pavement with a paper cup in front of us, wearing a medium-dirty green blanket and reading *The Idiot*. It's our birthright.'

Once they'd changed onto the Piccadilly line, they found themselves in an empty carriage. They sat side by side, Sir Cecil Chubb on the floor between them, her ears flattened as though she intended them to form a sort of protective shield.

'Do you have any pets?' Piper asked him.

'Not really,' he said. And then, because this answer still didn't bring the total tally of words he had ever said to her beyond about two dozen, he found himself adding, 'Unless you count the, um, mouse that watches me sleep.'

'A real mouse?' she asked, suddenly interested.

'Yes, it came with the room.'

'Don't you mind it?'

'I don't have any option – I can't find where it gets in. It doesn't seem to do any harm though, apart from eating sandwiches. It's quite nice, in a way, that it's there every morning, twitching and wringing its hands.'

'Maybe it's in love with you.'

Her mention of the word 'love' made him blurt out the truth, to hide his embarrassment.

'I think it might be my dead grandpa,' he said, then added, 'except I don't think that, because that's an insane thing to think.'

'Oh, I do that,' she said, looking pleased. 'You know, think things and not think them at the same time.'

'What like?'

She checked to make sure she wasn't being overheard, and then said, 'I think I'm the reincarnation of Mary Wollstonecraft *and* Emily Dickinson at the same time. Except I don't think that at all. It would be conceited and quite stupid.'

She waved the idea away, wafting the spirits of Mary and Emily to the end of the carriage.

Jonathon wasn't sure whether he was allowed to ask any more about this, so he said, 'Do you have any? Pets, I mean.'

'No, that's why I'm so excited about having these dogs for a bit. I was never allowed pets.'

'Why not?'

'Oh, wait... there was a rabbit. I called him Starsky – for obvious reasons...'

'Because he spent all his time hanging around a hutch?'

'Yes! You got it. I always say "for obvious reasons" and people always do a kind of weird half-smile and look away, so I never know whether they haven't got it or they just think it's stupid.'

'People are annoying like that.'

'Tell me about it. So are foxes. One ate Starsky.'

'That's terrible.'

'I was twelve. I still dream about him sometimes, even though...'

'What?'

'It feels terrible to say it, but he didn't really have much in the way of personality.'

'But then the animals with personality make riskier pets.'

'How do you mean?'

'Well, all rabbits can really do is gnaw, sleep and scamper. It's difficult to express much with that, but – if they live in a hutch – it's also difficult to do much wrong. Whereas a chimp, say, can do almost anything. So it could endearingly drink cups of tea or it could go mad and smash everything in your house.'

'And *that's* why we don't have a chimp,' finished Piper for him, as though it were the moral of a children's TV programme.

'Exactly.'

'Isn't it, Cess?' she asked the dog, who had looked around enquiringly at her.

'Have you worked for your dad for long?' asked Jonathon.

She put her hands over the dog's ears, as though to shield Sir Cecil Chubb from an awful truth. 'Nearly two years. And now I'm studying to become an accountant, even though it's almost exactly the last thing I want to do.'

'Oh, I was doing that – the last thing I wanted – in my old job. It's horrible.'

'But it's sensible, and I'm really good at it. I'm not being boastful, by the way – I'd rather I was less good at it. Then I wouldn't have to do it. But I don't have any control over what my brain remembers, and anything to do with accounting and finance just seems to worm its way in and stay there. Anyway, you have to live in the real world, despite how inconvenient it is. Even Dad says so,' she said, sadly.

'If only we could somehow avoid the real world.'

'Stupid real world.'

'What would you do, if you could get out of the real world?' he asked.

'Oh, I'd make things. I'd embroider mainly – I just really like doing it. It's so calming and absorbing.'

'But…?' he began.

'But what?' she asked.

'I mean, can't you do that in the real world?'

'No, it's so *niche*. It's barely even a thing. Who pays for embroidery?'

She gestured around, as though calling his attention to the lack of 'Embroiderers wanted' notices in the empty carriage. He nodded, taking her point.

'And that's why I'm studying accounting, working for my dad, and we don't have a chimp,' she concluded.

By this time, they had reached Piccadilly Circus. They left the Tube and a silence settled over them again.

He wasn't sure how the conversation had happened, how it had sneaked past his powers of awkwardness. Now it was over, he desperately wanted it to happen again. But when he looked into the part of his brain reserved for conversational topics, he saw only a blank, white space. And Piper didn't seem interested in continuing the conversation. Well, that was natural. After all, she was by some way the greatest and most beautiful being in the history of the universe, and he was an amateur beggar who lived with a mouse.

She guided him past Waterstone's, along the pavement where the tourists, the businessmen and the betweeded gentlefolk of St James slowly scattered through one another, like large billiard balls on a narrow table. Then she directed them left, down a narrow alleyway beside a church. Jonathon was glad that Sir Cecil Chubb seemed content to pad along near him, as though she just happened to be going the same way. He didn't know what he would have done otherwise. It seemed rather rude and gauche to yank someone else by the neck, even if they are a dog. Besides, she outranked him.

'This is Jermyn Street,' said Piper, as they emerged from the alleyway.

They were standing on a long street running parallel to Piccadilly, flanked by slightly grand and faded old-fashioned shops.

'And this is your spot,' she said, gesturing generously to a place on the wide pavement, next to some railings beside the church.

'I'll be in there,' she said, indicating a threadbare but upmarket cafe across the road, nestled beside a threadbare but upmarket menswear shop with a window full of hats, tweed and corduroy trousers.

It was by now ten o'clock and the street was quiet. Jonathon spread his blanket out on the pavement at the base of the railings and sat down cross-legged, trying not to take up too much room. To his left was the blue nylon bag. To his right was Sir Cecil Chubb, beating her tail slowly. Jonathon put the battered paper cup in front of him, weighed it down with a small stone, slipped the lead over his wrist and opened his book. Sir Cecil Chubb glanced at him and groan-growled.

And so they sat, for twenty minutes, Jonathon tensely reading, waiting for the moment when Sir Cecil Chubb would move on from growling to tearing his throat out.

'Hey!' someone shouted from across the street.

55

'Gentlemen – and lady – would you please be upstanding,' said Patrick Swire, the senior board member. They pushed back their heavy antique chairs, and the ebony groaned as they stood.

Patrick Swire cleared his throat and, in his most solemn and silly voice, said, 'It is with great pleasure that I announce Farynx's new Chairman and Chief Executive Officer, Mr Todd Stuckers.'

They applauded, and Todd felt that a weight had been lifted from him. He suddenly saw that all his life he had suffered – *suffered* – from not being a Chief Executive Officer. It had been an injustice. And today it had been put right. He had spent his life struggling for this. He had fought long and hard and bloodily. And today he had prevailed.

Todd moved to the head of the table, the place reserved for the CEO. He raised his hands and the applause pattered to a halt.

'Thanks, thanks. Please sit down,' he said. His heart was beating hard in his chest.

'This is a great honour, and I pledge to do everything in my power to achieve the vision set out for us by Chesborough O'Teece. I think it's fair to say that we're all still in shock that he's… no longer with us. And Patrick, I think you summed up what he stood for, and what he meant to all of us, better than I ever could.'

Todd gestured to the painting of Chesborough that had joined the other portraits on the wall. It had been painted just last year by Durden Myerscough, and it showed Chesborough staring out like a man of vision, though looking more than ever like a species of turtle. The board members glanced at it and bowed their heads. Only Dame Margery kept a straight back and direct gaze.

'Now, let's go upstairs to the dining room, where we have food direct from Le Gavroche, prepared for us by Rubio Louis Black himself, and let's pay tribute to Chesborough the way he would have wanted – by celebrating the success of this great company, and our forthcoming acquisition of United Biscuits.'

They applauded him again. Todd walked to the door and stood there as the board members solemnly filed past. First was Adam Ness. 'Congratulations, Mr Stuckers,' he said. 'We're all totally behind you.' Todd had the feeling that Ness would have kissed his hand if he could.

Then came Jackson Seward, brushing down his white moustache and saying, 'Todd, I just know the company is in great hands. Congratulations.'

Even Dame Margery said, 'Congratulations, Mr Stuckers,' as she walked past. Finally, Patrick Swire shook his hand again, and held the door for him.

'You go on ahead, Pat,' said Todd. 'I'll catch you up. I want to take a moment.'

Todd closed the door behind Swire and turned to the empty room. He surveyed the great oak table, the ebony chairs, the foolish tiles, the portraits and the silver plaque.

'I won,' he said. 'How do you like that? I fucking won.'

And then he left, because he had the sudden feeling that Chesborough's eyes were on him.

56

Jonathon looked up, his hand on the blue bag, guiltily ready to get up and leave.

'Oh, I'm terribly sorry. I didn't mean to startle you,' said a woman in her forties, with grey-blonde hair and a luxurious beige coat.

'No, it was my fault,' said Jonathon, starting to stand. 'I didn't mean to be startled.'

'No, don't get up,' said the woman. 'It must be fearfully tiring, your sort of… circumstances.'

'Well…' said Jonathon. Actually, they *were* fearfully tiring, his sort of circumstances. He had spent Monday surreptitiously carrying poo down a stairwell. And now he was having to spend all day with a dog who was his social superior while being spied on by the universe's most beautiful being. He remained sitting down.

'I just… I live around the corner,' she said. It amazed Jonathon to think of anyone actually living in a place like this. Where would you buy your mops and gaffer tape? 'And caught sight of you, and your… your *shoes*,' she said it as though she wasn't quite sure that was the word she wanted, 'and I suddenly realised that Jeremy, that's my husband, has an old pair I've been meaning to… find a home for, for some time, and, well…'

She brought out a John Lewis bag from behind her back.

'They're rather stuffy,' she said, 'but they're well made and will keep the water out *a treat*.' She paused for a second and gave a little smile, as though pleased with herself for saying 'a treat'.

From the bag she took a pair of shoes so heavy, smooth and fiercely shined that they could have been made of black steel.

'Oh, thank you very much,' said Jonathon.

The woman gave him her small smile again. 'I haven't any money, I'm afraid.'

'Oh no, I don't… I mean, I didn't…' He gave a little wave of his hand at the paper cup, as though that was just where he kept his stone.

And then he realised that the woman wanted him to put the shoes on now. He unlaced the comfortable old trainers he'd been issued and pulled them off.

'I've brought some spare socks, in case they're too large,' she said.

So Jonathon put on some smart, dark-blue socks and a pair of what he suspected were handmade shoes. And he stood up and walked up and down a few steps. Sir Cecil Chubb sat on the blanket watching him avidly, as though assessing whether the shoes gave him enough instep support. The shoes gripped his feet like vices, keeping them entirely immobile.

'Very comfortable,' Jonathon lied politely.

The woman beamed and fumbled about in her pocket, and then quickly bent to the paper cup, like she was curtseying, and smiled again and hurried off, over the road, past a grand but slightly threadbare shaving-supplies shop, and around the corner.

When she had disappeared again, Jonathon tried to meet Piper's eyes in her seat across the road, but she was hammering away at her phone's keypad with both thumbs. He picked up the paper cup and found the woman had left a fifty-pound note in it, which he put in the locked box he had been given for his takings. As he was doing so, Sir Cecil Chubb, who had sat still throughout the posh woman's visit, now got up and sniffed the shoes with huge interest, excitement and discernment, like a Picasso specialist who has just found an early study for *Guernica* has been left beside her on a park bench. Her tail wagged, and she growled only the very softest of growls, then looked up at Jonathon with a new respect in her eyes.

Jonathon sat down again in the almost empty street and returned to *The Idiot*. No one passed Jonathon for the whole duration of Prince Myshkin's lengthy reading and subsequent discussion of the poem about the sad knight, who was also poor and proud and disdainful of gain.

Jonathon slipped into the book, which was somehow boring and deeply enjoyable at the same time. He was only recalled to reality by the soft *chunk* of coins hitting the stone in his paper cup. When he looked up he saw two people in suits – a man and a woman, not much older than him – walking away. Sir Cecil Chubb gave Jonathon a very quiet, pleased growl and wagged her tail.

A couple of minutes later, a woman in a red coat using the nearby postbox glanced at his viciously uncomfortable black leather shoes, said, 'Oh darling, what *have* you got on your feet?' and gave him five pounds. She came back shortly afterwards with a pair of sound but outmoded trainers for him, saying that they were Jack's but she had been meaning to get rid of them for some time.

Jonathon gradually got used to the pattern: reading his book, stiffening self-consciously as he heard someone approach, then whatever it was they gave or didn't give, followed by Sir Cecil Chubb's softly growled commentary.

And then he looked up and Piper was standing over him.

'Hello, Jonathon,' she said brightly. 'What have you got?'

'Um, said Jonathon, 'a Kinder Surprise, a leaflet about Jesus, some chewing gum, these…' He opened his blue nylon bag and showed her the two pairs of shoes he had collected. 'Oh, and, er, some of this.' Jonathon gave her the cash box he'd been emptying his paper cup into.

'Goodness me,' said Piper, feeling the weight of the box, 'if I'm allowed to say *that* at my age.'

She took out a key and opened the box, quickly counting the notes and raking through the coins with her hand. 'There must be eighty pounds here!'

'Is that…?'

'It's lovely! I mean, it's amazing! The best we've had before was three pounds sixty-seven. And most of that was in foreign money. Jonathon, you were obviously born to, er…' She stopped, evidently not wanting to say, 'Beg on the streets'.

'And the shoes!' she said instead. 'What's going on with the shoes?'

'I don't know.'

'Bejesus, Jonathon. Just bejesus,' she said, looking at the money box. Jonathon glowed like a hot coal blown upon by her enthusiasm.

And then an idea announced itself in her eyes. 'Jonathon, would you perchance like to try somewhere busier? It's your first day, so we're allowed. No pressure,' she added, holding her hands up.

'Yes, let's try somewhere busier,' he said. He would have liked to say more, but she was being nice to him and that was making him dizzy. In many ways, liking someone makes it much more difficult to get on with them.

'Lovely and lovely. We just have to make sure we go to all our four places on a mixture of mornings and afternoons over the week. But that'll be easy. We always start with Jermyn Street because it's quiet and no one's ever been set on fire here. But there's a much busier spot on Piccadilly, just two minutes away. Let me show you.'

He put the blanket and cup into the blue bag, tucked the book under his arm, took a firmer hold of the lead, and moved off up the little passageway beside the church, Sir Cecil Chubb trotting quite happily beside him.

On Piccadilly, Piper pointed out a place for him to sit, next to a bin near the front of the church. He was only a few feet from an old man who made Jonathon feel like the fraud he was – with only one tooth, a purplish nose and a cough that sounded like the fabric of space-time was being ripped apart. Piper told Jonathon she would watch him properly this time, from inside the 'Sup sandwich shop across the street.

57

Henry had joined Todd for lunch, but they didn't linger afterwards with the board members. 'I process my grief by working through it,' Todd had said, 'and I am *stacked*.'

They stood at the top of the dark-panelled stairwell outside the dining room.

'Let's walk down,' said Todd. 'I don't trust an elevator that old.'

As they walked down, Henry said to Todd in a low voice, 'Positive news. The Fire Investigation Unit out in New Jersey has stopped work on the case. The cause has been labelled "undetermined", but results indicate the fire was not suspicious.'

'They still think it was the coffee machine?'

'They say there's not enough evidence to conclude that. High winds caused the fire to burn rapidly.'

'And Flemke?'

'Filing for bankruptcy.'

'Buy it.'

Todd glanced around to check the stairwell was empty, then added, 'Any news on Chesborough?'

'The inquest has initiated and is expected to take approximately three months. They may wish to speak with you as a... friend of the deceased. I am monitoring a raft of sources to keep up to speed on all developments.'

'Okay. Keep me posted.'

They reached the bottom of the stairs. Their shoes clicked neatly over the tiled hallway as they walked past more paintings and charcoal portraits of the company's founders. Todd shivered.

'These old guys give me the creeps,' he said.

Todd pushed open the door, ignored the polite 'Goodbye sir' of the doorman, and almost tripped over a man sitting on the doorstep.

'Sorry, mate,' said the man, moving along a bit. He was holding a can of beer and had a sleeping bag draped over his shoulders like a robe of office. 'Suppose a donation's out of the question?'

'What the fuck?' said Todd. He turned to Henry. 'Is he allowed to sit there? I mean, this building's private property, right?'

'Ah, he is not, no,' said Henry.

'What, you going to sue me, mate? You'll get about 24p and half a can of Tennant's.'

Todd looked the man in the eye. The man tried to sprawl casually. Todd moved closer.

'You wanna die?' he asked.

'All right, mate, keep your hair on,' said the man, getting up and edging around Todd. 'Your step's shit. I was going to move anyway.'

He backed further off, hitched up his trousers, raised his arms and chanted, 'I wanna go home, I wanna go ho-o-ome, your step's a shithole, and so-o are you.'

Todd took a step towards him and the man ran off, still chanting.

'Jesus,' said Todd. 'What is *with* these people?'

'I will look into that,' said Henry. 'The car's waiting around the corner.'

'They think they can sit there on my property, and I will just hand them money for that? Why would I? You know, we all have the same chances in life. If you're wearing an eight-thousand-dollar suit and stepping out of a twenty-million-dollar building, you earned those things by talent, relentless hard work and refusing to give up. If you're sitting on someone else's step, asking for handouts, that's on you.'

'Well this is exactly what *Atlas Shrugged* is all about,' said Henry. 'You know, I really think you would have a positive experience with that book.'

'If I can do it, why can't they?' said Todd. 'You know how I got into Columbia University? It's because I went to my room after school and I studied – not just because my mom told me to, but because I wanted to be richer than my parents. And my allowance as a kid? I worked for that, at my dad's company. This country is lousy with socialism – the National Health Service and whatnot. They don't realise that if you tax the talented and relentlessly hard-working folks that make all the money, they're going to give up. You want talents like Jeff Skilling and Bernie Madoff sitting on the street begging? Fine, keep on taxing them, keep on with the free handouts for deadbeats.'

Todd gestured towards a young man sitting on a corner across the street, a dog at his side.

'Maybe it's a little different if there's an animal involved – I mean, it's not their fault. But then look at that guy – just sitting there reading a book. You can't expect to get paid for sitting around reading books.'

'Which guy?' said Henry, looking around.

Todd rubbed his eyes.

Prince Myshkin was deep into an extraordinarily maladroit proposal of marriage when Jonathon had the sudden sense of being watched. He could not help looking up to see if it was Piper. He gazed across the road and into the eyes of Todd Stuckers, whom he had last seen having the front of his trousers touched shortly before Jonathon had been fired.

Todd was staring at Jonathon with a look of unmistakable hatred. And Jonathon was afraid that Todd was going to charge across the road and thoroughly embarrass him for either a) being a beggar or b) not being a beggar.

Jonathon saw Todd rub his eyes, and decided in an instant that he could not face being embarrassed by a man who had recently fired him. In a single fluid motion he stood up, stuffed the blanket and cup into his bag of shoes and vanished down the alleyway with Sir Cecil Chubb at his heels.

59

'Which guy?' repeated Henry.

Todd looked again. There was no one there. On the other side of the street, by the bin, where he was sure he had just seen the spy, there was now only a space.

'Todd, you okay?' said Henry.

'You see that guy with the book?'

'What? Er, I don't believe so. Where?'

'The guy begging. He was reading a book—'

'This crazy socialist something-for-nothing culture—'

'For Christ's sake, did you see him? Am I going crazy? I think it was the spy, dressed up as a beggar.'

'Uh, I don't really register beggars.'

Todd shoved his briefcase into Henry's hands and ran across the first two lanes of the road, narrowly avoiding hitting a cyclist. He vaulted the railings in the centre and dashed in front of a bus. There was the bin. The empty space. The alley. He ran down the alley, pushing aside tourists, daytime drunks and men in red corduroys. He emerged in a street beside a postbox. He looked around. The street was quiet, the spy nowhere to be seen.

Todd ran down another road and reached a park in the middle of a large square. He jogged around the park, looking intently at the office workers eating sandwiches together in small, chilly clumps. There was no one who looked remotely as though they had recently been sitting beside a bin, simultaneously reading, begging and spying. He looked around the square. At least five streets led away from it. He couldn't see the spy.

Todd had lost him, if he had been there at all. He leaned against a bench, catching his breath. *When I find that guy,* he thought, *I am going to come up with a* really *creative way to kill him.*

Back at the office, Todd flopped into his chair and Henry poured him a coffee.

'You're sure it was him you observed?' asked Henry.

'No. I am not *sure*. But I saw someone who looked a lot like him. And he saw me and took off in the time it takes someone who went to Harvard to casually mention that he went to fucking Harvard. So, put two and two together, it was probably the spy.'

'A lot of pressure has been placed upon you recently...' began Henry.

'Sure. That's part of my job. I'm paid to take pressure without start-ing to hallucinate people on the street watching me. Believe me, I am keeping up my end of the deal.'

'Sorry, it was never my intention to—'

'Henry, I need to you to work with me here and give me a little support. So, maybe the guy across the road wasn't the spy. I couldn't swear he was. But whoever it was, he was there. And he was watching me. We have got a spy problem. And I need you to take that problem off of my shoulders. I want this company to get serious about security. Change everyone's system passwords. Get some seriously high-quality surveillance cameras in this place – and I want to see the model you choose before you go ahead and place the order.'

Henry took out his PalmPilot and began to make a note.

'And,' said Todd, 'one more thing. About Lance and Plover at LPA...'

Plover was glad when the phone rang. He and Lance, after trying to follow up the acting agencies in the hope of finding someone who had met Fairfax that Wednesday, had drifted off into an increasingly competitive game of throwing screwed-up paper into the bin.

'Bob Plover speaking,' he said.

'Bob, this is Todd. You found this Fairfax guy yet?'

'We have made significant progress…'

'And what is that progress?'

'We have tracked down a name and address for his father, we've found another address where he used to live, and we've hunted out someone who went to university with him.'

'Uh, that sounds like mostly nothing. Listen, I'm sending Henry over to take charge of this. He has some new information and some new instructions. I want you to do whatever he says, just like it was me telling you to do it. Understood?'

'Yes of course, but—'

'Great. He's getting in the car now and he'll be with you in five minutes.'

Fortunately, Henry's car ride took an hour – long enough for them to tidy away the paper and finish calling the acting agencies. They met him at the lift doors.

'Henry,' said Plover, stepping forward to shake his hand, wearing his most tiredly cheerful expression.

'Robert. Lance,' said Henry, shaking hands with Lance and looking around with a forced smile, as though determined to put the best possible construction on their corporate poverty: the carpet tiles easing away from one another, the flickering strip lights on the ceiling.

'So,' said Henry as they walked him down to LPA's area, 'you guys own a quantity surveyors' business too, huh?'

Plover decided to answer this by smiling at him in a 'you know how it is' sort of way. It was a look he had developed for times like this when he didn't want to risk an outright and easily discovered lie, but also didn't want to say, 'No, we're being slowly squeezed into a smaller and smaller fraction of the floor space in this dilapidated hovel by rising rents and failure.'

Nonetheless, by the time they reached the hessian enclosure that was Plover's office, Henry probably suspected the truth. Henry sniffed and left the coffee they brought him, then sat down, clacked open his briefcase and said, 'Okay, I have news. First, Todd has assumed the role of CEO following the accidental death of Chesborough O'Teece. Second, he has delegated oversight of this operation to myself. Third, Todd observed Fairfax, or persons unknown, engaged in a surveillance activity centred upon him.'

'Right,' said Plover.

'Could you be less specific?' Lance asked Henry.

Henry narrowed his eyes.

'I think Lance means "more specific",' said Plover.

'Surveillance activity was carried out,' said Henry. 'And it was observed.'

'Okay,' said Plover. 'So, just a couple of questions: where was this?'

'Piccadilly Street.'

'And what was the means of surveillance?'

'The surveillance was carried out through an optical modality.'

'So someone looked at him?' said Lance.

Henry looked as though he was turning something upside-down in his mind. 'I guess it could be put that way.'

Plover stepped in to save the situation. 'Okay, so could you just walk me through this. How did Todd realise he was being... optically surveilled?'

'The surveiller was observed by Todd in a seated posture on the obverse side of the road, outside a place of worship. He was attired in a green-coloured blanket, a book was being read, and a canine was seated by his side. It is believed he was Fairfax, in disguised form.'

'So Todd thought he saw Jonathon Fairfax sitting watching him on the other side of Piccadilly, outside a church, in disguise and with a dog?'

'That is correct, in substance.'

'How did he know this was Fairfax?'

'There is not absolute clarity on the identity of this person. But whomever this was took off as soon as he became aware he had been observed.'

'So it wasn't definitely him?'

'Not definitively.'

'Right,' said Plover, clapping his hands and standing up. 'Thanks a lot, Henry. That's very helpful.'

Henry remained sitting. 'So, what is your intended solution, based off of this intelligence?'

'Well,' said Plover, 'we'll carry on trying to find Fairfax, track down where he works, and discover whether he – or person unknown – is surveilling Mr Stuckers.'

'So you propose no changes to your modus operandi?'

'Oh, of course we'll make changes,' said Plover, looking to Lance for help.

'But they'll be qualitative ones,' put in Lance, 'rather than quantitative.'

'Exactly,' said Plover, relieved. 'The whole investigation will have a completely different texture.'

Henry looked from one of them to the other. 'I need you to shift into a different operational mode. This needs to become a counter-surveillance operation.'

Plover and Lance exchanged glances.

'What does that mean?' asked Plover.

'I need you to shift resource from telephone investigation to maintaining physical proximity to Todd Stuckers, enabling you to scan his vicinity for Fairfax.'

'So you think if we stay close to Todd, we'll find Fairfax?' said Plover.

61

Henry had insisted that they begin immediately, so Lance and Plover went with him to Farynx's Arundel Street offices. They immediately set to work hanging around in the coffee area, waiting for Todd to go somewhere so they could follow him and fail to spot the spy who Lance knew would not be there.

But then Henry asked them if they had physically examined the outside perimeter to ascertain whether Fairfax was involved in optical stakeout activity. Lance pointed out to Henry that one of them would have to stay near Todd in case he left the building at short notice, and then suggested to Plover that they play scissors-paper-stone to see who would go outside in the drizzle. Lance won, of course.

His reward was to hang around the coffee area on his own, drinking an almost inhumanly large amount of coffee and trying to understand what the *Harvard Business Review* was. He was leaning casually against the counter, reading about structure modelling in the pharmaceutical industry, when a woman in a suit came in and began making a coffee.

Lance had almost forgotten the power of the suppressed erotic charge that builds up in big corporate offices. The woman didn't look at him, but he could sense how desperate she was to strike up conversation. He almost did it for her, but he was curious to see how long it would take and in what form it would come.

'Hope it's not going to rain all day, ha ha ha,' she said eventually, stirring a Bolivian.

'Me too.'

'Ha ha ha,' she said. 'Nasty wet stuff, ha ha.'

'It's especially inconvenient,' he said seriously, 'when you don't have an umbrella.'

This conversation, which consisted of pretending to laugh at statements about the weather, lasted fifteen minutes and ended with an exchange of business cards. Her name was Rhiannon, and she was a Senior Manager in Strategic Delivery Management Services.

It was the highlight of his time at Farynx.

A few minutes later he took a desultory walk up the corridor past Todd's office. He almost bumped into a woman leaving, smoothing down her skirt.

She glared at him, then said, 'You must be Lance Ferman. I'm Livia Cavendish.'

'Hey, good to meet you. You spoke to my colleague, Bob, on the phone, didn't you? You gave him some great background on this Fairfax character. Really helpful, especially the bin stuff.'

'Oh, it was nothing. Really,' said Livia flipping in a picosecond from sternness to girlish smiles.

'Well, if you've got any more nothing, give us a call,' he said, handing her an LPA card.

She gave him her card, and a moment later the office door opened and there stood Todd, filling the doorway with his mighty shoulders.

'Lance, good to see you,' he said.

'Todd, great to see you too.' They shook hands. 'Congratulations on becoming CEO. I'm very sorry to hear about Chesborough.'

'Thanks. We're working through our grief.'

'You must be *stacked*, with this United Biscuits acquisition coming up too.'

'I am. The share price seems to be going through the roof since news of my promotion got out – it hit ninety dollars this morning in New York, and fifty-five pounds in London. This is an all-share deal, so we need to do a little renegotiating with the guys over at Biscuits.'

'You'll kill them.'

Todd caught his eye for a fraction of a second, as though sizing Lance up, but he smiled to cover it.

'Right,' he said. 'You know who else I'll kill? This Fairfax guy, whoever he turns out to be.'

'You're absolutely sure he's a spy?'

'At this point, I don't care,' he said, looking at Lance with brutal sincerity. 'If he isn't a spy, I'll kill him for all the sleep he's cost me.'

Thursday

62

'Uuuurggh,' said Lance. It was a strong opening. Now he just needed something to back it up. 'Hedda?'

'Yes,' said the voice on the other end of the line.

'It's Lance.'

'Lance? You sound terrible.'

'I am. Food poisoning – I've been up all night. Can you tell Bob I won't be able to make it this morning? Hate to let him down. I'll try to get in later on.'

'Don't you dare,' said Hedda. 'You need to stay in bed today. Squeeze a lemon into a glass of hot milk and add some Coke – that's what you need for tummy troubles.'

This suggestion made Lance feel genuinely ill, which added nuance to his performance as he groaned, 'Okay, thanks Hedda,' and put the phone down.

He jumped out of bed, patiently unwrapped another tiny bar of hotel soap, showered, dressed and headed for the Tube, stopping off on the way to buy a coffee, some pins and a copy of the *Financial Times*.

Lance walked up the grimy steps of Leicester Square station, past all the people asking for money, and strolled on towards Piccadilly Circus.

He stopped beside the mysterious watery statue of the naked child firing arrows indiscriminately into the crowd. He needed to check he wasn't being followed, so he sat down on the edge of the fountain, between a crowd of Italian schoolchildren and a party of American tourists in shorts and brightly coloured raincoats. After two minutes he was reasonably satisfied, so he continued across Lower Regent Street into Piccadilly itself, a thoroughfare so self-assured that, like Prince, it's able to pull off a one-word name.

Lance was on his way to look for Jonathon in the place where Todd said he'd been. On balance, it seemed more likely that Jonathon had become a beggar than that he had ever been a spy. But it was even more likely that a beggar there looked a bit like Jonathon.

Lance stopped to look in a travel agent's window, really checking the reflection of the pavement opposite and using his peripheral vision. *Clear*, he thought. He lit a cigarette, telling himself it helped to obscure his face in case anyone was following him.

Lance had to find Jonathon before Plover or Todd did, to warn him. But he also needed to stay close to Todd and Plover to keep up with what they knew. He hoped his absence today wouldn't rouse their suspicions.

He took up a position in the window of 'Sup with a coffee and a Danish at his elbow, watching the street through carefully placed pin-holes in his *Financial Times*. Across the road was St James's Church, with its green roof and spindly clock tower, the only church Todd could possibly have meant.

It was fun, being back in business.

After about an hour, it was no longer fun being back in business. Lance had tired of the pinhole technique. He bought another coffee and Danish, and then he sat back and watched London unfurl before him. A man in red corduroy trousers was berating a cyclist. A party of Japanese tourists carrying Burberry bags was stepping over dirty, ill-looking men holding out paper cups. A woman with black hair and great legs was shoulder-barging an elderly punk.

Could Todd really have seen Jonathon here? Last time Lance had seen Jonathon, there had been no possibility of mistaking him for a homeless person. But on the other hand, he had now lost his home. In fact, he had moved out on the same day Emma had broken up with him. Was it even possible to find a place to stay in London at such short notice? Had Jonathon, perhaps, just moved politely and unobtrusively under a bridge? Or into the porch of a church? That was just the sort of old-fashioned thing he might do.

Someone punched Lance hard on the arm.

'Hey, jerk.'

He looked up. There, standing over him, was the girl with the art-deco cheekbones, her black hair almost obscuring her perfect blue eyes. He would have known that punch anywhere.

'You again?' he said, surprised.

'Nice to see you too,' she said, sitting down beside him with her coffee.

'What are you doing here?' he asked.

'I'm in London all the time. I told you. I work in couture logistics.'

'I made sure I killed all the brain cells that ever took in that information.'

She blew on her coffee, seemingly perfectly at ease and not feeling the need to reply.

'Well,' he said, 'did you burn down my flat and steal my stuff?'

'Wait and see. I want it to be a surprise for you.'

Lance nodded patiently and said nothing, hoping she would get bored and go away.

'So, what are you doing?' she asked.

'Drinking coffee.'

'Don't let on more than you have to.'

'And eating a Danish,' he said, taking a bite of the Danish.

'You read the *Financial Times*?' she said, indicating the paper.

'Sometimes,' he said through a mouthful of Danish.

'What's the little hole for?'

'How can you see the little hole?'

'Eye for detail. I told you, I work in couture. Is it spy stuff?'

'No.'

'You told me what you do for a living, you know. Former private investigator turned presenter of *MTV Undercover*, development hell then cancelled because you're not as exciting as a house fire.'

'Fine, yes, it's spy stuff.'

'How's it work?'

'You make four pinholes on the front page, and you position them so that by making tiny casual movements and swapping pinholes, you can keep a wide area under surveillance without anyone seeing your face. And the small size of the pinholes helps to keep what you're looking at sharp and clear.'

'What? How?'

'Some optical process that I don't fully understand and suspect is bullshit anyway.'

'Cool.'

'There's this problem with watching people: they just turn for no reason and look right at you. This way, all they see is the *Financial Times*, which most people can't help but ignore.'

'But why do they turn and look?'

'No one knows. I don't read anything into it – except, of course, for the widespread existence of almost entirely useless psychic powers.'

'You believe that?'

'Oh no. I just notice that it's true. I'll show you. See that group of middle-aged women on the other side of the road?'

'No. Ah, oh, hold it. Yes, I got them.'

'We'll both stare at the one on the right, holding the pair of men's shoes.'

'They're all holding men's shoes.'

'Oh. Oh, yes. Weird. Okay, well the one with the pink scarf.'

Lance checked that the girl who had taught him about microrelationships was staring, and then joined in the stare himself. The woman with the pink scarf was on the outer fringe of a group of seven. In her other hand she was holding a comb, and she was tentatively trying to get closer to something propped against a wall. Some*one* propped against a wall. There was also a white dog who seemed shyly protective of whoever it was.

Lance picked up his *Financial Times* and raised the pinhole to his eye. Using the optical process that he did not understand and which was almost certainly bullshit, he found the crowd and searched for the person sitting against the wall.

And there he was.

63

At six o'clock that evening, Jonathon stood outside the door to Albatross's offices, the blue bag on his shoulder heavy with shoes and change. He looked around, feeling again that someone was watching him. But the concrete council flats on the other side of the road looked back, blank and uncomprehending.

Tzzz.

The door buzzed and Jonathon let himself in, coaxing Sir Cecil Chubb, who was always reluctant to cross a threshold, after him. Gus was waiting at the top of the stairs.

'Might I, er, have a word?' he asked.

'What shall I do with Sir Cecil Chubb?'

'Bring Cess with you. There's nothing I wish to say that's unsuitable for her ears, except in the sense that I intend to speak in human words.'

Piper, still at her desk, wouldn't meet Jonathon's eye as he passed, ripping a great chunk out of his heart. What had he done to make her hate him? They had seemed to get on so well the day before, on the Tube. Perhaps she had guessed the way he felt about her.

He suddenly noticed that her arms matched the rest of her perfectly, in shape and texture. They seemed suddenly miraculous. He shook his head. Once you start marvelling at the existence of a woman's arms, all hope is lost.

Jonathon and Sir Cecil Chubb followed Gus up the cast-iron spiral staircase, which the dog negotiated surprisingly well. *Is this about all the shoes?* he wondered. He didn't know how to explain that he just couldn't prevent it from happening. People seemed horrified to see him in either shoes or trainers, and would then donate a pair of trainers or shoes, which Jonathon would wear until someone else was horrified and the whole cycle began again.

'Jonathon,' said Gus, when they were seated, 'how much have you taken today?'

Did Gus suspect him of stealing? 'Um. I don't know. About four hundred pounds?'

'You have a quite remarkable natural talent for begging.'

Jonathon flushed with unexpected pride. 'Oh, thank you.'

'This is no idle compliment, Jonathon. It's true that we have only two other people in our pilot project here, but in your first two days you have, as well as bringing us a quite incredible quantity of shoes, collected more than twenty times as much money as our previous top performer.'

'Really?'

'Yes, really. Your performance, Jonathon, is in every way excellent. Except that it poses a possibly fatal problem to our operation.'

'Ah.'

'Our other two people have collected only a tiny amount of money. They have suffered a large amount of verbal abuse and one of them was briefly set on fire. This is fully consistent with the experience of real homeless people we have spoken to. We expected teething troubles, and to build gradually from a low base.'

Jonathon nodded. He was pleased to find he was good at something, but apprehensive about where this was going.

'As you know, we're trying to discover "begging technologies" – simple rules, tricks and techniques that can readily be transmitted to the neediest homeless person, so that they can capture more of the untapped demand for street donations, and so that the people who give can feel better about themselves. I was thinking our work might eventually lead to a programme to lend out dogs of a certain breed, or that we could advise on particularly favourable times of day, locations or blanket colours. But your results suggest that there's a huge factor – perhaps several of them – at work here which we're just not taking into account. So, please, Jonathon, tell me what you're doing.'

'Er, I'm reading the book?'

'The other two are reading the book: same book, same edition, same condition. We're very thorough.'

'Could it be Sir Cecil Chubb?'

'Cess was out with one of our other people last week, producing our lowest donations so far. She was taunted for looking like the ghost of a wolf, which upset her.'

'Um. I don't know, then.'

'Show me. Sit on the floor as you would on the street.'

Jonathon obligingly sat down with his back to the wooden cupboards on the other side of the room, facing Gus. He wrapped the blanket around his shoulders, set the blue bag beside him, put the cup in front of him with the stone in it, and got Sir Cecil Chubb to come and sit next to him. Then he opened his book and began reading. Gus watched him.

'Is,' said Gus, 'and I don't mean that "is" to sound dismissive, but is that all you do?'

'Yes, I think so.'

'The problem appears to be worse than I suspected. I want reproducible results. The very last thing I want to discover from this exercise is that some people just have a certain something that makes others want to give them money and shoes.'

'Are you sure the others didn't get any shoes? I mean, I'm wearing the same kind they did, aren't I?'

'We have never before received even a single pair of shoes. Are you sure you aren't saying anything to people?'

'Not till they start saying things to me.'

'Extraordinary. Perhaps there is an eloquence to your silence. Have you had any dramatic training? Any acting experience?'

'Well, only accidentally,' said Jonathon.

Gus raised his eyebrows.

'Well, in my last job I forgot my pass one day, and, well, one thing led to another and I got sort of pulled into something the company were filming in an empty floor upstairs. But it was nothing really and I haven't done any other acting.'

'What did this nothing consist of?'

'I had to pretend to be a computer operator on a pretend trading floor.'

'A pretend trading floor?'

'Yes.'

'Why didn't they use a real trading floor?'

'I don't know.'

'How mysterious. What were they filming? And was this your last job, at...' Gus hunted through some papers till he found Jonathon's CV '... Farynx?'

Jonathon was suddenly unsure whether to answer. He had a sort of superstitious feeling that talking about Farynx could bring it back into his life. And he was so glad it was gone. He was much happier reading *The Idiot* on the streets of London, discovering he had a natural talent for begging, and having even this limited contact with Gus, Piper and this eccentric but essentially human company.

'It doesn't matter,' said Gus, smiling apologetically. 'I'm getting distracted from the real business of trying to find out why you're so remarkably good at this.'

'That's all right,' said Jonathon. Of course he would answer. 'It was Farynx, and it was some sort of corporate thing. An advert, maybe? It was a bit strange though, because some analysts walked through while the filming was going on. And after they'd left, they stopped the filming and sent everyone home. A friend of mine thought it was fraud.'

'Extraordinary. And what were they trading? Stocks?'

'Internet bandwidth.'

Gus's eyes expanded to fill the lenses of his glasses. 'Can you tell me more?'

64

Lance pretended to knock on the door. He was standing in the open walkway of a four-storey block of council flats, giving him a good view of the streets around.

No one answered of course: it was a Thursday afternoon. Lance tutted, sighed, unfolded his newspaper and pretended to resign himself to a long wait. He was actually watching the elaborate Victorian building into which Jonathon had disappeared.

It was the dog who had alerted Lance to the fact that something strange was going on – stranger than Jonathon becoming homeless. Lance could just about imagine Jonathon sleeping in a church porch. But he couldn't imagine him immediately getting a timid white wolf to help him beg. That was why Lance had decided to follow Jonathon rather than talk to him.

Lance shook his paper out again and pretended to read a story titled 'Treasury yields firm up', all the time keeping his eyes on the building into which Jonathon had gone.

But something wasn't right. He had a sensation like the slightest of slight itches on the inside of his skull. Was he being watched? He checked his peripheral vision. There was a movement, like someone subtly ducking out of sight. It came from the building next to this one – a similar block of 1950s brick and concrete.

Lance pretended to impatiently check his watch. He tutted, folded the newspaper and trudged down the steps. At the corner of the stair-case, he scanned the other building for signs of movement. There was a flicker, a tiny movement on one of the walkways.

Lance emerged onto the street, wandered casually along and then quickly ducked into the other building's stairwell. He climbed with silent steps to the second floor, where he had seen the flicker of movement.

'Hello Bob,' he said, as he stepped out.

Plover, who had been crouching behind the parapet, stood up.

'Afternoon Lance,' he said. He had that slight squint that he did when he was annoyed, but his voice sounded friendly and composed, as tiredly cheerful as ever.

'Good follow?' enquired Lance, lighting a cigarette.

'Not so bad.'

'Anyone I know?'

'A colleague of mine, as it goes.'

'Oh. Why are you following him?'

'Well, he lied about whether he knew someone we're meant to be tracking down.'

'Why do you think that?'

'A few little things. For example, this note he left for someone we interviewed.'

Plover pulled a piece of paper out of his pocket and unfolded it. It was the note Lance had written to Emma.

Lance nodded. *How does Plover have that?* he thought. But he said, 'Pretty compelling evidence. So what next?'

'Thought I'd wait a bit, watch him and the person he's following. Reckon LPA might have found where our spy works.'

'If this colleague of yours knows the spy, why's he following him?'

'Just the sort of thing that nobhead would do.'

'Wait a minute,' said Lance, with mock stupidity, '*I'm* a nobhead. This is *me* we're talking about, isn't it?'

Plover turned to him and sighed, suddenly serious. 'Why, Lance mate?'

'Let's go for a drink. I'll explain.'

'By "explain" do you mean "make up some new lies"?'

'No.'

Plover sighed again. 'Okay, but first I want to watch until Fairfax comes out.'

Lance also wanted to watch, so he could find out what was going on and whether Jonathon worked for the company that occupied these offices. There was, realistically, nothing he could do to prevent Plover watching too.

And so they stood, Lance propped up against the wall of the stairwell, Plover on the walkway, watching a Victorian house while pretending to read their copies of the *Financial Times* and impatiently wait for someone.

65

When Jonathon had explained exactly what he had seen at Farynx, and answered many questions, Gus sat back, took off his glasses and said, 'Well.'

'Well,' said Jonathon, not wanting to be left out.

'I must confess,' said Gus, 'that when I read about this bandwidth trading in the *Financial Times*, I wondered how they could possibly have solved all the problems involved in it. Bandwidth, after all, isn't much like a commodity. It's not something you can load onto a train and send off to a delivery point for your buyer to collect. Bandwidth is more like the track that the train runs on. And that's not a commodity, because no one would ever buy, say, transport for a hundred miles on grade-one track. You care about where the track is and when you can use it.'

'Um, and whether there's a train running,' said Jonathon.

'And *whether there's a train running*,' said Gus, taking off his glasses again and staring with slightly squinted eyes into the middle distance.

Jonathon followed his gaze, but saw only a wall.

'I thought they must be geniuses to have solved that problem: a distressingly lazy assumption. But what you've told me makes me suspect that they – like most other purported geniuses – are in fact frauds.'

'So Farynx is definitely committing fraud?' asked Jonathon.

'I'm afraid so. This is further proof that investors – and the whole financial system – have become too stupid and lazy to ask the most basic questions. Everyone believes that prices incorporate all publicly available information, which means there's no point in doing any due diligence at all. And what pair of words could be more exciting to investors, or better sum up the spirit of the age, than "bandwidth trading"?'

'Um. Harry Potter?'

'No,' said Gus, ignoring Jonathon's suggestion, 'I doubt Farynx even has any intellectual property in this area. In fact, I suspect that if I wrote the sentence, "Bandwidth trading is currently impossible," on a piece of paper and locked it in this petty cash tin, I would have far more intellectual property in this area than they do.'

'Um, would that count as intellectual property?'

'Oh yes. There are five main types of intellectual property, of which one is "trade secret". My piece of paper amply meets the three requirements for being a trade secret. One, it is not generally known to the public – otherwise Farynx's share price would not have gone up so startlingly in the past few days. Two, it confers an economic benefit on its owner – by preventing me wasting money investing in Farynx shares. And three, I have made reasonable efforts to maintain its secrecy – viz. locking it in a box.'

66

After Jonathon had left the office, Gus sat back in his old but preternaturally adjustable chair, playing with a paperclip. Then he sat up, wrote, 'Bandwidth trading is currently impossible,' on a piece of paper and locked it in his petty cash tin.

He picked up the phone on his desk and dialled a number. He didn't get straight through, of course, but a few minutes later he got a call back.

'Gus, Donald Eade here, HBCI.'

'Ah, Donald. Thank you so much for calling me back. Listen, I'd like to make a last-minute change to Albatross's stock-market prospectus.'

'I'm afraid that will be rather difficult, Gus – impossible even. The IPO is on Monday, and we already have our institutional investors lined up.'

'It's just that I've developed some new intellectual property. I wanted to keep it hush-hush until I was absolutely sure of it, but it's ready somewhat sooner than I expected. It's in the area of bandwidth trading.'

'*Bandwidth trading*? Sounds exciting. Do go on.'

67

Almost twenty minutes later, Jonathon emerged again, this time in a large black coat, but otherwise apparently just wearing very slightly different versions of the clothes he'd been wearing when he went in. He had no bag and no dog.

'There he goes,' said Plover, putting a small pair of binoculars to his eyes. 'Hm. *Albatross: The Ideas Company*. Write this number down, will you?'

Lance put the number into his phone and dialled it. There was no point further antagonising Plover.

'Good afternoon, Albatross,' said the jaunty voice that answered. 'Piper speaking. How can I help you?'

'Hi, uh… Wait, sorry, I thought you said "Piper speaking."'

'I did. My mum's American and my dad has some sort of personality disorder that doesn't have a name yet.'

'Great. I've always loved the name Piper. Like a mellow lark.'

'Like a what?'

'Never mind. Listen, I'm a friend of someone who works for you, Jonathon Fairfax. Is he still there?'

'No, sorry. You've just missed him.'

'Ah, damn, well can I—' And then Lance pressed the red button to end the call.

'Well, that's our job done,' said Plover, standing up and making for the stairs.

'What?' said Lance, turning to follow him.

'It's clear this is where Jonathon Fairfax works. That was the question Todd employed us to answer. Once we tell him, we get the second half of the fee.'

'Right. But this is what I need to talk to you about,' said Lance, descending the stairs after Plover.

'No,' said Plover, without turning, 'what you need to talk to me about is why you lied to me.'

'But the reason I lied to you is that Jonathon Fairfax isn't a spy. I know it.'

'Well if he isn't a spy he's got nothing to worry about,' said Plover, leaving the stairwell and striding into the street.

'He's got Todd to worry about. Todd said he would kill him.'

'Todd's an American CEO. He says he's going to kill everything. That's just how he speaks.'

'This wasn't a metaphor. He was serious.'

'And you're an expert on seriousness all of a sudden, Mr I'll-just-sleep-with-my-friend's girlfriend?'

'But they had broken up and— How did you know about that?'

'It was written all over your faces. Since then I've just been waiting for you to lead me to Fairfax.'

'But... don't you think there's something not right about Todd?' asked Lance. They were heading away from Albatross now, towards Rosebery Avenue and, beyond it, Angel Tube station.

'Of course I do. But that's not my problem. My wife and daughter and everyone at LPA are my problem. They're relying on me to bring the money in, and the company's fighting to survive. This is LPA's big chance to work for the blue-chip corporates. So, thanks for the introduction, and you'll get your finder's fee. But I'm not going to let you ruin this opportunity.'

They stopped beside a long narrow park lined with trees, over which loomed a statue of an angel with outsized wings. Plover was framed by the entrance to one of those concrete public toilets that were built in the aftermath of the war, when people couldn't shake the habit of making things indestructible.

Plover pulled his phone out of his pocket and was about to press a button when Lance made a swipe at it, narrowly missing.

'Are you really trying to grab my phone off me?' asked Plover, turning to face him.

'No,' said Lance, but then he immediately undermined the credibility of this claim by trying to grab Plover's phone again. Plover hid it behind his back.

Lance said, 'I'm just trying to get you to talk about it before you make the call. Come on, it won't matter whether you make the call now or in the morning.'

'Except that if I call him now, we'll definitely get the bonus. Who knows what could happen overnight. I'm not taking any chances.'

'Well, just leave it half an hour.'

'He might have gone home in half an hour.'

'What, at seven? He's the CEO of a major multinational corporation.'

'Well…' said Bob uncertainly, as though he was about to give in. But it was just a ruse. He ran into the toilet.

Lance followed him. The door of the middle toilet cubicle slammed shut and locked.

'If you try calling Todd,' said Lance, walking into the cubicle to the right of Bob's, 'I will flush this toilet, so help me God I will. And he won't be able to hear you. And if you try calling again while this toilet's filling up, I'll flush the other one. I'm prepared to stay in here all night, flushing toilets.'

Plover said, 'Hello, could I speak to—'

Sssscccchhhoooooooosssshhhh!

'I warned you,' said Lance.

'To—' began Plover.

Sssscccchhhoooooooosssshhhh!

'Hello?' said Plover.

'Oh, did they hang up?' asked Lance.

Plover said nothing.

'Instead of spending all this time here, we could just spend half an hour talking about it in a nice cosy pub, and then you could call him,' said Lance.

'You don't have the patience to wait here flushing toilets for half an hour,' said Plover. 'That's the problem with you. Me, I'm happy to spend the night sitting in my car outside your hotel, so I can spend the day following you. But you can't even be bothered to check properly to see if you're being followed.'

'What are you talking about?' said Lance. 'I spotted you, didn't I?'

There was a long silence, then Plover said, 'Only when it was too late.'

'Come on, Bob,' said Lance.

There was no reply.

'It doesn't have to be this way,' said Lance.

Again, there was a long silence.

'Bob?'

There was a silence again, then a clack as the cubicle door was unlocked.

'Finished,' said Bob as he walked out, holding his phone.

'What do you mean?'

'Nokia Communicator 9110, mate. It does email.'

'What? But you were in there less than ten minutes.'

'Yep,' he said, flourishing the instruction manual. 'And that's all the time it takes to choose "Mail", press the "Select" button, type a few lines, enter the recipient's email address, choose "Make Data Call", establish a connection, press "Send", go to the document outbox, press "Open" and then press "Start". Done.'

'Shit,' said Lance. He was smiling though, in spite of himself, because Bob's phone really was pretty impressive.

'Let's go for that drink and I'll show you,' said Plover.

Friday

68

'What's this?' asked Todd, looking up from the piece of paper Henry had just given him.

'This is a list of three firms with an investigative services offering. I believe LPA's services are suboptimal.'

'You want to use a different company to find where this Fairfax guy works?'

'That would be affirmatory.'

'Why?'

'I specifically tasked them with shadowing you, to pick up on any surveillance activity going on, possibly involving Fairfax, as you observed. They came Wednesday for less than one quarter of a day. Yesterday, they sent a guy named Barry *Lenin*, if you can believe that. Today, who's showed up? No one.'

'Oh, I guess they didn't copy you in on the email.'

'There was an email? I specifically tasked them with communicating through myself.'

'Henry, I don't have time for this. If you can't get along with them, that's your problem. They already tracked Fairfax down and found out who he's working for.'

'Huh,' said Henry. 'Right. So who is his present employer?'

'Company called Albatross. I'll email you the address. I need you to do a little desk research, see what you can find out about them.'

'You're not going to get LPA to do that?'

'No. Why would I? I got you.'

'Right.' Henry seemed to be on the point of leaving, but didn't. 'Don't you think it's a little *off*, that my oversight is introduced and then all of a sudden they find Fairfax? A little too convenient?'

'No. It seems like you told them to do the wrong thing, and they ignored you and did the right thing. I don't know how many times

I've got to say this: all I care about is results. I don't want you to do what I say; I want you to get me what I want. And what I want right now is to know all about this Albatross.'

Henry returned an hour later.

'Okay,' said Todd. 'So what have you got?'

'Albatross is a privately owned company based in Garnault Place, London EC1R. In the financial year ending April 1999, it declared revenues of three point eight million pounds. It has twelve employees and one office. It self-describes as an "ideas company" and claims to have invented the wheeled suitcase. That claim has been contested. Other service offerings include placebo design and public policy creation. Its IPO on the London Stock Exchange Main Market is scheduled for Monday. But here's the item of greatest potential significance: its IPO prospectus was altered yesterday. Its sponsor, HBCI, is attempting to leverage some last-minute bids from institutional investors off of the back of it.'

'So?'

'That prospectus now claims they have intellectual property related to bandwidth trading.'

Todd jumped from his chair. 'Son of a bitch!'

Henry nodded.

'I knew it,' said Todd. 'They're the spies!'

'Couldn't be clearer,' said Henry. 'Although…'

'Although what?'

'Well, bandwidth trading is not actually actively carried out by us. So they can't have misappropriated our intellectual property.'

'Which is exactly why they have to be spies. It only makes sense to claim they've got the IP if they know we haven't. Best-case scenario: they've been snooping around and know about the fake bandwidth trading. Now we can probably ride that out and cover for it, but it's bad timing. I don't want anything to happen that could get in the way of our acquisition of Biscuits. Worst-case scenario: they've taken a look at our accounts. Whatever, we need to get rid of them.'

'I anticipated aggressive action might be desired, therefore I created a robust plan that could potentially be executed in a timely manner.'

69

A thin man, wearing a green blanket (medium-dirty) over his shoulders and carrying a bag of shoes, was walking with a shy white dog. He rounded the corner. Lance stepped out from the shadows, nonchalant but dramatic.

'Hey J-walk,' he said.

Jonathon glanced at him, involuntarily pulled a hurt and regretful face not entirely unlike Céline Dion's, and carried on walking.

'By which I mean,' said Lance, 'hello Jonathon.'

Lance fell into step beside him. The dog, on Jonathon's other side, looked up at Lance and bared its teeth.

'I'm sorry I slept with Emma,' said Lance.

Jonathon said nothing.

'I'm also sorry I did it when I was meant to be meeting you in the pub. I would have been late anyway, because I arranged to meet Todd at six. I told myself that it would only take twenty minutes from Farynx in a cab, but I knew that wasn't true. So, I apologise.'

The dog glared at Lance then gave Jonathon a comforting look and a groan-growl of solidarity. Jonathon kept his eyes fixed on the pavement ahead.

Lance said, 'It just happened. I didn't mean it to. But then also I didn't really do anything to stop it happening once it started. And… well, never mind. Sorry.'

Jonathon upped his pace. They had already been walking quite fast.

Lance said, 'Fine, you don't have to talk to me yet. But I need to warn you about something. This is serious. Todd Stuckers has found out where you work.' Lance decided Jonathon didn't need to know how Todd had discovered that. 'He thinks you're a corporate spy and that you have information that could really fuck up Farynx. He's got a bit paranoid and obsessive about the whole thing. He says he'll kill you and I think he's serious. He's now CEO, by the way, in case you hadn't heard. And he got his last two promotions because of people dying in accidents. I seem to be the only person who finds that suspicious. Everyone else says that only a madman would believe he could get away with that, so it can't have been murder. But that implies you can become CEO of a major multinational corporation without being a madman – and Todd drinks forty coffees a day and only sleeps four hours a night.'

Jonathon walked even faster, his mouth a thin, tense line, his eyebrows gathered in close to their eyes.

'He's also really ruthless, cunning and powerful. He's in charge of a seventy-billion-dollar company. He could squash the company you work for like it was yesterday's pork pie. They say he made the CEO of United Biscuits cry – and *he* used to be in the army. I sort of get on all right with Todd though, for some reason. Maybe it's because I made him believe I'm more famous and successful than I am. Anyway, I think I can help. Oh, and by the way, did you know your dad doesn't have any photos of you?'

Jonathon began to jog. Lance did too, which reminded him that he smoked and rarely exercised – he just looked really healthy because of all the genetic lotteries he had won.

'Come for a beer,' said Lance, 'just one, and I'll explain it all properly.'

Jonathon broke into a run, the white dog at his heels, and Lance fell back, breathing heavily.

'I've got your phone charger,' he called. But Jonathon was already gone.

Lance knew there is nothing that can't be solved by means of charm and huge self-confidence. So he went to a pub, recovered his breath over a cigarette and a beer, and then called Todd.

'This is Todd,' said Todd.

'Hi Todd. Lance here. How about we get together some time?'

'Yeah, I'd love to. But I am *stacked* with this United Biscuits thing. And I'm out of the office all next week. Maybe the week after?'

'Great,' said Lance, though it wasn't quite as great as he would have liked. 'What day?'

'Ah, I'll get my PA to put some options together. Now, I've got to shoot. I have a meeting in like *minus* ten minutes.'

'Good one,' said Lance.

Saturday and Sunday

70

Some things happened. Others, not so much.

Monday

71

It was half past seven on Monday morning, and Gus was in a state Piper had never seen him in before. As a rule, he was a man who favoured sitting down and mulling things over. This had worked out very well for him over the years, since he charged relatively high mulling fees. But this morning, sitting – much less mulling – seemed entirely beyond him.

He kept walking about, climbing up and down the wrought-iron staircase, going into rooms and out of them. He smiled and clapped his hands and swung his arms. He even occasionally seemed to be on the verge of dancing.

There was no talking to him either. Piper had tested him out on an easy subject.

'Would you like a cup of tea, Dad?' she called from the reception desk.

Gus came bounding over from the other end of the office, where he had been bothering someone who worked for him. Everyone was in early because of their stock-market launch.

'What's that?' he asked, excitedly.

She said, 'I said, "Would you like a cup of tea, Dad?" Dad.'

Gus smiled hugely, but his eyes seemed to be focused on a spot about six inches behind her head. 'You look lovely today, Piper. What a… what a splendid young lady you've turned out to be.'

She felt quite pleased by this, in spite of the part of her that hated it. Compliments from parents simultaneously don't count and matter a great deal.

'Tea?' she persisted.

'Hmm? What?' he asked. He had picked up a mechanical pencil from her desk and was examining it minutely, jigging from one foot to the other.

Piper smiled at Jonathon, who had appeared behind Gus, but he wouldn't meet her eyes. *Why?* she wondered. He looked like he had barely slept.

'Um,' Jonathon said to Gus, 'could I have a word with you?'

'What's that?' said Gus. 'A word? Of course, of course. Dear me, yes. A word.'

The front-door buzzer sounded and Piper stood to answer the intercom.

'That'll be him,' said Gus, bounding downstairs like a dog given the sudden chance to jump in some dirty water.

Jonathon seemed to give up on the idea of talking to Gus, and disappeared into the basement. He was on the early shift today. Was that why he looked so sad?

Seconds later, Gus returned, dragging with him a plump-faced man with neat, thinning hair and a blue pinstriped suit. The man carried an excitingly chunky metal case, which Gus could not help staring at.

'Donald Eade,' said the man, extending his hand to shake Piper's. Gus was in such an excitable state that he intercepted the man's hand and shook it himself.

'This is Donald Eade,' said Gus, 'from HBCI, the bank that's sponsoring us through our stock-market flotation.'

Piper moved around the desk, gently extricated Donald Eade from her father's clutches and guided him towards the desk they had cleared in the main working area.

'Will this be all right to set up your... equipment?' she asked.

'Oh yes, fine, absolutely perfect,' said the man in a voice so extravagantly posh that he seemed to swap around and extend his vowel sounds as the fancy took him, like an experimental jazz musician. *Ooayisfainepslooootlypuffic-t.* Piper had to strain to understand.

She took his order for tea and made Gus observe an exclusion zone around the man while he set up his equipment. Then she went to the kitchen.

She returned minutes later with Donald Eade's tea and a bucket of ice in which nestled the bottle of chilled champagne Gus had insisted on. All fourteen people in the office had crowded around the desk. Donald had by now unpacked and set up his equipment. The excitingly chunky metal case sat open and empty on the floor beside the desk. Inside, there was expensive-looking black foam with shapes cut out of it for three pieces of equipment: a power supply, a faded black box with a serial number stamped on it, and a slightly bulky and old-fashioned-looking laptop. A wire trailed from the black box to one of their telephone sockets.

On the laptop's screen, in various shades of acidic green, there were lists of letters and numbers. Every single person in the office stared fixedly at them.

'There's really nothing to it,' Donald Eade was saying, noodling through a bit more vowel-freestyling. *Thyarsrellynyethingtut.* 'When the market opens at eight, ownership of the shares is transferred to your roster of institutional investors. The money is transferred from them to you. Then Albatross's stock ticker – ALBT – will appear in the listings, and thus on this screen. And at that point secondary trading will begin as some of the investors sell off part of their allocation. Now, of course, that secondary trading doesn't directly benefit you, since you've sold all your shares, but it's an important indicator of market sentiment towards your company. You're looking for a bounce of around ten per cent in valuation by COB.'

'COB?' asked someone.

Donald Eade looked in surprise at the questioner.

'Close of business,' explained Donald. *Clioseffbisuns.* 'We're hoping that when the market closes for the day at half past four, Albatross's shares will be worth about ten per cent more than the two pounds fifty that the institutional investors paid for them.'

'Oh. Why?'

'Never mind. The important thing is that when ALBT appears on the screen, the money will be in Albatross's bank account.'

'And at that point,' said Gus, 'I'll tell you how much we've raised.'

'But you know already?' said someone else.

'I know already – we agreed a new final price yesterday. But I don't want to reveal it until we actually have it. I have an irrational fear of jinxing or hexing the whole thing.'

When Piper returned with champagne glasses, a tense, expectant silence had fallen over the throng. Everyone was staring at the green screen, hypnotised by its flickering numbers, its lists of letters. People licked their lips, checked their watches, shifted their weight from foot to foot. Gus was sitting in a chair beside Donald Eade, clutching the neck of the unopened champagne bottle. He was motionless now but so tense he seemed to vibrate finely like the string of a violin. Donald lounged beside him, but the muscles of his face were set, his lips pursed.

The clock ticked down to eight o'clock.

The clock stood still at precisely eight o'clock.

The clock ticked on past eight o'clock.

People exchanged worried glances. A little rash of coughing broke out and passed. And Gus sat there still, unmoving, not even blinking now, his knuckles white around the bottle's neck.

'And there she goes,' said Donald. *Yendtheshigairs*.

Piper could not see what had happened on the screen, but evidently 'ALBT' had appeared, because everyone then reacted exactly as though a super-concentrated football team had scored the final goal of all time. As one, they stood, raised their hands in the air and shouted, 'YEEEEERRRRSSSSS!!!'

Gus was fumbling with the champagne bottle, his hands shaking, while Freelance Jenny who was helping them with marketing hugged his arm. People cheered, hugged and jumped up and down. And then there came a loud, satisfying *bock!* and the bottle was open. Gus was pouring it into a glass as Donald pushed his machine a little further out of range.

Gus poured three or four glasses, laughing all the while, and then Piper took over for him, with some more bottles. Everyone clinked glasses and said, 'Cheers,' and, 'To Albatross PLC.' And there was laughter and smiling.

'Tell us how much, Gus!' someone said.

'Yes, how much?' said everyone else.

Gus took a gulp of champagne, adjusted his glasses and beamed around at all of them.

'Friends,' he said, 'oh, and of course, Donald. Donald and friends, today Albatross has received a little over forty-one million pounds.'

People turned to one another and either said, 'Oh my God,' or repeated the amount incredulously. One or two people managed to do both.

'This means,' continued Gus, 'that we will finally be able to use our ideas to make the world a better place.'

He poured himself some more champagne and went on. 'It looked for a while as though the absolute maximum we could get, even in these insane times, was seven million. But then I made a few last-minute improvements to our prospectus, which led to a new surge of interest from institutional investors – that is, large firms, financial institutions and so on – on Friday. That got us up to fifteen million. And then they began to enquire whether we would release more shares – that is to say, give up control of the company. I agonised long and hard on Saturday, but finally concluded that I cannot fault my initial

218

analysis. In America there's a dotcom company that has lost fourteen million dollars delivering goldfish to people's doors, and only succeeded in delivering seven fish. Its shares are currently worth twenty million dollars. A crash is bound to come. There will never be another opportunity like this. We have simply to wait for the crash, buy back our shares at a much lower price, and then set about using some of this immense pile of money – which would surely otherwise have been wasted – to do good.'

There was wild applause and people looked wonderingly at Gus.

'He's a genius,' said Freelance Jenny who was helping them with marketing, shaking her head, 'a genius.'

'That's very strange,' said Donald Eade, *thyetsvairstraaaange,* staring at the green figures on his screen. 'None of the institutional investors has sold on a single one of its shares – despite the demand.'

72

On Garnault Place sat a large Mercedes painted a copyrighted shade of blue. And in one of the buttery leather back seats, in what was effectively a generously sized mobile living room, sat Todd Stuckers.

'There,' said Henry, from the neighbouring seat, pointing his finger.

A green door had opened, and a man with thinning hair, a pin-striped suit and a large metal case was descending the short flight of steps to the street.

'You got everything?' Todd asked.

Henry patted the attaché case on his lap.

'Then let's do this,' said Todd.

There was the luxurious sound of air-sealed doors popping open, leather-soled shoes meeting the street, doors swinging gracefully shut. Todd and Henry walked to the green door and pressed the buzzer.

The speaker sprang into life, relaying some tinny background laughter before a somewhat flushed voice said, 'Good morning, Albatross PLC?'

'Good morning,' said Henry. 'Mr Todd Stuckers, CEO of Farynx, is here to see Augustus Palgrave.'

'Oh,' said the voice, 'well… please come up.'

Tzzz.

The lock fizzed and Henry pushed the door open. When they reached the top of the staircase inside, a young woman with large eyes and a black-and-white dress was waiting for them, smiling nervously.

'Good morning,' she said. 'How can I help you?'

Todd looked her dead in the eye, curled his lip and said, 'Well you can start by welcoming your new owners.'

Five minutes later, they were sitting in a meeting room. On the other side of a large old table sat a man in tweed, his eyes like blue fish swimming in a pair of big square aquariums. On one side of him sat a middle-aged woman in yoga clothes, and on the other side sat a man in a crumpled linen shirt.

'But what do you mean "new owners"?' asked Gus, the man in tweed. 'Surely you're using the phrase in some other sense than its everyday, literal one.'

'Show him,' said Todd.

Henry sprung open the catches on the attaché case that lay on the table in front of him, and removed a sheaf of papers. He dealt them like a hand of cards in a neat row facing Gus.

'The share certificates,' he said.

Gus picked one up and examined it closely.

'I don't know where you got these,' he said, replacing the certificate, 'but any transfer of share ownership – unless conducted on the open market – must be approved by the board of this company. And I happen to know that, unusual as it may seem, none of our institutional investors has sold a single share.'

'Yeah, I know that too,' said Todd, 'because I am your institutional investors. They're all companies we own.'

Todd signalled to Henry, who reached into the attaché case and withdrew a single sheet of paper. Henry handed this to Gus.

'Recognise the names?'

Gus skimmed through the list of company names. The pale blue fish quivered in their aquariums. He looked at Todd.

'Are you saying that the roster of institutional investors, carefully negotiated and composed by our sponsor, HBCI, are all companies that belong to you?'

'That's exactly what I'm saying.'

'So you were behind the demand that we sell a larger stake in the company?'

Todd allowed his eyes to close for a second in silent

acknowledgement.

'Well,' said Gus, 'this cannot possibly be legal. I shall consult my lawyers.'

'Be my guest,' said Todd. 'But don't spend too much of my money on it. That forty-one million belongs to the shareholders, you know. And you have a legal duty to run this company in their interests. You ignore that, we can sue. We can also replace the management around here.'

Gus gave him an angry look but kept his voice under control. 'Let's imagine things are as you suggest. Why?'

'Cut to the chase. I like that. Well, I've come to give you a choice. It's an easy choice. In fact, to make it as easy as possible, I've made one option *real* bad and the other one *real* good.'

'Well?'

'The bad option. Your shareholders – i.e. me – call an "extraordinary general meeting". At that meeting they dismiss the current management and replace them. The new management sack everyone else. So, that's part of it: we kick you out of your own company and fire everyone who works for you. This company retains the rights to all your intellectual property. So you lose everything you've worked for and all your future income. If you try to have any more ideas in future, you'd better be careful that none of them are even a tiny bit related to ones that we own, or we will sue you for every penny you don't have. In fact, whatever you do, we will find ways to take you to court, and you will spend every penny on lawyers. If it costs me ten million to take a million off of you, I will consider that a bargain. And we will do our level best to ensure that no one who works here ever gets a job again.'

Todd leaned back and continued in a deliberately casual tone. 'There are a lot of companies who want to do us favours, by the way. Not just HBCI. Everyone wants to lend to us, do consulting for us, get in on our deals and just generally do business with us. We're the world's most successful company.'

'I see. And the good option?'

'You keep your company, you keep your life's work, you keep the money you just raised. Everyone – bar one – gets to keep their jobs. We're your shareholders but you never hear so much as a whisper from us.'

Gus and the other two exchanged looks. 'But presumably you want something in return.'

'Yes. You tell us why you were spying on us and what you found out. And we use Sodium Pentothal and polygraph tests to make sure you're telling the truth. You hand over everything you've got on us. You sign watertight contracts preventing you from revealing whatever you know, or think you know. And you give me your spy, this Fairfax guy. I want his real name, his real address, and I want to sit down in a room with him and have a long talk.'

'Wait a minute. Have you gone to these extraordinary lengths because you think we're spying on you?'

'I know you're spying on us.'

'But, that's preposterous. Why ever would we—'

'You're telling me it's just a coincidence that you suddenly decide to put bandwidth trading in your prospectus, right before the IPO? We know Fairfax snuck into our little demonstration. Come on.'

Gus looked startled.

'But, I could have… that is to say, I *did* read about your bandwidth-trading venture in the newspapers. And I suddenly realised we had some intellectual property that could be applied to that activity. I was trying to take advantage of the same unthinking herd mentality among investors as you were.'

'That only makes sense if you know that we…'

'Can't really do bandwidth trading?' suggested Gus.

'I'm not saying that,' said Todd, heatedly. 'I did not say that. But you did, and that proves you've been spying.'

'So you can do bandwidth trading?'

'Yes. Of course we can.'

'But you're saying that we must have been spying because we know that you can't do bandwidth trading?'

Todd stood up. 'This meeting is over. You've got a choice to make. I need your answer by close of play tomorrow.'

73

Over the weekend, Jonathon had decided to resign from Albatross. After what Lance had told him on Friday, it seemed the only way of protecting Piper, Gus and everyone from Todd Stuckers. He had tried to talk to Gus about it that morning, but Gus had been too excited. So he had to do it now – fresh from his shift, before he even checked in his box of cash and bag of shoes – no matter what state Gus was in.

Tzzz.

The front door buzzed and Jonathon pushed it open, with Sir Cecil Chubb as ever shying back from it as though she suspected it was a trap. In the hallway, the quietness struck him. Where that morning everyone had been laughing and shouting at the tops of their voices, now there was silence. They had probably all gone to the pub. Or maybe they had all come back from the pub and were lying unconscious on their desks.

When he got to the top of the stairs and looked around, he was surprised to see that at least half of Albatross's employees were still at their desks. They were grim and silent.

Piper looked up and said, 'Jonathon, Gus would like to see you in the meeting room.' Her voice was quiet and her eyes were round and sad.

Jonathon looked at the dog, who looked equally back. 'What shall I do with Sir Cecil Chubb?'

'Let's just take her in.'

As Piper pushed open the door to the meeting room, Jonathon was again hit by a wave of unexpected silence.

'Here's Jonathon,' said Piper in a sober tone, as though she were wheeling his body in to be identified by relatives.

Seven people, including Gus, were sitting around the gleaming but battered antique table in the meeting room. They looked up slowly from the pads of writing paper they had been staring at.

'Ah, Jonathon,' said Gus. 'Come in, sit down. Something unbearably disastrous has befallen us, and I'm afraid it very much affects you. You had better sit down to hear it. Oh, hello Cess – who's a good girl?'

Jonathon said, 'Oh, ah…' and took a seat. Piper and Sir Cecil Chubb sat beside him, the dog looking from one to the other, as though for reassurance.

At this point Jonathon noticed that one of the people sitting around the table was Lance. He was sitting with his back to the door, which was why Jonathon hadn't spotted him sooner. Lance winked roguishly and Jonathon looked away.

Gus then launched into a long account of Todd's visit. He ended it by glancing at his watch and saying, 'So we now have somewhere in the region of twenty-four hours to give Todd our decision. We have debated the matter extensively, and have gone through all the stages you might imagine: denial, defiance, determination to pursue the matter through the courts, desperation – we briefly thought an eloquent letter in the *Telegraph* would rally public opinion to our side – and finally, resignation. I hope it is otiose to say that we didn't for a second consider giving in to Todd when it comes to you. Are you listening to me, Cess? Who's a clever dog? Look, she has one of her ears cocked.'

'I still don't understand how we're in this position,' said Tim, folding his arms and crumpling his linen shirt. 'We haven't done any spying. We've been taken over illegally. And now, because we won't admit to the spying we haven't done and won't fire someone who hasn't done it, we're all going to lose our jobs and our futures, the company's going to be shut down, and Gus is going to lose his life's work. This literally cannot be happening.'

'Ah, back to denial,' said Gus sadly, looking at his watch again.

'The fact is, you have been spying,' said Lance.

Almost everyone in the room turned to him simultaneously and gave him their own personal variation on the theme of an incredulous, '*What?*'

'Tell them, Gus,' said Lance.

'Wait a minute,' said Tim, who had been the handsome one before Lance's arrival. 'Can we trust him? I mean, he claims he came to warn us about Todd, but…'

'I did warn you about Todd,' said Lance, 'just too late – I underestimated how fast he would move. And if you want to know whether you can trust me, ask my friend Jonathon.'

Everyone in the room, including Sir Cecil Chubb, turned to look at Jonathon.

'Um, you can trust him,' said Jonathon. After all, Lance couldn't sleep with *all* their girlfriends, could he? And he definitely wasn't working for Todd.

'What did you mean by your spying allegation?' Tim asked Lance.

'Well, it's just too much of a coincidence. Jonathon sees the fake bandwidth trading, gets a job here, and then Gus adds bandwidth trading to his IPO prospectus and gets an extra thirty-four million.'

'We have not been spying,' said Gus. 'That is, I never employed Jonathon to infiltrate Farynx and steal its secrets, as Todd believes. But I have, as it were, retrospectively employed Jonathon as a spy. That is, he happened to have observed something odd at Farynx and told me about it. And I made use of that fact.'

'What are you talking about, Dad?' asked Piper.

'I suppose, since we're in this position, no further harm can come from telling you about it. Jonathon observed what I took to be a fake trading floor. Farynx's entry into bandwidth trading is what's behind the huge increase in its share price since Todd announced it last Wednesday. So, not to put too fine a point on it, I added to our IPO prospectus a last-minute mention of our intellectual property in bandwidth-trading.'

'You mean you *lied*?' said Freelance Jenny who was helping them with marketing.

'Absolutely not. I stayed within the letter of the law and the truth. I merely chose to temporarily disregard their spirit – with the best of motives. And it would have worked. My only failing was in not being aware of Todd Stuckers' paranoid fantasies about my company and its newest member of staff.'

'Why don't we just tell the truth now?' said Jenny. 'You and Jonathon could go to Todd Stuckers and explain the whole thing.'

'Not a good idea,' said Lance.

'And why's that?' asked Jenny, crossly.

'Because I asked Todd what he would do if it turned out that the spy wasn't a spy, and he said he would murder him for all the sleepless nights and stress he's caused him.'

'And what did Todd say he'd do if Jonathon was a spy?'

'Ah, in that case he said he would murder him,' said Lance.

'Right. But what does that mean? Obviously Stuckers isn't going to actually murder Jonathon.'

'I don't know about that,' said Lance. 'He had this look in his eye…'

'Oh well, of course we should make decisions about all our futures based on the look in someone's eye,' said Tim.

'I'm just saying. Also, Todd's last two promotions have been the result of accidental deaths. Again, I'm the only person who seems to find this suspicious. Could he not just have a talent for making murders look like accidents?'

'I'm afraid you're being fooled by randomness,' said Gus. 'Accidental deaths aren't evenly spread out. There's absolutely no reason why there wouldn't be two among executives in the same company. Besides, the previous CEO had already, according to the *FT*, acknowledged Todd as his successor. What would he have to gain?'

'Surely in this situation we can go to the police,' said Tim, completely ignoring Gus's point. 'I mean, this is scary. Isn't this what the police are there for? We've got two suspicious deaths, a man threatening murder, and our company's just been illegally taken over.'

'We could try,' said Lance. 'But I don't know what the police could do. One of the deaths is in a different country and is officially not suspicious, and there's already an inquest into the other. Todd would just deny having said he would murder Jonathon, and – like you say – looks in eyes are inadmissible as evidence. And the police don't deal with illegal company takeovers. We'd have to go to court. It'd be bollock-rinsingly expensive, and there's no way Gus could win a court case against one of the richest corporations in the world.'

'I'm afraid he's right,' said Gus. 'And as CEO I have legal duties to act in the best interests of my shareholders – which currently means Todd Stuckers – so he could probably sue me for even trying to bring the case. The same thing prevents me from disposing of all our money. It wouldn't be in the best interests of the shareholders, so they could sue me for it.'

'Do we really not have anything we could use against Stuckers? I mean, he thinks we've got access to his accounts—'

'Oh,' said Jonathon, 'I do know how to get into their accounts.'

There was a sudden loud burst of silence, as though everyone in the room had been struck slightly more than dumb in unison.

'Did you say you know how to get into their accounts?' said Gus.

'Er, yes. I did it to check some figures for their annual report. There's a subfolder that only top management can see, but I know Mr Stuckers' password. Shall I get into it? I mean, they think I've been spying anyway, so I might as well actually spy.'

Everyone around the table exchanged silent glances.

'Why didn't you mention this before?' asked Tim.

'Um, everyone was talking.'

'So, I mean, how do you do this?' asked Tim. 'Is there anything you need? Do we just sit you down in front of a computer and leave you for a couple of hours?'

'Oh, no,' said Jonathon, 'I can't hack into their computers from here.'

'I thought you could do computers,' said Tim.

'I can do a bit of computer programming. If you need someone to make a screen border go green under certain circumstances, I can do that. But hacking into a corporate network is a bit out of my league.'

'So what were you talking about? How can you get into the management accounts?'

'Well, I'd have to get into Farynx somehow and use one of the computers in the Data Services Department, in the basement. I know the password for the computer and Todd's password.'

Piper said, 'Don't go into Farynx, Jonathon. It's too dangerous.'

Gus agreed. 'It is a valiant notion, Jonathon, but it would be wholly and entirely illegal and wrong.'

'But what's the alternative?' asked Alan, who had short hair and a yellow sweater.

Gus took off his glasses and gazed with naked and suddenly small eyes at the questioner.

'When a course of action is clearly wrong,' he said severely, 'one should discard it as a possibility. The fact that there is no effective alternative is entirely irrelevant.'

'So we just accept that we're beaten and wait to have our lives ruined?' shouted Alan.

Gus sighed. 'That seems to me to be the only honourable course of action open to us. Let's all go home, have something to eat and an early night, and hope we think of something by morning. Thinking is, after all, supposed to be our strong suit.'

After that, the meeting broke up. Two people burst into tears. Tim and Alan began a brief, tired and uncommitted fistfight. Piper took Gus to his office and made him a cup of tea. And everyone else went home.

Jonathon numbly took Sir Cecil Chubb to the kitchen and fed her, then changed his clothes and left the office.

Outside, leaning against a lamppost, was Lance.

Jonathon was too tired to pretend he couldn't see him. He stopped, looked at him, and then started to walk towards Farringdon station. Lance silently fell into step beside him.

'I've got your phone charger for you,' said Lance, handing Jonathon the largest and most ungainly charger in the world. It looked like it had been designed in a North Korean lead mine.

'Thanks,' said Jonathon. He was too tired to not say it. He awkwardly clutched the huge device and carried on walking.

'That was brave,' said Lance.

Jonathon said nothing.

'Back there. Volunteering to infiltrate Farynx.'

Jonathon said nothing.

'Todd's out of the office all week, but it would still be dangerous.'

'I'm not afraid of *danger*,' said Jonathon. 'I'm afraid of *offending people*.'

'Hey,' said Lance, 'I know. I heard all about that time at the Ritz five years ago.'

'Which didn't happen.'

'Whatever.'

They walked in silence for a while.

'I'd never have got in anyway,' said Jonathon. 'I had to give in my Farynx pass when they fired me, and God knows it's impossible to get in there without a pass.'

'What if I could get you a pass?' asked Lance.

Jonathon looked at him sharply. Then he hung his head again. 'What if they looked up my name and employee number on the staff register? They wouldn't let me in.'

'What if we could find someone else's name and staff number and put them on the pass?'

'Well then I would do it,' said Jonathon. 'As it is, I've inadvertently destroyed one of the very few benign companies in the world, and the life of a man who saved me from becoming homeless and desti-tute – even if it was by giving me a job pretending to be homeless and destitute. And all because I was trying to take my mind off…'

Jonathon trailed off, deciding not to complete the sentence.

'What if someone recognised me?' Jonathon asked suddenly.

'I also know someone who could help with that.'

74

It was almost eleven by the time Plover arrived at the Faltering Fullback. He was too old for this late-night stuff, really, but he enjoyed a bit of forgery, especially if it might help someone annoy Henry, who had that morning told him there would be no more work for LPA. Plus, Lance had said he would forget his finder's fee.

Inside, the pub was busier than anywhere Plover had ever seen on a Monday night. Every table was occupied. There were people leaning against the ancient wooden panelling around the bar, and standing everywhere he wanted to walk. He found Lance and his friend at a table in a back room full of lampshades and old books. They had saved him a seat and a fresh beer sat on the table.

Lance stood and Plover gave him a matey half-hug, then turned to the friend, whom he suddenly recognised.

'You again!' he said. It was the kid he had watched from a block of flats four days ago. The kid he had been hired to find. The kid who, apparently, could not be photographed.

'Bob, this is Jonathon,' said Lance. 'Who did you think it was going to be? I gave you a photo of him for the…' He trailed off, obviously not wanting to say, 'Forged identity card'.

'It didn't look anything like him. And I thought you'd be working with a professional on a stunt like this. Unless he is a professional, and you've been lying to me again.'

'No more lies. Jonathon knows Farynx's offices, and we have a bulletproof plan. Plus, Todd's away. The worst that can happen is that they sue him for trespassing. If he gets a fine, I'll pay it.'

'Well,' said Plover, 'he has earned me forty grand, so… All right, Jonathon mate.' Then to Lance, 'Cheers for the beer.'

'No problem,' said Lance. 'Have you got the…'

'Check your pocket, mate.'

Lance gave him the tiniest hint of a surprised look – which pleased Plover no end – before turning it effortlessly into the expression of a man who needs a cigarette. Lance took out a packet of cigarettes and then patted his pockets as though looking for a lighter.

'Sorry,' said Plover, 'I should have said, "Check your wallet."'

Lance pulled out his wallet and checked inside. There, nestled among the notes, was a Farynx identity card. Luckily Lance had the easy kind of wallet and the easy kind of pocket. It was just a question of getting the angle right.

Jonathon gasped and then looked embarrassed. Lance turned to Plover with an expression of amazement. For once, he didn't try to hide it.

'Bob,' Lance said, 'you're a magician. How come you can do that but you need a manual to use your phone?'

'Embrace the mystery.'

They all drank some beer, and then Lance said, 'We're also looking for some tips on how to disguise Jonathon. He needs to go back to Farynx without being recognised by anyone he worked with.'

Plover studied Jonathon carefully, taking in every aspect of his appearance.

'I recommend no disguise,' he said.

'What?' said Lance.

'A disguise would be counterproductive,' said Plover.

'But why not use some make-up?'

'Because it can run when you sweat. And because he's pale, so the only way to change his skin colour is to make him darker. But if he looks tanned in March he's more likely to attract attention than if he's the colour he is now. Plus, make-up is hard. People do it for a living, you know.'

'Okay, but what about a fake nose?'

'If you add something to his nose to change its shape you'll just make it bigger and more interesting, so people are more likely to look at him. Right now his nose is barely noticeable. It's almost like there's no nose there. No one's going to look at it.'

'Can we at least change his hair colour.'

'What? His hair's perfect. He's got dark brown hair. If you made it black or slightly lighter brown it's not going to make any odds. The only way to make a difference would be to go blond – and again if he walks around with bleached blond hair it'll only draw attention to him, which is what you don't want.'

'I thought you said you were a master of disguise. Is this what you always advise – just doing nothing?'

'No, Lance mate, it's just him. If he had blond hair and a tan I'd be advising you to dye his hair a boring dark brown and give him pale, sweat-proof makeup. As it is, this man has almost no distinguishing features. He's got one of those faces that sort of looks a bit like every-one and a bit like no one. Even I'm wondering whether I've met him before – I mean, before this case. That face is a gift. His best chance of not being recognised is just to walk in as he is now, but in a suit.'

'False moustache?'

'Good idea. If the company's in Iraq. Otherwise he'll be the only person there with one. Plus they fall off.'

'Glasses?'

Plover looked again at Jonathon. 'All right, I'll let you do the glasses.'

'Great.'

'They won't make any difference though.'

Part Three

We Have Biscuits

Tuesday

75

Jonathon checked the watch he had synchronised with Lance's the night before. Ten minutes to eight. It was time.

He took a firmer hold of his briefcase, adjusted his fake glasses and stroked his fake moustache. They had decided to ignore Plover's advice about that.

And then he walked in. Empty, the lobby seemed to soar even higher, to flow to horizons yet more distant. Jonathon walked rather unrealistically towards the security barrier, the forged identity card gripped in his hand. The security guard – not Carl, he was relieved to see, but a genial, bald man in late middle age – bobbed closer.

'Good morning, sir,' said the guard, taking Jonathon's pass.

He studied it. Time stopped. Nothing in the universe moved. The planets ceased their restless orbit. The very air stilled.

At length the guard said, 'Thanks very much, sir,' handed back the pass and clicked the button on the turnstile. Jonathon walked through, making for the staircase beside the lift.

'Hold on, sir. Not so fast,' said the guard. He was holding up a clipboard and beckoning.

Jonathon walked back slowly on shaking legs.

'Michael Bartagharsley?' said the guard.

'Yes?' said Jonathon, trying to sound definite but accidentally adding a question mark.

'Etan Lajtha said to give him a bell when you arrive.'

'I'm, um, gots a work to do,' mumbled Jonathon, checking the time on the wrong wrist. *I'm gots a work to do?* If that was the best speaking he could manage, he should probably keep quiet for a bit, till he had himself under control.

'Good morning, Mr Lajtha,' said the guard into the phone on the desk beside the turnstile. 'Yes. Mr Bartagharsley's here… Exactly that.

233

Yes. Thanks, Mr Lajtha.'

The guard put down the phone and said, 'He'll be up in one minute.'

Jonathon nodded. The two of them stood there. The guard's pink face was not obviously unkind, and Jonathon had a sudden impulse to confess everything to him, to ask if he could just come back through the turnstile and go home. He restrained himself.

The guard said, 'See Arsenal–West Ham last night?'

'Ah,' said Jonathon regretfully, his football-bluffing instincts kicking in.

'Missed it?' asked the guard.

Jonathon nodded.

'Know the result?'

'No,' said Jonathon. 'Not yet.'

'Well, I don't want to spoil it for you.'

'No, that's fine. I don't mind.'

'Two-one, West Ham,' said the guard, with a pride that burst out around the edges of his official bearing.

Jonathon gave it his usual couple of seconds, as though considering, and then said, 'It was always going to happen.'

The guard grinned. 'Too true, mate.'

Jonathon decided to risk one of his six rote-learned football opinions.

'The trouble with Arsenal,' he said, 'is that they want to walk it into the net.'

The guard laughed. 'Too true. Now there's one problem with that, and its name is Mr Trevor Sinclair. Now I don't care who you are, when you see Sinclair take a touch and send it cross-field…'

'Ah, Michael Bartagharsley?' said a voice.

Did he know any football facts about Bartagharsley? *No, idiot, it's meant to be you.*

'Oh, um. Yes?'

He turned and saw a man with a thin face, blond hair and wire-framed glasses, like one of the four main types of Hollywood Nazi.

'Hi, Etan Lajtha,' said the man in an almost exactly American accent. 'Sorry to ambush you like this, but Kendrick Buttercorn reached out to apprise me that you're our new expert on the Japan approach to the automotive value chain. We've been pulling an all-nighter trying to get our pitch to Nissan Europe into shape. I would appreciate if I could walk you through it and hear your reaction with your Japan hat on.'

Etan smiled and began to turn, assuming Jonathon would agree.

234

'Ah,' said Jonathon. 'I… um, I'm stacked.' *Well done*, he thought. *That's what they say.* The football bluffing had obviously inspired him.

'It'll take two minutes, max,' said Etan.

'Michael,' corrected Jonathon, not wanting to be caught out.

'I meant "max" as in "maximum". Seriously. One minute, Michael.' Etan suddenly looked tired and irritable.

'Of course,' said Jonathon, buckling under the pressure. He agreed mainly to be helpful, and only secondarily to avoid making Etan suspicious. But as he followed Etan to the lift, he realised that he couldn't be helpful because he had no idea how to talk about automotive value chains with his Japan hat on, and that this would make Etan much more suspicious than continuing to claim that he was stacked.

'Pleasure talking to you, sir,' called the guard. 'Have a very good day.'

'Thanks, I will,' said Jonathon. 'You too.'

The lift doors closed behind him.

76

Lance, who had arrived at six to secure a parking spot, checked his watch and was horrified. There was a scratch on the glass, right over the words 'Vacheron Constantin'. How had that happened? He would have to get it polished, though – depending on how today went – he might have to put that off until he got out of prison.

It was one minute to eight o'clock, and thus time to stop leaning against the getaway car, Cary-Grantishly smoking a cigarette, and instead begin a daring data heist. If all went to plan, he would be back out here in half an hour, sitting at the wheel of the car, laptop at the ready. He ground out his cigarette and moved smoothly into action.

He walked through the revolving door without slowing and strolled across the huge lobby, swinging his briefcase, making for the receptionist with the largest smile.

'Good morning, sir. How may I help you?' said the receptionist, swishing her hair.

'Hi. I've got an eight fifteen with Rhiannon Henley.'

'And your name is?'

'Ferman, Lance Ferman.'

'Lovely,' she said, giving him another big smile. 'Here's your guest pass. If you could just take a seat, I'll let Rhiannon know you're here. She'll be down to collect you shortly.'

'Great,' he said. 'Shortly's my favourite way of being collected.'

'Mine too,' she said, blushing and knocking over a stapler.

Lance was just limbering up for the prodigious feats of flirting he might be called upon to perform in the course of the mission.

77

For Carl it was hate at first sight. He walked into the lobby and was seized by a wild yearning to punch the man in the face as hard as he possibly could. Unbidden, the words surged into his mind: *I want to give that fucker a right crack in gob.*

The man was sitting in one of the big blue sofas near the reception desk, one arm trailing casually along the seat back, the other brushing a speck of dust from his trousers.

Even at this distance, Carl could tell that the man's jacket and trousers were not the kind you could buy in any shop Carl went in. He was somehow wearing a spring morning in a French village. This made Carl angry.

And where to start with his hair? He had a hairstyle instead of a haircut. No clippers had been involved. The place probably didn't even put a price in its window.

Carl had been in London for two years now: long enough to have almost forgotten the phrase *soft southern ponce*. But here, unquestionably, was one – the sort of man who goes to a gym that offers manicures.

Carl was halfway across the lobby when Alison, his favourite, came out from behind the reception desk with a coffee for the southern ponce. She giggled at something he said, smoothed her skirt over her hips and flicked her hair about.

Alison had never brought anyone a coffee before. Carl hadn't even known there was a machine. *And what's this ponce said to make her giggle?* He doubted it was possible to tell a whole joke that quickly.

Carl had to force himself not to walk up to the man and punch him in the head. But getting this job had been hard, and he didn't want to lose it. So he headed for the security barrier.

'Morning, Carl,' said Jim.

'Morning.'

They stood for a while, side by side.

'See that bloke over there?' said Carl.

'What? Yeah. What about him?'

'Right ponce, he is.'

'Suppose so. Probably don't do him no harm with the ladies. See Arsenal–West Ham last night?'

'Keep your eye on him. I'm going basement, to finish me round.'

At that moment the lift arrived. A temp got out and walked through the barrier, over to the southern ponce. He shook her hand and said something that made her giggle. *Where did he get so many short jokes from? How had he memorised them all?*

And now they were walking this way. Carl, fully back under control, gave the southern ponce his best parade-ground stare, the sort that could knock a man over. But the southern ponce only flicked his eyes over the very top of Carl's head, showed Jim his guest pass and said, 'Nice day for it.'

To Carl's fury, both the temp and Jim laughed at this. *So that's his game!* He wasn't even saying jokes, just normal things that didn't quite make sense, in a voice that made them sound like they might be jokes. And people let him get away with it.

Carl saw the temp press the button for the fourth floor, and decided to follow them upstairs. Who knew what the ponce might be up to?

But before he had taken two steps, he heard Jim say, 'I'm sorry, sir, we already have a Mr Bartagharsley inside. I'll have to ask you to come this way.' Then, 'Carl! Could you mind the barrier for me?'

It was going to be one of those days.

78

The temp showed Lance into a small meeting room with glass windows. Rhiannon jumped guiltily in the act of closing the last of the blinds.

'Lance, ha ha ha,' she said, advancing on him with an outstretched hand. He remembered that she was one of those people who feel that saying the word 'ha' in a jolly way is exactly equivalent to laughing, and that laughter is the best way of setting people at ease.

Lance shook her hand.

'Rhiannon, ha ha ha ha!' he said, going one better.

His role in the plan required him to keep this meeting going, come what may, until he got a text from Jonathon. He didn't know when that might be.

'Please take a seat, ha ha,' she said.

The suppressed erotic charge was perhaps even stronger today than when they'd exchanged business cards in the coffee area the week before.

'Have you offered Lance a drink, Nicci?'

'Oh, no, I…' said Nicci.

Rhiannon gave Nicci a threatening smile.

'I am sorry, Lance, ha ha,' said Rhiannon. 'How unwelcoming of us, ha ha ha. Would you like coffee, tea, water?'

Lance jumped at this chance to add some precious extra seconds to the meeting – both now and when the drink arrived.

'A black coffee, please. I've got a bit of a tummy upset today, and I always find coffee settles it.'

He hoped this lie would help him leave in a hurry later.

'Oh. Nothing contagious, I hope! Ha ha ha.'

'It should be fine as long as our tummies don't touch,' said Lance.

Rhiannon seemed both delighted and flustered by this idea. She laughed, went red in the face, and then, seeing Nicci still lurking by the door, shooed her out.

'Milk or sugar?' asked Nicci, standing outside the room and speaking through a crack in the door.

'Just milk please,' said Lance, enjoying once again Nicci's confusion, glimpsed as the door closed.

'So,' said Rhiannon, 'we meet again, ha ha ha.'

'Yes,' said Lance. 'It was Thursday wasn't it, when we last met?'

'Yes. No, Wednesday.'

'Wednesday?'

'Yes, Wednesday. Ha ha ha.'

'Ha ha ha.'

This was going almost miraculously well. The longer they could spend naming days of the week and pretending to laugh, the easier it would be.

Unfortunately, the very next thing Rhiannon said was, 'So, ha ha, you wanted to talk to me about…?'

'Yes, thanks for agreeing to this meeting at such short notice.'

Lance wasn't going to fall into the trap of saying what he wanted to talk about.

'Not at all, ha ha,' said Rhiannon. 'It's an intriguing... er, opportunity.'

'Thanks. And when it comes to the size of this opportunity, well the sky's the limit. Year one, I project sixty per cent, minimum.'

'Sixty per cent?' asked Rhiannon. For a second Lance thought she might be about to ask what he was talking about. But then she said, 'That's big.'

His instinct had been right. Years of sitting in meetings had made Rhiannon very comfortable talking about vague, undefined abstractions that she didn't understand.

'That's right,' said Lance. 'And we expect that to grow both incrementally and exponentially over a three- to five-year period.'

'That's significant growth,' breathed Rhiannon.

'And there's a potentially tumescent role for you in this,' said Lance, instinctively pushing for a little less sense and a little more sex.

'Well, I have critical experience in roles that are highly relevant to this undertaking.'

'That's great,' said Lance, wondering how relevant her experience could be to something he hadn't explained and which didn't exist. 'Could you elaborate a little?'

'Well,' said Rhiannon, 'I have a strategic oversight role within the enterprise currently, with an absolute focus on KPIs, ensuring timely delivery and delivering stakeholder value 24/7 going forward. That includes significant exposure,' and here she leaned forward a little, 'to B2B initiatives, both inter- and intra-enterprise.'

For a second Lance was stunned into silence. He was in the presence of a master. He felt suddenly that Rhiannon deserved her well-paid job attending meetings if this was the sort of thing she could pull out of the air at a moment's notice.

But Lance was determined not to be outdone.

'Our aspiration for this venture is for it to move beyond enterprise into a whole new sphere that we're calling "extrasocietal". It collapses boundaries between business and non-business, being and non-being, and ultimately transcends notions of form, scale and coherence. In that sense it is a radical reimagining of reality.'

Lance sat back. Had he peaked too early?

Rhiannon fanned herself lightly with one hand as Lance's black coffee with milk arrived. He had made it through minute four. When would Jonathon's text come?

'… thus hinges on the fulcrum of capability maturity viewed from within the prism of the competitivity standpoint,' finished Etan.

Jonathon was in a first-floor room which smelled of men who had been drinking coffee and typing all night. Beside him was a man called Kasabian with wild hair and wilder eyes. And, despite Jonathon's protests that he really was stacked, Etan had just spoken for four and a half minutes about automotive value chains. This had blown a neat hole in the heist's schedule, painstakingly planned by Jonathon and Lance in the pub the night before.

Kasabian clapped slowly and sincerely. '*Very* strong,' he said, shaking his head as though awed by the power of Etan's argument.

Etan looked at Jonathon. 'So what do you think?' he said.

Jonathon nodded slowly, reeling at the idea of anyone being able to think anything about the stream of words he had just heard.

Etan raised an eyebrow, and Jonathon realised he was going to have to do more than slow nodding. His life and the wellbeing of a large proportion of the people he cared for depended on him somehow extending his football conversation skills into business. *What do they say, apart from being stacked?*

'Well,' said Jonathon, 'viewed from within the prism of my Japan hat, I'd say this adds some serious value.'

Etan restrained a proud smile. 'But would you add anything, to really cover off the Japan angle? I mean, do you perceive any downsides?'

Jonathon thought for a while, pensively nodding his head to hide any panicky twitching he might otherwise have done. He would have liked to borrow and adapt some of the words from Etan's speech, but they had all just slid off his brain.

'Well,' said Jonathon, 'the trouble with Japan is that it just wants to walk the car into the automotive value chain.'

Etan stared at Jonathon. Then he and Kasabian exchanged glances.

'My God,' said Etan, 'that is *so true*. So, do you see the problem as one of overcapacity?'

Jonathon gave it a couple of seconds and then said, 'It was always going to happen.'

'That is so right. But there's an answer to that, right? And its name is second-generation inventory-management systems. Now I don't care who you are, when you see...'

Jonathon pulled a regretful face and looked at his watch. 'Guys, I have to shoot,' he said. 'I am *stacked*.'

'Hey, thanks for your time,' said Etan. 'I've got to say, you really do know your stuff. Colour me impressed.'

He hurried down the stairs to the basement, badly behind schedule. Lance would be waiting for the coded text message telling him Jonathon was in place.

In the basement, he scooted into the men's toilets and bolted the cubicle door behind him. His first objective was attained. Had Lance succeeded in keeping his meeting about nothing going this long? Jonathon sent the text that should trigger the next part of the plan: 'yo bro awesome lol.'

Jonathon's phone vibrated disappointedly.

'MESSAGE SEND FAIL,' it reported.

Jonathon tried again, with the same result. Then he realised the first flaw in their plan: his phone had no signal in the basement. There were three texts he needed to send Lance at various stages in the operation, and he would have to make the hazardous journey upstairs for every single one of them. The only way to tell Lance that he was in place and ready was to be not in place and therefore not ready.

Again, a small voice in his mind asked if there wasn't just a way of apologising and going home. But of course there wasn't. Or rather there was, but it wouldn't solve anything. He could text Lance the abort code – 'yo dude thats totally rad' – and they would both probably get out. But then Todd Stuckers would destroy Albatross, ruin Gus's life, stymie Piper professionally and then come and, if Lance was to be believed, kill Jonathon. And it would all be Jonathon's fault.

He checked the room was clear, then set out for the stairs.

80

Rhiannon's upper lip was dewed with sweat, her eyes sparkled and her cheeks glowed. She breathed in little gasps. Lance had maintained his description of the undefined and non-existent thing for a heroically long time now. In fact, he had entered a sort of tantric trance, where the words just flowed out of him.

'The climax of this project,' Lance was saying in a soft voice, blowing erotically on his coffee, 'will be a state of profound realisation, in which companies simultaneously experience oblivion and total sensation – and understand that these are not opposites, but the same thing. We're calling this—'

RURR-RURR-RURR, his phone vibrated, breaking the trance.

He checked it. Finally, the text. Time to swing into action.

'You're calling this what?' breathed Rhiannon.

'Hmm?' said Lance absently, putting his phone away.

'What are you calling it?'

'Oh, something.'

'I *need* to know.'

'Er, Business…' he said, running through the next steps of the plan in his mind, '… Infinity… Point Zero?'

'Wow. *Business Infinity Point Zero*. This is the most exciting venture I have ever heard of. Please tell me more.'

Had he gone too far? He needed to lower the temperature a bit so that he could get out of the room and move on to the next stage of their plan.

'It's a, er, website,' he said. 'Did I mention that?'

She looked disappointed.

'Listen,' said Lance, patting his midriff and wincing, 'you know that stomach upset I mentioned earlier?'

'Oh, yes?'

'Well, I'm afraid it's come back. I really need to…'

'To…?'

'Use the bathroom.'

'Oh.' Her smile was gone.

'I'd better take this,' he said, picking up his briefcase. 'It's got my medication in.'

'Can't you just take the medication with you?'

'There's a lot of different kinds.'

He backed towards the door and opened it. They both did a yink.

'Well,' she said, 'see you… soon. Ha ha.'

'Definitely. Ha ha ha.'

Lance closed the door behind him and made his way through the open-plan working area to the carpeted section at the end, where there was an oil painting of what looked like a moist yellow penis.

There was also a fire alarm.

Todd clacked a coffee pouch into the machine, rubbed his eyes and leaned back in his chair. Henry stood beside him, PalmPilot at the ready.

'Okay,' said Todd, 'this is why I cleared out my schedule to deal with the takeover. Everyone thinks I'm out of the office till after tomorrow's press event?'

Henry nodded.

'So, yeah,' said Todd, 'if Sir Philip Rose wants to try some last-minute negotiation, bring it on. What does he want?'

'He's claiming our proposal undervalues the long-range earnings potential of classic British properties such as ah… something called *Jaffa Cakes*, and *Mini Cheddars*. Also, he claims the deal excludes packaged exotic nuts.'

'So this is just price stuff. He's still okay with an all-share deal?'

'That would be affirmatory.'

'Then this stuff is detail. I mean, I will push that fucker hard on it – I don't want him thinking he can get away with this kind of last-minute bullshit.'

'Sure.' Henry made a note.

'But basically, once we've done this deal, we will be unstoppable. Biscuits is a major part of the UK economy – I mean, we're talking ten billion pounds in flour factories, egg works, chocolate hubs, custard processing units – plus logistics, offices, you name it. Cut the staff, strip out the assets, sell them off, book it as income – that'll keep our quarterly growth at fifteen per cent for a long time. And if our growth figure stays high, so does our share price. We can move on with the plan, take over more companies – put ourselves so far ahead of the game that no one can ever catch us.'

Todd put his feet up on the desk, took a sip of coffee and massaged his temples with his fingertips.

'You want a masseuse?' asked Henry.

'What? No. I got to stay sharp. After tomorrow, with this deal signed and announced, we're golden.'

'Golden,' said Henry, making a note on his PalmPilot.

'You know, I feel like life keeps pitching them – the spy stuff, that whole Chesborough thing – and I keep hitting them out the fucking park. I mean, I am CEO. And I totally crushed that spy situation. That is *dealt* with.'

'You think maybe you'll take a vacation? After tomorrow, I mean.'

'What, and leave you in charge? That what you're thinking? You'd like that, huh?'

'That's not what… No. I was just saying—'

'Well, we'll see. Right now, get me Biscuits on the phone. Tell Phil Rose it's urgent.'

Henry hurried out of the office. A few seconds later the phone on Todd's desk rang.

'Yes?' said Todd. 'Phil. Hi. Phil, I've got one question for you: do you think I'm a fucking idiot? Are you *trying* to insult me?'

82

Jonathon, on his way back down the stairs, suddenly leapt a foot into the air. The fire alarm had suddenly turned the air into noise.

BRRRRRRRRRRRRRRRRRRR, it went, and at the same time, *EEEEEEEEEEEEEEEE*.

How had Lance managed to set it off so quickly? Jonathon suddenly regretted not telling him that his phone didn't work in the basement. But then they had no code for that. It was another flaw in their plan.

'Attention please,' said a voice in the air. 'This is a safety announcement to all colleagues. The fire alarm has been activated. A drill is not in progress. Would all colleagues please leave the building immediately. All personal belongings and effects are not to be collected prior to responding to this announcement.'

Jonathon knew he only had the length of time it would take everyone to rebelliously collect their personal belongings and effects before the corridors filled up with people moving in the opposite direction.

He ran through the noise, pushed through the fire doors, turned right, tripped, saw every door on the corridor open almost simultaneously, stumbled to the toilet door and then – just as everyone emerged into the corridor, loaded down with coats, laptops and papers – he slipped inside and disappeared into the nearest cubicle.

BRRRRRRRRRRRRRRRRRRR, went the alarm. *EEEEEEE*.

He closed the toilet lid and climbed onto it, squatting down so that no one would see his head or his feet.

The toilet door opened, and the sound from outside rushed in louder. A woman's voice, Essex-sounding, called, 'Fire warden. Anyone in there?'

'Ooh, listen to you: *fire warden*,' said a voice from outside, someone about Jonathon's age.

'But I am,' said the Essex woman. And then, as the door closed, 'What am I meant to say?'

He didn't hear the reply, but he did hear the woman loudly say, 'So why does it say "fire warden" on my tabard?' And that set off a shriek of laughter and young voices mockingly repeating the word 'tabard' as they receded down the corridor.

When the voices had gone, Jonathon cautiously left his perch and eased open the door to the corridor, where Carl was standing.

83

After Lance had set off the fire alarm, there had been a moment of silence. And then it felt like someone had thrown a bucket of sound over him, so that he stood there soaked in the stuff.

Now Lance needed to get downstairs and out of the building. He calmly trotted down the stairs, people streaming out all around him. He merged with the crowd, moving at exactly the same pace. They were on the ground floor now, where the higher ceiling somehow made the noise of the alarms more bearable. The security barriers were all open. Lance sailed through, out of the main door and into the comfort of his rented BMW, his ears still ringing.

He couldn't get over how easy all this was. Why wasn't everyone pulling audacious data heists? The only real downside to them was the cost of the parking.

He settled back to wait for Jonathon's next coded text message.

At the sight of Carl, Jonathon froze, barely breathing. Carl, his back to Jonathon, was covering one ear and bellowing into his walkie-talkie over the shriek of the alarm.

'C5381 to Control. Sector Minus One is code E. Proceeding to Sector Zero. Over.'

The person he was talking to must have said something, because Carl added, 'C5381 to Control. I've got a hunch that someone's up to no good. Proceeding to Sector Zero. Over.'

At that, Jonathon hurriedly withdrew back to the toilet lid.

After two minutes, he decided that Sector Zero must be somewhere other than this toilet. Again, he crept stealthily to the door, hesitated, then pulled it open. The corridor was empty.

Along the corridor, turn left – still no Carl – and into the DSD.

There was something eerie about seeing the room empty, without even a single Blount in it. Jonathon walked nervously over to Alan Handler's computer.

Looking at the Post-it note stuck to the monitor, Jonathon was surprised to see that it had changed. It no longer said 'Mallard1938', but instead 'Bittern1937'. He pressed a key to wake the computer, then typed in Alan's name and the new password.

Jonathon opened his briefcase and took out the Zip drive, contributed by Lance, though he wouldn't say why he happened to have it. There was something pleasingly futuristic and chunky about it, with its exciting grooves, its little rubber feet, and the fact that – according to Lance – a single Zip disk had the same capacity as between ten and a thousand floppy disks.

Jonathon plugged the drive into the big rectangular port on the back of Alan's computer. Then he unfolded the ten-step Easy Installation Guide.

'Shit,' he said.

He should have turned the computer off first. This was exactly the time when he least wanted computer problems. The fire brigade was probably here already.

Jonathon breathed deeply. *One step at a time.* First shut down Windows 95: 'Start', 'Shut down', 'Shut down'. The computer began the customary crisis they suffered in this situation, fretting about some things that had stopped responding. He eased it through its panic until it told him it was safe to turn it off.

Jonathon reattached the Zip drive. He was already on step six. *Perhaps I'll get to step eight before the firemen appear and I'm arrested*, he thought. Then, *Can firemen arrest people?* He turned the computer on and watched as it laboriously fretted itself back into wakefulness, mumbling to itself about some caches it was checking.

After some hard thinking and an acre of time, the computer showed him a grey box and Jonathon entered the username and password again. He waited.

He was in. There was only a little more waiting to do as the computer dealt out the icons on its screen. Now he was at step nine. He inserted a floppy disk, ran the 'Guest' program, and waited while the computer chugged away. Finally, it said, *'Congratulations! Your Zip drive is now mounted and ready to use.'*

He clicked on 'My Computer'. There it was: that familiar feeling of shock and betrayal as he realised that the computer had entirely failed to do what it was meant to do. The Zip drive was nowhere to be seen.

He should leave now, while he could. It was, after all, better to get out without any data than not get out at all. Instead, he took up the Easy Installation Guide once more and feverishly scanned it for anything he might have missed.

There it was! In step six, an embarrassingly clear instruction to make sure he turned on the Zip drive after turning on the computer, but before it began its start-up sequence. As far as he could work out, this gave him a window of roughly half a second to attach the power cable.

A minute later, once the computer had shut down, he was lying under the desk, poised over a long power strip, the Zip drive's adaptor in his hand. He reached up to the desk, pushed the computer's 'on' button and, as soon as it made its little electronic twitching noise, pushed the drive's adaptor into the power strip. He climbed back into the chair and stared at his watch, his leg jiggling with apprehension.

Again the grey box, the password, the waiting. Running the 'Guest' program, checking 'My Computer'.

This time it was there. He could barely believe it.

'Zip drive (G:),' it said, as though it were the most natural thing in the world. This was, by some measures, the third thing that had gone right that morning. Perhaps the plan could be salvaged after all.

Now all he had to do was log in to the Internal folder of the Accounts shared drive, and copy as much of it as he could onto the pleasingly chunky Zip disks.

He clicked on the Internal folder.

A grey box appeared, saying, '*Please enter username and password*.'

Jonathon had rehearsed this moment a thousand times in his imagination. He typed 'todd_stuckers' and 'Marmaduke021280' with a shaking hand.

'*Access denied. Error 4302. Check your password and try again. Attempt(s) remaining: 2.*'

He entered the password again, using one finger and watching carefully to see that he was pressing the right keys: 'Marmaduke021280'.

Again the 'access denied' message appeared.

'*Attempt(s) remaining: 1.*'

Jonathon clutched his ears in horror. 'No,' he pleaded softly. 'Please let me in. Please.'

Todd Stuckers had changed his password.

This seemed such an insultingly obvious and simple thing to go wrong that Jonathon immediately regretted everything he had done that day. It had all been for nothing – the early morning, the fear, the deceit, the hiding – because this central and essential part of the plan had been doomed from the outset.

He had one chance to try another password. But which one?

Alan had changed his password from 'Mallard1938' to 'Bittern1937'. Both passwords followed the same pattern – the train's name and the year it was built. Jonathon's passwords also followed a pattern: the name of one of his favourite Edwardian illustrators and a number corresponding to the size of their moustache. Maybe Todd had a pattern too.

Todd's old password was Marmaduke, which was, Lance had said, his son's name. The numbers must be his date of birth. Was there anyone else who might be as important to Todd? Did he have a daughter? Jonathon didn't know. There was only one other person Jonathon knew of who Todd seemed to like: Livia.

And of course he knew her birthday: that Thursday three weeks ago when he had bid her happy Christmas. It had been the twenty-sixth of February. But what year was she born in?

How had he got himself into a situation where, in order to have even the most microscopic chance of saving his own life and protecting the people he cared about, he had to correctly guess the age of a female executive?

85

Todd sat on the back seat of a Farynx Mercedes. It had been brought out of the garage so he didn't have to mix with the employees who covered the pavements all around.

'I thought I tasked you with de-meating this business,' Todd said to Henry, irritably.

'I'm progressing that,' said Henry. 'As you know, the whole of the seventh floor is vacated.'

'So how come there's still so many of them? I want this building sold in time to put it in our third-quarter earnings. And I don't see how you're going to get rid of that many people in time.'

'Ah, you know the number of people on the street here is not reflectionary of the number of employees. A lot of this building meat consists of temps and contract workers. All the admin staff are temps. The cleaning, facilities and security staff are on contract. They can be gone within a week, within a day.'

'You better give me a report by the end of the week telling me how we're going to get this building into our third-quarter earnings.'

'Absolutely. I will absolutely execute on that. It will be on your desk Friday.'

Todd grunted and carried on looking out of the window at the sea of people.

'Look at this bunch of mutants. Why can't they do what they're told? The announcement says leave your stuff, so what do they do? Drag out their cheap coats, cell phones... model trains.'

He glanced at the man with fluffy hair whom he had somehow neglected to fire on Friday.

'I left my stuff in there. Why can't they? If the building might be on fire, why would you stay an extra two minutes to go back to your desk and pick up your cell phone? I mean, I should be yelling at Phil Rose right now...'

A fireman pushed his way out through the revolving door, walking laboriously in his heavy equipment. He looked at someone in one of the fire trucks and gave a thumbs up. A moment later, the whoop of the siren inside the building died away.

86

'Come on, come on, come on,' muttered Jonathon to the computer.

The progress bar for saving to the last of the Zip disks stood at ninety-seven per cent, and had done now for almost a minute. This is what computers always do when they stop working. But it is also what they sometimes do when they are still working. If Jonathon didn't leave now, someone would find him there, and he really didn't want that to happen. But nor did he want to just abandon the ninety-seven per cent he had already saved to disk seven.

The alarm fell silent, and Jonathon's muttering suddenly sounded like a shout.

'Come on, COME ON, COME ON.'

He stopped. The silence seemed offensively and stupidly loud at first. And then his ears caught up with what was happening and were extremely grateful.

But the gratitude of his ears was a minor thing compared with the appalling tension generated by wanting a computer to do something faster than it wants to do it. Jonathon's whole being was as tense as the skin of a fine umbrella.

'Please, Lord,' he said to the ceiling, to the god who didn't exist but nonetheless constantly fucked with him. 'Please make it work.'

And then, divinely, the progress bar skipped on: ninety-eight, ninety-nine, one hundred. *Chug chug chug.* And finished. Jonathon laughed.

He thanked the ceiling, ejected the disk and put it in his briefcase, followed by the chunky blue drive with its adorable little rubber feet. Then he wiped the sweat off his face with a tissue, hurried through the door and ran along the corridor, making for the toilet.

He could already hear the voices of the returners. From the top of the stairs came the sound of the fire doors opening. People were coming. They would see that he had been there during the fire alarm, clearly up to no good. *Okay, stop running. Walk normally.*

Someone rounded the corner.

'Why don't you put it in your tabard?' the young man was saying.

The woman who had checked the toilet said, 'That's what it's bloody called, you dickwad.'

'Ooh, I'm busting for a tabard,' said someone else behind them,

'I'll just go to the tabard.'

Jonathon tried to make his face look like he was paying the people no attention, as though it was completely normal to be walking out of the basement after a fire alarm. *Be casual.* He casually stroked his moustache and almost screamed: it was gone. Now his only defence was the glasses, and anyone could see through them.

He tripped. *Forget the face, just stay upright*, he told himself. Luckily, the people he was pretending not to notice were genuinely not noticing him.

'Yeah, I drank a bit too much tabard this morning. I could do with a tabard too,' said one of them.

'Well I tabard tabard tabard tabard tabard the tabard tabard,' said another.

'Ben?' said the first man.

'What?'

'You always have to take it too far, don't you?'

They disappeared into the toilet, and the woman in the tabard went into the ladies' on the opposite side of the corridor.

They hadn't challenged him, and he was in among the crowd now – going the wrong way, but no longer obviously having been there throughout the fire alarm. The immediate danger was over. He pushed on, up the five steps, on to the landing. On to the longer flight of stairs. Make for the fire doors. Make for the surface. Make for the daylight. Step and step and step and step. Freedom drawing nearer. Step and step and step.

And then there he was. At the top of the steps. Past the lifts. The security barriers were ahead. Of the five sets of gates, four were being used for people getting into the building, with a security guard on each checking their passes. Only one was open for people going out, and there was already a short queue for it. The man checking passes was the pink-faced security guard who had let him in. Jonathon could not believe his luck.

He got out his phone and laboriously hammered out the code to Lance in many tiny key presses: 'awesome dude 4 realzz'. *I'm on my way out.*

Send.

He looked up, directly into the eyes of Todd Stuckers. It startled him so much that he knocked his glasses off.

87

Todd stared straight into the eyes of the spy, who turned and began pushing his way through the crowd, heading for the stairwell.

'There,' he said to Henry, pointing.

'What? Where?' said Henry.

All the security guards were on Todd's side of the barriers. There was no one to stop the spy disappearing back into the building. On the other hand, there was no one to know he had ever been in the building. If Todd left security out of this, he was free to do whatever he wanted to the spy – if he could catch him.

He called to the pink-faced security guard, 'Hey, get these people out of my way. I need to get in.'

'Let Mr Stuckers through, please, folks,' the security guard called. 'Please, move to the right. No, the right.'

The people queuing at the security barriers, waiting to get in, turned, recognised Todd, and tried to let him through. And Todd was getting through, though he was finding out that a dense crowd of people all trying to get out of the way is as difficult to traverse as a dense crowd of people all not trying to get out of the way.

Todd had to make sure he didn't fall too far behind, otherwise the spy could double back and get out while Todd was chasing up the wrong staircase.

'Tell security not to let anyone out,' said Todd to Henry.

88

With his streamlined body and inoffensive air, Jonathon was perhaps better adapted for politely pushing his way through dense crowds than for any other activity. He held his briefcase at shoulder height and – lubricated with a film of *sorry*s, *could I just*s, *excuse me*s and *oops can I*s – he poured himself through the mass like a glass of water through a shoal of herring.

As he set foot on the upward staircase, he glanced back and saw that Todd was wading through the security barrier, eyes fixed on him.

Jonathon ran up the stairs two at a time, dodging around the other people. On the first-floor landing he looked around. Where could he hide? The stairwell rang with the sound of Todd's footsteps – gaining on him. *Keep going*, he decided.

He passed the second floor. Very soon now he would need to cut through a floor and try to reach the other stairwell. The fourth was out of the question, because Livia or Victoria might see him.

He reached the third. Todd's steps were louder. It was now very likely he would be caught. He needed to hide the disks before that happened. Then there would still be a chance for someone to get the disks and perhaps save Piper, Gus and everyone else. And if he wasn't caught he could come back for the disks himself.

But where to hide them? The toilet? No, it would still be full of people returning from the fire alarm. Where did no one ever go? He thought of his moment of shame, after the 'Happy Christmas' debacle. *The knowledge-management area.* He rushed through the fire doors, past a watery picture of Big Ben, through the next fire doors, slowing so as not to attract attention, then turned right and opened the door to the room of unread brochures.

In its still, chill air he looked wildly around for a hiding place. He opened the large, blank-faced cupboards, but their long metal shelves were completely empty: useless for hiding things in.

And then he had it: on the top left-hand shelf was a brochure with a title so boring that he could not even think it. When he tried to read it, the words just fell straight back out of his eyes. Even the letters of the words were somehow boring.

Jonathon took the disks from his briefcase and dropped them down behind the row of copies, between them and the wall.

He fumbled with his phone. There was no code for what he had to say.

'Lance?'

'JJ-Cool-J. Where are you? I'm in the car with the engine running.'

'Don't call me JJ-Cool-J. Listen, I think I'm about to be caught. I've hidden the disks behind the brochures on the top left-hand shelf of the third-floor knowledge-management area. It's just beside the door from the right-hand stairwell. If I'm not out in ten minutes you'll have to find a way to come in and get them.'

'You've what the what now?' said Lance.

Jonathon didn't have time. He ended the call, grabbed his now-empty briefcase and hurried out.

He glanced through the glass of the two sets of fire doors. His heart was already stamping violently against the wall of his chest, even before he saw Todd running up the last few stairs.

Jonathon turned back, into the third-floor work area. He broke into a run, hoping he looked like he was late for a meeting.

He ran through rolling swathes of hot-desking pastureland, past the lifts and the reception booth, past the coffee area and breakout rooms, through more hot-desking and past the other knowledge-management area. He banged open the far fire door, ran through the carpeted area and stopped before the stairwell door, just in time to see Todd's friend, the one who had given the threatening pep-talk, running up the stairs.

Jonathon looked back through the fire door behind him. Todd, walking fast and purposefully, had just reached the lifts. Jonathon was trapped.

From the toilet behind him he could hear loud, confident voices saying the word 'optimisation' a lot.

He pushed back through the fire door and ducked into the second knowledge-management area. It was an eerily exact copy of the one in which he had hidden the disks. He opened the doors of the blank-faced cupboard, climbed in beneath the lowest of its four metal shelves, empty briefcase still in hand, and pulled the door closed behind him with his fingertips.

89

'… I can show you where. Be in the lobby in five minutes,' finished Lance, and hung up.

He had tried Rhiannon first, but Nicci told him she had fainted just before the fire alarm went off, and had been taken home. So Livia it was.

Three minutes later, he strode into the lobby. Livia was already there. She signed a new guest pass and led him through the security barrier, to the right-hand stairwell.

'So, Mr Ferman,' said Livia, 'exactly where are we going?'

Lance didn't answer, mainly to conceal how out of breath walking upstairs was making him. He led her up to the third floor, through the fire doors, past a painting of a brick penis with a clock on it, through the other fire doors, and turned right.

'In here,' he said, indicating the knowledge-management area.

Livia did a little double-take, as though seeing it for the first time. Lance led her inside and began taking brochures off the shelves and feeling around behind them.

'This is what I was talking about,' he said, withdrawing a handful of the pleasingly chunky Zip disks.

90

Jonathon lay still in the dark. His fingertips hurt from gripping the edge of the steel door. His whole body was a gigantic subwoofer unit for amplifying the sound of his heart beating.

He heard the door open. An American voice, speaking quietly, said, 'That's a negative from me on a stair intercept, Todd.'

Jonathon carried on trying to breathe as little as possible, hoping that his heart really was quieter than it sounded in his ears.

'Well, I saw him run into this floor,' said Todd. 'If he didn't pass you, he must have reached the stairs before you and gone up.'

'But you're sure security should not be alerted?'

'No. They'll want to get the cops involved. And I want to kill him. Jonathon Fairfax must be destroyed. This is our chance to deal with him without anyone knowing.'

Jonathon's breath stopped. He felt he was slowly suffocating himself in this metal tomb.

'Todd. Is that the optimum move? Is it possible others are apprised of his current location?'

'We'll find out. First we make him talk, then we figure out a way to kill him.'

Keep breathing. Don't think about being trapped in a tiny dark space right next to a man who wants to kill you. Keep breathing. But quietly.

'Sure. I mean…'

'Don't get soft on me, Henry.'

'Todd, I am stone.'

'Right. Here's what we're going to do. I'll take the nearest staircase. You take the furthest. We go up one floor, sweep it, ask a few discreet questions, pick up our cell phones and then swap staircases. And we'll ask security if they stopped him on the front gate yet. Then we keep on up like that, floor at a time, sweeping and swapping staircases, trying to drive him up to the seventh, where we can do whatever we want. Okay?'

'Okay.'

'Right, now go, go, go.'

The footsteps moved towards the door.

DADDLE-A-DADDLE-A-DADDLE-A-DOO. DABBLE-DABBLE DAA-DAA, DABBLE-DABBLE DAA-DAA. DADDLE...

Jonathon scrabbled in his pocket and pressed the button, but it was too late. The door to his hiding place had been ripped open and large hands were hauling him roughly out by his collar and hair.

91

'Hi Bob,' said Lance. 'I've got the material, so I'll bring it straight back for analysis.'

Lance said it in a steady, businesslike voice, for Livia's benefit, because he was really calling Jonathon. Keeping up the voice was going to be quite difficult though, because of what he could hear on the other end of the line.

Bang. Crumpf.

The fucking spy! It's the fucking spy!

Ow! Um, sorry.

How should we process him?

'Will do,' said Lance to his imaginary interlocutor. 'Is the lab clear?'

Yark! That's my leg. Could you...? Ow!

Henry, you go find one of those supplies trollies the facilities people have. We'll take him to the seventh floor.

Ung! That's my...

But what about shouts and other verbal presence-markers, Todd?

Unconscious guys can't shout, Henry.

He's not...

Bang. Umf.

'Great,' said Lance.

You were saying?

Nothing.

'About twenty minutes,' said Lance, giving Livia a thumbs up. 'Depends on the traffic.'

And now he had to decide whether to take the disks and get out, or risk everything by telling Livia a lie that would take them to the seventh floor.

92

Jonathon woke, safe and warm in bed, from the deepest sleep of his life. He felt as though he had been shut down and rebooted. The ceiling looked odd, he noticed. But that would be because he was in his new bedroom, which had a blue wall on the ceiling.

What? he thought, suddenly hearing what his brain was saying to itself.

He was facing a blue wall. And he was sitting up, not lying in bed. He tried to turn over and go back to sleep, but neither his arm nor leg would move properly. *Ah*, he thought, looking down, *I'm tied to a chair*. A supportive, mesh-seated swivel chair.

Jonathon looked around. To his left was a window showing a piece of grey sky and an office block. By the window, his phone and wallet lay next to a computer. To his right, a set of brushed-steel blinds covered the corridor window. In that corner stood a table with some stationery and a complimentary coffee tray on it. In short, he was tied to an executive chair in an executive meeting room.

Jonathon deduced that he must have been knocked out. He had never suspected it could be so relaxing. But now his body was just beginning to tell him that his jaw and the back of his neck were extremely painful. There was a shooting, throbbing ache in both.

'Todd, he's back,' said a voice.

'Turn him around.'

Someone swivelled the chair around to face the opposite direction. There was a white wall with a clock on it. His briefcase lay on a large meeting table that took up most of the room, with other luxurious swivel chairs clustered tightly around on both sides. In the corner, near the door, was a flip chart. Beside it was a cleaner's trolley. And looming inconveniently in front of it all was Todd Stuckers.

Todd stood with his very large arms crossed, displaying a set of jewelled cufflinks and one of those huge, chunky watches favoured by the rich and brutal.

'Glad you could join us,' said Todd.

'Oh, not at all. Thanks,' said Jonathon. *Is it weird to say that?* he wondered. *What are you meant to say?* His life really was just an unbroken succession of awkward social situations.

'Are you being smart with me? Can you believe this guy, Henry?' Todd asked his friend, who was standing beside Jonathon, massaging his fist.

'I can't believe him, Todd,' said his friend, Henry.

'I'm not being smart,' said Jonathon.

Todd stared into his eyes, evaluating his smartness.

'Okay,' said Todd. 'So then let's begin with the basics. What's your name?'

'Um, Jonathon Fairfax?' he hazarded.

Todd tensed his jaw.

'You still think you can get away with that, huh? Well, until you decide to tell us your real name, you're Maggot. What's your name?'

'Oh, Maggot,' said Jonathon eagerly, relieved to have an easy question.

Jonathon could hear his accent convert it from a humiliating American insult into an English surname of perfectly standard middle-class absurdity, probably spelled 'Margethwaite'. Henry laughed and Todd's eyes started forward in their sockets.

'I warned you about being smart. Seems like you both need to learn that this situation is serious,' said Todd.

'Um, *I* know it's serious,' said Jonathon, but he sounded like an overeager pupil sucking up to a teacher. Henry laughed again.

'Okay, that's it,' said Todd. 'Cut his ear off.'

'What?' said Henry.

'You heard me. You want to be a tough guy? Cut his ear off.'

'But what…?' asked Henry.

'Oh right, you think you're a natural like me but you can't even cut off a guy's ear in a meeting room?'

'Sure I can, but…' Henry looked helplessly around the room.

Todd pulled Jonathon's tie off and crumpled it into a ball.

'Put this in his mouth so no one hears him.' Todd put the tie in Henry's hand. 'And use this to keep his mouth shut.' He handed Henry a roll of Sellotape. 'That'll stop him getting smart.'

'I'm not getting smart,' said Jonathon. 'I'm just awkward. Some people think I'm slightly autistic, but I'm not – just really, really awkward. It's probably because of my childhood or something. We moved around a lot. My parents divorced. I had asthma. But I'll answer any questions, honestly.'

'Just awkward, huh? Just the world's only socially awkward corporate spy?'

'I'm not a spy.'

Todd tensed his jaw again. 'That is disappointing, hearing you say that. I thought maybe we were getting somewhere, Jonathon.'

'Maggot,' corrected Jonathon, automatically. And again, there it was, as though he were Mr Margethwaite of The Aspens, Kenilworth Gardens, Bognor Regis.

Todd took a ruler from the stationery tray and tested it on his finger.

'Could be sharper,' he said. 'In fact, it's totally blunt. I guess it could take a little time to saw through an ear with this. You'll just have to be patient with us.'

'There's really no need,' said Jonathon.

Todd's anger ratcheted up a notch. 'Oh, *there's really no need*, is there?' he said in a terrifying falsetto that Jonathon guessed was meant to sound like an English accent. '*Oh, pass me my cup of tea your majesty while I ride my croquet pony to the palace, because there's really no need* to CHOP MY FUCKING EAR OFF!'

'But I'll tell you the truth,' said Jonathon.

'Great,' said Todd, with a sudden icy self-control. 'So then tell us you're a spy.'

'I'm a spy,' obliged Jonathon.

'And who do you work for?'

'Ah technically I suppose I'm now an employee of Farynx but then my contract says Albatross on it but then today's the first time I've spied and no one's asked me to do it and it's all a mistake.'

Todd looked from Jonathon to Henry. 'Sounded to me like about five different stories came out there all at the same time.'

'No, it's all the same answer—'

'Are you arguing with me?'

'Um, in a way, but only to—'

'Okay, we're going right back to the ear-chopping plan,' said Todd.

He squeezed the sides of Jonathon's mouth, forcing it open, while Henry pushed the tie in. And then Todd's hands held his jaw closed while Henry wound the tape over his lips. It was very definitely the weirdest thing that had ever happened to Jonathon.

Henry took Jonathon's right ear in his hand and began sawing at where it was joined to his head. It hurt incredibly, like a rope burn that just kept on happening.

'How's that ear coming?' asked Todd, impatiently.

'Uh, this may be a little time-intensive.'

'I have an idea that's a little more immediate. Break his little finger.'

'What? How?'

Todd pushed Henry aside, grabbed the little finger of Jonathon's right hand in his powerful fist, then pushed the palm down and the finger up. There was a sickening *click* and a jolt of pain shot up Jonathon's right arm.

'Like that,' said Todd. 'You do the other one.'

Jonathon tried to signal with his eyes that this was unnecessary. Nonetheless, much more slowly and ineptly than Todd had, Henry broke Jonathon's other little finger.

'Okay,' said Todd, 'and now we get back to the ear project.'

Henry picked up the ruler and got back to work. Jonathon tried to keep his eyes fixed on a point on the far wall, as though he were at the dentist's, as the hot pain began again in his ear.

'Once that's done, I think he'll be ready to tell us what he knows,' said Todd.

Henry grunted and bent to his work.

And then there was the sound of the door opening and Lance's voice saying suavely, 'Is there anything I can do to help?'

93

Lance had expected Jonathon to be slightly crumpled after being knocked out and transported upstairs in a cleaning trolley. He had not expected to find him patiently, and with an expression of offended regret, having his right ear sawn off with a ruler by a senior Farynx executive.

As Lance stepped into the room, Henry looked up from his work and frowned. Lance turned to Livia, who had followed him in. Her eyes were wide open. She stared at Jonathon, who reddened with embarrassment. He sat there with his little fingers sticking out from his hands at crazy angles, tape all over his face, and the end of a striped tie lolling from the corner of his mouth.

'*What* is going on here?' said Livia, very quietly.

Todd turned his gaze full on her.

'We caught the spy,' he said, his voice slow and serious. 'I know how this looks, but I will do whatever it takes to defend Farynx.'

Livia was silent for several seconds, looking into Todd's eyes. She glanced at Lance, then back to Jonathon. His ear was bright red, and a thin line of blood had trickled down to his jaw and dried.

'So it's true,' she said. 'Jonathon, how could you betray us like this?'

'That's exactly what we're trying to find out here,' said Todd.

Lance snapped his fingers. Everyone looked at him.

'Word of advice,' he said. 'Interrogation is quite a lot easier if you don't tape the subject's mouth shut.'

'Yeah?' said Henry. 'What the hell competency do you have in the interrogation space?'

'I'm the best interrogator you'll ever meet,' said Lance, as though revealing a simple truth. 'But surely you don't need an interrogator as unbelievably good as me to tell you that you won't get anywhere by trying to chop someone's ear off with items of office equipment.'

Henry looked meaningfully at Todd, but said nothing.

Todd said, 'The spy needed a little convincing that we were serious.'

'This guy is a professional,' said Lance, indicating Jonathon. 'All this little display does is convince him you're *not* serious.'

Todd said, 'What do you mean?'

'Well, leaving aside the ear thing, there's the fact that this place is not secure. Anyone could wander by.'

'There's nothing else on this floor,' said Henry. 'No one's going to wander by.'

'What about facilities people?' said Lance, throwing a glance at the coffee supplies on the corner table. 'What about cleaners and security guards? Do they *never* come here? It's probably going to take days to get this guy to crack. Years, if you do it.'

Todd and Henry exchanged glances.

'So what do you recommend?' asked Todd.

'Well,' said Lance, 'I know this guy. I'm the one who tracked him down.'

Livia said, 'He also found some data Jonathon was trying to steal.'

Lance held up his briefcase and said, 'Not so fast. We don't know yet whether he was trying to steal it, or trying to put it on your system. It could be some kind of virus.'

'Let's see that,' said Henry, taking a step towards him.

Lance strode past Henry, put the briefcase on the table, beside Jonathon's dowdier one, and flicked open the catches with a flourish.

'Here,' he said, fanning out seven Zip disks. 'I've booked time in our technology lab to analyse them. We'll be able to find out what he was planning to do.'

'They were hidden behind some brochures,' said Livia.

Jonathon frowned.

'Not so happy about that, is he?' said Todd.

'Nope,' said Lance, replacing the disks and closing the briefcase, which he kept his hand on.

Henry pushed past and made his way through the clutter of swivel chairs to a computer by the window. *Good sign*, thought Lance. *He's trying to distance himself from what's happening.*

'Here's what we're going to do,' said Lance. 'I'll smuggle him out of the building in this cleaner's trolley and take him to LPA's dedicated debriefing facility. We'll have him talking within twenty-four hours. Guaranteed.'

Lance pushed the trolley beside Jonathon and set to work on the knots that bound him to the chair.

RURR-RURR-RURR, went the muted phone in Lance's annoyingly full jacket pocket. He pressed a button to stop the noise, and went back to the knot on Jonathon's left wrist.

'That your phone?' asked Henry.

'It'll be the office,' said Lance, 'calling to tell me the facilities are ready.'

'I have a hunch you're about to receive a callback,' said Henry. 'In five, four, three, two, one…'

RURR-RURR-RURR.

Lance took the phone out and stopped the noise. He had a missed called from Jonathon, but he tried to look unruffled. *Everything is fine.* Todd turned to Henry, a questioning eyebrow raised.

'I did last number redial on the spy's cell phone,' said Henry. 'The last person he called was Mr Great Interrogator here, thirty minutes ago.'

Lance looked at Henry with a pained expression. '*Obviously* he called me. I've spent weeks getting him to trust me. How do you think I knew about the disks?'

'You've spent weeks?' said Todd. 'So you started before I asked you to work on the case?'

'Obviously I don't mean weeks,' said Lance. 'I mean *days*.'

He cast his eye around the room. Henry wasn't an immediate threat, as he was still in the corner by the window and would need to negotiate the swivel chairs to reach Lance. Todd was on the other side of Jonathon. And Livia was by the door, on the other side of the trolley.

Lance eyed the door and wondered whether he had the time and agility to leap to it, open it, grab Jonathon by the chair and then pull it with him to the lift before Todd, Henry and Livia could stop him.

No. That was the answer.

Just then the door opened.

94

Carl felt a surge of excitement run through him, like an attack dog let off the leash. Unlike an attack dog, he stepped into the room and said a simple, 'Good morning.'

It had been great, that moment peering through the gap between the blind and the window frame, when he had seen the body language in the room abruptly change. When the southern ponce – *Lance* – had visibly considered running. That was when Carl knew he had been right to suspect him.

Mr Stuckers took advantage of the distraction to grab the phone from Lance's hand. Then Stuckers looked around at Henry, the American to whom Carl had been reporting suspicious behaviour.

'What is this?' Stuckers said. 'Did you call, like, Dwarf Security?'

'No. But since he's here: arrest that man,' said Henry from the corner of the room, pointing at Lance.

Carl was delighted to be asked to do something that might involve punching Lance in the head. He resented the crack about his height, but he would take out that resentment on Lance. He stepped forward menacingly. Then, like an attack dog who has been on a day's seminar about its legal position, he stopped.

'I've got power to make a citizen's arrest but I need clear evidence he's committed a crime. Then I can take,' Carl cleared his throat, '*reasonable steps* to detain him until police arrive.'

'Just get him,' said Henry.

'Hi,' said the ponce, pushing a kid in a chair towards the white wall and grabbing the trolley. 'I'm Lance. Two things: one, you don't want to go to prison for assault; and two, did you hear what he said about Dwarf Security?'

Carl hesitated. Lance took off his jacket, carefully folded it, and pushed it down behind the kid's back. *What kind of bellend worries about his jacket at a time like this?* thought Carl.

Stuckers turned to Carl. 'What's your name?' he asked.

'Carl Barker.'

'Hey. I'm Todd, your boss. We don't need to get the police involved. In fact, we don't need to get you involved. But thank you so much for stopping by. So you just go on with your rounds, and I'll be along later with a *substantial* bonus for being so… vigilant.'

Lance, taking advantage of the distraction, grabbed a flip chart and moved the trolley to secure his right flank. He pushed the kid in the chair further up behind the table, jamming him against three other chairs to secure his left flank. Then he pulled the paper off the flip chart and held the stand like a spear, covering the ground in front of him.

Despite himself, Carl was impressed with the ponce's deployment. The move also drew Carl's attention to the state of the embarrassed-looking kid tied to the chair, with blood running down his ear and his little fingers sticking out at grotesque angles.

'Who did that?' Carl asked, indicating the kid.

'He did!' said Todd, pointing at Lance.

Lance made a gesture that took in his whole person, as though asking if he were capable of tying anyone to anything, much less breaking a finger. Carl would have respected Lance more if he had been that sort of person, and would have wanted to punch him in the face less. But no, Todd was clearly lying to him. Carl knew this even without the kid's frantic head-shaking.

'Did I mention that the bonus is a hundred grand?' asked Todd.

That decided it for Carl. For a thousand pounds he might have considered it. But a hundred thousand pounds was an amount of money that did not exist in his world. Anyone rich and powerful enough to offer it was almost certainly also mean and powerful enough not to pay it.

'A serious assault's been committed,' said Carl. 'I'll tell head of security and he'll report matter to police.'

Carl pulled his walkie-talkie from his lapel and Todd knocked it to the ground. Carl stooped to pick it up and Todd kicked him in the side of the face, throwing a cloud of silver stars in front of Carl's eyes and sending him staggering across the floor like a drunken crab.

Carl shook his head, which just about restored his vision, allowing him to see Todd stamp on his walkie-talkie, crushing it to plastic splinters. Behind him he heard a *chock*: the tanned woman had locked the meeting-room door and was standing in front of it. At that moment a heavy object hit him on the back of the head, sending him sprawling forward.

At Carl's feet lay a heavy beige desktop PC that could have killed him if it had not been hindered by the wires that connected it to the monitor, keyboard and power supply.

The position looked bad. On the other hand, Carl had been in worse situations on nights out in Doncaster.

He let instinct take over. Reaching to the corner table behind him, he grabbed a glass and threw it at Todd, forcing him to use the monitor as a shield instead of throwing it. With his other hand, Carl threw the jug of water in the woman's face. Then, while she was spluttering, he put out his leg and gave her a shove, deftly tripping her over.

'Throw us your spear!' Carl shouted to Lance.

After a split-second's hesitation, Lance threw the metal flip-chart stand over to Carl, who leapt onto the table, wielding it like a scythe so that Todd and Henry were forced to take cover among the swivel chairs.

Lance pushed the trolley over Livia, trapping her on the floor. He then sat on it, preventing her from getting up, while he reached for the door catch. Meanwhile the kid in the chair had, at the cost of a huge effort, managed to use his left hand, now only loosely tied, to pick up the remote control from the edge of the table. This was of very dubious benefit in this sudden, desperate and inexplicable fight, but at least he was doing something.

Todd broke cover, but Carl got in a good kick at his face. He knew it wasn't a good idea from a legal or career perspective, but it seemed to offer the best chance of immediate survival.

Chi-chick went the door as Lance unlocked it. Then Lance spun around on top of the trolley and dashed over to the kid in the chair, pulling it after him as he raced to put his weight back on the trolley before the tanned woman could rise.

Carl wielded the flip-chart stand, covering Lance. Todd and Henry attacked but the kid pressed a button. Distracted by the projector's blue start-up screen suddenly shining in their eyes, they went down like bowling pins.

The door was open and the kid was now in the corridor. But Todd grabbed the end of the flip-chart stand, trying to yank it from his grasp, and Henry was crawling under the table.

'Come on!' called Lance from the corridor. 'And get the briefcase!'

'Which one?' shouted Carl.

'The cool one.'

Carl released the flip-chart stand and Todd toppled over. Then Carl grabbed a briefcase and leapt over the trolley. But the woman's foot lashed out, tripping him, and Henry, emerging from under the table, grabbed his ankle.

Carl fell, dropping the briefcase. Lance was waiting for him at the door, ready to close it. Carl crawled desperately towards it, hoping Lance wouldn't shut him in.

'Get the briefcase!' said Lance again.

'Get your own chuffing briefcase!' shouted Carl.

He kicked against Henry's grip. It faltered, but then he felt the hands take a firmer hold. Carl grabbed the doorframe and pulled his body into the corridor. Henry pulled Carl's leg back.

Thud. Lance had slammed the door on Carl's leg, below the knee. The pain bit like a man-trap, clanging through Carl's shin bone.

'You dickhead,' he shouted at Lance.

'Just pull your leg through.'

Carl jammed his free leg against the doorframe and pulled at the other leg. His ankle flamed in pain and his foot slid unwillingly from its shoe, but then his foot was out and the door banged closed. He was free.

Lance pulled his whole weight against the door to stop it being opened. Carl got to his knees, shooed Lance out of the way, and pushed his shoulder up against the horizontal metal handle, preventing it from turning.

'Thanks,' said Lance.

Carl looked him in the eyes.

'That there is a victim of assault,' he said, pointing to the kid in the chair. 'Minute he's safe, I'm gonna punch your fucking face in. Right?'

Lance looked as though he was thinking up something smart, but instead he just said, 'Right.'

'Now get him out of here,' said Carl. 'I'll stop these as long as I can.'

Todd and Henry were banging on the door, shouting threats at him, pushing down on the handle. Lance wheeled the kid down the corridor at a run. The pressure from the door handle on Carl's shoulder was intense, but as long as he kept himself wedged against it, it wouldn't move.

The pressure on his shoulder suddenly disappeared.

'The handle's non-operative – it's snapped off!' said Henry's voice.

'Okay, listen up. Out of the way, people. I'll deal with this,' said Todd's voice.

At that moment, Lance appeared again at the far end of the corridor.

'We're holding the lift!' he shouted. 'Come on!'

There was a loud bang on the window behind Carl. He got to his feet and began running, ignoring the sickening pain in his ankle.

There was another bang behind him, this time followed by the soft *scoosh* of breaking safety glass. Footsteps pounded down the corridor.

Carl dashed past the floor's reception area. As he did so a huge fist of sound belted him one in the ears. He saw that Lance had set off the fire alarm with a stapler, and that the kid was sitting, still tied to his chair, on the threshold of the lift, preventing the doors closing. Lance reached the lift and pushed the kid inside, and Carl hurled himself towards the closing doors.

95

Jonathon watched as Carl leapt in slow motion through the closing lift doors. The guard's bullet-head hit him in the midriff, knocking the wind out of him.

'Oof,' he would have said, if someone hadn't Sellotaped his tie into his mouth.

On the positive side, the lift doors had now closed and the braying of the fire alarm was muted and distant.

'*The fire alarm has been activated,*' said the lift. '*This lift will return to the* GROUND *floor.*'

'Sos, mate,' said Carl, standing up. 'You all right?'

Jonathon could say nothing, but tried to forgive Carl with his eyebrows.

Lance checked his shirt was all right, then turned and tried to remove the Sellotape wrapped around Jonathon's mouth. After much effort, he managed to pull the tape down to chin level, allowing Jonathon to spit out some of the soggy tie.

'Wuh hlun u-fingull hake nuh…' began Jonathon. He spat out some more of the tie. 'How long do you think it'll take Todd and Henry to get down all those stairs?'

'Depends how fast they run,' said Carl.

'We need a plan for when the doors open,' said Lance.

'You what?' said Carl. 'We'll just tell other security guards what's happened. That were a serious assault. They'll call police.'

'What if Stuckers tells the guards we're lying. Who will they believe? What if he gets them to take us to a room, where we can be murdered? And who would the police believe anyway? I've been arrested before, Jonathon was fired from here last week and you're a northerner.'

'So what do you suggest then, Mr Know-It-All?'

'As soon as the doors open, you use your securityguardness to get us through the lobby as quickly as possible. I've got a car parked outside. We put Jonathon, chair and all, into the back seat and then head straight to the nearest police station to report this without needing to worry about being murdered by Todd Stuckers while we're doing it.'

Carl looked at Lance for a second.

'Right,' he said in a resigned voice.

And then the doors opened, and they saw ahead of them a sea of people all pushing their way through the open security barriers and out onto Arundel Street.

'Security!' called Carl. 'Coming through! Make way!'

96

Todd's momentum drove him on towards the lift doors. He slammed into them, tried to prise the shiny metal sheets apart with his fingertips, slapped the buttons next to them. But it was too late.

'I'll call the police,' shouted Livia over the scream of the fire alarm.

'No!' shouted Todd. 'No police! Not till we've got our story straight. Call security. Make them stop these guys leaving the building. At all costs. Fire alarm or no fire alarm.'

'I thought we didn't want security involved,' shouted Henry.

'We don't. But I don't want these guys leaving the building even more.'

Todd slammed through the first fire doors, slid over the carpet in his leather-soled shoes, slammed through the next set of fire doors. His hands were on the bannister rail, grabbing it and taking the whole flight of stairs in two big jumps. Henry struggled after him.

There in front of him, on the sixth floor, was a huge crowd of people, arms full of coats and PalmPilots, curling with unbelievable slowness down the stairs.

'Hey!' he shouted, pushing into the crowd. 'Out of the way! I got an emergency here!'

'Er, yes, it's called a *fire alarm*. We've all got it,' said a man nearer the fire doors, obviously not knowing who Todd was.

'Okay,' he shouted. 'Whoever said that is fired. The rest of you get the hell out of my way.'

He tried to grab the handrail and get down the next flight of stairs as he had the last, but there were too many people in front of him, holding the handrail and looking at him in surprise, instead of moving out of his way.

'Sorry,' said someone.

'Oops, do you want…?'

'Which way…?'

'What is wrong with you people?' screamed Todd.

A voice with some authority cut through. 'Everyone, this is our CEO, Mr Stuckers. Please move away from the inner handrail so he can get down.'

'The *inner* handrail?'

'He means move away from the wall.'

'No, move towards the wall.'

Todd pushed and jostled his way through the people who were now all trying to move in incompatible directions in front of him.

'Get out of the way you fuckheads!' he shouted.

Gradually people started to get the message. The number of people standing directly in front of him decreased. He accelerated as he went, though still hampered by the crowds.

Finally, he made it down the last few stairs to the ground floor. He could see the elevators, all four standing with their doors open, displays saying, 'OUT OF ORDER.'

Where were the three fugitives? He scanned the loaded, fleeing throng as he shoved his way through them, making for the security barriers. Surely the fugitives couldn't have got out of the building already?

Then he saw it: a hole in the crowd just big enough for a chair and a very short security guard. And there was Lance's hair.

'Hey! Security!' he shouted. 'Stop them!'

A pink-faced guard turned and said, 'Stop who, sir?'

'The dwarf, the kid in the chair and the handsome guy!'

The pink-faced security guard looked around blindly. Todd pushed through the barrier, towards the hole in the crowd, which was now at the lobby door.

'Is this him, sir?' called the pink-faced security guard, holding a passable-looking man by the arm.

'No, over by the door, jagweed! They're getting out!'

There were two guards near the door. Todd shouted and waved to them frantically. They started to push their way through the crowd towards him.

'Not towards me, you fucking goons! Get the guy in the chair going out the door!'

But it was too late. As Todd continued to wade through the treacly crowd, he saw Lance, on the other side of the street, open a car door. Then Lance and the short security guard manhandled the kid and his chair into the back seat, slipping and struggling, as Todd fought his way towards the street.

Todd spilled out onto the pavement. He started running. The passenger door slammed shut. The car reversed two feet. Todd was a single pace away. And then the car curved out, beeping its horn to clear people from the street. Todd ran behind it until it turned the corner, slotted dangerously into the space behind a speeding taxi, and accelerated, its horn still blaring.

97

The top of Jonathon's head was pressed uncomfortably against the car's door panel. He was crammed on the back seat, still largely tied to the chair. Something was digging into his back. His little fingers were loudly telling him there was something very seriously wrong with them. And his ear burned. But what hurt most was having left the briefcase full of disks – their only chance, and a horribly slim one at that – in the meeting room.

On the other hand, they were free, stuck in a sunny traffic jam beside a park on Theobald's Road. The relief and pain bickered with each other, like Lance and Carl in the front seat.

'There's a fella in back of car seriously injured,' Carl was saying. 'He needs urgent medical treatment.'

'I'm all right,' said Jonathon, working at the knots on his right wrist.

Lance said, 'But there won't be anything to treat if we don't get to the police and tell them our side of the story before Stuckers does.'

'He's probably talking to them right now, dickhead. First priority is force protection. "If in doubt, ensure welfare of members of your unit first."'

'I can wait,' said Jonathon.

'Didn't someone say, "The first priority is attack"?' said Lance.

'No,' said Carl.

'It sounds like someone said it,' said Lance.

'They didn't.'

'That's what we should do though.'

'Bollocks we should. What you talking about, you?'

'The first thing we should do is take the disks to someone who can use them. Then we go to the police, then hospital.'

Jonathon said, 'But we haven't got the disks. We left them in the meeting room.'

Lance turned and said, 'We left *some* disks in the meeting room. The ones you hid are in my jacket. It's still wedged behind you, isn't it?'

'Are the disks what's digging into my back?'

'I hope so.'

Jonathon's brain flipped like a pancake. They had their horribly slim chance back.

'What...' he began. And then, 'But... how?'

'I brought some other disks in with me. And then on the way up to the seventh floor I put your disks in my jacket, even though it meant ruining the line of it. I had a feeling they would want me to hand them over, so I gave them the wrong disks.'

Carl said, 'So I lost my chuffing shoe trying to get wrong disks?'

'Yes,' said Lance. 'I didn't want them to suspect. Also, that was a Conrad Andersen briefcase. And I didn't want to lose the other disks.'

'What was on them?' asked Jonathon.

'Nothing,' said Lance.

'What, they're blank?'

'Sort of. Don't worry about it.'

'You need a right crack in gob,' concluded Carl.

98

Piper sat at her computer in the large bay window where her desk was stationed. She was doing Albatross's accounts and wondering whether there was any point in this if the company had been subsumed by evil.

Her dad had failed to come up with any brilliant ideas overnight, and was now shut up in his office with a hollow look in his eyes. And, because of all the bickering and tension in the office, he had told everyone, quietly and firmly, to go home. She had never seen him like this before. It was frightening.

What would he do, without his company? And what would she do, if Todd did his best to ensure that she never worked again? She was trying not to think about it, but was secretly pleased that she might have to give up on being an accountant. It had always been a very mixed blessing, having a talent for something lucrative, stable and in demand, but which she didn't much like. Perhaps Todd would so effectively close off all her career options that she could just sit and embroider, without that feeling of guilt that she should be doing something more sensible. The rabbit she was currently working on lay locked in her top drawer, for after she'd finished the accounts.

The 'quote of the day' she'd been emailed that morning was, 'Find what you love and do it for the rest of your life.' Instead, Piper had locked what she loved in a drawer until she'd finished all the stuff she didn't love but nonetheless felt she had to do.

She looked out of the window and thought about how hopeful she had been for her future, two years ago, before university finished. What had happened to her confidence? Why wasn't she showing off her midriff and wearing combat trousers, like everyone else, instead of saying 'goodness' and embroidering rabbits?

In the street below, a black car drew up. It looked smart, but there was a set of castors in its back window. In the passenger seat was a man who looked like being strong might be his job. And from the driver's side emerged another man, who resembled an early 1960s imagining of what the captain of a moon rocket would look like: all cheekbones and fringe. Then she recognised him as the man from yesterday. Lance, that was his name, as though his mother had known that he would turn out looking like the captain of a moon rocket.

The rocket man was carrying a badly creased jacket and seemed somehow lackadaisical and determined at the same time. The buzzer sounded.

'Hello, Albatross?' she said, in her best professional voice.

'Hi, I've come to save your company.'

'Oh, come on up.'

Tzzz.

A minute later Lance was standing in front of her desk. She stood up to greet him, breathing in and glad she was wearing her green dress. He was not her type, but she nevertheless felt obliged to be as good-looking as possible in his company.

'Good morning,' she said.

'Good morning,' he said.

'How can I help you?' she asked.

'I don't know,' he said, reaching into the crumpled jacket's pockets and taking out some unusually chunky disks. 'But I can help *you* by giving these high-capacity disks to Augustus Palgrave.'

'High-capacity,' she repeated. 'Goodness. Are they Zip disks?'

Lance gave her a look. 'Is he in?'

'Yes, let me get him for you. Would you like a seat? Coffee?'

'I would like a coffee more than almost anything else in the world.'

'Our machine's broken. Is instant all right?'

'No,' said Lance cheerfully, sitting down.

'Right,' she said, dithering. Her legs wanted to take her to the kitchen to somehow make him a non-instant coffee, but her upper body wanted to fetch her dad and find out what was going on. The upper body won. And after all, what could be less like an instant coffee than one that never arrives at all?

Two minutes later, she was conducting Lance into Gus's office.

'Piper said something about high-capacity disks, and something else about saving the company,' said Gus, looking over at Piper. She was standing in the doorway, too curious to leave. Gus met her eye meaningfully, but didn't say anything.

'Yes. I have in my hand some Zip disks—'

'Are those the ones that can hold the equivalent of ten floppy disks?'

'A hundred,' said Piper. 'Sorry, I don't know why I know that.'

'Something like that,' said Lance. 'But listen, I don't have much time—'

'Sorry.'

'As I have to take Jonathon to hospital and then go and report a crime—'

'What, *our* Jonathon?' said Gus.

'What?' said Piper.

'Yes. Did I mention I don't have much time? I—'

'I do apologise.'

'Sorry.'

'No problem. The point is, Jonathon got into Farynx and copied their real accounts on to these disks, though he got his little fingers broken and his ear partially sawn off in the process—'

Piper gasped. She had never believed gasping was real, but now it had happened to her: out of nowhere her body had suddenly decided it needed to take in a colossal lungful of air as noisily as possible.

'Is he all right?' she asked.

'He's fine – he's designed for sawing and breaking. But the point is that you now have Farynx's accounts.'

99

Lance had been driving for a long time now. Jonathon was sitting in the back seat looking tired, with a pained expression on his face and occasionally glancing at his oddly splayed little fingers.

Their inability to find a hospital in one of the largest cities on earth was now manifest. From Albatross's offices, they had followed signs to Moorfields Eye Hospital, reasoning that there would be at least a token non-eye facility, and further reasoning that any doctors who could fix something as complex as an eye could surely deal with something as straightforward as a finger bone. Their reasoning, however, had turned out to be faulty.

Lance had been away from London for a year, and had forgotten much about it, including a great deal of painfully acquired knowledge of its one-way systems. He had no map, had never been to a hospital in London, and was sharing a car with a stoical ex-soldier and a man who didn't want to bother anyone. In other words, they were perhaps the three people in London with the least knowledge concerning the whereabouts of its hospitals.

Lance's plan was to drive on large, easy roads until he saw a big 'H' symbol appear on the signposts, and then follow that. Since then, they had followed many 'H' symbols, but not one had produced a hospital.

Still, Lance pursued the plan. It was the only one they had.

That was why, almost an hour after leaving Albatross's offices in Clerkenwell, they pulled in at Whipps Cross Hospital, nearly ten miles away.

They got out and began the hunt for the Accident and Emergency department. The signs suggested a way, disappeared, reappeared, and eventually deposited them outside, at the bottom of a staircase in an alleyway in the rain. After that, they spent a long time discovering that the 'A&E' signs were actually pointing to the large 'Urgent Care Centre' which they had already hurried past three times.

Inside, they queued up for a ticket to stand in a queue, which, after fifteen minutes, resulted in Jonathon being given a ticket for the real queue. Then they sat in a windowless room, waiting for Jonathon's name or number to appear on the display that beeped or possibly the other one that didn't beep, or possibly to be called by a nurse.

After twenty minutes of this, Lance realised it was going to take a very long time indeed for someone to do anything about Jonathon's fingers.

'I'm going to the police station,' he said.

Jonathon gave a pained nod. Carl gave a slight flicker of the eyelids that might have indicated that he had heard.

'Will you stay with Jonathon?' Lance asked Carl.

'Is he Jonathon?' Carl asked.

'You still don't know his name?'

'It's not my job to know people's names.'

'Okay. But will you?'

Carl nodded.

'I don't need anyone to stay with me,' said Jonathon. 'All I'm doing is sitting down waiting for a beep, or not a beep, or a shout.'

'Okay then,' said Lance. 'I'm going to the police.'

'A word outside,' said Carl.

Lance nodded and walked outside, into the wasteland of old hospital buildings, cluttered with Portakabins, odd extensions, old signs and a slight drizzle. He turned and Carl punched him in the face.

'Fuck,' said Lance.

'I told you,' said Carl, and walked back inside.

'Gus,' said Todd into the phone, 'I am going to end you. Your company is over, your life is over, the lives of all your employees are over. None of you will ever have a job or money or anything good happen to you ever again. And Jonathon Fairfax will be destroyed.'

'Ah—'

'Shut up. I can only assume that is what you wanted, and that is why you sent your spies back here the day after I made you a very generous offer. Well guess what? Your spies may have gotten away, but I have the disks.'

'Ah, now I can explain—'

'Shut up. I've got something to attend to this week, but from next week on, I'll be making ruining your life one of my top priorities – and I have the resources to do a *very* thorough job.'

'Oh, but you see, it was—'

'Shut up. And goodbye, Gus. Next time I see you, you'll be begging on the street. Maybe I'll throw you a dime.'

Todd put the phone down.

There was a knock at the door and Henry marched in. Todd was back in his temporary office on the fourth floor.

'Chip Balenciago is in transit to the airport,' said Henry. 'He'll arrive by morning, and will commence analysis of these encrypted disks. We should be apprised of the material they were trying to steal or upload by early afternoon. And I have engaged a real US detective agency to find Ferman and Fairfax, or whatever their real names are, and keep Albatross under surveillance.'

'Great. Shame the police here know I'm associated with them and that I have a motive to kill them. Probably lucky they got away, or right about now I would have two dead bodies on my hands – not what I need before the big event tomorrow. But I guess we have plenty of time to work out how to kill them.'

'Okay,' said Lance. 'I've filled in the form. Now what do I do?'

He was standing in a sort of glass compartment in the closest police station to Whipps Cross Hospital. It was more a police room than a police station: a former shop on Walthamstow High Street, with a police sign above the door. Inside, there was a small corridor with a receptionist's window at one end. The receptionist controlled access to the glass compartment, where you could stand while you talked to the same receptionist again through a different window. Lance handed over the form he had filled in.

She took the form from him and said, kindly but in one of those accents that makes each syllable sound like it has tripped over the last one and fallen flat on its face, 'What is the nature of the offence?'

'I told you when we talked at the other window,' said Lance. 'And I've written it down on this form.'

'Yeah, but I got to fill in this computer screen now, innit?'

Lance took a deep breath. It had all seemed so simple in the lift after the fight: they just had to get out of Farynx, deliver the disks, get Jonathon's hands fixed and go to the police. He had imagined rejoicing at Albatross, then a team of dedicated but wisecracking medics rushing Jonathon along hospital corridors on a gurney, if that was what it was called, and then a couple of tough cops asking tough questions before jumping in the car with him and taking him off to arrest Todd and Henry. But things are rarely as simple and satisfying as you imagine, and almost always involve much more admin.

'The nature of the offence was assaulty. I want to report an assault or grievous bodily harm—'

'Which one?'

'I don't know the difference. It was—'

'Someone punched you in the face, yeah?'

'No, that was… That's something else.' Lance put delicate fingers to the swelling under his eye. 'I'm not the main person who was assaulted. That's Jonathon Fairfax, but he's in A&E. I've already written all this down on the form.'

She picked up the form and glanced at it, then let it fall back to the desk.

'And how were you assaulted by this John Fellfax?'

'I wasn't. He was assaulted by Todd Stuckers.'

'Todd…?'

'Stuckers.'

'How are you spelling that?'

It was going to be a long afternoon.

102

'Mr Stuckers, you do not have to say anything. But it may harm your defence if you do not mention, when questioned, something which you rely on in court. Anything you do say can be given in evidence. Do you understand?'

Todd nodded. 'Sure,' he said.

The policeman, who looked to Todd like a mid-level business analyst with half the money sucked out of him, adjusted his paisley tie and ran a hand through his gelled hair. It was dark outside and the narrow windows of the houses opposite, above Tiffany's and Gismondi, were lit up gold.

'The caution's purely a formality, you understand, Mr Stuckers. It's because certain counter-allegations have been made by… er, certain parties. Thanks very much, by the way, for making the time for this informal chat.'

'No problem. Happy to oblige.'

The policeman smiled nervously at Todd and his lawyers. There was Nicholas Hoy Tooth, a man with white hair, half-moon glasses and sharp teeth. Beside him was Camilla Parr Longrigg, with her grey hair, pastel jacket and a nose she had borrowed from a hawk.

The lawyers tolerated each other in a slightly theatrical way, like a pair of cats. They sat side by side on a large green sofa in the sitting room of Todd's suite at Brown's Hotel. Todd sat in a matching green armchair to their right. The policeman was on a smaller floral armchair near the window, with a spare policeman sitting on a nearby stool.

The policeman wiped the palm of his hand on his trouser leg, and took up his pen again.

'Could you, er, run us through the events of this morning, Mr Stuckers?'

Nicholas Hoy Tooth intervened. 'Our client has provided a full written statement of the events.'

'Yes, great. But it would be helpful just to hear it,' said the policeman.

'It's fine,' said Todd to the lawyer.

The policeman smiled again, and flipped to a fresh page in his notebook.

'So,' said Todd, 'we've been having a little spying problem – corporate espionage, you might call it. A temp in our recruitment team, Jonathon Fairfax, turns out to be an employee of Albatross—'

'9a Garnault Place, EC1R,' said Camilla Parr Longrigg.

'Right. Thank you, Camilla. And he's reporting on us to this other company. So we fire him. But yesterday this Fairfax guy pretends to be a different employee, and he gets into our offices. We have videotape evidence of him in the lobby, wearing a fake moustache and glasses, and in certain corridors in the basement. So we know he went into our Data Services Department during a fire alarm, set off by this other guy, Lance Ferman.'

'Employed until recently by the American broadcaster MTV,' said Nicholas Hoy Tooth.

'Right. Thank you, Nicholas. Now as I'm coming back into the building after the fire alarm, I spot this Fairfax guy, and you better believe I chase him. But I can't find him. Now Ferman has left the building during the fire alarm – again, we have the video footage. But he comes back in afterwards. He has called Ms Cavendish here and told her that he knows where this spy has stashed some data he stole from us—'

'Obviously this would be a crime under the Computer Misuse Act of 1990,' said Nicholas Hoy Tooth.

'Right. Thanks, Nicholas.'

'And what was this data?' asked the policeman.

'We have a specialist coming to analyse it, but we don't yet know,' said Todd. 'Ferman takes Livia to a knowledge-management area on the fourth floor—'

'A knowledge-management area?' asked the policeman.

'What we might call a very small library,' said Camilla Parr Longrigg.

'Right. Thanks, Camilla,' said Todd. 'So, he takes Ms Cavendish to this knowledge-management area and he extracts a device and some disks. Now we have been paying this guy to track down our spy, right, so Ms Cavendish trusts him when he says he needs to take the disks back to his office to analyse them.'

'He claimed to own an "investigative solutions agency" called LPA, of which he was an employee until five years ago,' said Nicholas Hoy

Tooth.

'Right. Thanks, Nicholas. He makes a call and then he changes his mind and says he needs to go upstairs, to meet me on the seventh floor. So he goes upstairs, and there's a meeting room up there. Who's in there? A security guard working on a short-term contract for us named Carl Barker, and this guy Jonathon Fairfax—'

'Was anyone else present?'

'No, just Carl Barker, Jonathon Fairfax, Lance Ferman and Ms Cavendish. Now, Jonathon Fairfax is tied to an office chair, he has tape around his mouth and a couple of his fingers appear to be broken. When Ms Cavendish arrives, Barker pushes her to the ground, and Ferman pushes a cleaning-supplies trolley on top of her so she can't get up.'

'A cleaning trolley,' said the policeman, making a note.

'Yes,' said Todd. 'I forgot to say that, after chasing Fairfax, Henry and I grew suspicious that he had tampered with this trolley in some way on the fourth floor – bugged it maybe – so we pushed it up to the empty office on the seventh floor, where it couldn't do any harm.'

'I see,' said the policeman, making a note. 'And what happened next?'

'They smash the room up and leave. Then they set off the fire alarm, take the elevator down to the first floor—'

'What we would call the *ground floor*,' said Camilla Parr Longrigg.

'Right. Thanks, Camilla. They push this Fairfax guy through the lobby and out the building, put him in a car and take off. Now Livia gets out from under this trolley and finds me—'

'Where were you at this point?' asked the policeman.

'On the stairs just below the seventh floor, talking to Henry.'

'So how did you react?' asked the policeman.

'I was pretty mad—'

'What we would call *angry*,' said Nicholas Hoy Tooth.

'Right. Thanks, Nicholas. I ran down those stairs to try to stop these guys, but they had set off the fire alarm so I couldn't get past all the folks in the stairwell. I was just too late. Saw the car take off.'

'And do you have any idea why these people may have acted as they did?' asked the policeman.

'Well, the way I read it, they stole our data and attempted to get away with it by saying that we assaulted them.'

'I see,' said the policeman. 'And is there anything else you think I ought to know, Mr Stuckers?'

'Not that I can think of right now. As you can imagine, I have found these allegations deeply—'

RURR-RURR-RURR.

Todd looked down at his phone. There was a text from Henry saying, 'Acquisition finalised. We have Biscuits.'

Todd had won.

103

'Thank you, Jonathon and Lance,' intoned Gus sadly, 'but I'm afraid your heroic effort and your sacrifice have been in vain. The situation is quite hopeless.'

This was a dispiriting thing for Jonathon to hear, especially after the day he'd just had. It was midnight, and they were sitting in Albatross's office, where Lance had brought Jonathon after his fingers had been splinted. They had all drawn up chairs in the main office space, around the computer Piper had used to look at the data from the Zip disks.

'How can it be hopeless?' asked Lance. 'We have Farynx's secret accounts. And Piper's just explained Todd's scheme. I mean, I still don't get it—'

'How can you not understand it?' asked Piper, putting her hands to her cheeks in horror. It was exactly the pose an Edwardian illustrator would have chosen, which naturally appealed to Jonathon.

Lance shrugged. Piper stared at him. She seemed tired, and her beautifully drawn eyes were getting the sad look that Jonathon wanted to find a way to erase. After spending hours working out what Farynx's data meant, Piper had just spent another half an hour explaining it to them. Jonathon now saw her understanding of the financial system as a deeply attractive quality, a marvel equal to the existence of her arms.

'I'm not a detail person,' said Lance. 'Can you leave all the details out?'

'If I leave all the details out, all that's left is a sort of low moan,' she said. 'You understand it, don't you? Dad? Jonathon?'

She looked desperately from one to the other. Jonathon tried to nod knowledgeably, but the guitar had started up and they were sitting in a tree, watching the sunset...

'Okay,' said Piper, shutting down his montage with a wave of her hand. 'The accounts show that Todd's selling Farynx's buildings and things and pretending that's normal income, so it looks like the company's growing at fifteen per cent a year, when really it's losing money. Then he's using mark-to-market accounting to make it look like Farynx still has huge assets. And then he's paying his auditors so much for other services that they're letting him get away with it all.'

'Yada yada something assets something,' paraphrased Lance.

'It's dangerous and illegal,' said Piper.

'*That's* what I was looking for,' said Lance. 'So if the world knew about it, Farynx would be finished. These accounts are lethal.'

'They should be lethal,' said Gus, 'but unfortunately we have been quite unable to do anything with them. I have talked to journalists at all the major newspapers, and none of them is interested. After all, we can't prove we got the accounts from Farynx. And the papers are worried about losing advertising and being sued – everyone knows Farynx has deep pockets.'

'Which is really annoying,' said Piper, 'because the accounts show that Farynx doesn't have any pockets at all. It's not even wearing real trousers.'

'Fake trousers: that's a story right there,' said Lance. 'We should have no problem getting this out.'

'But if none of the newspapers will print it, what can we do?' said Gus. 'They all know Farynx is the most successful company in the world. They think anything which contradicts that must be wrong.'

'It's a scoop,' said Lance. 'I'll call people tomorrow.'

'But tomorrow's too late anyway,' said Piper.

'Why?'

'Because Farynx is taking over United Biscuits tomorrow. The event's in' – she checked her watch – 'twelve hours – that's when they're announcing it and formally signing the deal.'

'What difference will that make?' asked Lance.

Her eyes expanded a little, as though they were on the point of bursting. 'Were you not listening to this bit either, when I explained it?' she asked quietly.

'I was *listening*,' said Lance patiently. 'I just didn't take any of it in.'

She glanced at Jonathon, who gave her an encouraging smile.

'Right,' she said, holding her head with her hands, exactly as Tenniel would have drawn her. 'The whole reason Todd's plan works is because Farynx always hits its earnings targets. For a bit it looked like they wouldn't manage that for next quarter, because they didn't have enough big assets to sell. But then they managed to do the deal to buy United Biscuits.'

'Is it really that big a deal?' asked Lance.

'I'd imagine so,' said Gus. 'Biscuits are the backbone of the British economy.'

Piper said, 'It's true. They account for two per cent of our gross domestic product. Sorry, I don't know why I know that. Anyway, everyone's obsessed with internet companies at the moment. All the non-internet companies are really unfashionable, and there's nothing less internet than a biscuit. So United Biscuits' share price has sunk really low – and they have a huge amount of assets that could be sold off: transport depots, box factories, chocolate-chipping plants. So Todd's buying their really cheap shares with his really expensive shares. After this deal, Farynx will look even more successful, its shares will be worth even more, and it can buy more huge companies. One day it'll have swallowed so many companies that it might even start making a genuine profit.'

'But surely Todd's scheme – whatever it is – can't just keep working forever,' said Lance.

Piper looked sad – either because of Lance's repeated failure to grasp her explanations of Todd's scheme, or because they were all going to be destroyed.

She said, 'It'll keep working till either someone stops it or Farynx swallows the world economy.'

'The situation is quite hopeless,' said Gus.

'It's not hopeless,' said Lance. 'There must be something we can do. We just need to think.'

'I can't think any more,' said Piper, resting her face on the desk. 'I'm too tired. I've explained the plan too many times.'

'If only we were more like Todd,' said Jonathon. 'Then we could just tell everyone we'd already destroyed Farynx and they'd believe us.'

'What did you say?' said Piper, lifting her face. Hope crept into her eyes. It took a long time: they were big eyes.

Wednesday

104

Todd stepped onto the stage, into the spotlight. The crowd rose to its feet, applauding. He raised his hands above his head. His brain felt lit up, as though it had been plugged into a higher-capacity power source. Pleasure coursed through his whole body.

Beyond the stage, a dark mass of people stretched back – three hundred journalists, shareholders and investment professionals, subtly sketched in by the lighting. The glint of a glasses lens, the gleam of a poised pen, the flash of a polished shoe, and everywhere energetically clapping hands.

Standing in the centre of the stage, Todd lowered his hands, smiling: time to start calming it down.

David Evans, the event's host, was standing at a small lectern at one side of the stage. He leaned into his microphone.

'Mr Stuckers will now say a few words.'

An assistant passed Todd a cordless microphone.

'Thanks, David,' said Todd. 'Hey, big hand for Bloomberg TV's David Evans. We're lucky to have him here. You got time off for this, David?'

There was more applause. Evans leaned into his microphone again and said, 'Wouldn't have missed it for the world, Todd.'

Todd chuckled into his microphone, then turned on his serious face. 'This is a very exciting day for me. I am proud to say that Farynx Global Limited is acquiring United Biscuits PLC in an all-share deal worth seven point four billion pounds, equivalent to around eleven point nine billion dollars. This deal is a testament to the great vision of its CEO and Chairman, Sir Philip Rose. So please join with me in welcoming Sir Philip to the stage.'

A second spotlight lit up a silver-haired man in a navy suit, hurrying purposefully from the other side of the platform. He arrived beside Todd and made a short, dull speech which Todd entirely edited out of his consciousness.

After the speech and the applause, the two men clasped hands. The lighting was adjusted subtly, fading down while a small spotlight added its glow to their handshake.

'We will now take questions from the floor,' said David Evans.

The lights on the walls were faded up halfway. Hands raised. David Evans looked out into the crowd and pointed to a nearby hand.

'Lady there on the front row.'

'Mr Stuckers, what would you say to people who talk about a "Curse of Farynx"?'

Todd smiled. 'At this point, I think we can safely say that the "Curse of Farynx" has lifted.' There was laughter, which he silenced with a wave of his hand. 'But seriously, we had two incredibly sad deaths. You know, we lost two incredibly talented colleagues. But that's life. It throws accidents at you. And I think it's a testament to the quality of the company we built that neither of those tragic losses drove down the stock price.'

Todd looked over to David Evans, who pointed to another questioner.

'Yes, gentleman there on the second table.'

A nearby assistant hurried in with a microphone.

'Hello,' said a loud, nasal voice, 'Ambrish Dont, *Business Insider* magazine. Maybe we could have some colour on how the deal came together. So maybe, "Why now?" is the question?'

'Great question, Ambrish,' said Todd, and sleepwalked his way through a prepared answer. He ended, 'So, Ambrish, I guess you could say the real question is, "Why the hell *not* now?"'

There were another couple of questions in this vein, and then Evans said, 'Yes, gentleman over by the door.'

'Um, ah, hello. Is this turned…? Oh right, like this. I'd like to ask um… a question?'

'Yes, go right ahead. That's why I pointed at you,' said Evans. 'Begin with your name please.'

Todd had frozen. He knew this voice. He looked out into the crowd where a small spotlight had alighted on a thin young man.

Todd felt the blood boiling up in his body while it simultaneously drained from his face, giving him a burning, sweaty sensation around his neck. It was the spy. That face. That face with no real distinguishing features. And his hand with its splinted fingers, which he had held up to get Evans' attention, was still in the air, as though carelessly forgotten. He had a plaster stuck over one ear.

'I'm um Alan Sample, from Banquo Investments.'

'And what's your question?'

'I'd like to ask about the illiquid risk-return profile of the stock and in particular whether it has a two-notch positive spread in terms of contrapuntal exogenous capital outflows within tightly delineated floor value constraints going forward.'

Todd stared at him. The question was gibberish. What was going on? Was he imagining this? Why was this man not in hiding? Was this part of some new plan?

Most of the crowd were continuing to do their serious business faces, but a few exchanged quizzical glances. And then Todd realised that those glances were because he was standing there silent in the middle of the stage, jaw clenched. His heart was pounding in his chest. He pictured himself leaping into the crowd and throttling the kid.

'Hey. Great question,' managed Todd. He ground his teeth and glanced at Evans to step in.

David Evans laughed. 'That question's perhaps a little... technical, so let's come back to that later. Er, yes. The young lady standing up there.'

The microphone was passed to a young woman with large eyes and chestnut hair.

Where's Henry? wondered Todd, looking around. *Can he grab the spy?* Todd didn't want to lose him again.

'Hello. I'm, um, Wanda Plinge, from a magazine called *Financial Intelligencer*. I've got a question for Mr Stuckers. Mr Stuckers, I was wondering why Farynx's New York share price has fallen fourteen dollars in the last few minutes?'

A perfect silence rippled out across the large room, stilling it.

Todd, still distracted by seeing the spy again, took a moment to replay the woman's question in his mind. Why was she making out the share price had fallen?

'Ah, that is just not true, uh, ma'am,' said Todd, glancing over to check whether the spy was still there. Henry was unobtrusively making his way around the edge of the room to him. 'Where are you getting your information?'

'I've got WAP on my phone,' she said. 'Wireless Application Protocol – sorry, I don't know why I know that. Anyway, it's like a little internet for phones, so I can see the stock prices live. The price has fallen on the London Stock Exchange too.'

People were starting to mutter to each other now. Had someone said the word 'sell' or was that just his imagination? He needed to squash this.

'We will check that out, sweetheart, but I can tell you right now it is not true. We have some pretty sophisticated models for our stock price and a fall of that magnitude is just not possible. Not possible.'

'*Sweetheart?*' said the young woman indignantly. 'Goodness. I've got a follow-up question: is Farynx a black box?'

There was an intake of breath around the room at the phrase 'black box'. There it was again, that phrase, turning up to haunt him like the spy.

'Hey,' said Todd. 'If some assho—' He pulled back from the edge, correcting himself unconvincingly. 'If some *assorted* people want to call us a black box, I'm fine with that. As long as we're a highly profitable black box, right guys?'

Todd looked around the room at a sea of somewhat tense smiles. He could see he had misjudged the mood slightly, saying 'black box' in such a cavalier way right after someone had mentioned a fall in the share price. These people were like sheep: they responded to simple stimuli, and they scared easily.

'What I mean,' said Todd, wiping his brow, 'is that the way in which Farynx makes money, its business model, is a key piece of our intellectual property. We just can't release that.'

Evans intervened, saying to the crowd, 'I think it's best if you try to restrict your questions to the acquisition of United Biscuits.'

'I've just got one last question,' said the young woman. 'Do you think the fall in the share price' – she held on to the microphone, turning her body from the shy assistant who was trying to take it back – 'has got anything to do with the fact that Farynx's internal accounts were released onto the internet when this press conference began?'

Todd could see Henry had switched course and was now making for the young woman.

'The information includes memos, internal reports and things,' she continued, 'and they're much too detailed to be fake. They answer all the questions that people really should have been asking for years.' She swung around to avoid another embarrassed grab at her microphone. 'Have a look at www dot farynxsecrets dot com.'

At this, a convulsion gripped the room. Everyone started talking at once, several people realised that gasps were real, a few left the room and many made urgent, whispered phone calls. One man stood up and said, 'Wait, my phone's got WAP too – I can check this. I just need to make a data connection, hold on…'

'So have I,' called another, trying to type an internet address with a numeric keypad. 'Wait a minute…'

Evans appealed for calm by talking loudly into his microphone: 'Folks… Er, folks… Ladies and gentlemen… Could everyone please calm down.'

Calm did not return, but people managed to bring the volume of their excited panicking down to a level that allowed Evans to add, 'Now Mr Stuckers has been asked a question, and I think we should hear his reply. Mr Stuckers…'

'Thanks, David,' said Todd, struggling to hold in his anger, divided between the spy and this hack, whoever she was. 'I have two things to say to that question. Firstly, whatever it is you say is out there, they are not our real accounts. They are absolutely fake. And secondly, I am gonna find out exactly who you are and how you knew about them first and I am gonna bury you. I am gonna *end* you. Do you understand that, Little Miss *Asshole*?'

On the other side of the hall, she was still managing to hang on to her microphone, despite the bashful efforts of the young assistants in their blue blazers. Henry was trying to push his way through them.

'Well, I understand that you're threatening me,' she said. 'And Sir Philip! Are you sure you really want to sell your company to a man like this?'

An assistant with a phone had been whispering something in Sir Philip Rose's ear. The biscuit magnate turned to face the audience, cranked up his smile and said, 'I'm very glad you asked me that because I absolutely, at this moment, intend to move ahead with the deal which we have agreed in principle with Farynx…'

Todd interrupted, smiling with bared teeth. 'I think what Phil means is that this is not just an agreement in principle that we have here. This is a deal, signed and witnessed.'

Sir Philip Rose attempted to out-smile Todd as he said, 'Absolutely, Todd. We do not intend to back out of this deal, legally possible though that is. Of course, as a fiduciary measure, we will fully investigate these false rumours, just to reassure the investment community that they are not real.'

'What?' said Todd. 'Are you getting fiduciary on me?'

At that moment a man in the audience said loudly, 'Hey, I've got the stock price on my WAP phone – eighty-three dollars.'

'Hey, don't anyone listen to that,' said Todd. 'WAP is a piece of shit.

And she said the price had fallen by fourteen dollars. That's barely seven.'

'My office says the same thing,' said another man. 'I've got them on the phone right now: $82.41. Wait, no, $78.27.'

'Okay. People!' shouted Todd. 'This is not happening! There is literally no way our share price can be dropping like this! I've seen the models, okay? It is just not possible. So would you all please just get real and congratulate us on this acquisition…'

'*Potential* acquisition,' said Sir Philip Rose.

'Hey, you want a *potential* punch in the face, asshole?' said Todd, grabbing him by the lapels.

At this, there was another gasp, sufficient in its volume and intensity to convince even the most hardened sceptic that gasps exist. As one, the audience rose to its feet, got its phones out, jammed them to its collective face and began to talk as loudly as possible to make itself heard above the noise of all the other people.

'$73.20!' someone shouted.

'Did you hear me?' shouted someone else. 'I said dump our Farynx stock!'

Sir Philip Rose haughtily pulled his lapels from Todd's grasp, whereupon Todd punched Sir Philip Rose in the face. Henry jumped purposefully onto the stage, but then stood dithering, obviously torn between helping Todd punch Sir Philip Rose in the face again and saving Todd from himself by dragging him away.

'Everyone stay calm!' shouted David Evans into his lectern microphone. 'Assistants, please call security and er… help out with the situation on the stage.'

Everyone ignored him. The very young blazered assistants who had been trying to inoffensively wrestle the microphone away from the young woman had lost heart and withdrawn behind the refreshment tables.

'It's down to $65.89!' shouted one of the voices.

'Sell all our Farynx shares,' shouted another.

'As the share price fell to $65.89, one shareholder was heard to plead with her broker, saying, "Please sell all our Farynx shares,"' dictated one of the journalists at the top of his lungs.

'Excuse me, I didn't plead,' shouted a voice.

'Will everyone please calm down!' shouted David Evans. 'And call the police!'

'It's called *colour*,' shouted the journalist. 'Tempers frayed despite

Evans' frequent appeals for calm. Security personnel were unable to enter the room as the audience surged towards the single exit.'

The self-absorbed crowd surged towards the single exit, jamming up in the doorway, knocking over tables, getting coffee on its trousers and continuing to shout.

'$54.12!'

'My phone does WAP too!'

'Dump Farynx!'

'Police were observed entering through a backstage door and arresting Stuckers. "I am ashamed," he said, as the handcuffs were fitted.'

'Hey! I did not say that!' shouted Todd, as he was led off stage.

105

'Well,' said Gus, coming out of his office. 'Well,' he added. 'Well.'

'Three wells: something pretty special must have happened,' said Piper, getting up from her reception desk. She was still wearing her blue dress and the blazer she'd managed to buy especially for the event earlier that day. She and Jonathon had arrived back only twenty minutes before.

'It has, somewhat,' said Gus. He walked down the spiral staircase from his office and was unable, at the bottom, to resist saying 'well' again.

Jonathon emerged from the kitchen, where he had been trying to make Piper a coffee. Otherwise, the office was empty. It was half past six, and all the employees were in the pub, celebrating Todd's arrest and the collapse of Farynx.

'So what is it?' Piper asked.

'I've just bought Albatross back.'

'What?' piped Piper in an embarrassingly high-pitched voice. 'How?'

'Well, since Stuckers was sacked and arrested, it seems Farynx has been selling its holdings in other companies – it's probably using the money to buy back its own shares, to raise the price and prevent a complete collapse and takeover. Luckily, we are now seen as an internet company, and our shares have thus become totally worthless. I instructed my broker to start buying any Albatross shares that were offered, and now I have all of them.'

'How much did it cost?' asked Piper.

'About forty-one thousand pounds in the end.'

'So, wait a minute,' said Piper, 'you sold the shares on Monday for forty-one million pounds, and now you've just bought them back for forty-one thousand?'

'That's about the size of it,' said Gus agreeably, polishing his glasses on the lining of his pocket. 'That's what the market decided a company that has forty-one million pounds in cash was worth.'

'So you now have forty million nine-hundred and fifty-nine thousand pounds left?'

'If that's what the maths say then yes, I do. Or rather we do. It's the company's money, after all. I do, however, own the company again. So in that sense it's my money.'

'But that's insane!' shouted Piper, running up and giving him one of her patented sideways hugs.

'It is a bit, isn't it? Did I ever mention that the economy and everything to do with it, and thus all of modern life, is entirely irrational and makes no sense at all?'

'Yes,' said Piper and Jonathon.

'Good,' he said. 'I was worried I might have neglected to point it out.'

'*So*,' said Piper.

'Ah, yes. Good point,' said Gus, producing some notes from his wallet, 'would you be a wonderful… er, daughter and run out and get us some champagne?'

'Champagne? Of course I will.'

'I'll help,' said Jonathon.

Piper looked at his splinted hands and said, 'You can't carry anything. Remember your fingers.'

'I can carry things without using my fingers.'

'*Mi man marry mings mimout musing my mingers*,' she repeated childishly, her tongue stuck in her lower lip. Jonathon looked slightly crushed.

'Don't worry,' she said, 'I'll get the best champagne available to entirely irrational modern life, and I'll carry it all by myself.'

106

Todd stood on the high ledge, looking down through the drizzle onto the jumble of old architecture below – and, below that, the hard, distant street. It was a desperate act, what he was about to do. The act of a man who, released on bail, returns to find he is now worth barely one million dollars. The act of a man overcome by rage and shame, abandoned by everyone.

He took a deep breath. *Go.*

107

When Piper had gone, Gus remembered that Cess hadn't been fed. Jonathon volunteered for the job, which he seemed confident could be done using very few fingers. Gus, meanwhile, prepared a victory tea to fortify himself for the victory champagne, and then took it to his office.

There he sent a general victory email, inviting everyone that very evening, and telling them to bring anyone they liked. He should probably arrange a better-thought-through party, in a proper venue, with… what, a *band*? He shuddered. It would turn into just another item on his to-do list, and the moment would be lost. Far better to have a party now, when he actually wanted one, than to laboriously arrange a less fun one for a time in the future when he would no longer be in the mood.

Did he dare call Freelance Jenny who was helping them with marketing? He rather thought he did. He picked up the phone. He put it down. *I'm worth forty million pounds*, he thought. He picked it up and dialled.

'Hello, Jenny speaking?' said the voice on the other end of the line.

'Yes it is,' said Gus.

'Sorry?'

'You always say "Jenny speaking" as though you're asking a question. It's extraordinarily charming.'

'Oh, hello Gus.'

'Jenny, how would you like to come to a… Hello? Jenny?'

The line had gone dead. She had hung up on him. He sat there in shock for a second. Then he realised there was no dial tone. He pressed the button on the phone repeatedly, but there was no sound at all.

'Jonathon!' he called. 'Have you seen my portable telephone?'

'Hello Gus,' said Todd. He was standing in the doorway to Gus's office.

'What?' said Gus. 'How…?'

'How did I get in here? I did a little climbing – all the elaborate stucco and decorative features made it pretty easy. If you'd been in a decent modern building I wouldn't have had a hope. Then I stood on a ledge for a while and let myself into the room next door.'

Todd carefully closed the office door and stepped towards Gus, who remained in his chair. Gus watched, carefully timing Todd's steps.

'I'm not going to hurt you, Gus. I just want you to do me a favour.'

Gus continued to sit in his chair, his hands limp by his sides, as though paralysed by terror. One step. Two steps. Three steps.

When Todd was about a foot and a half away, Gus suddenly pulled the controls on either side of his chair. It dropped to the floor and the back flopped down, allowing Gus – in an ideal world – to roll under his desk and out the other side, seize the floor lamp and knock Todd out with a single powerful blow. But it was not an ideal world. The old chair's collapse was more sudden than he had imagined, dumping him painfully and inelegantly on the floor, where Todd immediately set upon him and tied him up.

108

Jonathon, having fed Sir Cecil Chubb, returned to the office part of the building. What should he do with himself while he waited for Piper?

'Jonathon!' called Gus's voice from upstairs.

'Yes?' Jonathon called back, moving towards the spiral staircase.

'Jonathon, call the *oof*.'

Jonathon stopped in the middle of the floor. *What?* he thought. What could Gus possibly mean by 'call the *oof*'? He climbed the staircase and knocked on Gus's door. It swung open.

Jonathon walked inside and the door slammed shut behind him.

'Hey, Jonathon,' said Todd, moving in front of the door.

Jonathon looked wildly about and saw Gus, tied up tightly and lying under his desk.

'Regular nemesis, aren't you, "Jonathon Fairfax"?'

'Not regular, I don't think. Oh, but you probably mean it in the American sense—'

'I am going to kill you, Jonathon Fairfax. And I mean that in the American sense of "smash your fucking brains in and then make it look like an accident by setting the building on fire".'

Todd ripped the power cable from the back of a combined printer and fax machine. He pulled it taut, wrapping the ends around each of his huge fists, and took a step forward.

'Ah,' said Jonathon, edging away from him, trying to keep Gus's desk between them.

'Lot of nice toys in here,' said Todd, looking around. 'Which should be the one that started the tragic, accidental fire that killed you and Gus?'

'None of them?'

'Not an option.'

Todd took another step towards Jonathon, who took another step to keep them apart. Jonathon feinted to his left, luring Todd into trying to grab him. Todd took the bait, made a lunge and fell over Gus's chair, which was still lying collapsed on the floor.

Todd kicked it furiously against the bookcase, causing a large and precarious pile of books and papers to topple onto the floor. Jonathon took advantage of this distraction, which had put Todd on the far side of the desk, to rush to the door.

A heavy book hit the door just as Jonathon opened it, pulling the doorknob from his grasp. But Jonathon's foot was in the gap, painfully preventing the door from slamming shut. He flung it open and turned to see Todd charging forwards.

Jonathon reached, found a weapon and threw it. Todd reared back, hands up to protect his face from what turned out to be a tiny jug of milk. Jonathon then picked up the teapot and threw the contents at Todd. But instead of burning Todd's face off with scalding water, Jonathon succeeded only in splashing approximately a cup and a half of quite warm tea over his shirt.

'What the fuck?' said Todd, looking down at his tea-stained clothing.

'Um, sorry. I don't know how to fight,' said Jonathon. And with that he stepped out of the room and shut the door.

Jonathon pulled on the doorknob with his whole weight, bracing himself against the wall with one leg. There was a turn and a tug from the other side of the door, but somehow Jonathon hung on with his six good fingers.

Then Jonathon remembered Gus, tied up and unconscious. What if Todd did something terrible to him to force Jonathon to open the door? *Time for a change of plan.* Jonathon let go of the handle and pushed the door open as hard as he could. There was a loud bang and a shout of pain.

Todd's face appeared around the side of the door, blood pouring from his nose. Again Jonathon grabbed for a weapon. He hit Todd in the face with a packet of digestive biscuits and made for the spiral staircase, half-running, half-falling down it, hoping to lure Todd away from Gus.

Above him, Todd rushed out of the office with a roar and vaulted the railing, landing on the sofa and then executing a commando roll. It was not a particularly expert commando roll. Todd grunted, 'Ah, fuck,' and knelt, knee cradled, for a few seconds, breathing through his teeth in tight little gasps.

Making a dash for the front door was out of the question: Todd was in the way. But Gus's phone was lying on the desk beside Jonathon, and behind him were the steps leading down to the cellar, and then up to the family kitchen.

Jonathon dialled 999, and sprinted for the cellar door. His left hand scrabbled with the slippery doorknob. He looked back. Todd was on his feet again and coming for him.

'*Emergency. Which service?*' asked a voice from the mobile phone.

'Um, hold on a sec,' said Jonathon, using his right hand to help the left.

The door opened and Jonathon slammed it behind him and slid the bolt. He leaned back, breathing heavily, and then descended the cellar steps.

'Hello?' he said. 'Are you still there?'

'*...ich ...vice? ...lo?*'

'I'd like the police, please.'

He reached the bottom of the stairs. The bolt from the door at the top flew off under the force of a powerful blow. Jonathon ran. The heavy base of a swivel chair landed where he had been standing. He rushed along the short corridor, past the room full of begging supplies, towards the steps up to the kitchen.

'Hello? Hello?' he said. *No signal.*

As he ran up the steps he slowed and, with shaking hands, dialled 999 again.

'*Emergency. Which service?*'

'Hello. I'd like the police, please.'

He had reached the top of the steps, and another doorknob challenge. Todd was at the bottom of the stairs behind him. Jonathon again helped out his beleaguered left hand with his right. The kitchen door swung open, Jonathon stepped through and slammed it behind him.

Sir Cecil Chubb got to her feet, ears alert, eager to find out what was going on. Beside the kitchen door hung the old key that no one ever used. Jonathon put it in the huge ancient lock and tried to turn it. The metal hurt his fingers. The dog came and stood next to Jonathon, looking at him inquiringly as he did his fascinating human stuff. The key was cutting into his sweaty, slippery skin. Then *clunk*, it turned, locking the door.

Jonathon crouched down with his back to the door, hoping to slow Todd with the weight of his body.

'… *line until you tell me there is no emergency,*' said a voice from his phone.

'Sorry, I missed that,' said Jonathon. 'Could you say it again?'

'*What is the location of the emergency?*'

'It's a kitchen,' said Jonathon, distracted by the shock of Todd's kick on the door at his back. Sir Cecil Chubb retreated a couple of steps and began to bark.

Rrrr… Wroaah!

'*What is the address?*'

Rrrr… Wroaah!… Wrroaaagh!

'Sorry, my address, or…?' A pane of the door's glass shattered, covering him with shards. The barking continued. *Roooaaauuuff! Wrooauff!*

'*What is the address of the emergency?*'

'It's 9a Garnault Place, London EC1R something something something. It's a company called Albatross, but I'm in the family house bit at the back.'

Rowf! Rowf! Rowf! Rowf!

'*What is the emergency?*'

'Um, a man's trying to kill me.'

The other pane of glass shattered. Sir Cecil Chubb sprang back.

'*Okay, stay calm. Can you repeat the address?*'

Wroaah!… Wrroaaagh!… Rrrr…

'Yes, sorry, it's 9a Garnault Place, London, echo, cocoa? No, Charlie, um… one, Romeo. EC1R. Sorry I can't remember the last bit.'

'*Okay, I'm Andy. Is the man with you now?*'

Roooaaaaauuuff! Rowf! Rowf!… Rowf!

'Yes. He's smashing the door I'm hiding behind. Um, I don't suppose you'd be able to send someone, would you? The man's name's—'

Jonathon's injured fingers were wrenched back. The phone disappeared from his hand.

'Hey, sorry about that,' said Todd's voice above Jonathon. 'Crank call. My son does this all the time. We're trying to work through the problem, but… *kids*. What can you do, right?'

Rrrrr… Wroaaagh!… Wrroaaagh!

Todd reached through the empty window for the lock. Jonathon grabbed a stout stick from the kitchen table and hit Todd's hand. The stick disintegrated, revealing itself to be a baguette, but Todd reflexively drew back.

'Sure, my name's Gus Palgrave,' said Todd.

'Er, don't listen to him, please,' called Jonathon. 'I'm not his son and he is trying to kill me. His name's Todd Stuckers.'

Sir Cecil Chubb backed away from the door. *Woaaagh! Wooaaaggh!*

Todd reached his hand through the window. Jonathon picked up a wooden breadboard with a handle and smacked it against the door, narrowly missing Todd's retreating fingers.

'He's nearly through the door. Please send someone. If that's all right!' shouted Jonathon.

'That's great,' said Todd into the phone, smiling unsettlingly at Jonathon through the door's smashed window. 'Thanks for your understanding.'

Jonathon's heart sank. He hefted the breadboard in his hand.

'Of course,' said Todd. 'Oh, it'll come out of his allowance, you bet.'

Jonathon thought of his hopeless crush on Piper, his career as a fake beggar, his dad who had no pictures of him. Perhaps it was for the best. But then he remembered Gus, lying under his desk. And that Piper would arrive back soon to find a killer in her kitchen.

Jonathon put the breadboard down and pulled his splints off, giving him a total of eight useable fingers. He grabbed the bread knife off the table.

'Thanks again, er, Ross,' said Todd. 'So long.'

He dropped the phone on the floor and stamped on it.

Jonathon opened the cupboard beside him and took out a can of dog food. He threw it through the smashed window, forcing Todd to duck. Sir Cecil Chubb looked at him in alarm, forgetting to bark.

Todd stood back and kicked the door, putting his whole weight into it. The door shuddered, but held. Jonathon threw another can, buying him another few moments. Todd's second kick produced a long crack running down the centre of the door. Another can. On Todd's third kick, the door burst into two pieces and fell into the kitchen.

Jonathon took a firmer grip on the bread knife. His little finger was telling him that he was doing something seriously wrong, but Jonathon ignored it. Sir Cecil Chubb moved closer to Jonathon, hackles up, shaking.

'That's what you got, huh? A bread knife and a shy dog?' said Todd, stepping through the doorway.

'It's all I need,' said Jonathon, suddenly realising that in this situation, it no longer mattered about saying the wrong thing. He really didn't need to worry about offending Todd or sounding like an idiot.

'Right,' said Todd. 'You know, I am still learning stuff about this murdering thing. For example, if you're going to kill someone in a kitchen, take a moment to locate the knife block. I can't emphasise that enough.'

Todd moved to the counter by the fridge and drew two large and viciously sharp knives from the block. Jonathon kicked himself for not remembering it was there.

'Also, you want a knife you can stab with,' said Todd. 'A bread knife is designed for sawing.'

'Come over here and I'll saw through you,' said Jonathon, suddenly enjoying his liberation from having to worry about what he said.

'You fucking what?' said Todd.

'Your face looks like a loaf of bread did a shit on top of an idiot.'

Pure rubbish. But how great to die liberated from politeness and self-censorship.

'Oh, you little fucking shit,' said Todd, and launched himself across the kitchen at Jonathon.

As he did so, Sir Cecil Chubb, who had been standing quivering next to Jonathon, leapt for Todd's throat. Todd instinctively brought up his right arm to defend himself, and the dog's jaws clamped around it. The knife fell from Todd's right hand, but his other knife was in the dog. Jonathon rushed in, leg behind Todd's ankle, and they all went over on the suddenly slippery floor. While Todd struggled to free himself from the dog's jaws, Jonathon was on top of him, hammering at his hand. Todd's knife skittered across the floor.

Jonathon went after the knife, but slipped over in the blood. Todd rolled over and managed to stand, the dog hanging from his arm, the lower part of her white coat now pink.

Jonathon was lying on his back. The dog dropped from Todd's arm and lay motionless on the kitchen floor. Breathing heavily, Todd stood over Jonathon, who was groping for the dropped knife.

Jonathon saw something through the window, a flash of white. *Focus on the room.*

And then Todd was on him, his hands around Jonathon's throat, cutting off the air, his whole weight on Jonathon's chest. Jonathon grabbed at Todd's wrists, trying to shake the chokehold. It was no use: the wrists were only marginally thinner than his own neck.

This was it. He was going to die.

His legs were flailing. His face felt like it would burst. His lungs were straining to pull in air that would not come.

There was a great white light all around. A feeling of peace and limitless space.

Ahead of him was a group of figures. He moved closer. They were smiling and waving. Among them he recognised his grandpa, wearing a checked shirt and a pair of trousers that had bagged at the knees, despite his care.

'Um. Hello,' said Jonathon.

'Hello,' they all said, smiling but slightly self-conscious, as at a family reunion.

'It's nice to see you,' said his grandpa, 'but it's not your time yet. Go back. You can do it. Roll, then give him a kick in the trousers.'

They began to retreat, as though Jonathon were being pulled away from them.

'And stick with the guitar!' called his grandpa.

'That's David,' called Jonathon. 'I do the drawing.'

But the white light had gone. He was back in the kitchen with the gigantic hands around his windpipe.

Jonathon stopped clawing at the hands. He rolled, turning himself into a pivot for Todd's tense arms. As Todd crashed down, Jonathon got in a kick to his trousers, making him roar.

Jonathon crawled away, taking in great gasps of sweet, painful air. But Todd was on his feet again, a knife in his hand. Jonathon looked around for a weapon.

Behind Todd, there was a thud, a crunch and a loud bang as the back door flew open and a man toppled into the room under the momentum of his own kick. He wore a white shirt and a bulky black waistcoat with a walkie-talkie clipped to it.

'Evening, mate,' said the man in an easy-going way. 'Everything all right?'

Todd didn't answer. He was breathing hard, his eyes, tunnels of hatred, were fixed on Jonathon. He lunged forward, the knife held high and shining.

A short, stocky woman with ginger hair walked into the kitchen. She crossed the floor in two businesslike strides and almost casually passed her baton over the backs of Todd's knees, bringing him down. Jonathon could not account for the speed with which this happened. She then sat on Todd while the easy-going man helped her to wrestle his hands behind his back.

'You're under arrest, sonny Jim,' said the policewoman.

'That's right, mate,' said the policeman. 'Now, you do not have to say anything. But it may harm your defence if you do not mention, when questioned, something which you rely on in court. Anything you do say can be given in evidence. Do you understand that? It's important.'

'Hey, I want a lawyer,' shouted Todd. 'I am a rich man, and you do not want to fuck with me.'

'Oh, a rich man, are you?' said the policewoman chattily, putting the handcuffs on him. 'That's nice.'

She looked up at Jonathon. 'You all right, love?' she asked.

109

By half past ten, when Jonathon and Gus returned from the police station, the house was completely full.

There were people sitting on the smashed sofa on which Todd had done his commando roll. There were people in Gus's office amid the scattered papers, the toppled books and the tea service that had been turned into offensive weaponry and smashed. There were people among the desks that Todd had turned over while auditioning them for use as battering rams. There were people in the small office kitchen, which had survived unscathed, and in the large domestic kitchen, which had been quite disastrously scathed and which, despite having been mopped, still contained more dog's blood than is conventional at parties. There were, in short, people everywhere. There were far, far more people than would ever have responded to an invitation to a properly organised party in a fully intact home.

Gus was so pleased by this that he immediately drank two glasses of champagne and spontaneously recited the greater part of Robert Southey's 'After Blenheim'. Then he stood at the top of the spiral staircase, outside his office, and began hitting his champagne glass with a fork. People turned and quieted.

'Friends, family, and er...' he looked around '... other people. Thank you very much for being here. I would like to thank the people who have made this possible. Firstly, Todd Stuckers, who has definitely been arrested this time. Mr Stuckers may have tried to kill me, but he has also inadvertently given me forty million pounds. I pledge that I will use his money to make the world a better place.'

Everyone cheered and clinked glasses.

'Secondly, I would like to thank my lovely daughter Piper, for understanding what Farynx's accounts meant and working out the plan that rescued Albatross. By putting Farynx's secret data online and then telling a group of financial experts that this had already caused panic selling, she caused a real wave of panic selling that has now destroyed Farynx and burst the dotcom bubble.' Everyone began to raise their glasses again, but Gus added, 'Oh, and of course thanks for her sterling work on reception.'

There was an extremely loud cheer, a great emptying of champagne glasses, and much shaking of heads at Gus's ability to undercut anything nice he said about his daughter, even at a time like this.

'Thirdly, I would like to thank Lance Ferman for bringing us the disks with Farynx's accounts on them, enabling Piper to save the company.' There was more cheering.

'And finally, I would like to thank the caterers, who have done such a great job at very literally no notice at all.'

Another cheer rose, amid more clinking and polite thanking of the people pouring the champagne and handing out the pizza.

While Gus was making this speech, Jonathon was floating through the house on a cloud of relief. It seemed incredible to him that he should be both alive and not in a police station, and these twin facts made him so happy that he couldn't stop smiling. He needed to see the kitchen, just to check that the whole thing hadn't been a dream.

Its state immediately convinced him that it had all really happened.

And such was his state of mind that this realisation made him laugh.

'Jonathon!' Lance shouted, turning around and also laughing. 'You're alive!' He hugged him. 'I'm so sorry again for sleeping with your girlfriend.'

'That's all right,' said Jonathon, because everything was now all right. 'You did save my life, after all.'

'Having first endangered it,' said Lance.

'Never mind. She looks like she's got over it too.'

He pointed to where Emma was sitting, on one of the less broken kitchen chairs, talking to Carl.

Lance and Jonathon exchanged glances.

'How come she…?' began Jonathon.

'I invited her,' said Lance. 'And Carl?'

'We bumped into him at the police station.'

Emma and Carl began to kiss.

'Do you think he'll try and hit me again?' asked Lance, indicating the dashing bruise that now emphasised his left cheekbone.

'Wouldn't have thought so.'

The kissing became slightly more graphic, so they turned away.

'She's finally met someone who really is the strong, silent type,' said Lance.

'Well, that gets us off the hook.'

'Phew.'

'Lance. There's one thing I don't understand.'

'What's that, J-doc?'

'Don't… Actually, that's fine. Call me what you like. But how come you had a load of spare high-capacity Zip disks with you in the heist?'

'I thought I might need my laptop, and they were in the bag. I mainly use them because they look good. They're just so chunky.'

'Yes, but what was on the ones you left in the meeting room?'

Lance looked at the floor. It was the first time Jonathon had ever seen Lance even remotely embarrassed. He snapped out of it and smiled.

'I've been writing a screenplay. I like to have backups.'

'Oh. What's it called?'

'*Deadly Information*. It's about…'

But at that moment they were joined by a woman holding two glasses of champagne. She looked like someone would almost certainly pay her to advertise swimsuits, but she would refuse because she had a proper job.

'Ah, Jonathon. I want you to meet Arlene. She may have burned down my apartment and stolen all my stuff. I just don't know.'

Jonathon went for a handshake, and Arlene laughed and hugged him. 'Jonathon Fairfax! I have heard so much about you!'

'Oh,' said Jonathon.

'All good,' she said. 'You're a hero! Here, have this champagne.'

Jonathon suddenly realised how greatly he needed champagne, so he suppressed his natural urge to awkwardly refuse it and instead drank half of it at a gulp.

'We've expanded our microrelationship. This is our second date,' said Lance, proudly. 'Or third if you count the one in 'Sup.'

'Of course I count it, *jerk*,' said Arlene. Then to Jonathon she said, 'We've moved up to a nanorelationship.'

'Wouldn't that be smaller than a microrelationship?' asked Lance. 'And was that my champagne you gave away?'

During the bickering that ensued, Jonathon realised that he needed to find some more champagne and Piper, so he made his excuses and slipped away.

In the office part of the building, it was impossible to avoid being given champagne. As he looked for Piper, he was very surprised by all the people who were there. He said hello to Donald Eade, who had, out of guilt, signed them into Farynx's event that morning. Then the elegant boxer introduced him to the real Alistair Fordham as one of the most interesting performers he had ever seen. Jonathon apologised to Alistair for using his pass, but Alistair said it had all worked out for the best. He had been free for a last-minute audition, and as a result had just been cast in a one-man version of *As You Like It*, told from the forest's point of view.

Jonathon eventually found Piper standing by her desk, looking down into the street.

'Hello,' he said.

'Jonathon, you're safe,' said Piper, throwing her arms around him. 'Ah, thank god.'

'Yes, I'm in love with you.' He didn't immediately realise what he'd said. It had just come out, as though it was how you're meant to reply when someone says, 'You're safe.'

A small silence occurred.

He had ruined a moment of closeness with her, spoiled a moment when they were both just two people who were glad to find each other safe and alive.

'Sorry,' he said. 'I didn't mean to say that.'

On the other hand, it was liberating, saying what he felt, like that moment in the kitchen with Todd. And perhaps she didn't want to hear it, didn't want him to feel it. Perhaps it was inconvenient for her to deal with this on the day that her dad had almost been murdered and her favourite dog had been stabbed. But that was nothing compared with the immense burden of saying nothing.

'It's completely true though,' he said. 'I am in love with you. But you don't need to think of anything to say. I just wanted you to know. I should go and say hello to Blount.'

Who invited Blount? he wondered.

'Jonathon?' she said, looking at the desk.

'Yes?'

'I'm in love with you too. You had me at "hup um oops".'

Jonathon's mind flipped itself neatly inside out and vanished.

'You don't remember,' she said, 'but we met on the Tube about three weeks ago. That's what you said. I fell in love with you at first sight, so I remembered.'

'I remember,' he said. 'I thought you'd forgotten, or not noticed, or something.'

'Well I hadn't and I didn't and I somethingn't,' she said. 'I mean, I did wonder if it was wrong of me to feel that way. I thought maybe you were the silent type, or just really… stupid. But then you got the Starsky thing – as well as saving all our lives, destroying Farynx and defeating Todd.'

'You're the one who did all that,' he said. 'But why do you go quiet on me?'

'Because you go quiet on me, and I always think it's because you don't like me.'

'But I go quiet because you… Oh, I see. It's a loop.'

'Stupid loops,' she said.

'And why did you give me that look of infinite pity, when I came for my interview?'

'I think you're probably referring to my *seductive* look. I practically threw myself at you, giving you tea in a special cup and saucer. It was pathetic.'

'Oh, was that throwing yourself at me?'

'*Yes.* And you didn't even notice me.'

'I did. I have. I something. I'd just decided I wasn't cut out for relationships. Women always end up either marrying a French farmer or thinking I'm a completely different person than I am. I mean, that's what's happened before.'

'Well I promise I'll never go farmer. And I've been waiting all my life for someone who's as ridiculous as you. And here you are. Are you?'

His arms had, without asking his permission, reached out for her.

'Oh dear,' said Jonathon.

'What?' asked Piper, a look of worry creeping into her eyes. It took a long time to creep in, for obvious reasons.

'I've got my watch caught in your hair.'

'Will it stop you from kissing me?'

'I hope not.'

They kissed and Piper softly said, 'Ow, my hair.'

110

They would almost certainly have kissed again immediately if they had not been distracted by a loud noise from above, on the other side of the room. They looked up and saw that it was Gus, standing at the top of the spiral staircase and hammering a fork against his champagne glass so energetically that the glass was already quite badly damaged.

'I'm sorry,' he said, 'I didn't mean to thank the caterers earlier on – invaluable though their services have been.' Everyone looked at the caterers and smiled apologetically for Gus's insensitivity. 'I had a fit of absent-mindedness brought on by champagne, relief and the nature of my mind. I meant, of course, to thank Jonathon Fairfax, "who art a light to guide, a rod, to tumpty-tumpty-something who art victory".'

Gus looked around, beaming, but discerned that no one else had read the poem he had half-forgotten. He cleared his throat and resumed his speech.

'Jonathon saved my life today, and willingly risked his own yesterday, carrying out the daring heist that saved my company and the livelihoods of myself and all my employees.'

At this he paused and everyone cheered. Gus waved his arms to signal that there was more.

'But I believe he has done far more than that. Jonathon – and Lance – acted just in time. Since Todd was fired yesterday, rumours have spread that several more of the world's largest companies are, like Farynx, accounting frauds – conceptual businesses that are essentially malign figments of our imagination.'

'Malign figments!' toasted some of the more drunk people.

'But your actions, Jonathon, have brought all this to light. The internet bubble has burst, conceptual business has been exposed. Now, finally, we have a chance to rebuild our economy – perhaps even our civilisation – so that it makes sense. Ladies and gentlemen, a toast please to Jonathon Fairfax.'

Everyone raised their glasses and roared.

'Has anyone seen Jonathon, by the way?' asked Gus, in the aftermath of the cheer.

Six months later

111

New York

'Hey, Jerk!' she called.

Lance put his head around the bathroom door, into the steam and the sweet clean smell.

'I can't believe I'm living with a woman whose pet name for me is "Jerk",' he said.

'I can't believe you're living with a woman,' she replied agreeably. 'Soap my back, will you?'

She was lying in an impressively full bath. It contained that gigantic, luxurious volume of soap bubbles that only women are able to attain. Lance sat on the side of the bath, took the soap from her hand and worked it to a lather.

'Why couldn't you have burned this place down and stolen my stuff,' he asked, massaging the soap into her back as she leaned forwards, 'instead of moving in?'

She gave a happy sigh and stretched out her toes, her feet resting on either side of the taps.

'Well, if I'd done that I wouldn't have a soap-monkey, would I?'

'And I wouldn't have a tyrannical harpy occupying my bathroom the whole time.'

'Ah, the soap-monkey and the tyrannical harpy, trapped in their abusive pico-relationship.'

'There's only one thing that could make it worse,' said Lance, soaping her shoulders.

'That screenplay you sold?'

'Nope. I said "worse".'

'Then that would have to be if the harpy dragged the soap-monkey into the bathtub and made out with him,' she said.

'That would be my ultimate nightmare,' said Lance.

She grabbed his arm and turned, looking up at him. His shirt was already damp with steam.

'Welcome to hell,' she said, and pulled him so that he slipped down the side of the bath and sloshed into the water with her, completely soaking the bathroom floor in a way that neither of them cared about at all.

112

New York

Beige walls, scuffed tiles, voices shouting words he couldn't quite make out. He pushed through the faded green doors and looked around. And there was his dad, sitting at the white-topped table on an orange plastic chair, underneath a huge number six that hung from the ceiling. He was wearing prison-issue green trousers with a green sweatshirt.

'Hey Dad.'

'Hi Duke.'

'There's no hugging here, right?'

'No, but sit down. It's good to see you.'

Marmaduke pulled out an orange plastic chair and sat down.

'So how you doing?' said Todd. 'You look good.'

'Thanks. I cleaned up my act, got a job. Well, you know, I work at Discount Computer Warehouse. But I'm renting an apartment, so...'

'That's great. Good for you.'

'You look good too, Dad. You lost weight.'

'Really. You think I needed to lose weight?'

'Dad, I am not going to get into a fight with you about how much you used to weigh. We only have ten minutes, and I am just not.'

'Hey, I'm not like that any more. I've done a lot of work on myself and I can accept that maybe I needed to lose a little weight. I'm a new man.'

'Really?'

'Yeah. I sleep well. I had no clue I was so sleep-deprived. When I got here I just slept for like two weeks. I have regular meals. You know, the food's a little plain but it's good. And I work out and play chess and… get this, I *meditate!*'

'No! You remember how much you mocked me when I tried meditation?'

'I don't specifically remember that, but I… Okay, I haven't been the greatest dad in the world, or the best role model. But that has all changed. You know, trying to get ahead, it just made me crazy: the pressure, the meetings, those weird conference phones, the booze, the competition, always wanting to win, I was drinking way too much coffee, I wasn't sleeping – I mean, Jesus, I thought every hour I slept was an hour of lost productivity, and I had got it down to, like, three hours a night…'

'Three hours? No wonder you were killing people.'

'Hey! That was never proved. I am in here for *attempted* murder. And conspiracy and securities fraud.'

'Dad, we both know…' Marmaduke stopped himself. 'Okay. Fine. I'm sorry. I misspoke: no wonder you were *attempting* to kill people.'

'I know, right? I was under a lot of pressure, and I still had a lot to learn about myself. I really wanted to get on the cover of *Forbes* magazine, and it just made me crazier every time I saw some other business guy on there…'

'Well, you did make the cover of a few magazines in the end.'

'Yeah, and that was nice. I mean, it wasn't for the reasons I wanted…'

'No, but that one *Wired* cover, "The Man Who Killed the Internet (And Maybe a Bunch of People)", that was pretty cool.'

'Yeah. A little negative still, but I deserved that. I was not in a happy place.'

'So, that… woman you were seeing. She visit you?'

'No, she's mad at me because I *attempted* to murder those two guys, so… I probably won't see her again.'

'Oh, that hurts,' said Marmaduke.

'Yeah, but… she's right. I made a bad call.'

'Speaking of calls. You could pick up the phone once in a while.'

'Yeah, I know. I am, like, the *worst* at keeping in touch. I'll fix it though. It's just, a lot of my phone allowance goes on making trades—'

'You're playing the stock market?'

'Sure. A little.'

'Is that even allowed?'

'Well, I can't conduct a business. But my PA does all the buying and selling for me. I just study the companies, I look at the way the market's moving, and I tell her what to do. Don't worry though, I am *very* conservative. Here's a tip for you. There's this super-safe way you can get into mortgage investing: they put a lot of mortgages together, pool the risk and turn it into a bond. It's called a CDO.'

'Okay, well, I'll look into that maybe, when I get a little money together.'

'You know, the way things are going maybe I could start up your allowance again pretty soon.'

'Oh.'

'What? You're not pleased?'

'Sure. It's just… I got myself together now. I thought you'd be, like, breaking rocks or something.'

Todd laughed. 'I sew a few mailbags, you know. It's good to do something with your hands. Good for the soul.'

'I thought it was meant to be hell in here.'

'I don't want to come off like a douche, but I started my career in Goldman Sachs, so I'm kinda comfortable in a high-aggression environment. And this is way less intense than Goldman: here you get to sleep.'

'But what about, you know, all the shankings, gangs, drugs…'

'That is way overplayed. There's like three stabbings a week, *max*.'

113

London

Either Gus had suddenly become much more sensitive or his ex-wife had talked to him. In any case, he had offered to split the forty-one million pounds with Jonathon and Piper. They had turned it down, Jonathon out of polite awkwardness and Piper out of a prudent worry that she would end up spending a lot of time managing it. And after all, Gus did mean to spend it all on righting society's ills. In the end, though, they had accepted the offer of a house and a modest income.

As a result, they lived – slightly embarrassingly – in Hampstead. It was a bit like being in an unrealistic ideal of an English country village, but set incongruously in the middle of north London. There was even a gigantic slab of English countryside beside it in the form of Hampstead Heath. Granted, there were more lawyers, politicians, actors and general rich people than you might choose for the population of your ideal village, but there it was. Nothing is perfect, even if all your cares have been magicked away.

It was a medium-sized stone cottage with a green door, a small front garden, and a middling back garden, in which two friendly apple trees grew and a small tabby cat hunted things that no human eye could see.

It was September. Clear, golden daylight seeped in around the edges of the curtains. In the trees beyond the curtains, the birds made their neat little observations to one another. Jonathon woke from a dream in which he'd been comfortably sleeping on this pillow, in this bed. He frequently dreamed now of his actual life. The dream cottage was his cottage. Its old and only approximately rectangular doors that did not automatically slam themselves shut with a terrifyingly loud bang were... well, you get the picture. Its skirting boards, wainscoting, architraves and picture rails were all his – or rather his and Piper's. And perhaps he didn't know what wainscoting was, exactly, but he knew it was in the house, and that made him happy.

The alarm clock was silent apart from its comfortable murmured ticking. He had forgotten to ask it to wake them, but it didn't matter. This was probably the time he would have chosen anyway: quarter to nine. He turned to look at Piper, whose hair stretched out across her pillow like a dark, slumbering starfish. And he lay there like that for a while, watching her breathe, marvelling at his good fortune, at his happiness.

He had always assumed he was just not made for happiness, that it was somehow impossible for him. And so it was a shock to find that it existed and that he could feel it, nestled warm in his stomach and lazing in the deep furrows of his mind. Who would have thought that just getting rid of commuting, worry, a horrible job and a relationship with someone totally unsuited to him could possibly have made such a difference?

Cess, sensing the day beginning, nosed her way into the room and laid her chin restfully on the end of the bed, joining Jonathon in watching Piper.

And Piper's eyes opened, just a crack, then a little wider. She blinked twice. He liked to watch this, her beginning to piece herself together. He smiled at her.

'Good morning,' he said.

'Guh fmufneg,' she replied indistinctly.

311

She burrowed her face into the pillow, then scooched along in bed, wrapped her arms around him, nuzzled into his ribs and closed her eyes again. She seemed to like lying in his armpit like that. He didn't fully understand it, but he was very glad of it. That was now true of much of his life.

After a while she half-opened her eyes and said, 'I want tea now. Please bring me some tea.'

Jonathon leaned over and switched the kettle on. This single thing – having the ability to make tea without getting out of bed – had improved his life almost as much as living in an improbable dream cottage with wainscoting. In thanks, Piper kissed the bit of his armpit where her lips happened to be.

When the tea was ready, they found a way to sit up in bed with their arms around each other, holding their mugs. It took a bit of manoeuvring, but they managed it, this morning as every morning, with only a modest amount of tea spilling onto the sheets. He asked about her dreams and she unfurled a tapestry of talking trees, wise apples and giant thumbs. As ever, it delighted him.

'What are you drawing today?' she asked.

'I'm doing some rabbits in waistcoats for a slightly eccentric illustrated edition of *The Idiot*.'

Although he was being paid to do this, he also wanted to. This still surprised him.

'What are you embroidering today?' he asked her.

'I'm still working on those dress panels inspired by seventeenth-century Persian cloud collars.'

'That's so niche.'

'*We're* so niche.'

They kissed, and she muttered 'ow' because he had got his watch caught in her hair.

'And what are we going to sing in the shower this morning?' he asked.

'How about "Perfect Day" by Lou Reed, and we'll just pretend that it isn't actually about heroin addiction and death?'

'Perfect.'

The End

A note from the author

Like many people, I've always found the world quite a difficult and confusing place. So, ever since I learned to read, I've been escaping into books. I've read and enjoyed lots of different sorts of books. But there's a particular kind that has really helped when the world has been at its most baffling and intractable.

I was nine or ten when I read *The Hitchhiker's Guide to the Galaxy* by Douglas Adams. It immediately made me think, 'Oh, maybe it isn't all my fault. Maybe it's just that nothing makes any sense.' It was a huge comfort and relief.

And then when I was in my mid-twenties and had a horrible corporate temping job, I found a 1932 *Jeeves Omnibus* by PG Wodehouse in a second-hand bookshop. I read it to soothe myself when I woke in the night, dreading the next day. Since then a few other books have worked the same magic. They include *Augustus Carp By Himself*, by the excellently named Henry Howarth Bashford, *Three Men in a Boat* by Jerome K Jerome, and *The Understudy* by David Nichols.

There aren't many of these books, but I love them. To me it feels like the authors are whispering reassuringly that, if we're finding things difficult, it may well be because the world is senseless and absurd.

I would like to convey the same thing, however incompetent my whispering technique may be. I just want to write something that would have made me feel better if I'd read it when I was twenty-four and sitting full of dread on a District line train.

I hope it worked for you. But in any case, thank you for reading.

Christopher Shevlin

To get in touch, find out more, or sign up for information about the next book, please visit:
www.christophershevlin.com

Novels by Christopher Shevlin

The Perpetual Astonishment of Jonathon Fairfax

Jonathon Fairfax Must Be Destroyed

CPSIA information can be obtained
at www.ICGtesting.com
Printed in the USA
LVHW092231100521
687067LV00019B/319

9 780956 965639